The Further Adventures

of

Sherlock Holmes

(Part I: 1881-1891)
The Complete
Jim French
Imagination Theatre
Scripts

The Further Adventures

of

Sherlock Holmes

(Part I: 1881-1891)
The Complete
Jim French
Imagination Theatre
Scripts

Compiled for the Benefit of the
Restoration of Undershaw

by Jim French
Edited by David Marcum

MX Publishing
2019

ISBN Hardback 978-1-78705-490-5
ISBN Paperback 978-1-78705-491-2
ePub ISBN 978-1-78705-492-9
PDF ISBN 978-1-78705-493-6

Published in the UK by
MX Publishing
335 Princess Park Manor, Royal Drive,
London, N11 3GX
www.mxpublishing.co.uk

Cover design by Brian Belanger
www.belangerbooks.com and *www.redbubble.com/people/zhahadun*

Illustration by Sidney Paget
Danse Macabre by Camile Saint-Saëns

David Marcum can be reached at:
thepapersofsherlockholmes@gmail.com

CONTENTS

Forewords

Adventures

(Continued on the next page . . . .)

Appendix

COPYRIGHT INFORMATION

<u>NOTE</u>

The following scripts by Jim French have been published in text form in the previous volumes:

- "The Inspector of Graves" in *The MX Book of New Sherlock Holmes Stories – Part III: 1896-1929* (2015)
- "The Man Who Believed in Nothing" in *The MX Book of New Sherlock Holmes Stories – Part V: Christmas Adventures* (2016)
- "The Adventure of the Apothecary Shop" in *The MX Book of New Sherlock Holmes Stories – Part VI: 2017 Annual* (2017)
- "The Tuttman Gallery" in *The MX Book of New Sherlock Holmes Stories – Part VII: Eliminate the Impossible: 1880-1891* (2017)
- "The Curse of the Third Sign" in *Imagination Theatre's Sherlock Holmes* (2017)
- "The Coughing Man" in *The MX Book of New Sherlock Holmes Stories – Part X: 2018 Annual (1896-1916)* (2018)
- "The Abernetty Transactions" in *The MX Book of New Sherlock Holmes Stories – Part XII: Some Untold Cases (1894-1902)* (2018)
- "The Mystery of the Patient Fisherman" in *The MX Book of New Sherlock Holmes Stories – Part XIII: 2019 Annual (1881-1890)* (2019)

<u>NOTICE</u>

These scripts are protected by copyright.

The following adventures appear in the companion volumes:

Imagination Theatre's
Sherlockian Legacy
by David Marcum

A week or so ago, a Sherlockian author asked me about what I'd recommend for a young friend of his who had just been cast as Sherlock Holmes in a school play. I suggested some of the various book series that recount Holmes's own adventures as a child, in the days before he became the world's best and most famous detective. I also listed some of the series that tell stories of The Baker Street Irregulars, and other children who so ably assisted Holmes in his endeavors. But I had one important piece of advice, along with the recommended books: Don't give a child some watered-down abridged edited ruined version of The Canon as his or her first experience of meeting Sherlock Holmes and these incredible stories. Give him or her the real thing, because he or she will only have one chance to meet the true Sherlock Holmes for the first time, and it should be done right.

Having advised this, I thought back to how I first met Holmes. I don't recall when I first became aware of him specifically, but I vaguely knew of him from a very young age, because he's an archetype. An icon. A hero who is instantly recognized all over the world, for what he represents as much as for himself. His representation was everywhere – and it still is. Alfalfa of *The Little Rascals* (or *Our Gang*) wore a deerstalker to be a Junior Detective. Laurel and Hardy wore them as detectives too. On *Gilligan's Island*, the Professor once dressed as a Holmes-like character in deerstalker and full Inverness, and Peter Brady donned a deerstalker to solve a mystery on an episode of *The Brady Bunch*. Daffy Duck was Holmes (to Porky Pig's Watson), and the deerstalker in that particular cartoon was what instantly defined him. I saw all of those portrayals and others long before I ever read an actual Holmes story – and yet I knew who he was supposed to be, even if only in the most vague of terms.

With a general idea of Holmes in my mind, it's no wonder that I was so primed to enjoy his adventures when I received my first Holmes book, a copy of *The Adventures*, when I was ten years old in 1975. I've never thought that the original (and pitifully few) sixty adventures were enough, and I always sought more, but it was very difficult in those days to find Holmes pastiches in print form – and just as hard to find accurate media representations. This was before VCR's (and later DVD players), and one had to hope that something related to Holmes would show up on television – and it occasionally did, but only every couple of years of so. Fortunately, I had some better luck at finding old Holmes radio shows from the 1940's on records at our local library. Thus, even as I was able to read about the Canonical Holmes, I was able to encounter the incredible Basil Rathbone as the first Holmes that I ever *heard.*

As I wrote in my foreword to *Imagination Theatre's Sherlock Holmes* (2017), Holmes and radio have had a long and incredible association. Holmes was first portrayed on radio on October 20th, 1930, when – quite fittingly – William Gillette, the legendary stage actor who defined Holmes for a generation or more, starred in NBC's version of "The Adventure of the Speckled Band". This was the beginning of an amazing body of work representing that most amazing of men, Sherlock Holmes, that has continued to the present.

This is sadly not the place to completely discuss Holmes's entire history on radio – that would take volumes, and someone with much better knowledge about it than me. I'd like to explore the amazing contributions of Edith Meiser, who did so much to further Holmes and keep his memory green during those early years of the twentieth century when the flame might have fizzled – and to prove that Holmes pastiches can be just as great as The Canon. I'd love to write about how Basil Rathbone and Nigel Bruce portrayed Holmes and Watson on the air, initially when they filmed two 1939 Holmes movies that were set in the correct Victorian period, and then continuing on radio even after the films temporarily ceased, and so on through that period until their films resumed in 1942, produced by a different studio and incorrectly updated to a 1940's setting. While the rest of the Rathbone and Bruce films were ostensibly taking place in or just after World War II, the radio shows continued to be set in the correct years of the 1880's, the 1890's, and the early 1900's. The two actors continued in these career-defining roles until 1946, when Rathbone left. Even then, Bruce remained with the show for one more season, this time with Tom Conway as the Great Detective.

There were so many actors who contributed over the years, including Carlton Hobbes and Norman Shelley on the BBC in the 1950's and 1960's. And of course, there are the giants in the field, Clive Merrison and Michael Williams, the Holmes and Watson representing the team led by Bert Coules. This group was finally were able to broadcast, with the support of the BBC, the entire

Holmesian Canon with the same two actors in the title roles – an amazing feat with two amazingly perfect portrayals.

Holmes and Watson have appeared a staggering number of times on radio, all the way back to when radio first became viable. An incomplete (and out-of-order) list of the acting duos that have portrayed them includes:

- Basil Rathbone and Nigel Bruce
- Tom Conway and Nigel Bruce
- Clive Merrison and Michael Williams
- Clive Merrison and Andrew Sachs
- John Stanley and Alfred Shirley
- Sir John Gielgud and Sir Ralph Richardson
- William Gillette and Leigh Lovell
- Richard Gordon and Leigh Lovell
- Louis Hector and Leigh Lovell
- Richard Gordon and Harry West
- Carlton Hobbs and Norman Shelley
- Roy Marsden and John Moffett
- Barry Foster and David Buck
- Graham Armitage and Kerry Jordan
- Robert Hardy and Nigel Stock
- Robert Langford and Kenneth Baker
- William Gaminara and Walter Hall
- Edward Petherbridge and David Peart
- Jim Crozier and Dave Hawkes
- Simon Callow and Nicky Henson
- John Neville and Donald MacDonald
- Christopher Newton and Leon Connell
- Tim Pigott-Smith and Andrew Hilton
- Roger Rees and Crawford Logan
- John Gilbert and Lawrence Albert,
- *and of course that great team of* . . . . John Patrick Lowrie and Lawrence Albert of *Imagination Theatre*

This three-volume set, *The Further Adventures of Sherlock Holmes: The Complete Jim French Imagination Theatre Scripts*, is about the Holmes stories that are presented to us as *"Movies for your mind!"*, as written by the legendary Jim French.

I don't recall the date, but I suspect that I discovered *Imagination Theatre* in approximately 2002, when a box set of the first sixteen episodes of their *The Further Adventures of Sherlock Holmes* was released on cassette tape. Of course, I bought it (and later replaced them on CD). Those initial episodes featured the *first* actor to play Holmes in the Imagination Theatre series, John Gilbert, and Larry Albert as Watson, a role he has portrayed wonderfully to the present. I was mightily impressed from the very beginning, both with the production values, and also how Holmes and Watson were shown – particularly Watson. Larry and Jim French understood that Watson was not a buffoon or a comedic figure. (This was often a problem as adapters, uncertain how to include Watson when translating him from the observer and narrator of the stories. Their solution was often to use him for comic relief, *a la* Nigel Bruce. And Watson is NOT comic relief.)

Another thing that I liked about *The Further Adventures* was the fact that such care was taken to get things right in terms of *chronology*. I've collected literally thousands of traditional Holmes pastiches since the mid-1970's, and since the mid-1990's, I've organized them into a chronology that arranges both Canon and pastiche by book, chapter, page, and even paragraph (or the equivalent for other formats, such as radio broadcasts) into years, days, and even hours. It's an ever-changing document, now over nine-hundred dense pages stretching from 1844 (when Holmes's parents meet) to 1957 (the year of Sherlock Holmes's death), and as an initial basis of that effort, I used the chronology established by famed Sherlockian William S. Baring-Gould in his seminal biography, *Sherlock Holmes of Baker Street* (1962). I don't agree with everything Baring-Gould established, but it's a great jumping-off place. One thing that he espouses that I completely support is that Watson had a first wife named *Constance* from 1886 to late 1887, before his second (and more famous) marriage to Mary Watson *née* Morstan from 1889 to 1893. (Constance's existence helps to explain a great many chronological inconsistencies within The Canon.) I was amazed and wonderfully pleased to discover that, as I listened to those *Further Adventures* broadcasts, Constance was acknowledged as Watson's *first* wife, and even mentioned by name upon occasion.

I quickly found that the new *Imagination Theatre* episodes were streamed online, and I checked every week to see if it was a Holmes week, and listened with rapt attention. (And this was a true commitment in those days, I assure you, when we had dial-up internet, and the twenty-plus minute shows sometimes ran for an hour or more as I sat through endless buffering.)

By this time, John Gilbert had left the show, and Holmes was being portrayed by someone who sounds exactly like Holmes should – John Patrick Lowrie. (I was amazed, years later, to learn that Mr. Lowrie isn't British.)

I continued to enjoy each new entry, completely confident that these versions of Our Heroes wouldn't disappoint me with some behavior that would steer things off the cliff – such as presenting him as a murderous sociopath or a tattooed drug addict.

Over the years, I've been fortunate to write (so far) fifty traditional Canonical pastiches. Not long after the first volume of them was published, I sent a copy to the folks at *Imagination Theatre*, partly in thanks for all the great work that they had done, and also with the idea that I might be able to convert one or more of the stories into scripts, as several other authors had done with their Holmes pastiches.

Not too much later, I received an email from Larry "Dr. Watson" Albert indicating that he had received my book and would read it with an eye toward seeing if anything there was worthy of being a part of *Imagination Theatre*'s *Further Adventures*. Over the next few years, we exchanged emails as I chipped away at a script, and he read through my various drafts, acting as a wonderful and encouraging mentor, always being patient as I shaped and reshaped the manuscript. We also had a few telephone calls, and it was really fun to actually speak with him (and also sometimes Jim French.)

Finally, my first script, "The Terrible Tragedy of Lytton House", was recorded, and then broadcast nationwide on Sunday, November 24th, 2013. *Imagination Theatre* wasn't on any of my local radio stations, and I didn't want to wait to hear it on the internet stream in a week or so. Therefore, I hunted until I found a station broadcasting it that night, and my family and I listened, huddled 'round our computer in the same way that families in generations past had surrounded their radios, once again enjoying Old Time Radio as we experienced "movies for your mind". It was then that I was able to, in my own small way, contribute to the great Sherlock Holmes radio legacy.

The next round was easier, and that second script, "The Singular Affair at Sissinghurst Castle", was finally finished, recorded, and broadcast nearly a year after the first, November 23rd, 2014. And just like when the first was broadcast, I was thrilled to be a part of it all.

I became busy with other projects after that, but stayed in touch with Larry. In early 2015, I came up with the idea of a series of Holmes anthologies, *The MX Book of New Sherlock Holmes Stories*, which I would edit. The stories would be about the traditional Holmes, a push-back against those adaptations that maligned Holmes and tried their best to greatly damage his reputation by making him a creep and a modern-day killer and an all-around jerk – along with all the other associated characters. The author royalties from these anthologies would go to support the Stepping Stones School for special needs children at Undershaw, one of Sir Arthur Conan Doyle's former homes. I reached out to Larry about including one of Jim French's Holmes scripts in the collection. He happily helped me out, and that became the first of many of Jim's scripts that have since appeared as the MX anthology series continues to grow.

In the meantime, *Imagination Theatre* continued from success to success. Throughout its initial run, there were 128 episodes of *The Further Adventures of Sherlock Holmes*. (This number temporarily paused before *Imagination Theatre* closed its doors in early 2017, due to Jim French's poor health. The company has since come back, with new broadcasts – including new Holmes adventures – appearing on an irregular basis.) Additionally, between 2005 and 2016, John Patrick Lowrie and Larry Albert also recorded the entire Canon, as *The Classic Adventures of Sherlock Holmes*, with all scripts being adapted by one person, Matthew Elliott, and with the same two actors as Holmes and Watson – only the second time that has ever been done, and the only time with American actors. John and Larry have also become the two actors who have portrayed Holmes and Watson for the longest stretch of time.

In late 2016, I approached both Larry and publisher Steve Emecz with the idea for *Imagination Theatre's Sherlock Holmes*, which would include a representative Holmes script from every author who had written one for the series. Both Larry and Steve were very encouraging, and I got busy. I found that, even though there were a large number of Imagination Theatre Holmes scripts, there really weren't that many of us Imagination Theatre Holmes writers – just sixteen, and some of those had been as co-writers. I began contacting them – most were easy to find, as I had worked with them on previous MX Anthology projects, while a few others were more difficult. We are a diverse group, living in both North America and Great Britain. I eventually found everyone, and all agreed to donate a script to the proposed volume, which was published in late 2017. Like the MX Anthologies, the royalties for *Imagination Theatre's*

Sherlock Holmes went to support the Stepping Stones School. The earlier anthologies have raised almost $50,000, and this book has added to that growing amount.

Sadly, just as the books were published, and before he could see a copy, Jim French passed away on December 20th, 1887, at the age of eighty-nine. A legend in radio, he first began his career in 1959. He was responsible for keeping broadcast radio drama alive when it was faltering all around him. He was the creator of the popular radio detective Harry Nile, and in support of Sherlock Holmes, he personally wrote forty-eight scripts about Our Heroes, Holmes and Watson – all of which are included in this three-volume collection. (Additionally, he co-wrote two others with Gareth Tilley, who has graciously allowed them to be included as well, making for an even fifty!

It was sometime in late 2017 that Larry Albert sent me a box of Jim French's scripts for use in future MX anthologies. That started me thinking, and I realized that – with another boxful to round out the first – I'd have access to all of Jim's Holmesian output. It would be a lot of work on my part – a massive amount, really – but worth it to have these preserved in this format, to complement the performed and broadcast versions.

In each case, I had to scan each individual script page-by-page into a computer file, and then run each of them through text-conversion software – which didn't work very well, especially considering all the unique indentations and handwritten notes that were on each original script – all of which came from the *Imagination Theatre* files, or were Larry's own personal working copies, used during the performance. After the scanning was complete, they had to be formatted for consistency, to fit with the overall book, and then finally edited. All of this occurred around real life, and family, and work, and also while editing a number of other Sherlockian volumes and writing pastiches of my own. But I chipped away at it, script by script by script, and finally, after taking much longer than I would have liked, it's finished. Errors have certainly crept in here and there, and if I had time to go through it yet again and look for them I would, but I hope that tolerant and patient readers will forgive me, in the spirit of being able to read these collected scripts, and appreciate the genius that was Jim French.

The group of script-writers who wrote the various Holmes adventures for *Imagination Theatre* all did it as a labor of love, and those individuals involved with this book have been no different.

Personally, I'm so very fortunate at having been a small part of *Imagination Theatre*'s Sherlock Holmes, contributing to that incredible body of work that makes up the entirety of Sherlock Holmes on Radio. It's continuous legacy stretching back for decades – no approaching a century! – and I'm incredibly proud to have been a small part of it.

Personally I'd like to thank the following:

- My wife Rebecca and son Dan, who continually support me as I'm able to be a part of this Great Sherlockian Party! You are both everything to me!

- Larry Albert – From the enjoyment you've given me playing Watson the CORRECT way, to the time we started corresponding about my first Holmes book, to the incredibly helpful advice you gave as I started writing scripts, and then the monumental bend-over-backwards effort you made to gather materials for use in this book: Cheers to you, sir!

- John Patrick Lowrie – Likewise, for giving such an amazing performance as Holmes, and for the help and encouragement as this project progressed.

- Jim French – His work and efforts were amazing, and he truly deserves all the admiration that people have for him.

- Matthew Elliott – You have written the greatest number of Holmes scripts for *Imagination Theatre* – both *Further Adventures* and *Classic Adventures*, as well as the scripts since the company has been revived following Jim's death. I've enjoyed your Holmes stories from way back, when I first found them in various publications such as the old *Sherlock* magazine, and later when I found *Imagination Theatre*. I always knew that I could count on you to write a story about the *Correct* Holmes. Then, when the idea for the MX Anthologies came along, you were incredibly

8

supportive. I was very glad to get the opportunity to meet you at the MX Anthology launch part in London in 2015, and I hope to get the chance again someday.

- Gareth Tilley – Much appreciation for providing information on how you and Jim French divided the writing duties on "Lord Halsworth's Kitchen" and "The Ten-Pound Notes" while you learned about creating scripts. Your generosity in letting me include these scripts in this collection, as well as works by you in other volumes, is very much appreciated.

- The other Imagination Theatre Holmes script writers (besides Jim, Matthew, Gareth, and me) who also contributed Holmes scripts to *The Further Adventures*. You gave me hours of entertainment, and presented Mr. Holmes exactly they way he always should be:

  o Larry Albert
  o John Patrick Lowrie
  o Matthew Booth
  o J.R. Campbell
  o Jeremy B. Holstein
  o Roger Silverwood
  o Teresa Collard
  o John Hall
  o Steven Phillip Jones
  o Daniel McGachey
  o Iain McLaughlin and Claire Bartlett

- Brian Belanger – Thanks once again for such wonderful work. I've enjoyed working with you on many projects now, and look forward to many more. And one of these days, I'll visit your part of the world and shake your hand. You have been warned!
- Steve Emecz – As always, you are incredibly supportive with these various ideas that pop into my

9

brain, and you've helped me to explore different corners of the Sherlockian Sandbox in ways that I would have never had otherwise. I can't wait to see what happens next. Thanks, my friend!

And last, but certainly *not* least: **Sir Arthur Conan Doyle**. Author, doctor, adventurer, and the Founder of the Sherlockian Feast. Present in spirit, and honored by all of us here.

This book demonstrates once again why Holmes and Watson have been so popular for so long. These are just more tiny threads woven into the ongoing Great Holmes Tapestry, continuing to grow and grow, for there can *never* be enough stories about the man whom Watson described as *"the best and wisest . . . whom I have ever known."*

David Marcum
July 27th, 2019
The 139th Anniversary of
The Battle of Maiwand,
where Watson was injured,
leading to his meeting
Mr. Sherlock Holmes
on January 1st, 1881

Questions, comments, or story submissions
may be addressed to David Marcum at
thepapersofsherlockholmes@gmail.com

Writing for Sherlock Holmes
An Interview with Jim French
(From July 2017)

Jim French passed away on December 20th, 2017, at the age of eighty-nine. Several months before his death, he was asked to write a foreword to Imagination Theatre's Sherlock Holmes, *a volume collecting a representative scripts from each of the writers who had contributed to* The Further Adventures of Sherlock Holmes *over the years. Instead of a foreword, he answered a series of questions presented by Larry Albert . . . .*

J*im French is now eighty-eight years old, and sadly not the best of health. When it was suggested to him that he write a piece for this volume, he was ready, but ultimately unable to do so. However, you can't keep a good radio man down, and he asked if it could be done as an interview instead, and if that could be used that to fill the bill. Brilliant!*

Below is that interview – not in its entirety, as that would take too many pages. It's not a comprehensive story of his life, for that would fill a different volume. The man started in radio back in the mid-forties as a teenager, and has only retired this year, with over seventy years in the medium. He wrote his first dramas in the late nineteen-forties for Armed Forces Radio while stationed with the occupation forces in post-World War II Japan, and he really never gave up on the idea that good audio drama has a place in the lives of the people. Some say that almost single-handedly, Jim reintroduced professional quality dramatic radio back onto the American airwaves. Jim doesn't like that idea and denies it almost vehemently.

But I digress. Now it's Jim's turn to talk . . . .

Lawrence Albert

WHY DID YOU WANT WRITE A RADIO PLAY ABOUT SHERLOCK HOLMES?

Why does any serious writer want to see if they can copy the style of a master like Conan Doyle? To see if he can do it and do it well. Several people suggested the idea to me over the years, so after I left daily broadcasting, I thought I'd give it a try.

IS THAT PLAY INCLUDED IN THIS COLLECTION?

Heavens no! I never finished it. Can't recall why just now, but it sat in the files for quite a long while. As matter of fact, I'd forgotten all about it. It wasn't many years later that my friend Larry (Albert) was going through the drawers, trying to straighten out my filing system, that the thing resurfaced. Being a Holmes fan, he asked if he could read it.

HOW DID HE LIKE IT?

Well, his feelings as I recall were mixed. He liked the story, but he hated the treatment of Watson – said it was too *Nigel Bruce*. I was up front with him and said that the Rathbone and Bruce films were my main source of information when it came to writing about Holmes and Watson, and that I'd never read a real Sherlock Holmes story. He came in the next day with a complete collection of Conan Doyle's stories and told me to read some of these and then finish the script.

I did, and this time I got Watson down correctly, at least according to Larry. It was all easy after that. Another friend of mine, the late Bill Brooks, was able to direct me to the attorney who handles the rights to the characters for the Estate of Doyle's daughter, Jean. Through him, we arranged to do five or six plays and pay a royalty for each. This allowed us to use the tag *"With permission from the Estate of Dame Jean Conan Doyle"*.

TELL ME ABOUT CASTING THE SHOWS.

(Laughs) Well, that was fairly easy. Larry, who worked with me full time as my operations manager, as well an actor and director, and I went to lunch to discuss that very thing. Turns out, we were both in sync when it came to casting Holmes: John Gilbert.

WHY HIM?

John in real life was Sherlock Holmes when it came to intensity, focus, and the ability to make the most mundane seem exciting. I'd used him several times over the years in different types of roles, and he never disappointed. Plus I knew his stage work, so there was never any doubt who should be Holmes.

AND WATSON?

Well, now that wasn't so easy. When I asked Larry that question, he didn't miss a beat. He named himself. Apparently, I hesitated just long enough for him to start selling me on him as Watson. I finally said yes, and we scheduled the first session in front of a live audience. People loved John and the script, but I wasn't all that sure about Larry and in the next week, I held some quiet auditions for the role. However, the night of the broadcast, I heard Watson through Larry's voice and knew I had the right guy.

HOW DID JOHN PATRICK LOWRIE JOIN THE CAST?

Well, sadly after eighteen episodes as Holmes, John Gilbert's health started to deteriorate, and he decided to give up acting. Naturally, that left me with the decision of either ending the series or finding another actor. I decided to recast, and again Larry and I were in line with each other. We both chose John Patrick Lowrie and he agreed. Unfortunately, he was touring in the East with a production of *The Diary of Anne Frank* and wouldn't be back for a few months.

Rather than go so long without a Holmes story, I wrote two shows that featured Dr. Watson as the main hero, assisted by Mycroft Holmes, as played by Ted D'Arms. Then John returned, and that's when the show really took on a life of its own. He and Larry were a perfect match as far as I'm concerned, and John's interpretation of Holmes stands with the best.

HOW DID YOU DISCOVER M. J. ELLIOTT?

Matthew told me that he'd been surfacing the Internet for Holmes audio and ran across our website. I don't recall if he managed to hear any episodes, but he was curious enough to send us one of his scripts. Now, that alone is not too unusual – folks had been sending plays to me for years – but Matthew's was from England via snail mail. I opened the envelope, read the piece, and told Larry we were going to record it without any changes. This is the first time in my career I'd ever done such a thing.

After that, M. J. Elliott became a familiar name to our listeners, and over the years he wrote for several of our series, and as well as Holmes, we even let him create his own successful show, *The Hilary Caine Mysteries*. By the time we closed our doors, the man had

13

written and we had produced over two-hundred of his plays, including his adaptations the entire Holmes Canon.

Of even greater value, as I see it, is the fact that he opened the doors for others to join our ranks as writers and make real contributions – not only to Holmes, but also to the libraries of truly well-done mysteries. Matthew Booth, Iain McLaughlin, Claire Bartlett, J. R. Campbell, David Marcum, Daniel McGachey, Steven Phillip Jones, John Hall, Roger Silverwood, Teresa Collard, Jeremy Holstein, Gareth Tilley, and on a couple of occasions John Patrick Lowrie and Lawrence "Larry" Albert.

NOW THAT IT'S OVER, DO YOU HAVE A SENSE OF SPECIAL ACCOMPLISHMENT?

To a small degree perhaps. I don't know. Our job was to produce and syndicate quality audio drama, and in that, yes, there is a sense of achievement. We did it for twenty-one years, one thousand-ninety-three weeks, without missing a week. As far as Sherlock Holmes – well, we aired one hundred and twenty-eight new stories and all sixty of the stories from The Canon, so you could say we added more to his body of work then just a small amount.

Oddly enough, even though *The Further Adventures* ran for nineteen years and *The Classic Adventures* ran for ten, and even though John and Larry are the longest running Holmes and Watson in the history of American radio, and Larry is the longest running audio Dr. Watson anywhere, we are quite probably the least known of the all the audio series ever done, and it really doesn't matter. We did it with seasoned professionals, with marvelous writing, with attention to detail, with dedication, and determination to get it right, and most of all with humor and heart.

Jim French
July 2017

14

Jim French

Foreword
by Lawrence Albert
"Dr. John H. Watson"

Jim French (1928-2018), wherever you are old son, thank you for your courage, creativity, desire to continue to the art of full cast audio drama, for the gift of Watson, and your incredible friendship.

When I was cast as Dr. John H. Watson back in 1998, I never seriously gave any thought to the idea I might still be playing the role twenty-one years later, or that anyone would be interested in preserving the efforts of the work done by the many writers for the character in not one but several books. Yet here we are, because of the remarkable David Marcum and his dedication the world of Sherlock Holmes pastiches. "Pastiche" a word defined by Webster as:

1. A literary, artistic, musical, or architectural work that imitates the style of previous work. *His building designs are pastiches based on classical forms.* Also: Such stylistic imitation.

2. A musical, literary, or artistic composition made up of selections from different works: POTPOURRI: *The research paper was essentially a pastiche made up of passages from different sources; and* HODGEPODGE: *The house is decorated in a pastiche of Asian styles.*

However, to many it means a "lesser" work done in the style of the original. To some it is a continuation of the work, and in some cases a better work then the original. Now don't misunderstand me. I am in no way saying that the scripts you'll find in these volumes surpass the writings of Sir Arthur. No, but I am confident the many will be found by the reader to be close to, and perhaps as well executed. Plus, if the reader ever has the chance to hear the actual produced version of the plays, they just may find themselves transported back to the late Victorian Age of the Baker Street duo in a slightly more tangible manner then a well-written short story. Why? It's not difficult to explain: The tales you'll read here were

16

designed to be performed out loud, with music and sound effects adding to the creation of a nineteenth century England that is now only seen in grainy out-of-sync films from the period, or what we read about in written memoirs.

In the written piece, the reader is required to create the sounds and costumes themselves, right down to the voices of Holmes and Watson. In the world of audio drama, the listener is given a bit of help via the voices working in tandem with the effects and music. The script, as in the short story or novel, has to create the world in a manner that transports the individual. However, in our medium, John Patrick Lowrie, myself, and all the actors, have the extra-added duty to be as believable as possible to aid in that transportation. Mostly I think we succeeded, but it all starts with the play. In these volumes, I'm sure you'll see why our jobs gave us as much joy as we hope we gave the listeners.

Enjoy.

Lawrence Albert
March 2019

Forward
by John Patrick Lowrie
"Sherlock Holmes"

Where would we be without Sherlock Holmes? It took almost two centuries of The Age of Reason before a character like Sherlock could emerge. For, though he is largely seen as a detective and crime fighter, a force of good versus evil, his revolutionary contribution to the human dialogue is a voice of reason: Reason versus superstition, reason versus bias, reason versus assumption. Rigorous thinking, taking nothing for granted, doubting everything, assuming nothing.

How have these ideas and practices affected our social structures? Can we even quantify it? If I tried to list the superstitions, biases, and assumptions that shaped the 19th Century, I would certainly still be writing this in the 22nd, and many of those biases and assumptions still plague us today.

And yet Sherlock was subject to biases of his own. He is a complex character, a flawed character, and for all his genius and rigor a very human character. When we read Sherlock we know that we can only aspire to objectivity, never achieve it. Even when we bring every intellectual tool in our arsenal to bear on a problem, we will still view the world from our own tiny perspective. We will trip on our own prejudice. With all his arrogance, he teaches us humility.

It has been my privilege, honor, and more than anything else, pleasure to voice Sherlock Holmes in Jim French's *Imagination Theatre* audio dramas for the last two decades. With any luck at all, I will get to continue for many years to come.

John Patrick Lowrie
June 2019

John Patrick Lowrie and Lawrence Albert

Recording
Imagination Theatre

Photos Courtesy of Larry Albert

20

Photos Courtesy of Larry Albert

The Further Adventures

of

Sherlock Holmes

(Part I: 1881-1891)
The Complete
Jim French
Imagination Theatre
Scripts

ANNOUNCER: *The Further Adventures of Sherlock Holmes*, starring John Patrick Lowrie as Sherlock Holmes, and Lawrence Albert as Dr. John H. Watson!

MUSIC: *DANSE MACABRE* (UP AND UNDER)

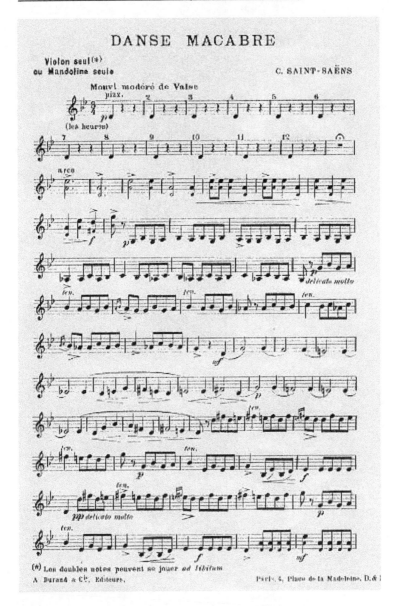

School for Scoundrels

CHARACTERS

- SHERLOCK HOLMES – *Age twenty-seven. He sounds a bit younger than he usually will in this series*
- DR. JOHN H. WATSON – *Age twenty-nine. In the narration he is the middle-aged Watson already established, but in the scenes he should sound a little younger, almost matching Holmes's age*
- MRS. HUDSON – *Scot dialect. She is around sixty*
- JEAN SAMSON – *About thirty. She runs the family publishing business, and is trying to be independent, for the time*
- ROBERT MASON – *About twenty-four. A spoiled son of a successful businessman. Lazy but plenty charming*
- PETER SIDNEY – *A chum of Mason's, not terribly bright*
- *EMILY CALKINS – Highborn accent*
- PROFESSOR MURDOCH – *Mason and Sidney's teacher*
- BARMAID – *Low class Cockney. Very young and coarse*

SOUND EFFECT: OPENING SEQUENCE, BIG BEN, STREET SOUNDS

ANNOUNCER: *The Further Adventures of Sherlock Holmes . . . .*

MUSIC: *DANSE MACABRE* (UP AND UNDER)

WATSON: My name is Doctor John H. Watson. The story I'm about to tell you happened very early in my association with Sherlock Holmes. It was in the year 1881, just after Holmes had successfully concluded the case I called *A Study in Scarlet*, and on an April afternoon, Holmes was absorbed with one of his odious chemical experiments, when our landlady, Mrs. Hudson, tapped at our door.

SOUND EFFECT: DOOR OPENS

MRS. HUDSON: Excuse me, Doctor Watson, but a message has come for Mr. Holmes – Good gracious! What's that smell?

WATSON: It's one of his experiments.

MRS. HUDSON: Well!

HOLMES: (OFF-MICROPHONE) Ah, Mrs. Hudson. Have you come about the collection of dirty dishes you left after last night's supper? You'll find them in the kindling box.

WATSON: (UP) No, she has a message for you.

HOLMES: Then read it to me please, both of my hands are occupied at the moment. And then remove the plates if you please.

MRS. HUDSON: Well!

HOLMES: You've already said that. The message?

SOUND EFFECT: LIGHT PAPER ENVELOPE OPENED, SHEET WITHDRAWN

MRS. HUDSON: Here, Doctor.

WATSON: Hmm. It says, *"To Mr. Sherlock Holmes: I am in possession of information too delicate to entrust to the police, but which must be addressed before any more women like me are victimized. Trusting in your discretion, I request an audience with you at the earliest moment. I shall await your reply and am prepared to come whenever you can see me."* And it's signed *"U.S.".*

MRS. HUDSON: The messenger is waiting, Mr. Holmes.

HOLMES: And so am I, for the process of fulmination, which should – take – place right – now!

SOUND EFFECT: A SHARP EXPLOSION, BREAKING A GLASS

MRS. HUDSON: Mercy!

WATSON: What on earth . . . ?

HOLMES: A-ha!

WATSON: Good grief, Holmes . . . There's smoke up to the ceiling! I'll get a window open!

<u>SOUND EFFECT: WATSON STRIDES TO THE WINDOW, SLIDES IT OPEN. BAKER STREET IN BACKGROUND</u>

MRS. HUDSON: (OFF) Really, Mr. Holmes! Do you know what you're doin' with that mess?

HOLMES: I know precisely what I'm doing. What you have just witnessed will advance the science of crime investigation by years! And it was first performed under your roof! Now: Tell the messenger twelve o'clock noon. That should give me time enough to put things right. And do take the dishes away, Mrs. Hudson.

<u>SOUND EFFECT: UNDER: SHE WALKS ACROSS ROOM, GATHERS PLATES AND SILVERWARE AS SHE MUTTERS, RETRACES HER STEPS</u>

MRS. HUDSON: (OVER ALL THE ABOVE, MOVING OFF) I tried to come for the dishes last night but you were playing your violin so loud you didn't hear me. First it's noises from the fiddle and now it's stink from your chemicals . . . I don't know how much more a body can take, I truly don't!

<u>SOUND EFFECT: DOOR SLAMS</u>

HOLMES: (MOVING ON, LAUGHS GOOD-NATUREDLY) Now let's have a look at that message, Watson.

WATSON: Here you are.

HOLMES: (PAUSE) Yes. (SNIFFS) Hmm.

WATSON: Do you think it's anything interesting?

HOLMES: Oh, certainly. It's most provocative. Here we have a well-educated woman, a strong woman, unmarried and independent, not accustomed to appealing for help, especially from men.

WATSON: You got all that from the note?

HOLMES: (BORED) Yes, Watson, the words have a message and the paper and ink have another. Help me clear away these things.

SOUND EFFECT: (UNDER) BOTTLES, TUBES AND VIALS BEING PLACED IN A SMALL WOOD BOX

HOLMES: Her language is direct – none of the apologetic manners of a stranger begging help from a professional, as I've seen so often. She "requests" rather than "begs" an "audience" – businesslike and formal. No, this is a strong and purposeful individual. (By the way, try not to shake the fluid in that tube.)

WATSON: This tube?

HOLMES: Yes. Put it in the corner of the box and put that cotton around it, there's a good fellow. Now – as to the note itself. She wrote it rapidly. The pen slashes show that she didn't linger over the composition. And the paper is of high quality, with a high rag content. And it has just a faint smell of lavender, which means that the writer, for all her assertiveness, still has feminine characteristics.

WATSON: What do you make of – ?

HOLMES: Careful there! That gray dust from the explosion will eat your skin away if it gets wet.

MUSIC: SHORT BRIDGE, SEGUE TO

SOUND EFFECT: BAKER STREET FAINTLY IN BACKGROUND. MANTEL CLOCK STRIKES TWELVE (UNDER). MRS. HUDSON KNOCKS ON THE DOOR

HOLMES: (SATISFIED SIGH) Ah. Another characteristic I expected from our new client is punctuality. (UP) Come in, Mrs. Hudson.

MRS. HUDSON: This is the lady who has an appointment with you, Mr. Holmes.

HOLMES: Yes indeed. Do come in.

SOUND EFFECT: (UNDER DIALOGUE) FEMALE STEPS IN

MRS. HUDSON: This is Mr. Sherlock Holmes and Doctor Watson.

JEAN: How do you do. Thank you for seeing me.

HOLMES: That will be all, Mrs. Hudson. Thank you.

SOUND EFFECT: DOOR CLOSES

WATSON: Won't you take a seat, madam?

JEAN: I won't take much of your time, so I prefer to stand.

HOLMES: As you wish.

JEAN: Which one of you is Mr. Holmes?

HOLMES: I am Sherlock Holmes.

JEAN: Yes, well, due to the nature of my – situation, I would prefer to share it with the fewest possible people.

HOLMES: Doctor Watson is a physician as well as my trusted associate. We work together.

WATSON: Dear lady, please have no concern that I –

JEAN: Very well, if I must, then I must. Here is my problem. Well, if it were only *my* problem, I would bear the shame in private and never speak of it to another person. But since a friend of mine has suffered the identical experience, I know it's my duty to help put a stop to it.

HOLMES: And so let us begin by being totally and completely candid, starting with your name.

JEAN: Jean Samson.

HOLMES: Watson, will you please write down these particulars?

JEAN: Must he?

HOLMES: He must. Now, your problem. In minute detail, Miss. Samson, and from the very beginning, if you please.

JEAN: Well, I work for the family publishing house, and I'm an editor. Perhaps you can understand why I'm reluctant to have anyone take this down – the written word is rather indelible . . .
.

HOLMES: And transferable, but you must rely upon us to respect your privacy. No one will see Watson's notes except for me.

JEAN: (PETULANT SIGH) All right. To get to the point, I met a man.

HOLMES: Ah.

JEAN: It's not as you may think. He was an author. Or, well, he brought in a manuscript which he said he'd written. I read it. It was charmingly done – Memoirs of an English lad brought up in California. It needed a good deal of work, but the core of it was good.

HOLMES: The man's name?

JEAN: Robert Mason. His story was about Indians and cowboys and the Gold Rush. Not original subjects, but nicely treated. We decided to publish it, so I was obliged to work with Robert on a daily basis.

HOLMES: And?

JEAN: And we began to see each other socially. He seemed the perfect gentleman, and we got on quite well. And in time, he proposed marriage.

HOLMES: And did you accept?

JEAN: Yes. I hadn't expected to marry. I'm educated, enjoying more independence than most women. I'm an only child, so Father pinned his hopes for maintaining the family's fortunes on me. And . . . . and that's where the shame of it comes in. After our engagement was announced, one day Robert took me to see a house that he'd found, a true honeymoon cottage . . . (BEGIN FADE) . . . and it was perfect! A dream of a place . . . .

SOUND EFFECT: (FADE IN) HANSOM CAB IN MOTION

ROBERT: Then you liked it?

JEAN: I loved it! But can you afford it?

ROBERT: Well, when I knew I'd found the girl of my dreams . . . that's you, Jeannie . . . I wired to the States for my money. It's in a bank in San Francisco. I have nearly ten-thousand dollars there!

JEAN: My goodness!

ROBERT: But poor old Dad, he got things mixed up somehow, and now I have to sign a release form to authorize the shipment of silver certificates to the Bank of England, and it's apt to take weeks to get here! And I'm afraid I may lose the house if I can't pay the agent. So, I hate to bring it up, but . . . Jean?

JEAN: Yes, dear?

ROBERT: Do you suppose your father could advance us the money to put down on the house, just until my money arrives? (BEGIN FADE) It'll just be temporary, and this way we can start married life in our own little nest . . . .

33

JEAN: (FADE IN) Well, you can imagine what happened. Father handed Robert a thousand pounds, and that was the last I ever saw or heard from him!

WATSON: The blackguard!

JEAN: And after he disappeared, Father and I drove to the house to see if it was still available, and there was someone else living in it. They said they'd never heard of Robert Mason.

WATSON: What a rotter!

HOLMES: Do you have a photograph of him?

JEAN: No.

HOLMES: Do you still have his manuscript?

JEAN: Yes.

HOLMES: Excellent. I want to see it immediately. Now, what about this friend of yours?

JEAN: Emily Calkins.

HOLMES: What happened to her?

JEAN: Almost the same thing. Will you try to help her too?

MUSIC: BRIDGE

SOUND EFFECT: COUNTRY GARDEN (BACKGROUND)

EMILY: His name is Peter Sidney. We were to be married in June. His parents live in Canada, and Peter needed the money to pay for their passage to come to the wedding, so I gladly lent him fifteen-hundred pounds. It was only a loan. And I never heard from him again. (PAUSE) Oh, I feel such a fool!

JEAN: I know. I shall never trust another man again.

HOLMES: How did you meet Peter Sidney, Miss Calkins?

34

EMILY: At the Literary Circle.

HOLMES: What is that?

JEAN: It's a charity. It pays for tutors to teach foreigners and the poor how to read. Emily and I both belong. That's how we met.

HOLMES: I take it the members are all rather well-to-do?

EMILY: Well . . . .

JEAN: I wouldn't say well-to-do. Not all of us are.

EMILY: Our parents all have money, though. We do have that in common.

MUSIC: UNDERCURRENT

WATSON: Holmes took further information from the two women, and then we rode back to Baker Street. I thought he'd find the case of the two jilted women a bit trifling, but it turned out to be much more involved than it looked at the outset.

MUSIC: FAST FADEOUT

HOLMES: Poke up the fire a bit, will you Watson?

SOUND EFFECT: POKER ON THE GRATE, IRON DOOR CLOSES

HOLMES: That's better. Took a bit of a chill in the cab.

WATSON: How are you going to go about solving this one, Holmes?

HOLMES: The one piece of evidence available to us is Robert Mason's manuscript. That is where I shall begin.

MUSIC: UNDERCURRENT

35

WATSON: In the late afternoon, we were visited again by Jean Samson, who brought Holmes the manuscript. Mrs. Hudson brought in hot tea and biscuits, and Holmes sat by the fire, studying the huge stack of pages. Being something of a writer myself, I took an interest in the work, which was neatly written on lined copybook paper.

MUSIC: OUT

HOLMES: I wonder if he wrote it or got it from someone else. Have you a sample of Mason's handwriting, Miss Samson? Other than the manuscript?

JEAN: Let me think. No, I don't think so.

HOLMES: No love notes you might have saved?

JEAN: No, Mr. Holmes. There was nothing to save, and if there had been, I would have burned it.

HOLMES: Then first thing in the morning, I need you to contact all the publishing houses in London, and inquire if any of them have seen this same manuscript. Does it have a title?

JEAN: Uh . . . yes. *A Briton in the Gold Rush.* But Mr. Holmes, there are nearly a hundred publishers in London!

HOLMES: Then Watson will be glad to help. Give him half your list. We must make haste, Miss Samson, before the culprit swindles any more women!

MUSIC: UNDERCURRENT

WATSON: Fortunately, most of the thirty-seven firms on my list were located along Fleet Street, and I was footsore when, at well past teatime, I limped back up to our rooms, having found no one who'd seen the manuscript.

MUSIC: OUT

SOUND EFFECT: DOOR CLOSES

WATSON: Holmes? Holmes, are you here? Hmm.

<u>SOUND EFFECT: SOFT FOOTFALLS ON RUG UNDER</u>

WATSON: Eh? What's this? A note on the gasogene? Now, how would he know I'd be wanting to mix myself a whisky? What does it say?

<u>SOUND EFFECT: PAPER FLEX</u>

WATSON: *"Meet me at Sheldrake Arms, Oaken Road, Disston, and bring your notebook. Now enjoy your whisky."*

<u>MUSIC: BRIDGE</u>

<u>SOUND EFFECT: QUIET INN BACKGROUND</u>

WATSON: Ah, there you are, Holmes. Wh – ? I say! And Miss Samson! I didn't know you'd be here.

JEAN: Mr. Holmes thinks we're onto something and asked me to join him.

HOLMES: Sit down, Watson. I'll order you a pint.

WATSON: (DOWN) Well, I wore out my shoes for nothing. Nobody I talked with had ever seen the manuscript.

JEAN: But I had better luck. Regency Press was offered it and they turned it down. Only it turns out the manuscript wasn't really Mason's at all. When Regency looked at it, the author was a Professor Murdoch.

WATSON: Ah, Mason stole it, then.

HOLMES: Professor Murdoch teaches at Culverton College, a public school, which is situated a stone's throw from where we are sitting at this moment!

WATSON: Then you know the school?

37

HOLMES: Never heard of it until today, but the barmaid has been most instructive. (UP) Yes, over here, my dear!

BARMAID: (MOVING ON) 'Ello, luv. What'll it be?

HOLMES: Bring him a pint of your brownest ale, my girl.

BARMAID: Comin' right up.

HOLMES: (PAUSE) She is a delightful fountain of gossip. She says Culverton is small and expensive, with a clientele largely made up of rich men's sons who couldn't earn the marks for the better universities. According to her, they bestow diplomas to anyone who can write a large enough cheque. And furthermore, she says Professor Murdoch is a regular patron here at the Sheldrake. He usually happens by after his last class of the day, along with some of his students.

WATSON: But how does this get us any closer to Robert Mason?

HOLMES: It's the manuscript that links the professor to Robert Mason. If Murdoch showed his manuscript to another publisher and Mason showed it to Miss Samson, unless Mason stole it, obviously he and Murdoch know each other.

JEAN: Yes. I could have figured that out.

WATSON: But you don't suppose this Murdoch will give you the goods on Mason, do you?

HOLMES: He might not want to talk to Sherlock Holmes, the consulting detective, but he should very much wish to talk with Sir Hugh Courtney, sole proprietor of British Heritage Press of Coventry.

JEAN: Who? I've never heard of British Heritage Press.

HOLMES: Sir Hugh, at your service.

WATSON: How's that?

JEAN: You're going to pretend you're a publisher?

HOLMES: A publisher with a great desire to print his book. A book Miss Jean Samson was about to throw in the dustbin.

JEAN: Well, you needn't tell him that.

HOLMES: Oh, indeed! I want him to believe every word I say, and when you blend ten percent truth with ninety percent fiction, it makes the fiction sound more like truth.

JEAN: I know, but –

SOUND EFFECT: (UNDER) BARMAID WALKS ON-MICROPHONE, STOPS

BARMAID: 'Ere you go, Ducks.

SOUND EFFECT: HEAVY GLASS SET DOWN ON TABLE

BARMAID: Will you be wantin' anythin' to eat?

HOLMES: Not just now, thank you. But I would like to ask a small favor. I need to know if and when Professor Murdoch comes in.

BARMAID: Well, you're in luck. 'E just walked through the door not a minute ago. You'll find him up front at the bar with some of 'is boys.

HOLMES: Here's a sovereign, my girl. Come back in a minute and describe the professor and the "boys" for me, will you? Tell me what they're wearing so I can . . . surprise them.

BARMAID: Well! Yes sir, right away! (MOVING OFF) I'll be quiet as a cat on a mouse.

JEAN: (PAUSE) What are you up to, Mr. Holmes?

HOLMES: I want you to stay in this booth while I talk with Murdoch.

JEAN: Alone? You want me to sit here alone?

39

WATSON: Actually, Holmes, it would look better if I were to stay here with her. A lady shouldn't be unaccompanied.

JEAN: If you are thinking it's necessary to protect me, please understand that I am a businesswoman, and I deal with reality on a daily basis.

WATSON: (CHUCKLES) Businesswoman! (CHUCKLE) Never heard that term before.

HOLMES: I'm not concerned with protecting you, Miss Samson, I need Watson with me to complete the impersonation. Watson, I'll introduce you as my editorial assistant. You'll have nothing to say except to agree with me. And here comes our barmaid.

BARMAID: (SECRETIVE) The professor is wearing a plaid scarf. The other two are dressed like young bankers.

HOLMES: Young bankers?

BARMAID: Like toffs. You know. Posh.

HOLMES: I see. Thank you. You've been most helpful.

BARMAID: Another pint all 'round?

MUSIC: STING AND UNDERCURRENT

WATSON: I followed Holmes to the front of the inn, where the party the barmaid had described was seated around a table. The three men were just raising their mugs in a toast when we arrived. They paused and looked up at us.

MURDOCH: Yes? Something we can do for you?

HOLMES: Oh, I do hope we're not interrupting. I'm looking for an author, Professor Murdoch.

MURDOCH: I'm Ian Murdoch. And who might you be, sir?

HOLMES: Sir Hugh Courtney, owner of British Heritage Press.

MURDOCH: Oh, a publisher?

HOLMES: Yes, but I fear we've intruded. Perhaps my editor and I can call on you at a more convenient time.

MURDOCH: No time like the present, Sir Hugh! Boys, find a couple of chairs.

HOLMES: No, we really can't stay.

MURDOCH: Well, you've come at a most propitious time, gentlemen. One of my students is about to take himself a bride! Where is that girl, Peter?

PETER: She's shopping. She'll be here directly.

MURDOCH: Now perhaps you'll tell me which of my humble scribbles interests you, Sir Hugh.

HOLMES: The title is *A Briton in The Gold Rush*.

MURDOCH: (PAUSE) Oh, that one.

ROBERT: May I ask where you saw that manuscript?

HOLMES: I rescued it from the dust bin of a fellow publisher who'd rejected it.

MURDOCH: Well, this is indeed a – a happy surprise.

HOLMES: If you will give me your card, I'll send our barrister round to work out the details. But now, we must let you get on with your celebration.

ROBERT: Uh, tell me, what is the name of the person who rejected the manuscript?

MURDOCH: Well, that's hardly important, is it, Robert? The important thing is, the book will be published!

HOLMES: Subject, naturally, to the laws of the Crown relating to copyright. And now that we've found you, there is just one other member of our firm who I'm sure would like to meet you. John, will you go back to our table and bring our – associate?

WATSON: Oh? Yes indeed. I'll be right back.

MURDOCH: I'm curious, Sir Hugh – how did you manage to find me?

HOLMES: You may not believe this, but I employed the services of Sherlock Holmes!

THE "BOYS" (CHUCKLE)

MURDOCH: I believe you're serious.

HOLMES: Oh, I am. Quite serious. Mr. Holmes was retained by a woman who had been defrauded by a despicable sort of fellow. Holmes reasoned that there was a connection between that thief and another chap who had done much the same thing to another woman. And through his remarkable powers of deduction, Mr. Holmes saw that there had to be a third conspirator, and even a fourth!

EMILY: (OFF, MOVING ON) Peter! Peter, I'm back. Sorry I took so long. The shops were crowded. Oh, am I too late for the party?

PETER: Uh, no, dear, uh the party's off. Why don't you go on back to the flat and wait for me?

EMILY: Oh? And who's this?

MURDOCK: (CLEARS THROAT) This is Sir Hugh, uh . . . . (CLEARS THROAT AGAIN)

SOUND EFFECT: CHAIR SCRAPE FLOOR (UNDER)

ROBERT: Look, chaps, I really have to go.

HOLMES: Would this be the bride-to-be?

PETER: Yes. Now really, my dear, you must run along . . . .

42

WATSON: (OFF, MOVING ON, EXCITED) Here she is, Holmes!

HOLMES: Ah, just in time.

ROBERT: Holmes? Did he call you Holmes?

JEAN: Emily! What are you doing here?

HOLMES: Yes. It's time to take off our masks. I am Sherlock Holmes, and this is my associate, Doctor John H. Watson. And the lady with us is my client, Miss Samson. Of course, you all know that.

JEAN: So, Robert, did you ever buy our honeymoon cottage?

ROBERT: I – I don't know her! I've never seen her before!

JEAN: And Peter! It is Peter, isn't it? From the Literary Circle?

PETER: I'm not saying anything! Come on, Emily.

JEAN: Wait! So you were in on it too, Emily? Were you? Were you part of the scheme?

EMILY: And what if I was, Jean? You have plenty of money. You can always buy another friend.

MUSIC: STING

WATSON: Facing criminal charges, Robert Mason and Peter Sidney wilted under Holmes's questioning.

ROBERT: The plan wasn't ours. I didn't think it up. Neither did Peter.

PETER: No. The whole idea came from Professor Murdock. We were failing our grades, you see, and then he said he had a way to be sure we passed.

HOLMES: So he taught you how to steal a thousand pounds from Miss Samson. How much was his share?

43

ROBERT: Half.

PETER: But he did give us passing grades.

HOLMES: And why did you select Jean Samson as your victim?

ROBERT: Oh, that was Emily's job.

PETER: Leave her out of it!

HOLMES: Emily joined the Literary Circle to get to know who had money and was unmarried. Correct?

PETER: That's all she did.

HOLMES: And the story Emily told Miss Samson, about your stealing her money?

PETER: Murdoch made it up so Jean would trust her. Look, Emily and I have been sweethearts for simply ages. We were about to get married on . . . our share of the money. Until Mister Sherlock Holmes butted in!

MUSIC: THEME *DANSE MACABRE* UP AND UNDER

WATSON: Holmes turned the men over to the police. But Jean Samson decided not to press charges against their accomplice, Emily Calkins. I fear I shall never fully understand women. Or the greed that drives some men. Well, I hope you've enjoyed this story, and I have another Sherlock Holmes adventure for you . . . *when next we meet*!

The Adventure of the
Dover Maiden

CHARACTERS

- SHERLOCK HOLMES – *In his late twenties*
- DR. JOHN H. WATSON – *In his late twenties*
- CAPTAIN CHILDS – *Sturdy merchant seaman, possible roots in Australia. Around fifty*
- DONALD TRENTHAM – *Head of a London shoe factory. Fifty-four. Blustery, take-charge type*
- JACK CASPAR – *Courteous, forty. Appears subservient to Trentham. Upscale Brit*
- DOROTHY CASPAR – *Jack's wife, thirty-five. Same regional dialect. Gentle and kind to "Mum"*
- ELOISE TRENTHAM – *Fifty-year-old. Very decent sort. Disapproves of husband Trentham*
- BROWNING – *From the London docks. Defensive, suspicious, reluctant. About eighteen*

SOUND EFFECT: OPENING SEQUENCE, BIG BEN, STREET SOUNDS

ANNOUNCER: *The Further Adventures of Sherlock Holmes* . . . .

MUSIC: *DANSE MACABRE* (UP AND UNDER)

WATSON: My name is Doctor John H. Watson. I don't believe I've ever told you the story of one of the first adventures that Sherlock Holmes and I ever shared, early in in our association. It was in the year 1881. We were much younger then, I was only twenty-nine and Holmes two years my junior. Holmes had concluded the case I would later publish under the title *A Study In Scarlet*, so his name was quite unknown at the time. Well, at any rate, a few weeks after finishing that case, a rather fat envelope arrived at Baker Street, mailed from Paris and addressed to Sherlock Holmes.

45

MUSIC: OUT

SOUND EFFECT: STREET THROUGH WINDOWS FAINTLY. ENVELOPE OPENED

HOLMES: What is this? It's stuffed with francs!

WATSON: Good heavens! How much is in there?

HOLMES: Well, well! Hmm. Listen to this, Watson: (READS) "*My dear Mr. Holmes. Word of your skill as a civilian detective has reached me via an English friend, Inspector Gregson of Scotland Yard, who very much admired your assistance in solving a difficult case . . . .*" (STOPS READING) He must mean the Jefferson Hope matter.

WATSON: Huh. Generous of Gregson to mention you at all. I thought he and Lestrade took all the credit!

HOLMES: No. Of a sorry pair, Gregson is the more honest of the two. I've known that all along. Well, back to the letter: (READING) "*A delicate situation is developing in a noble French institution which I direct. Reputations are at risk, so I dare not inform our police. If you will accept, it is urgent that you investigate immediately. The money is yours to keep, whatever your decision. I await your reply by telegram at the earliest hour.*" (STOPS READING) And it's signed (READING) "*M. Marment, 29 Rue de Lyon, Paris.*" (STOPS READING)

WATSON: I say! He expects you to accept without knowing a thing about the case? What a preposterous assumption!

HOLMES: Yes, quite preposterous, isn't it? How would you like a few days in Paris, Watson? With money to spend!

MUSIC: STING TO UNDERCURRENT

WATSON: Well, Holmes wired his acceptance, despite some misgivings on my part, and we proceeded to pack for an undetermined stay in France. But Fate had other plans. It seemed the channel boats were fully booked with winter-weary

46

Englishmen on a Continental holiday. No sailings were available for a week! But we were able to book passage on a night boat which carried freight and mail, with accommodation for only six passengers. Holmes and I took the last two berths on that evening's sailing.

<u>SOUND EFFECT: BUSY WATERFRONT SOUNDS</u>

WATSON: The evening was mild but cloudy as we arrived at the North Woolwich Dock on the Thames where a packet boat was taking on supplies. The name *Dover Maiden* was just visible on its hull. A man in a dingy uniform stood on the dock, marking off bundles and boxes being taken aboard. Across the brow of his cap, gold letters spelled out "*Captain*".

CAPTAIN: (EXTERIOR) Watson and Holmes? Right. Just go on up the gangway. You're in cabin number four.

<u>MUSIC: UNDERCURRENT</u>

WATSON: And with that began a brief but eventful journey which was to bring into play the brilliant powers of Sherlock Holmes, even before the ship brought us to the shores of France. Holmes and I went aboard the *Dover Maiden* and found our "stateroom" – if you could call it that – in the aft cabin house, which stood above decks at the stem of the ship, and housed four small cabins and a dining lounge, which was furnished with a central table and six chairs, all secured to the deck. Just forward of the deckhouse stood a tall funnel, which had begun to belch smoke. Forward were the hatches over the cargo hold, and forward of that was another deck house where they steered the ship. The galley and crew quarters were below decks. I should say the ship was about one-hundred-twenty feet in length, perhaps a thirty-foot beam. A working vessel, this, with little in the way of amenities.

<u>MUSIC: OUT</u>

<u>SOUND EFFECT: DOOR CLOSES. TWO SUIRCASES SET DOWN</u>

HOLMES: And which shall you have, Watson, the upper or the lower berth?

WATSON: Oh, I don't care . . . .

HOLMES: With that wounded leg of yours . . . hate to make you climb that little ladder . . . .

WATSON: Oh, I don't mind a bit . . . .

HOLMES: Of course it's not as if we're going to spend the night in here . . . .

WATSON: Of course.

HOLMES: Well, good. I'll put my things up there for now.

SOUND EFFECT: HEAVY SUITCASE PLOPPED ON A BUNK

HOLMES: There! Well. Should be cozy.

SOUND EFFECT: KNOCK ON DOOR

HOLMES: Oh? Come in!

SOUND EFFECT: DOOR OPENS

HOLMES: Ah. Captain.

CAPTAIN: Captain Childs is my name. And you would be Mr. Watson and Mr. Holmes.

WATSON: Doctor Watson, actually. I'm a physician. And Mr. Holmes is a detective. A consulting detective.

CAPTAIN: Detective? I'll make a note of that. Now, we should be getting underway as soon as our missing parties show up.

HOLMES: Missing parties?

CAPTAIN: The Caspers. Mister and Missus and her mother. Soon as they're aboard, we're off. Supper bell about eight. Should reach Calais before midnight.

SOUND EFFECT: DOOR OPENS

CAPTAIN: Pleasant journey, gentlemen. Glad to have you aboard.

SOUND EFFECT: DOOR CLOSES

HOLMES: (PAUSE) I feel stifled in this room, Watson. I think I saw a couple of chairs on deck. What say we take the air?

WATSON: Excellent idea.

SOUND EFFECT: THEY STEP TO THE DOOR, OPEN IT, STEP THROUGH IT, CLOSE IT. HOLMES INSERTS KEY IN LOCK, LOCKS THE DOOR

HOLMES: Now, let's see if those chairs are still free.

SOUND EFFECT: THEY WALK ABOUT TEN FEET, STOP. WATERFOUNT ACTIVITY SOUNDS SNEAK UP (UNDER – EXTERIOR)

HOLMES: Ah. Good.

SOUND EFFECT: THEY WALK TO THE CHAIRS AND SIT DOWN

WATSON: Well, they must have finished loading the ship.

HOLMES: Evidently.

WATSON: Just waiting for the – uh – what were their names?

HOLMES: Mr. and Mrs. Casper.

WATSON: Yes.

HOLMES: And here they come now, I should think – pushing the old woman in a wheelchair.

49

WATSON: Yes. They have her well bundled, don't they? Hat, muffler, robe . . . .

HOLMES: And pitifully weak. Her head nods with every bump.

WATSON: Yes, muscle atrophy is common in the very aged. Hmm. The daughter is pausing to talk to her . . . See if she's all right . . . .

HOLMES: You may want to offer your services.

WATSON: Well, there's little anyone can do about diseases of age.

SOUND EFFECT: (OFF) A MAN WALKS UP

TRENTHAM: (OFF, MOVING ON) Well, here they are at last. (YELLS) Ah, Jack! You made it! Need some help?

CASPAR: (CALLS FROM FAR OFF) No, we can manage.

TRENTHAM: (OFF) Hello, Dorothy. Welcome aboard!

DOROTHY: (OFF) Hello, Mr. Trentham.

TRENTHAM: Want some help with that wheelchair?

CASPAR: (CLOSER, SLIGHTLY WINDED) No, thank you, I'm doing fine.

(ALL MOVE CLOSER)

TRENTHAM: I was beginning to wonder if you were going to make it.

CASPAR: It took us a bit longer than we expected to fetch Mum and get her ready.

DOROTHY: And Eloise is aboard?

TRENTHAM: Of course. She's in the cabin feeling seasick already!

CASPAR: Oh, sorry to hear that.

DOROTHY: Poor thing. Which cabin is she in?

TRENTHAM: We're in number one. You'll be in number two, and your mother will be in number three.

CASPAR: I'll take her to her cabin right away. (LOUDER) This is Mr. Trentham, Mum.

TRENTHAM: (UP) Good evening, ma'am.

DOROTHY: She's very hard of hearing, Mr. Trentham. We'll get her comfortable in her cabin, and make sure she's warm enough. Here we go, Mum . . . (FADING OFF) . . . Have you tucked in nice and cozy in no time . . . .

TRENTHAM: These cabins are awfully small, but beggars can't be choosers, booking as late as we did. Lucky I could get tickets at all. (NOW ON-MICROPHONE) Ah. Good evening, gentlemen.

HOLMES *and* WATSON: Good evening.

TRENTHAM: And you'd be cabin four?

HOLMES: Yes, we have cabin number four.

TRENTHAM: Well, I'm Donald Trentham, and this is Jack Caspar.

HOLMES: How do you do? I'm Sherlock Holmes, and this is Doctor John Watson.

WATSON: Good evening.

TRENTHAM: Delighted to meet you both.

CAPTAIN: (EXTERIOR – FAR OFF-MICROPHONE) All right, cast off the bow line!

TRENTHAM: On holiday, are you, gentlemen?

WATSON: No. We're going to Paris on a criminal investigation.

51

CASPAR: You don't say! Are you the police?

HOLMES: I am a consulting detective, and I've been retained to investigate a case in Paris.

CASPAR: Then you don't work for Scotland Yard?

HOLMES: No. As I said, I am a consulting detective.

WATSON: The world's first and only.

CASPAR: Why, that's very impressive. Do you do that kind of work too, Doctor?

WATSON: I help where I can.

HOLMES: Doctor Watson is entirely too modest. I wouldn't care to undertake any investigation without him.

WATSON: Your mother-in-law is ill, I take it, Mr. Caspar?

CASPAR: I'm afraid so. Has been for some time. We're taking her to Lourdes.

WATSON: Oh, I see. Lourdes. For the waters.

CASPAR: For the miracles. People are being cured of all sorts of things. I – I don't know your position on these things, but we are a devout family and our priest gave us his blessing for the trip. Even if our doctor didn't.

HOLMES: And the Trenthams are going there with you?

TRENTHAM: No, I'm afraid my interests are commercial. I own a boot factory in London and I'll be in France on business.

HOLMES: I see. Well, we'll be seeing you gentlemen and your wives at dinner, no doubt.

TRENTHAM: No doubt. Well, I'm going in. Are you coming, Jack?

CASPAR: Eh? Oh, yes, Donald. Coming. Gentlemen.

MUSIC: BRIDGE

SOUND EFFECT: SHIP RUNNING (BACKGROUND INTERIOR). CABIN DOOR CLOSES

WATSON: (STRETCHING LUXURIANTLY) Well, Holmes, our cabin may be a third the size of the one on an ocean liner, but at least I won't have to dress for dinner. I've had enough travel to last me a good while. But you seem to thrive on it.

HOLMES: I thrive on the study of people and circumstances. There is a story hidden beneath the shirt-front of every man in the world!

SOUND EFFECT: A FAST, SURREPTITIOUS RAP ON THE DOOR

HOLMES: We have a visitor.

SOUND EFFECT: HE TAKES TWO STEPS, AND OPENS THE DOOR

CASPAR: Mr. Holmes?

HOLMES: Mr. Caspar.

CASPAR: May I come in?

HOLMES: Certainly.

SOUND EFFECT: HE TAKES TWO STEPS, THE DOOR CLOSES

CASPAR: I hope I'm not intruding.

HOLMES: Not at all.

CASPAR: This is most unusual, I know. But when you said you were a detective, I . . . I felt as if fate had brought us together, in a manner of speaking.

53

HOLMES: How can I be of service?

CASPAR: Mr. Holmes . . . Doctor Watson . . . I . . . I am in fear for my life!

HOLMES: How so?

CASPAR: Do you promise not to say anything to anyone else?

HOLMES: If you like.

CASPAR: For years I have worked faithfully for Trentham Boot Works. I've put Trentham Boots in some of the finest shops in England. And my wife, Dorothy, works in the head office as book-keeper. We devote our lives to the company.

HOLMES: I see.

CASPAR: But lately, Donald Trentham has become . . . well, odd.

HOLMES: In what way?

CASPAR: He . . . he as much as accused me of stealing from the company! I handle domestic sales and collections, and they've been off a bit lately, but he'd rather blame someone than look to the competition.

HOLMES: I see.

CASPAR: But that's not all! He's also made remarks about me and his wife, Eloise! Completely unfounded!

HOLMES: What sort of remarks?

CASPAR: Trentham has a vicious temper, especially when he's drinking, and more than once he's driven Eloise to tears when she's been at the office. All I ever did was offer her some sympathy. A kind word, here and there. But he chose to see something more, when there was nothing more to see!

HOLMES: Then why are the four of you traveling together?

CASPAR: And well you may ask! We had a holiday coming, Dorothy and me, and we'd saved our pennies so we could travel down to the south of France and bring her Mum to Lourdes. And I'd hoped to bathe along the French coast. Well, when Dorothy mentioned our plans to Eloise, Eloise wanted to come along with us, but Donald wouldn't hear of it. Apparently he suspected she just wanted to be near me, which is outrageous! I wouldn't think of looking at another woman, much less the wife of my employer! Anyway, there was a terrible row between the two of them, ending with him agreeing to come along and turn it into a business trip.

HOLMES: And what would you like me to do?

CASPAR: Just watch him, Mr. Holmes. I'm fairly fit, but he's half-again my size and strong as an ox, and with his temper . . . well, if anything should happen to me, I would appreciate it if you knew how the land lies.

HOLMES: I see.

CASPAR: All that Dorothy and I want is a quiet pilgrimage down to Lourdes, and some relief for her poor mother.

HOLMES: I understand.

WATSON: Mr. Caspar, would you like me to look in on her?

CASPAR: Oh, that would be so kind of you, Doctor. Let me slip back to her cabin and see if she's awake. She spends a lot of her time sleeping.

WATSON: Well, if you'd like me to visit her, just say the word.

CASPAR: I will. And thank you both for hearing me out.

SOUND EFFECT: TWO STEPS, DOOR OPENS

CASPAR: (WHISPER) And please, not a word!

HOLMES: (QUIETLY) Our lips are sealed.

55

SOUND EFFECT: DOOR CLOSES

WATSON: (PAUSES) Well! What was that you were saying about a story behind every shirt-front?

HOLMES: Yes! I had no hope for the hours we'll have to spend on this miserable little vessel, but now, I look forward to every minute!

MUSIC: UNDERCURRENT

WATSON: The *Dover Maiden* made its way down the Thames at a slow pace, for water traffic was a tangle and it was getting dark. We glided past docks and wharves, and many vessels of all sizes. I stood on the narrow portside promenade, where a deckhand was coiling a rope. From below, I could smell food being cooked in the galley. I'd been standing there only a few minutes when Holmes sauntered up.

MUSIC: OUT

SOUND EFFECT: BOAT (BACKGROUND)

HOLMES: (LOW) Ah, there you are. Watson, we have another visitor in our cabin. Care to join me?

WATSON: Who is it?

HOLMES: Mr. Trentham has taken me aside and asked for a private audience.

WATSON: Oh?

HOLMES: We're about to hear the other side of Mr. Caspar's story, I should think. He's waiting in the cabin right now. And I think he's had a bit to drink.

MUSIC: SWIFT BRIDGE

SOUND EFFECT: DOOR OPENS, THEY GO IN. DOOR CLOSES

TRENTHAM: Good of you to see me. Good evening again, Doctor.

WATSON: Mr. Trentham.

TRENTHAM: I need to say a word to you, Mr. Holmes.

HOLMES: Yes?

TRENTHAM: You've met Jack Caspar, the fellow traveling with us.

HOLMES: Yes?

TRENTHAM: I took him on five years ago as a salesman. Later made him manager. He brought in his wife to keep the books. Ideal employees, I would have thought. But in the past year, I've seen our profits begin to dwindle. Caspar has an explanation, of course – some of our credit customers aren't paying on time, or waste has gone up in the factory, or shipping costs have increased . . . .

HOLMES: But you don't believe it.

TRENTHAM: No. I've done some checking. I think Caspar and his wife are fleecing me, but I'm dashed if I can find out how they're doing it!

HOLMES: And you've spoken to them about this?

TRENTHAM: Of course, but they deny everything.

HOLMES: Well, once we're back in London I may be of some help, but I can do nothing about your business losses while we're away.

TRENTHAM: I understand that, but I'd like you to keep an eye on him all the same.

HOLMES: Well, I may be of some help.

TRENTHAM: But there's another thing . . . . (CLEARS THROAT)

HOLMES: Yes?

TRENTHAM: A man doesn't like to admit these things, but . . .
(CLEARS THROAT)

HOLMES: You may speak freely. It will go no further than this
cabin.

TRENTHAM: Well, the fact is – the fact is, I think Caspar and my
wife Eloise are more than just friends!

HOLMES: Really?

TRENTHAM: Yes. There are certain looks between them . . . Well,
it's hard to put a finger on it, but you know what I mean . . . .

WATSON: If I may say so, it's strange that you would be traveling
together, given your feelings about the Caspars.

TRENTHAM: Well, at first Eloise asked if she could go with them
alone. I refused, but she raised such a row, in the end I had no
other course than to let her go, and go along with her. So, Mr.
Holmes – you're a detective. Now that you know what I've told
you, I want you to watch the three of them, and tell me what
you think. I'll pay you of course. Will you do it?

HOLMES: I'll do what I can.

TRENTHAM: Good. See you at dinner.

SOUND EFFECT: DOOR OPENS, HE STEPS OUT, DOOR
CLOSES

MUSIC: (UNDER)

WATSON: (NARRATING) And with that, Trentham left the cabin,
and Holmes sat on the lower bunk, a smile beginning to crease
his face.

HOLMES: Ha ha! A routine channel crossing turns into a penny
novel! How delightful, Watson! How delightful!

MUSIC: UNDERCURRENT

58

WATSON: But at that moment, Sherlock Holmes couldn't have known the final twist that lay ahead! A bell rang aboard the *Dover Maiden*, calling us to the small dining lounge. As we passed the door to cabin number three, Dorothy Caspar stepped out.

SOUND EFFECT: DOOR OPENS

DOROTHY: I'll bring you your dinner as soon as it's served, Mum.

SOUND EFFECT: DOOR CLOSES

DOROTHY: Oh! Good evening, gentlemen.

HOLMES: Good evening, Mrs. Caspar. Going to dinner?

DOROTHY: Yes.

SOUND EFFECT: THEY START WALKING (UNDER)

(OFF-MICROPHONE, IN THE LOUNGE)

DOROTHY: I'm going to bring Mum her dinner when they serve it.

ELOISE: Donald, really!

TRENTHAM: No, it's time we had it out in the open!

CASPAR: I wouldn't be throwing these charges around, Donald!

TRENTHAM: Don't you think I know what you've been doing? You've been stealing my money and you're trying to steal my wife!

DOROTHY: (ON-MICROPHONE) Good heavens! That's Mr. Trentham!

(OFF-MICROPHONE IN LOUNGE)

ELOISE: Donald, you're drunk! Jack hasn't done a thing!

TRENTHAM: Oh yes, stand up for Jack by all means!

SOUND EFFECT: STEPS STOP. DOOR OPENS

(LOUNGE SCENE NOW ON-MICROPHONE)

TRENTHAM: Oh. And here's Dorothy. You've fixed the books, haven't you, Dorothy?

CASPAR: I won't have you saying that about my wife!

TRENTHAM: I'll say whatever I please about your wife and you and my wife!

ELOISE: You will not! You blame everyone but yourself, Donald!

TRENTHAM: I've got eyes to see with! You think I can't see what's been going on?

ELOISE: Be quiet, Donald, for heaven's sake! We're not alone!

CASPAR: Mister Holmes! Doctor Watson! I'm sorry you had to hear what this madman is saying!

TRENTHAM: Oh, madman, am I? Explain why my company started losing money the same year you came to work for me!

CASPAR: That's a lie! You made more money than ever before, right up until –

TRENTHAM: Oh yes, I would have done, with your wife keeping my accounts and covering up what you stole!

CASPAR: All right! That's enough! If you want to keep talking like this, come out on deck with me!

TRENTHAM: You want me to go out on deck?

SOUND EFFECT: SCRAPE OF FEET. TWO MEN WALK TO DOOR (UNDER)

TRENTHAM: Right, I'll go out on deck and we'll finish it!

60

ELOISE: Donald!

DOROTHY: Jack, don't go, he's bigger than you!

CASPAR: Stay inside, all of you! I can take care of myself, don't you worry!

DOROTHY: Stop them, someone!

SOUND EFFECT: DOOR OPENS

TRENTHAM: I'll be right back when I'm done with this scoundrel!

SOUND EFFECT: STEPS THROUGH, DOOR SLAMS

ELOISE: Oh, I'm so ashamed of my husband! Mr. Holmes, won't you stop them?

DOROTHY: No, Eloise! He's dangerous! Haven't you seen him in a fury before now?

ELOISE: But never like this!

CASPAR: (OFF-MICROPHONE, MUFFLED SHOUT) No, Donald! Don't do it! Please, don't do it!

SOUND EFFECT: SMALL CALIBER PISTOL SHOT FROM OUTSIDE

WATSON: Good Lord!

DOROTHY: Oh! Oh no! He's shot him!

SOUND EFFECT: HOLMES AND WATSON RUN TO DOOR, OPEN IT. BOAT RUNNING (BACKGROUND)

WATSON: (NARRATING OVER SOUND EFFECTS) Holmes and I dashed to the door, the women right behind us. Trentham was at the rail, looking down into the water. On the deck lay a small pistol, and Caspar was nowhere to be seen!

DOROTHY: What have you done, Donald? What have you done?

TRENTHAM: Confound it, I didn't do anything!

ELOISE: I didn't know you brought your gun, Donald!

TRENTHAM: I didn't! That's not my gun! Caspar had the gun! He shot in the air and then he jumped over the rail!

HOLMES: This is not your gun, Mr. Trentham?

TRENTHAM: Uh . . . well . . . it's something like my gun . . . .

ELOISE: Yes it is, Donald! See? Your initials on the handle! It's your gun!

TRENTHAM: But I . . . look here, this isn't the way it looks!

DOROTHY: We all heard you threaten Jack! You've killed him!

HOLMES: Take the gun and hold it carefully, Watson. (MOVING OFF) I'll be back directly.

WATSON: (NARRATING) Holmes disappeared around the stern of the ship. We felt the ship stop. A boat was lowered with two crewmen, to search for Caspar.

DOROTHY: Oh, Poor Jack! And mother! What must she be thinking? She must have heard the shot! (MOVING OFF) I'm going to her cabin! Oh, this is terrible . . . terrible . . . .

MUSIC: EXCITED UNDERCURRENT

WATSON: Dorothy Caspar hurried to her mother's cabin. In the lounge, Trentham sat at the table with his head in his hands, while his wife stood against the wall, visibly shaken. Captain Childs came in shortly after, and announced that as master of the *Dover Maiden*, he would conduct an investigation. The search boat returned, reporting no luck in finding Caspar's body. Then Dorothy Caspar wheeled her mother into the lounge. And finally, Holmes came back in, bringing one of the deckhands with him.

MUSIC: OUT

CAPTAIN: Now, since the crime was committed on a British vessel while in British waters, it's my responsibility to give a full report to Scotland Yard. But Mr. Holmes, here, being a detective himself, has offered to help.

HOLMES: With your permission, Captain, I've asked this sailor to tell me what he knows.

CAPTAIN: Very well, Browning.

BROWNING: Aye, sir.

HOLMES: Browning: I just came round to the portside and I saw a rope tied to the rail, trailing over the side of the ship

BROWNING: (PAUSE) Yes, sir.

HOLMES: Who put it there?

BROWNING: I did.

HOLMES: Why?

CAPTAIN: (AFTER A PAUSE) Speak up, lad!

BROWNING I couldn't see no harm in it, and he give me half-a-quid!

CAPTAIN: Who gave you half-a-quid?

BROWNING: Wull, I don't know his name.

HOLMES: One of the passengers? Is he in this room?

BROWNING (PAUSE) No, sir.

HOLMES: When did you throw the line overboard?

BROWNING: When you lot went into the lounge.

63

HOLMES: Did you see anyone climb aboard on that line?

BROWNING: No, sir, I was belowdecks.

HOLMES: Yes, your part in this was done. Now, here is what I saw: After the gunshot, while the rest of you were still on the starboard side, I walked round the stern of the ship and saw the rope trailing in the water. There was a puddle of water on the deck, and a clear trail of water and footprints leading from the deck to the door of one of the cabins.

CAPTAIN: Are you saying we have a stowaway on board?

HOLMES: Oh, no. We have the same number of souls on board at this minute that we had when we departed.

ELOISE: How can you say that? What about Jack?

HOLMES: Jack is safe and sound.

CAPTAIN: Well then, where is he?

HOLMES: Would you like to show us, Mrs. Caspar? (PAUSE) No? Then permit me to introduce you to your invalid mother, First, I'll just remove her hat and veil . . . .

CAPTAIN: What are you doing?

HOLMES: Then her wig . . . and muffler . . . .

TRENTHAM: My God! It's Caspar!

CASPAR: Oh, all right!

HOLMES: You may step out of the wheelchair now, Mr. Caspar.

TRENTHAM: What – what'd you do with the old lady?

HOLMES: There never was an "old lady", was there, Mr. Caspar? You recall that you told me you enjoy swimming, so I presume that after you fired the gun in the air, you swam round the back

64

of the ship and held to the rope until you were assured the rest of us were all on the other side, then you climbed back aboard and fled into your mother-in-law's cabin, where you stripped off your wet clothes and assumed the disguise. And so, Jack Caspar would have disappeared, the police would hold Donald Trentham for his murder, while you and your wife began a new life in Europe on the cash you embezzled from the shoe company. Is that how you planned it?

CASPAR: You'll never prove it!

HOLMES: I presume you also stole Trentham's gun from his office. Or did your wife do that? Captain, will you inspect cabin number four and locate a soaking wet pair of Trentham brand shoes, and a pile of wet clothes, along with a padded dressmaker's dummy, probably tucked into a steamer trunk.

CAPTAIN: I'll do that, Mr. Holmes. And I'll keep the Caspars under lock and key until we return to England.

WATSON: When faced with the evidence Holmes had found, the Caspars finally confessed. And Holmes and I sailed on to France and another adventure, which I'll tell you about another time. I have a different tale for you . . . *when next we meet*!

MUSIC: THEME *DANSE MACABRE* UP AND UNDER

The Speaking Machine

CHARACTERS

- SHERLOCK HOLMES
- DR. JOHN H. WATSON
- SIDESHOW BARKER
- PROFESSOR ALLESANDRO – *Big, fat, boisterous*
- LYDECKER – *A pompous highborn reformer*
- "VOICE" – *An important part of Allesandro's act*
- MAN 1 – *Cockney*
- MAN 2
- MAN 3

SOUND EFFECT: OPENING SEQUENCE, BIG BEN, STREET SOUNDS

ANNOUNCER: *The Further Adventures of Sherlock Holmes . . . .*

MUSIC: *DANSE MACABRE* (UP AND UNDER)

WATSON: My name is Doctor John H Watson. In reviewing the many sketches I've written about my partnership with Sherlock Holmes, I find I have given little attention to our earliest cases, except for the more noteworthy ones, such as *A Study in Scarlet*, the Dover Maiden matter, and the sad affair of my old friend Anthony Moltaire. All of these attracted some notice in the public press. But in the first year of our association, Holmes was still obliged to take some commissions simply to pay the bills. One such case occupied him for just one night in June of 1881. A traveling carnival had been set up a few blocks from our Baker Street digs, and Holmes, who was running low on his supply of the alkaloid he frequently injected, thought an hour spent among the bizarre attractions there might be a cheap way to escape his constant enemy – boredom.

MUSIC: SEGUE TO

SOUND EFFECT: CARNIVAL (BACKGROUND)

VARIOUS BARKERS: Toss a dart, win a prize . . . Roll up, roll up .
. . See the smallest man in the world . . . Hit the pig, win the
bacon . . . (Etc.)

WATSON: In heaven's name, Holmes, haven't we seen enough?
The juggler, the dwarf, the fire-eater, the bearded lady –

HOLMES: What say, Watson?

WATSON: I say, I've seen enough of this to last me a lifetime!

HOLMES: Hello? What's this? Something we've missed?

PROFESSOR: (OFF, SHOUTING) Ladies and gentlemen, the
wonder of the age! The invention of the century that science
cannot explain! Come see and hear the one, the only Speaking
Machine! The machine that knows all, tells all!

WATSON: Nothing but one of those new Gramophones, I expect.

PROFESSOR: (CLOSER) Imported direct from Italy! A machine
with the brain of a genius and the tongue of an orator! Do not
confuse this remarkable invention with the Gramophone! You
talk to it, it talks to you! It knows the future! It tells your fate!
Step right this way for The Speaking Machine, the next
performance is about to begin! Yes, ladies and gentlemen, for
the price of a pint of ale, you are about to witness the scientific
marvel of all time!

HOLMES: Two, please.

PROFESSOR: (DOWN) Thank you, sir! Step right into the theatre.

WATSON: Huh! Theatre, he calls it! An army tent is more like it.

PROFESSOR: (MOVING OFF) Hurry, hurry, hurry! Hear The
Speaking Machine! The wonder of Italy and the Continent of
Europe! Hurry hurry hurry, the performance is about to begin!
(REPEATS HIS SPIEL FROM THE TOP, UNDER):

HOLMES: Shall we go in and get a good seat?

LOW MALE CONVERSATION IN BACKGROUND

WATSON: (NARRATING) But inside, there were no seats and nothing but dim light, and a platform set against a curtain at the back of the tent. Ten or fifteen people were there, and one of them – a tall, somber-looking fellow – stared at Holmes as we came in, and then shouldered his way through the crowd until he stood beside us. He lifted his hat with deference.

LYDECKER: I beg your pardon. Are you not Mr. Sherlock Holmes?

HOLMES: I am.

LYDECKER: And you must be Doctor Watson! How fortunate that we meet! I believe that you and I –

SOUND EFFECT: A CYMBAL CRASH

LYDECKER: Well, the charlatan is about to begin, but I would very much like to have a word with you after he's done.

WATSON: Before he could say more, a giant of a long-bearded man appeared on the platform. He was grotesquely obese, and wore a huge shapeless smock as black as his beard, covered with gaudy ornamentation. He moved ponderously, swaying from side to side. I would have judged his weight at nothing less than twenty-five stone!

CROWD: A FEW CHUCKLE AT HIM

PROFESSOR: *Attenzione*! I am Professore Allesandro, of the Italian College of Science. I bid you welcome to my scientific demonstration! In a few moments, you will see that the final barrier between science and humanity has been broken! You are about to see my *macchina parlare*, or as you would say it, my Speaking Machine . . . a machine which sees, and hears, and speaks, as if it had a human mind and tongue! A machine which draws upon cosmic powers! A machine that will listen to you and speak to you, and tell you your future! And now, I present to you the perfection of my labors, my invention, *La Voce Mistero*, The Voice of Mystery!

68

SOUND EFFECT: CYMBAL CRASHES

CROWD: MURMURS

WATSON: (NARRATING) Through the back curtain, an assistant handed the professor a black metal box. It seemed to have eight sides, and was about eighteen inches high. In shape, it resembled a large lantern. He held it above his head so everyone could see.

PROFESSOR: Now, I must have absolute silence!

CROWD: MURMURS FADE

WATSON: (NARRATING) He slowly lowered the box until he held it in front of him, opened a lid on the top of it, and spoke into it.

PROFESSOR: *Voce*! There are many persons who have come to hear you speak. Who will you speak to first?

WATSON: (NARRATING) The professor turned the box to the left and then to the right, as if allowing it to scan the crowd.

VOICE: I will speak to the man in front, wearing a cap.

CROWD: SLIGHT REACTION

PROFESSOR: Yes, my good sir, he means you. Do you have a question for The Voice of Mystery?

MAN 1: Can he see us?

PROFESSOR: Why not ask The Voice?

VOICE: I am aware of everything and everyone in this audience.

MAN 1: Aw . . . I think it's a trick!

CROWD: REACTS IN AGREEMENT

PROFESSOR: The *Professore* does not trick!

69

MAN 2: Then have the machine tell me my name!

VOICE: Your name is John.

MAN 2: Heh-heh . . . that's right! How did he know that?

PROFESSOR: The Voice of Mystery has cosmic powers!

MAN 1: What's my name?

PROFESSOR: Voice of Mystery, what is this man's name?

VOICE: His name is also John, but he is known as "Jack"!

MAN 1: Well, that's right!

CROWD: REACTS WITH EXCITED RESPONSE

WATSON: (WHISPER) Holmes, I think I know how he's doing it!

MAN 2: (OFF-MICROPHONE, SHOUTS) How does it work?

PROFESSOR: Ah, but that is my secret!

MAN 3: (OFF, SHOUTS) It's the spirit of a dead man! He's got the spirit of a dead man in his box, that's what it is!

CROWD: MYSTERIOUS WHISPERS

VOICE: No, my friend, I am not dead, because I was never alive. I was created by Professor Alessandro.

WATSON: (LOW) Really, this is intolerable! Someone should challenge him! (SPEAKS UP) You! Professor!

PROFESSOR: Eh, *signore*?

WATSON: You've hired these men! They're working with you!

PROFESSOR: And can you prove that, *signore*?

MAN 1: I never seen him before in my life!

MAN 2: Neither have I!

WATSON: Then tell us, Professor: Can you drink while your little
box speaks?

PROFESSOR: *Signore*, I do not drink during a performance!

WATSON: Or is it that you cannot drink because you're throwing
your voice! It's called ventriloquism!

LYDECKER: (LOW) Good show, Doctor!

CROWD: MURMURS UP

HOLMES: (LOW) Watson, are you sure of your ground?

PROFESSOR: A-ha! The gentleman thinks The Voice cannot speak
by itself! Very well, it so happens that behind this curtain I have
a bottle of wine. I will now ask my assistant to hand me the
bottle. Antonio, *mi vino, prego*! (PAUSE)

ANTONIO: (OFF) Here you are, Professor.

PROFESSOR: Ah, *grazie*! (PAUSE) Now, you will hear The Voice
of Mystery speak to you as I drink! *Guardi*!

SOUND EFFECT: CORK PULLED OUT OF A BOTTLE

PROFESSOR: (AUDIBLY GUZZLES)

VOICE: (PAUSE) You must be very thirsty, Professor! Won't you
save some for me?

CROWD: LAUGHS

PROFESSOR: That was very good wine, it comes from Napoli. And
now if you wish for more proof, *signore*, I shall ask The Voice
of Mystery to speak while I am speaking! Speak for yourself,
Voice. Tell us what day this is.

71

VOICE: Today is Friday, the third of June, in the year or our Lord, eighteen-hundred-and-eighty-one. The moon is in its first quarter and the season is the last fortnight before summer.

PROFESSOR: (OVER ABOVE) And while The Voice is speaking, I also am speaking. Now what do you think? Are you satisfied, *signore*?

CROWD: LAUGHS AND BREAKS INTO APPLAUSE

WATSON: Well, he jolly well made a fool out of me!

HOLMES: Oh no, Watson, I think you managed quite nicely by yourself.

LYDECKER: Tut, tut, Mr. Holmes. I applaud the good doctor's attempt to expose this mountebank!

CROWD: SUBSIDES

MAN 3: The man outside said The Voice knows the future!

PROFESSOR: That is very true.

MAN 3: Awright . . . what's my future?

PROFESSOR: Will you tell this gentleman his future?

VOICE: You will live . . . (PAUSE) . . . a long and happy life. You will work hard for your living . . . (PAUSE) . . . And you will die an old man.

MAN 3: How – how old? How old will I be when I die?

VOICE: That is up to you. Live your life well and you will enjoy many years.

MAN 3: Thank you! Thank you!

PROFESSOR: And thank you, *mi amici*, for your kind attention. And now, The Voice of Mystery wishes to say one last thing.

VOICE: God Save the Queen!

CROWD: God Save The Queen! (THEY APPLAUD, THEN CHAT IN ASTONISHMENT AS THEY LEAVE)

LYDECKER: Oh, now, that's the last straw! Invoking God and the Queen after all his deception! Have you ever seen a more hypocritical display? Gentlemen, permit me to introduce myself. My name is Clive Lydecker. My writings have been published in *The Times of London*.

HOLMES: Letters to the Editor, I believe. Yes, I've read some of them. You're becoming quite a diligent reformer, Mr. Lydecker.

LYDECKER: You honour me. Yes, it is my mission to rid our city of such blights as these tawdry carnivals! They encourage all the Biblical evils, and lead the lower classes into debauchery . . . which is why I want a word with you. But first, let's get away from here! There is a perfectly awful café just outside the carnival but it will be quieter and we can have a glass of wine. Shall we?

HOLMES: Watson? Are you up to it?

WATSON: Lead on.

SOUND EFFECT: CARNIVAL UP, DOWN, SEGUE TO QUIET CAFE

LYDECKER: Your health, gentlemen.

SOUND EFFECT: THREE GLASSES CLINK (THEY TAKE A SIP)

LYDECKER: A lowly vintage, but what can you expect? I allow myself one glass of wine per day, for my digestion. But now, to my purpose: My purpose is to warn our people of the evils of these carnivals and sideshows that plague the city. That is why I was there among the tent-shows tonight, passing out these fliers I had printed. Have you seen them?

HOLMES: Yes. "The Devil's Playground" I believe was the headline.

LYDECKER: Yes, a clear warning to the dull-witted common folk that they are playing with fire!

WATSON: I'm afraid most of the people seem to be throwing them on the ground.

LYDECKER: But they are having their effect, make no mistake! Now, it may have been pure chance that led me here tonight, but I believe that I was meant to meet you gentlemen!

HOLMES: Is that so?

LYDECKER: Yes! It's all coming clear in my mind! We can help each other! With your powers of investigation, we can strip away the intrigue from the crystal ball gazers and this outrageous Italian fortune teller and his mystery voice. If you can discover how they deceive the gullible, I'll put it in the paper, giving you the credit for uncovering the chicanery! I will urge a boycott of such squalid attractions, and in time, these carnival people will have to pack up and move away! I presume you can discover how the Italian makes the box appear to talk?

HOLMES: I have already done so.

LYDECKER Then you know his trick?

HOLMES: Of course.

WATSON: Well, if he's not a ventriloquist, I don't see how he does it! It looks utterly impossible to me.

HOLMES: When you have eliminated the impossible, Watson, whatever remains, however improbable, must be the truth.

WATSON: Well then, how does he do it?

HOLMES: If you will accompany me back to the carnival, all will become clear.

LYDECKER: Excellent! Now I must hurry back there myself and take up my post by that "Voice of Mystery" tent. I still have a hundred fliers to hand out. Gentlemen: To the success of our mission!

SOUND EFFECT: THREE GLASSES CLINK

MUSIC: VIOLIN BRIDGE (END BACKGROUND)

WATSON: And as the three of us left the café, little did any of us know what lay ahead . . . and that before the night was over, only two of us would walk away! So that you may visualise the location of the carnival, its caravans had been drawn up in South Audley Street, which becomes Orchard Street and then Baker Street as you go north, placing the carnival about a mile from 221b, or just east of Hyde Park. The night was filled with greasy lamp smoke and garlic-scented frying meat. Barkers promised cheap thrills to gawking onlookers for a few pieces of copper. As the hour grew later the crowd grew larger. Lydecker had gone on ahead of us to distribute his literature, and Holmes and I took our time strolling back up Audley Street and into the milling crowd.

SOUND EFFECT: TWO MEN STROLLING ON PAVEMENT (UNDER)

HOLMES: Tell me what you make of our new friend, Watson.

WATSON: A sanctimonious firebrand, if you ask me.

HOLMES: My definition precisely.

WATSON: Then why are you doing this? After getting your name in the paper for solving sensational murder cases, here you are, about to expose a cheap showman? Why are you lowering yourself?

HOLMES: (WISTFULLY) Ah, Watson, because the coffers are bare. If you couldn't live on your Army pension you could go into medical practice again, but I have no such cushion. In other words, a favourable notice in the paper, as Lydecker proposes, will put my name before the public again and may attract a client or two – and just now I need clients. Paying clients.

WATSON: I see.

HOLMES: You disapprove.

WATSON: I hate to see you lower your standards.

HOLMES: Lofty principles are well and good when there's food in the larder, but Mrs. Hudson expects her rent on time, and I intend to pay my half of it . . . any way I have to. Now we'll speak of it no more.

SOUND EFFECT: CARNIVAL CROWD LOUDER, ALARMED VOICES

WATSON: Well then, tell me this: How does the Italian produce that voice from the box?

HOLMES: Just a minute . . . . Look there, Watson! Something's going on at The Voice of Mystery tent! I don't like the looks of that crowd!

SOUND EFFECT: CROWD NOISE INCREASES AS HOLMES AND WATSON WALK FASTER

WATSON: Isn't that Lydecker? Yes, it is! He's gotten into a dust-up right in front of The Voice of Mystery!

LYDECKER: (OFF, SHOUTING) Listen to me! These people are fakers and humbugs! Give them your money and you're throwing it away!

BARKER: All right you, move along!

LYDECKER: Listen to me! You men! You work hard for your wages! Some of you have wives and children. Would you take food out of their mouths to squander on the likes of this? This carnival is a hotbed of sin!

76

BARKER: Here, now, none of that talk! Get along with you or I'll send for the police!

LYDECKER: Take one of my fliers and read the truth! Turn away from corruption and immorality! London is being undermined by the likes of these mountebanks and fakers!

BARKER: I'm warnin' you, mister . . . !

HOLMES: Mr. Lydecker!

LYDECKER: Shun this indecent exhibition! Go back to your homes!

WATSON: Mr. Lydecker!

BARKER: Hoy, you men! If you know this loud-mouth bloke, you better take him away from here before he gets shut up for good!

HOLMES: Come along, Mr. Lydecker. You're placing yourself in danger.

LYDECKER: No! Someone has to stop all these indolent layabouts from pouring their money into sideshows like this! Fortune-telling is the work of the Devil!

BARKER: (OFF-MICROPHONE) All right, everybody, come see what the shouting's about! Inside this tent is the show they don't want you to see! The machine that knows the future! The machine that tells your fortune! * (MOVING FARTHER AWAY) For the price of a pint, you can talk to the machine that sees all, knows all, and tells all! The scientific demonstration that can't be explained! The invention of an Italian genius! The bosses of London don't want you to see and hear this! Why? Because you will learn something in this tent, ladies and gentlemen, something the bosses don't want you to know!

LYDECKER: (AT *) Look at them! Now these dolts are fighting to get into that tent! What have I done?

HOLMES: You've made people all the more curious to know what goes on in the tent, Mr. Lydecker. You've promised them the forbidden fruit, the fruit of forbidden knowledge.

LYDECKER: No! I didn't promise it! I told them they mustn't have it!

HOLMES: Which always makes it more attractive. Just read the book of *Genesis*.

WATSON: I remember as a boy, if I was told not to do something, I was tempted to do it just to see what would happen. Human nature, I think.

LYDECKER: Then you were a sinful boy, Doctor. Shame on you! Shame on all these people who lust after evil!

HOLMES: I think it would be wise to get you out of sight for a while. Here, over this way, perhaps.

WATSON: (NARRATING) Lydecker was quite rattled now. Holmes took him by the arm and led the way into a dark space behind the tent where the professor did his show. One of the caravan wagons was drawn up to the back of the tent, to serve as a dressing room and living quarters for the dwarf, the fire-eater, and the professor. But there, we came face to face with the object of Lydecker's fury, the hugely ponderous professor himself, preparing to go into his act! But when he saw us, his jaw dropped and his eyes widened in alarm . . . .

PROFESSOR: What are you doing back here? Get out! *Signori desiderano –* ?

LYDECKER: What do we wish? We wish you to be gone!

PROFESSOR: Oh. You understand Italian?

LYDECKER: Better than you do, I wager! You're nothing but London street scum! And I'm here to expose you and your like!

HOLMES: Come along, Mr. Lydecker. Nothing's to be gained here.

78

LYDECKER: I warn you! I will not stop until I've driven you and your cohort out of London!

HOLMES: Watson, take his other arm.

LYDECKER: Do you know who these men are? Sherlock Holmes and Doctor Watson! If you know anything, you know they are England's most famous detectives, and they've seen right through you!

PROFESSOR: Well, gentlemen, you'd better take this fellow away before he gets hurt! It's time for my next performance!

HOLMES: We're just leaving.

LYDECKER: (SHOUTS) But I'll be back!

SOUND EFFECT: THREE MEN WALKING ON PAVEMENT (UNDER)

LYDECKER: Did you see how brazen he is? He thinks nothing can stop him!

HOLMES: Try and calm yourself.

LYDECKER: Calm myself?

HOLMES: I'm sure your cause is just, but your methods leave something to be desired. You asked me to expose his trickery and I agreed. But confrontation produces the wrong results.

LYDECKER: But do you know how he does it?

HOLMES: Yes.

WATSON: Then tell us!

HOLMES: I should rather demonstrate it. Let's see if we can get into that tent for one last performance!

SOUND EFFECT: CARNIVAL (UNDER SLIGHTLY)

WATSON: Call it pride, or vanity, or what you like – Holmes enjoys an audience, and as we made our way once more into the crowded tent, there was a glint in his eye and a sudden twitch of a smile on his lips.

<u>SOUND EFFECT: CRASH OF CYMBALS. THE CROWD QUIETS DOWN</u>

PROFESSOR: *Attenzione*! I am Professore Allesandro, of the Italian College of Science. I bid you welcome to my scientific demonstration! In a few moments, you will see that the final barrier between science and humanity has been broken! * You are about to see my *macchina parlare*, or as you would say, my Speaking Machine . . . a machine which sees, and hears, and speaks, as if it had a human mind and tongue! A machine which draws upon cosmic powers! A machine that will listen to you and speak to you, and tell you your future!

HOLMES: (OVER ABOVE AT *) Mr. Lydecker! Where are you going?

LYDECKER: I want to get closer!

PROFESSOR: And now, I present to you the perfection of my labors, my invention, *La Voce Mistero*, The Voice of Mystery!

CROWD: REACTS AS THE BOX IS DISPLAYED

PROFESSOR: Now, I must have absolute silence!

LYDECKER: (CRIES OUT) It's all a sham! He's a humbug!

PROFESSOR: *Ascoltare*!

CROWD: REACTS AGAINST LYDECKER

PROFESSOR: *Silenzio*!

LYDECKER: You are being tricked! You should demand your money back!

CROWD: AD LIBS "AW, SHUT UP", ETC.

PROFESSOR: (OVER CROWD) *Ascoltare*! Listen to The Voice of Mystery!

VOICE: I am The Voice of Mystery! I speak to you from the cosmic world! I see all, hear all, and know all! I know the future and the past!

LYDECKER: This is nothing but a trick, and here is the man who will prove it!

VOICE: I know the man. His name is Sherlock Holmes!

HOLMES: Of course you know my name! You heard it only a few minutes ago, just outside this tent! The Voice of Mystery is no mystery at all! It belongs to a very ordinary human being . . . ordinary except for one thing! Professor, would you kindly remove your smock?

PROFESSOR: How dare you?

LYDECKER: (EXERTS) Do as he says!

PROFESSOR: Come no closer, Mr. Lydecker!

LYDECKER: (EXERTS) I'll take that talking box!

VOICE: Stay away or meet your doom!

LYDECKER: Give me that cursed box!

SOUND EFFECT: SMALL CALIBER GUN GOES OFF

LYDECKER: Uhh! Uhh!

SOUND EFFECT: LYDECKER FALLS TO THE GROUND

MUSIC: STING

WATSON: From somewhere came a muffled shot and Lydecker slumped to the ground.

81

CROWD: REACTS IN SHOCK

PROFESSOR: Lydecker!

HOLMES: He's been shot! Watson, get over here! The rest of you, stand back!

WATSON: Get back, all of you! (PAUSE) He's dead! Shot through the heart!

HOLMES: At pointblank range! One of you men! Go out and see if you can find a policeman!

CROWD: REACTS WITH CONSTERNATION

PROFESSOR: But . . . I'm innocent! I did not have a gun!

HOLMES: Perhaps you didn't.

WATSON: What? The man was shot! We all saw it!

HOLMES: Now will you remove your costume, Professor? Or shall I do it?

VOICE: Do not touch the professor or you, too will die!

PROFESSOR: No! No more killing!

HOLMES: Not quite yet!

PROFESSOR: What are you doing with that knife?

HOLMES: Nothing so lethal, Professor!

SOUND EFFECT: LONG RIP OF FABRIC

PROFESSOR: Aagh! My costume!

HOLMES: And there, ladies and gentlemen, is your "Voice of Mystery"!

WATSON: A dwarf! A dwarf hidden under the smock?

HOLMES: The dwarf from the sideshow next door, harnessed to the chest of the professor with leather straps and covered by this smock!

WATSON: Holmes! He still has the pistol!

HOLMES: Give it up now and you may be charged with shooting Lydecker in self-defense. Shoot me, and it is murder in the first degree, for which the sentence is death.

VOICE: (PAUSE) Here. Take it.

HOLMES: Yes. A pepperbox pistol. The only gun small enough to conceal. He fired it through the magic box, because he could see through the loose-knit fabric of the smock!

SOUND EFFECT: (IN DISTANCE) POLICE WHISTLE

CROWD: REACTS

WATSON: When did you know how he did it?

HOLMES: From the moment the professor appeared. The bone structure of his head is that of a slender, well-muscled man, not matching the corpulent appearance of his body, so I knew he wasn't really fat. The billowing black smock he wore was of light enough texture to see through. And the "Voice of Mystery" was clearly that of a miniature person, and the dwarf from the sideshow is advertised as being only thirty-one inches tall. Finally, the dwarf appeared in his own sideshow between performances by the professor, and he never spoke! The conclusion was inescapable.

MUSIC: *DANSE MACABRE* UP AND UNDER

WATSON: This is Doctor John H Watson. I hope you've enjoyed tonight's adventure, and I'll return to tell you another one . . . *when next we meet*!

MUSIC: THEME UP AND OUT

The Diary of
Anthony Moltaire

CHARACTERS

- SHERLOCK HOLMES
- DR. JOHN H. WATSON
- MRS. HUDSON
- ANTHONY MOLTAIRE
- SGT. THOMAS LEEMAN
- INSPECTOR LESTRADE
- JAMISON
- ANDREW CARSTAIRS

SOUND EFFECT: OPENING SEQUENCE, BIG BEN, STREET SOUNDS

ANNOUNCER: *The Further Adventures of Sherlock Holmes . . . .*

MUSIC: *DANSE MACABRE* (UP AND UNDER)

WATSON: My name is Doctor John H. Watson, and the story I'm about to tell you concerns one of the earlier adventures in my association with Sherlock Holmes. The year was 1882. The previous spring, we had been occupied with his first three cases – *A Study in Scarlet*, "School For Scoundrels", and "The Adventure of The Dover Maiden". But despite their successful conclusion, Holmes had yet to draw much attention in the press, and I was living on half-pay and a small Army disability pension, so by the summer of 1882 our financial circumstances were somewhat strained. Then I heard from Anthony Moltaire, an old comrade of mine from the Berkshire infantry regiment. He wired that he was in urgent need of my help, and I wired back to come ahead. And I mentioned it to Holmes.

MUSIC: FADE OUT QUICKLY (UNDER)

HOLMES: Then it's some kind of medical matter?

WATSON: I have no idea. I haven't seen Tony since I was shipped home from Peshawar back in '80. But the Berkshire Club keep pretty fair track of the old Regiment. They say he's been doing quite well for himself.

HOLMES: Well then, I judge the fellow I see down there alighting from a hansom would be your man.

WATSON: Hmm?

HOLMES: Dressed to the nines and in a bit of a hurry?

WATSON: Let me have a look . . . .

HOLMES: Too late, he's below our window now, but he'll be upstairs in a minute and you can see if I'm wrong. And since he's coming to see you and not me, shall I make myself scarce?

WATSON: Not at all, not at all. I don't know how he found out where I am, but I'm sure he must know we're sharing the same digs. At any rate, 1 wouldn't think of putting you out.

HOLMES: Most considerate of you, Watson.

WATSON: I must say, I'm curious. I don't know what he could want. We weren't exactly close. I seem to remember he could be a bit aloof, though I never had any trouble with him.

HOLMES: Is that so.

WATSON: He was the sort who always stood a round of drinks for the other officers. Always seemed to have plenty of money.

HOLMES: Interesting.

WATSON: He always carried himself well. We used to say he walked more like a colonel than a leftenant.

HOLMES: (CHUCKLES)

WATSON: He was with the regiment at Maiwand, but I was injured so soon after the fighting began that I lost track of him, and

85

after they took me to Peshawar with the fever, I never saw anyone from my unit again.

SOUND EFFECT: (OFF: STEPS ON STAIRS MOVE CLOSE)

HOLMES: Well, be sure to give me a sign if you want me to leave.

WATSON: I will.

SOUND EFFECT: STEPS STOP (OFF-MICROPHONE) KNOCK ON DOOR

WATSON: I'll go.

SOUND EFFECT: HE STEPS TO DOOR, DOOR OPENS

WATSON: Yes, Mrs. Hudson?

MRS. HUDSON: A Mr. Anthony Moltaire to see you, Doctor. He says you're expecting him.

WATSON: Yes. Come in, Tony, come in!

MOLTAIRE: Watson! It's like old times!

MRS. HUDSON: Will you be wanting anything, Doctor?

WATSON: Care for coffee, Tony?

MOLTAIRE: No thank you, I don't think so right now.

WATSON: Coffee, Holmes?

HOLMES: No thanks.

WATSON: Nothing then, Mrs. Hudson.

MRS. HUDSON: Very good, Doctor.

SOUND EFFECT: STEPS IN, DOOR CLOSES

WATSON: Tony, may I present my good friend and associate, Sherlock Holmes.

MOLTAIRE: A pleasure, Mr. Holmes. Oh, here – please take my card.

HOLMES: Gladly.

WATSON: Let me take your hat and cane.

HOLMES: Just sit anywhere. We don't stand on ceremony here.

MOLTAIRE: Thank you.

WATSON: What can I do for you, Tony? You look well. Your telegram said you have urgent business.

MOLTAIRE: Yes, it is urgent . . . confidential business.

WATSON: Of a medical nature?

MOLTAIRE: Medical? No. I come to you, not as a patient, but an old friend.

HOLMES: Excuse me. Perhaps you'd prefer to conduct your business in private, Mr. Moltaire, since you've traveled in such haste from the East India docks.

MOLTAIRE: . . . How would you know where I've been?

HOLMES: Simple observation.

MOLTAIRE: Well, you're quite right – I've just come from the North Key. But how did you know that?

HOLMES: By the aroma of Oriental spice on your clothes, I knew you had been aboard an East India ship. There is creosote on the tip of your walking stick and the soles of your shoes, and I knew the Bow Creek Pier was being re-paved. And the papers say a vessel from Bombay docked there last night with a cargo of cardamom. Perfectly logical deduction.

MOLTAIRE: You astound me, sir! That was the very ship I was visiting! One of my clients is a spice trader.

WATSON: Holmes is a consulting detective, you know. The first, and only.

MOLTAIRE: Oh, yes, I know. In fact, I must admit that the reason I contacted you, John, was because I thought I might reach Mr. Holmes through you.

HOLMES: Well, you've reached me. Now, what is your urgent business?

MOLTAIRE: If I tell you, I'll be placing my reputation – my very life – in your hands!

HOLMES: Nothing you may say will leave this room.

MOLTAIRE: Well, all right, here it is: I'm being blackmailed!

HOLMES: Yes? Go ahead.

MOLTAIRE: As you know, John, I served in the Afghan War. In the very battle where you were wounded, the enemy overwhelmed us. Our lads were dying all round! It was nothing but suicide!

SOUND EFFECT: (SNEAK UNDER) BATTLE SCENE

MOLTAIRE: I was terrified! I ran a few yards into the thick of it, and then . . . I threw myself to the ground as if I'd been shot! And I lay on my face pretending to be dead! And just a moment later, my batman, Sergeant Thomas Leeman, rushed up and turned me over on my back!

LEEMAN: Leftenant! Where were you hit? Leftenant!

MOLTAIRE: Leave me here, Leeman! Go on!

LEEMAN: Sir!

MOLTAIRE: Damn it, Sergeant, I wasn't hit! I'm trying to save my own life! Just go on and keep quiet about it!

LEEMAN: What?

MOLTAIRE: I'll pay you when it's over! Now, roll me over as if I'd been shot!

LEEMAN: (PAUSE) I ought to shoot you myself! You damned coward! (SPIT)

SOUND EFFECT: BATTLE SCENE FADES UNDER AS:

MOLTAIRE: After dark, the tide of battle turned and the Afghans retreated, and I got up and retreated with them. When they found a British officer among them I was afraid they'd execute me, but I gave them all the money I had with me and convinced them I wasn't a spy . . . only a coward.

WATSON: I say, Tony!

MOLTAIRE: They let me go and I was able to find my way back to our line. I made my way to regimental headquarters and made up a story that I'd been captured and fought my way out. Well, they believed me. And later, to my everlasting shame, I accepted the Victoria Cross! They awarded the medal to a coward! A liar and a coward!

WATSON: And your batman didn't report you?

MOLTAIRE: No. Leeman said he'd keep quiet about it "if I made it worth his while", so I gave him a few quid – twenty pounds I think it was.

WATSON: But it would have just been his word against yours!

MOLTAIRE: Oh no, John, that's the devil of it. You see, I've always kept a diary. Ever since I was ten and away at school, I've written down everything I did at the end of every day. The good and the bad.

WATSON: You don't mean you wrote down your – your –

MOLTAIRE: My act of cowardice? Oh yes. But the next night when I looked for my diary, it was gone!

SOUND EFFECT: (EXTERIOR) IN DISTANCE, MEN TALKING OUTSIDE

MOLTAIRE: Leeman?

LEEMAN: Sir?

MOLTAIRE: My diary. Have you seen it? It's not under my cot.

LEEMAN: That's right. I took it.

MOLTAIRE: You took it?

LEEMAN: For your own safety, sir. You shouldn't be leavin' it around where it might be found.

MOLTAIRE: Well, give it back this instant!

LEEMAN: Oh, you'll get it back in good time.

MOLTAIRE: What do you mean by that?

LEEMAN: After it's earned its' keep.

MOLTAIRE: You mean to blackmail me?

LEEMAN: Why don't you turn me in?

MOLTAIRE: (PAUSE) All right. How much do you want for it?

SOUND EFFECT: BACKGROUND FADES OUT (END EXTERIOR)

MOLTAIRE: Well, that was two years ago. By now I must have paid him something approaching fifteen-hundred pounds, and he still comes round for more.

WATSON: Good grief, that's a king's ransom!

90

HOLMES: Well, of course, the sure way to foil an extortionist is by confessing.

MOLTAIRE: No, Mr. Holmes, that's out. I'd be ruined forever! I can't face that. But a man as clever as you are must know some way to silence him!

HOLMES: And I just told you.

MOLTAIRE: No, that's out of the question. Aside from the shame, I'd face a court-martial. I'd be clapped into prison. Maybe even shot! Mr. Holmes, I'll pay you anything you ask if you'll get my diary back! Because if I don't get it back. . . I swear I'll kill him!

MUSIC: STING

WATSON: I confess I was utterly disgusted by my old friend Anthony Moltaire! And even more so when, as he was leaving, he opened his purse and tried to pay us!

HOLMES: We don't want your money, Mr. Moltaire. I don't mean to be harsh, but your predicament is of your own making. Your future is up to you.

MOLTAIRE: I see. Very well.

SOUND EFFECT: HE STEPS TO THE DOOR, DOOR OPENS

MOLTAIRE: Well, gentlemen, thank you for your counsel. I shan't trouble either of you again.

SOUND EFFECT: HE STEPS OUT. DOOR CLOSES

MUSIC: UNDERSCORE

WATSON: A week went by. Holmes immersed himself in various research projects, while I spent the days writing my manuscript for the case I called "A School for Scoundrels". But Moltaire's terrible admission kept haunting me. What choices did he have? What would I do if it were me? And then one morning, Holmes unfolded the newspaper that Mrs. Hudson had brought with our breakfast.. .

MUSIC: OUT

HOLMES: Watson!

WATSON: Eh?

HOLMES: Listen to this!

WATSON: What?

HOLMES: (READING) *"War Veteran Slain. The body of Thomas R. Leeman, a veteran of the Afghan War, was found in his flat in Franco Street, the victim of a vicious beating, according to Inspector Giles Lestrade of Scotland Yard."*

WATSON: Good Lord! So Moltaire's done it! What else does it say?

HOLMES: It just says the Yard's investigating.

WATSON: Well, this puts us in an interesting position. We promised him our confidence but we have evidence we should give to the police!

HOLMES: What we have is a rash statement made by a highly agitated man.

WATSON: You don't think he killed Leeman?

HOLMES: No, I think he probably did. But I know nothing. Shall we visit Inspector Lestrade and see what we can learn?

MUSIC: FAST BRIDGE – SEGUE TO

SOUND EFFECT: SCOTLAND YARD (TYPICAL OFFICE NOISES – BACKGROUND)

LESTRADE: Gentlemen? What brings you to Scotland Yard?

HOLMES: We read about the murder of Thomas Leeman.

LESTRADE: What about it?

HOLMES: Were there any witnesses?

LESTRADE: No, he was killed in his room. He'd been dead a day at least before anyone found him.

HOLMES: The paper was rather vague. Do you have any suspects?

LESTRADE: Not at the moment. What's your interest in this?

HOLMES: Purely academic at this point. Do you know the motive?

LESTRADE: Robbery.

HOLMES: Robbery?

LESTRADE: Yes, his place had been ransacked. Now, what is there in this that you find so interesting? Did you know the fellow?

WATSON: Actually, no. But a friend of mine had mentioned him.

HOLMES: Is his body in the morgue?

LESTRADE: Yes.

HOLMES: May we see it?

LESTRADE: I suppose so.

SOUND EFFECT: CUT TO ECHOING MORGUE. BODY DRAWER PULLED OUT

LESTRADE: There you are. Look to your hearts' content, gentlemen. I don't fancy gruesome sights as much as you do.

HOLMES: Watson? What do you see?

WATSON: Hmm. . . . the deepest indentation in the skull seems to be here, above the left ear.

HOLMES: That would have been the first blow. Notice the same mark at each point of impact. You see?

WATSON: Yes. The left zygomatic has been fractured. And the parietal and occipital bones. He was struck again and again –

HOLMES: By an object with a ring around it.

LESTRADE: There could have been two or more people who ganged up on him.

HOLMES: Only if all his attackers were left-handed and stood behind him to deliver their blows with the same object.

LESTRADE: What?

HOLMES: There are no wounds on his face, just the left side of his head and the top of the skull. How was he lying when you found him, Inspector?

LESTRADE: On his right side.

HOLMES: And was a chair beside him?

LETRADE: Yes, there was! How did you know that?

HOLMES: From the position of the blows. He would have been seated, and his attacker, standing behind him, swung his weapon at the back of his head, in an arc from left to right. Leeman topples to the floor, very likely dead at that instant. Inspector, Watson and I should like to see where Mr. Leeman met his end. I hope your men haven't tidied up the place?

LESTRADE: Now, Mr. Holmes, you know protocol forbids me from letting outsiders into the scene of a crime. It's enough that I've taken my valuable time to bring you down here. Obviously you know something about this, and I want to know what it is!

HOLMES: I can answer that only when I've been to where it happened. And then, I may be able to give you the name of the murderer. If, of course, you haven't already got him.

LESTRADE: . . . Oh, very well. I'll order a carriage.

SOUND EFFECT: ECHO OUT

MUSIC: UNDERSCORE

WATSON: Franco Street, where Leeman lived, was a middle-class neighborhood of substantial flats. Leeman's rooms were comfortably furnished. Not what you'd expect a criminal type to live in.

MUSIC: OUT

LESTRADE: (OFF) All right, the body was here, and that chair was tipped over beside him. There was a big spray of blood off to this side.

HOLMES: Which your fellows thoughtfully cleaned up. What other little housekeeping chores did you do before locking the place up?

LESTRADE: Everything you see is just the way we found it except for the body.

HOLMES: And the blood.

LESTRADE: Why do you go on about the blood, Holmes? We know he was bludgeoned to death – any fool could have seen that.

HOLMES: When blood is projected from the human body it can tell a great deal about the weapon and the person who wielded it. But all that having been obliterated, give me a few minutes to go round the place and see what I can find.

MUSIC: UNDERSCORE

WATSON: . . . And he poked and prodded into every nook and cranny of the apartment, while I encouraged Inspector Lestrade to step into the hall and describe some of his most recent victories over crime, which he was only too happy to share, possibly in the hope that I would write one of them into a

95

Sherlock Holmes story. Half-an-hour later, Sherlock Holmes emerged from Leeman's rooms, thanked Lestrade, and said we'd take a hansom back to Baker Street . . . .

MUSIC: SEGUE TO

SOUND EFFECT: HANSOM IN MOTION

WATSON: . . . and once in the privacy of the cab, I asked him what his search had turned up.

HOLMES: Four things stand out, Watson. Leeman knew his killer but didn't fear him.

WATSON: Knew him but didn't fear him? That could be Moltaire.

HOLMES: Leeman had a female friend who visited him quite frequently and left a few long black hairs.

WATSON: Oh?

HOLMES: And I found another trifle: Some bits of wax. And . . . let me see, there was something else – what was it? Oh, yes: I found Moltaire's diary.

WATSON: You did what?

HOLMES: Complete with the final entry, dated *"Encampment, Maiwand, 27 July, 1880"*, in which he described his acts of cowardice. Yes, it is definitely Moltaire's stolen diary.

WATSON: How in the world did you find it?

HOLMES: By imagining where a man like Moltaire wouldn't have looked – a most fastidious man who wears elegant clothes, a man who just committed murder and would be in a distracted state of mind and would be in a hurry to leave the scene of his crime. So I lay on my back and swept my arm under every piece of furniture in the bedroom – getting extremely dusty in the process – and sure enough, the diary was jammed under the bureau, where it's been collecting dust ever since Leeman moved in.

WATSON: Do you have the diary with you?

HOLMES: Right here in my coat.

WATSON: What are you going to do with it?

HOLMES: Well, I suppose I could just give it back to him. I'm sure he would be most grateful . . . and generous.

WATSON: You're not serious!

HOLMES: It is his property.

WATSON: And let him get away with murder?

HOLMES: No, perhaps you're right, Watson. There are some untidy remnants to address, such as – this.

WATSON: What do you have in your handkerchief?

HOLMES: Something suggesting that the late Mr. Leeman had expanded his business, and his killer may have found an alibi. But contain your curiosity, Watson, until we reach our rooms!

SOUND EFFECT: HANSOM OUT

MUSIC: STING

SOUND EFFECT: DOOR CLOSES

MRS. HUDSON: Ah, you're back just in time, gentlemen. It's not too early for tea, and I've just taken some biscuits out of the oven.

WATSON: No, no, not now, Mrs. Hudson. Holmes and I have some urgent business to take care of!

HOLMES: Tea is a wonderful idea, Mrs. Hudson! I have a ravenous appetite!

MRS. HUDSON: I'll bring it up in a minute. Oh! I almost forgot! What did I do with that . . . ? Oh, here it is, in my apron! This letter came by delivery while you were out! Addressed to you, Doctor.

WATSON: Oh? Thank you.

MRS. HUDSON: (MOVING OFF) I'll bring your tea right up.

WATSON: It's from Moltaire! His name is on the envelope!

SOUND EFFECT: HE OPENS THE ENVELOPE WITH HIS FINGER, REMOVES AND UNFOLDS THE LETTER

WATSON: (UNDER HIS BREATH, READS) *"John: By now you have read the news, and no doubt you and Mr. Holmes think I did it, but rest assured that I didn't, and I can prove it. Anthony Moltaire"*.

HOLMES: May I see that?

WATSON: Here.

HOLMES: (PAUSE) Upstairs, Watson. Things are falling into place!

MUSIC: QUICK BRIDGE

WATSON: Now, what did you wrap in your handkerchief?

HOLMES: I'm about to show you. Careful . . . there are several fragments here.

WATSON: Hmm! Bits of blue candle wax.

HOLMES: Purple sealing wax, from a sealed letter. Now, take my magnifying glass and look at the largest piece.

WATSON: All right.

HOLMES: Can you see anything familiar in it?

WATSON: What do you mean?

98

HOLMES: Look very carefully. See if you recognize that part of the seal that was stamped into the wax.

WATSON: Whatever it was, it was broken when the seal was broken . . .

HOLMES: Do you recognize it?

WATSON: No . . . .

HOLMES: Then take out one of your cards.

WATSON: One of my cards? From my practice?

HOLMES: Yes.

WATSON: Well . . . all right . . . I still carry a few . . . (EXERTS) . . . here. Here's one.

HOLMES: Now put it on the table beside the largest chunk of sealing wax.

WATSON: All right.

HOLMES: Do you see it now? Look at the emblem on your card, and look at this scrap of sealing wax.

WATSON: Yes! I see it now! The stamp was a caduceus! The emblem of the medical profession!

HOLMES: The Staff of Hermes or Mercury entwined with serpents.

WATSON: Yes! Apparently, whoever sent this letter was a physician.

HOLMES: And not just any physician, because it's the custom for ordinary letters to be sealed in red wax.

WATSON: What do you make of it?

HOLMES: Perhaps Mr. Moltaire can tell us. Let's wire him and tell him we'll be right over after tea, and solve this little mystery!

MUSIC: UNDERSCORE

WATSON: At that moment I wanted answers far more than tea, but while we waited for Mrs. Hudson, Holmes went to a book he used frequently, the *Directory of Royal Appointments*, looked in it briefly, and put it away. When Mrs. Hudson brought the tea, he sipped it with great delicacy, and sampled the biscuits like a gourmet, saying nothing more about his conclusions – all of which threatened to drive me mad! But at last we did leave Baker Street and rode to the exclusive address of Anthony Moltaire. He lived in a handsome townhouse in an expensive district of London. A smartly polished landau had been drawn up in front of his address, and when we were admitted by a manservant, we found ourselves in a spacious drawing room occupied by Moltaire and a gray-haired man of fifty or so, wearing a Van Dyke beard and a pair of spectacles.

MUSIC: OUT

MOLTAIRE: Mr. Holmes! Doctor Watson! I was so glad to get your telegram. The events of the last couple of days were so upsetting to me, I wanted to set the record straight. Let me introduce you to my old friend, Andrew Carstairs. Andrew, this is Doctor John Watson, my old friend from the regiment, and his associate, Mr. Sherlock Holmes.

ALL: (AD LIB RATHER STIFF GREETINGS)

MOLTAIRE: Won't you sit down? I have a well-stocked bar, and Jamison will fix you whatever you like.

HOLMES: Nothing for me, thanks. We won't be staying very long.

WATSON: Nor I, thank you.

MOLTAIRE: Well, all right. Then that's all, Jamison.

JAMISON: (OFF) Very good, sir.

MOLTAIRE: And just close the door on your way out.

JAMISON: (OFF) Yes, sir.

<u>SOUND EFFECT: PAUSE (OFF) A HEAVY DOOR CLOSES</u>

MOLTAIRE: It struck me that you might have seen the article in the paper about the death of my old batman, Sergeant Leeman, and drawn the wrong conclusion. And we can speak freely, gentlemen. Carstairs is an old friend. He knows all about my – regrettable act in the army.

WATSON: Well, your note said you could prove you didn't kill Leeman, and I, for one, would be glad to see that proof.

MOLTAIRE: Well, John, I won't pretend I'm sorry he's dead. I swore I'd kill him myself, as you know. But on the day he was murdered, I was spending a most pleasant weekend in Danthorpe, at the estate of Mr. Carstairs. Isn't that right, Andrew?

CARSTAIRS: Yes, that's right.

MOLTAIRE: So, as you can see, I couldn't have been the one who killed Leeman.

HOLMES: No, not if you were in Danthorpe. Do you go to Danthorpe very often, Mr. Moltaire?

MOLTAIRE: Not as often as I'd like.

HOLMES: I suppose you go boating?

MOLTAIRE: Boating?

HOLMES: On the river.

MOLTAIRE: We – we haven't been boating on the river.

HOLMES: Well, you really should take him boating, Mr. Carstairs.

CARSTAIRS: Yes, I . . . I shall do that, without fail.

101

HOLMES: And of course you know that Scandinavian sculptor who opened the inn right there in Danthorpe . . . What was his name again?

CARSTAIRS: I, ah . . . ?

HOLMES: You know the inn I mean. With the red-and-blue roof?

CARSTAIRS: Oh, that one. Yes, yes indeed.

HOLMES: Is the food still as good as it was?

CARSTAIRS: Oh, yes, excellent.

HOLMES: And the barmaid? Is she still as charming as ever?

CARSTAIRS: Oh, yes, charming as ever.

HOLMES: Betsy? Was that her name?

CARSTAIRS: Yes, Betsy, that's right!

HOLMES: And you, sir, are a liar, and a rather bad one!

CARSTAIRS: (PAUSE) W-what?

HOLMES: There is no river at Danthorpe, no Scandinavian sculptor. Or red-and-blue roofed inn, or a barmaid named Betsy! I made them up on the instant! Do you know whom you're trifling with? I am Sherlock Holmes! And I know who you are, with or without that false beard! You are Sir John Malcom, physician to the Royal family!

CARSTAIRS: No, no, there's been some mistake!

HOLMES: Yes, several! Mr. Moltaire. After you murdered Thomas Leeman when he wouldn't turn over your diary, you searched his rooms and couldn't find the diary, but you did find something else: Love letters mailed by Sir John Malcom to his mistress!

CARSTAIRS: You know about them? I'm a ruined man!

HOLMES: So Moltaire – always the sharp businessman – took those stolen love letters and decided to do some blackmailing of his own! What was the price?

CARSTAIRS: He . . . he said if I'd be his alibi, he'd give me back my letters! I had no choice but to agree!

HOLMES: And did he give your letters back to you?

CARSTAIRS: He said he'd give them back after I . . . after I . . . .

HOLMES: Lied for him. Watson, I see a telephone there beside you. I think it's time to call Inspector Lestrade.

WATSON: Right.

HOLMES: And by the way, Moltaire: I have your diary.

MOLTAIRE: You have it! How long have you had it?

HOLMES: Hmm. Approximately three hours.

MOLTAIRE: I'll pay you anything you ask! Sir John! I'll give you back your letters! I'll do anything! I'm rich! I'll make you rich! This is our chance to make everything go away!

WATSON: Yes, Tony. Everything except murder.

SOUND EFFECT: JIGGLE THE TELEPHONE HOOK

WATSON: Hello? Operator . . . Give me Scotland Yard!

MUSIC: BRIDGE

SOUND EFFECT: HANSOM TROTTING

HOLMES: It's been a long day, Watson.

WATSON: One thing, Holmes: Since you never saw the letters, how did you know what was in them?

103

HOLMES: What would any important nobleman fear? Scandal. The most common scandal involves illicit romance, and The Royal appointment directory not only showed a photograph of Doctor Malcom – it said he was married and had three children.

WATSON: I wonder how Leeman got his hands on the letters?

HOLMES: By wooing a black-haired maid or nurse who works for the doctor. He probably persuaded her to bring him letters the doctor had told her to mail. The woman left some hairs behind, and when Leeman broke open the seals and read the letters, he left a few crumbs of wax behind.

WATSON: I wonder to whom he wrote the letters?

HOLMES: Tut-tut, Watson. Two reputations have been destroyed tonight. Why go for a third?

MUSIC: *DANSE MACABRE* UP AND UNDER

WATSON: This is Doctor John H. Watson. I've had many more adventures with Sherlock Holmes, and I'll tell you another one . . . *when next we meet*!

MUSIC: THEME UP AND OUT

The Strange Case of Lord Halworth's Kitchen
by Jim French and Gareth Tilley

CHARACTERS

- SHERLOCK HOLMES
- DR. JOHN H. WATSON
- DR. RICHARDSON – *A friendly, energetic forty-five-year-old Londoner, good education*
- ELIZABETH HALWORTH – *Thirty-year-old daughter of Lord Halworth. Doesn't get along well with . . .*
- CHARLES HALWORTH – *Thirty-two-year-old son of Lord Halworth, very precise and domineering*
- LORD HALWORTH – *In constant painful distress, enjoys power, loves excesses. Sixty-five years old*
- DR. GORDON XAVIER – *The Royal Physician. Pompous and egotistic. About sixty years old*
- BUTLER – *Classic servant of aristocrats*

SOUND EFFECT: OPENING SEQUENCE, BIG BEN, STREET SOUNDS

ANNOUNCER: *The Further Adventures of Sherlock Holmes . . . .*

MUSIC: *DANSE MACABRE* (UP AND UNDER)

WATSON: My name is Doctor John H. Watson, and it is my great pleasure to recount another adventure I've had with my friend and colleague, Sherlock Holmes. It was the winter of 1884, it had been some time since he'd had a case to occupy his mind, and the cold rainy weather compounded his frustration. I, on the other hand, welcomed the opportunity to catch up on my reading. I was settled by the fire, perusing an article in the latest issue of *The Lancet*, when Holmes picked up his Stradivarius and started playing it . . . loudly.

MUSIC: SEGUE TO VIOLIN SOLO IN BACKGROUND

105

WATSON: When he wanted to, Holmes could play rather expertly, but on this occasion it interrupted my concentration. I bore it for a while, but then . . . (PAUSE) I say, Holmes . . . ? (PAUSE, LOUDER) Holmes!

HOLMES: (AS HE PLAYS) What do you want? I'm playing.

WATSON: And I'm trying to read a medical article.

HOLMES: (AS HE PLAYS) Go right ahead. Doesn't bother me a bit.

WATSON: But I can't concentrate – at least not the way you're playing!

MUSIC: VIOLIN STOPS PLAYING

HOLMES: And what is it that's so important?

WATSON: Rather interesting article by an old friend of mine. It's to do with anaesthetics. Seems he's developed a safer method of delivery for chloroform, by combining it with two other gasses of his own development.

HOLMES: Good for him.

WATSON: The article was written by Dr. Joseph Richardson. I knew him at St. Barts when I was a staff surgeon there.

HOLMES: Good for you. Now that you've interrupted my *musicale*, I think I'll go for a walk and burn off the rest of my tension. Coming with me?

WATSON: Go walking in this rain?

HOLMES: I tell you, Watson, if I don't get something to occupy me, you'll wish I were using the Strad instead of the needle! (MOVES OFF) Hello . . . we're having a visitor.

SOUND EFFECT: (OFF) THE BELL JINGLES

WATSON: There, you see? There's a diversion. Who is it?

106

HOLMES: I couldn't tell. A man, young, not well dressed.

WATSON: Maybe he's calling on Mrs. Hudson. One of her charities.

HOLMES: Most amusing.

SOUND EFFECT: (FAR DISTANT) DOOR SLAMS

HOLMES: No, now he's leaving. Must have been a messenger! Yes, there he goes, crossing the street. And Mrs. Hudson is on her way up with it.

SOUND EFFECT: HE STRIDES TO THE DOOR AND OPENS IT

HOLMES: (OFF-MICROPHONE, CALLS) Hello, Mrs. Hudson! You have something for me, have you? Bring it right up. (FARTHER OFF-MICROPHONE) Ah. A letter? Just hand it to me. Thank you, Mrs. Hudson.

SOUND EFFECT: DOOR CLOSES

WATSON: You didn't give her a chance to talk.

HOLMES: She talks enough. (BEAT) It's for you!

WATSON: Is it? Fancy that.

HOLMES: Here.

WATSON: Thank you.

SOUND EFFECT: OPENS AN ENVELOPE, REMOVES SHEET OF PAPER

WATSON: (PAUSE) Well! If this isn't a coincidence! Upon my word! What do you make of that?

HOLMES: (PAUSE) Well, what is it?

107

WATSON: The very thing I was just reading about in *The Lancet*! How incredible! It's from Doctor Richardson! He's inviting me to observe a major operation using his latest anaesthetic technique. And – Good heavens, it's tonight! He wants me to come tonight! And he says, *"Please bring your associate, Sherlock Holmes"*.

HOLMES: Invited to a surgical operation. Where's it to be, Covent Gardens? Tuxes and tails?

WATSON: No, it's to be at the home of his patient. And listen to this: The patient is none other than Lord Halworth of Knightsend!

HOLMES: Halworth? I've seen him. Elephant of a man! He's eating himself to death!

WATSON: Yes, extreme obesity is an illness in itself. Ah, and Richardson says he's also invited Doctor Gordon Xavier to observe!

HOLMES: The Royal Physician? My, my.

WATSON: This is astounding! Xavier has been criticizing Richardson's new techniques in *The Lancet*. I just read one of his letters they printed! Let me read it to you.

SOUND EFFECT: A STEP, MAGAZINE PICKED UP, A PAGE TURNED

WATSON: Yes, here it is – listen to this: (READING) *"Dear Sirs: With regard to the recent articles on anaesthetics by Dr. Richardson, I would like to voice my scepticism about the validity of his claims. To suggest that delivering a cocktail of different gases is more suitable for inducing unconsciousness than the simple application of chloroform."* Oh, he was really quite rude! Holmes, I must take this in. Will you come?

MUSIC: QUICK BRIDGE

SOUND EFFECT: LONDON STREET (BACKGROUND)

BUTLER: Yes, gentlemen, you are expected. I'll tell Doctor Richardson that you're here.

WATSON: Thank you.

SOUND EFFECT: DOOR CLOSES. STREET EFFECTS OUT. TWO MEN WALKING (UNDER)

BUTLER: Lord Halworth has been moved to a bed in the study downstairs, to make it more convenient. Doctor Richardson has asked me to show you to the drawing room, which is next to the study.

SOUND EFFECT: STEPS STOP, DOOR OPENS

BUTLER: Doctor John H. Watson and Mr. Sherlock Holmes.

RICHARDSON: (OFF) Watson! Welcome! Let me have a look at you! You've scarcely changed since our days at Barts!

WATSON: Oh, I've added a pound or two.

RICHARDSON: And Mr. Holmes! I can't tell you what a pleasure it is to meet you!

BUTLER: Will there be anything else, sir?

RICHARDSON: Not at the moment, Prentice.

BUTLER: (OFF) Very good, sir.

SOUND EFFECT: THREE STEPS, DOOR CLOSES

RICHARDSON: Now I'm sure you're wondering why I've invited you to witness this surgery, and why I'm doing it here instead of in hospital.

WATSON: Yes, the question had crossed my mind.

RICHARDSON: Well, I thought you'd be an ideal witness to the success of my anaesthetic process. And – if you should care to

109

write it up at some time. *The Lancet* would print your comments in an instant!

WATSON: That's most flattering. But why are you doing the surgery here and not in hospital?

RICHARDSON: Well, you see, Lord Halworth suffers from a case of morbid obesity, which has brought on a hernia – a tear – of the hiatal ring, and this has caused a deformation of his diaphragm and esophagus. I've tried to get him to diet, but to no avail. Surgery is our last resort. And yesterday his condition worsened. That's why I knew I had to operate as soon as possible. And why here? Well, the Royal Medical Society have to issue their stamp of approval, and – because of Doctor Xavier – they haven't seen fit to let me demonstrate my process to them. So, I can't do it in hospital.

WATSON: Interesting.

RICHARDSON: Oh, but I've trained Lord Halworth's own son and daughter to assist me. Elizabeth is a nurse, and a very good one. In fact, we met at St. Bartholomew. Met and – fell in love. Elizabeth has consented to marry me.

WATSON: Well! Congratulations!

RICHARDSON: And her brother Charles has studied hydraulics, so he very rapidly picked up the skills needed to make the valves that regulate the gas mixture. He's a very meticulous chap. Did most of the work in his shop down cellar.

HOLMES: May I ask, Doctor, why you included me in your invitation?

RICHARDSON: Because I believe Dr. Xavier may try to make this procedure fail. And if he does, it could cost Lord Halworth a great deal of pain . . . and possibly, his life!

SOUND EFFECT: DOOR OPENS. TWO PEOPLE WALK ON-MICROPHONE AND STOP

RICHARDSON: Oh, Mr. Holmes. Doctor Watson. May I introduce you to Elizabeth and Charles Halworth.

ELIZABETH: How do you do, gentlemen.

CHARLES: We heard the doorbell and thought it would be Dr. Xavier.

RICHARDSON: No, and frankly, I'm beginning to doubt if he'll come.

ELIZABETH: Oh, Joseph – I came to tell you. Father would like a word with you before we begin, and he wants to meet our guests.

RICHARDSON: Of course. Tell him we'll be right in.

CHARLES: Well, while you do that, I'll go in the kitchen and check the equipment one more time. Want to be sure everything's right.

RICHARDSON: Very good. Thank you, Charles. I'll be right in, my dear.

SOUND EFFECT: THEY BOTH WALK OFF. DOOR CLOSES

HOLMES: So Lord Halworth will be your first patient to be administered this new gas of yours?

RICHARDSON: Combination of gases. Yes, he'll be our first human patient. We've experimented on animals, of course, to learn the proper mixtures.

HOLMES: And you think it possible that the Royal Physician might do something to upset your anaesthetic procedure?

RICHARDSON: I believe he's entirely capable of it.

HOLMES: But, in view of the forces against you and your new methods, Lord Halworth still wants to go through with the operation?

111

RICHARDSON: Lord Halworth is prepared to finance a firm that would produce my new anesthetics. If this procedure works as I believe it will, he will invest hundreds of thousands of pounds!

HOLMES: I see. Interesting.

WATSON: Where will you perform the surgery?

RICHARDSON: His kitchen is well-lit and spacious, and I've equipped it with everything we'll need, so I'm doing it in there. Why don't we visit our patient now? He's keen to meet you both, and we must hurry along.

SOUND EFFECT: THREE MEN WALKING (UNDER). A DOOR OPENS

MUSIC: UNDERSCORE

WATSON: We walked into a generous-size study. The regular furniture had been pushed to the walls, and Lord Halworth lay on an oversize bed. He was indeed a ponderous figure.

MUSIC: OUT

SOUND EFFECT: DOOR CLOSES

HALWORTH: (OFF) Well, well. This is Doctor Watson, is it?

WATSON: Good evening, Lord Halworth. How are you feeling?

HALWORTH: Not well, Doctor. Anxious to get it over with. And then you, sir, would be Sherlock Holmes, I take it?

HOLMES: I am.

HALWORTH: What do you think of all this? Bit unconventional, isn't it? Being carved upon like a great turkey in my own kitchen, eh?

HOLMES: I'll be as interested in the outcome as I'm sure you are.

112

HALWORTH: You know, I've lived a good life. Denied myself nothing. Known every pleasure. The best of everything: Wine, food, diversions of every kind. You may say that's what's put me in my present condition. Well, I don't regret any of it. So . . . if I shouldn't wake up after Richardson turns off his gas . . . don't arrest him! That would put a damper on his wedding to my daughter, what? (WHEEZY CACKLE)

ELIZABETH: Father! Don't even joke about that!

HALWORTH: You met my children? Elizabeth and Charles?

WATSON: Yes, we did.

HALWORTH: Good. Now Mr. Holmes . . . ?

HOLMES: Sir?

HALWORTH: When a man faces . . . well, faces what I'm facing . . . he can't be too careful. What I mean is, it would be most convenient for my political enemies if I were not to survive.

ELIZABETH: Father!

HALWORTH: No no no! I have the utmost confidence in Richardson! After all, he's going to be my son-in-law! I requested that he use his new anaesthetic on me! No, Mr. Holmes, my concern is with the Queen's doctor, Gordon Xavier. He represents a bloc in Parliament that wants me out of the picture.

HOLMES: Then why have him here?

RICHARDSON: When Xavier sees my methods are safe and successful, he'll be forced to drop his objections to them for general use, and countless lives will be saved as a consequence!

HALWORTH: And so will be born a business enterprise in which I will have a major interest. Supplying the gas formula to the surgeons of the world! There'll be money in that. A lot of money!

BUTLER: (OFF) Excuse me, sir.

HALWORTH: What is it, Parsons?

BUTLER: Doctor Gordon Xavier has arrived.

HALWORTH: So he did come after all. All right, show him in.

BUTLER: Yes, sir, I'll bring him right in.

SOUND EFFECT: DOOR CLOSES

ELIZABETH: (SOTTO) Now, father, please try and control your temper. If he says anything to –

HALWORTH: Don't lecture me, Elizabeth! I've dealt with him before! He'd like nothing better than to discredit our anaesthetic, since he won't make a shilling out of it!

RICHARDSON: You see, Watson, when it comes to medical developments, if Xavier didn't come up with it, it can't be any good!

WATSON: I see. Greed, again.

HALWORTH: Precisely that. But Mr. Holmes: Apart from the enjoyment of meeting such a celebrity as yourself, I want you to be on the watch for anything Gordon Xavier may do to cause this operation to fail!

CHARLES: Well, you're certainly not having him in to watch the surgery?

HALWORTH: Don't tell me what I shall or shall not do!

SOUND EFFECT: SHORT DOOR TAP

HALWORTH: Ah. Here he is now.

SOUND EFFECT: DOOR OPENS

114

BUTLER: Doctor Gordon Xavier.

HALWORTH: Come in, doctor.

SOUND EFFECT: HE STEPS IN. DOOR CLOSES

XAVIER: Good heavens, a crowd!

HALWORTH: Oh, come in, Xavier, we've been waiting for you.

XAVIER: I do apologize. At the last minute, I was called to consult with Her Majesty.

RICHARDSON: Nothing serious, I hope?

XAVIER: Thankfully, no, but you know how Her Majesty relies on me. Now, Lord Halworth: It is my duty as Royal Physician to warn you that any unproven anaesthetic is dangerous! There is nothing wrong with chloroform. I delivered Prince Leopold while the Queen was under chloroform! I have only your best interests at heart!

RICHARDSON: And so have I. Remember, Doctor Xavier, I invited you here so you could witness for yourself the effectiveness of my methods, just as I invited these gentlemen. Let me introduce you. This is Doctor John H. Watson and this is Mr. Sherlock Holmes.

XAVIER: Sherlock Holmes? You are Sherlock Holmes?

HOLMES: That's correct.

RICHARDSON: They are here to witness the dawn of a new day for the comfort and safety of surgical patients.

XAVIER: (DRILY) And I am here to save a man's life. I have taken the liberty of reserving an operating suite at St. John's Hospital, Lord Halworth, and an ambulance can be at your service at a moment's notice!

HALWORTH: So tomorrow you could tell the press how you saved my life! Come on, Richardson, let's get on with it before my stomach explodes!

<u>MUSIC: STING AND UNDER</u>

WATSON: And those were the circumstances that led to the bizarre consequences which were about to take place. Richardson, Elizabeth, her brother Charles, Xavier the Royal Physician, and Holmes and I crowded into the kitchen, where there was a table in the centre of the room, laid out with the surgical instruments on glistening white linen.

RICHARDSON: You are free to inspect the arrangement, gentlemen, but I must caution you not to touch anything.

WATSON: (NARRATING) A narrow bed was positioned next to the table. At its head were three large cylindrical tanks, each with gauges and a bizarre interconnection of tubes. Each tank was fitted with a valve, through which gas would be admitted into a manifold with three more valves. Exiting the manifold was a single rubber hose about three feet in length, which ended in a curious mask, shaped to fit over the patient's nose and mouth.

<u>MUSIC: OUT</u>

XAVIER: And just what is in these tanks, Doctor?

RICHARDSON: I'm reluctant to reveal the formulae for my gases until I secure a patent, but the biological properties – when combined in a particular way – are not dissimilar to those of ether, but without the side effects.

HOLMES: And its chemical properties? I happen to have some passing knowledge of chemistry.

RICHARDSON: As I say, one of these gases is highly flammable and heavier than air, but perfectly safe when combined with the others, although it is a more complex molecule with both alcoholic and carboxylic groups.

HOLMES: Fascinating.

XAVIER: Very interesting I'm sure, but all this equipment – the tubes and valves – how do you intend to use them?

RICHARDSON: The three cylinders are connected via the rubber tubing to the mixing valves. Then the gases are regulated and combined in a particular way and released to the patient through this mask of my own design.

XAVIER: And how is the gas flow maintained?

CHARLES: I can explain that, Doctor. That's my field. You see these valves on the top of each cylinder?

XAVIER: They look like ordinary kitchen water taps.

CHARLES: The same principle, but they are much more finely made. And I've fitted them with special gaskets to prevent the gas from escaping.

XAVIER: May I examine them?

RICHARDSON: Go ahead. But please be careful.

XAVIER: (OFF SLIGHTLY) Hmm. Then these valves feed into –

CHARLES: Don't touch them, man, for heaven's sake!

ELIZABETH: Charles! Watch your tongue!

XAVIER: I was just trying to understand the way they are connected. What would happen if there's a leak from one of these valves?

CHARLES: Well . . . (PAUSE)

XAVIER: The tank would blow up, wouldn't it?

RICHARDSON: Only if there was a spark to ignite it.

117

CHARLES: But there's no danger of that. My gaskets are made of India rubber, and when the gases are mixed, that removes any danger.

XAVIER: And you, young woman. What is your job here?

ELIZABETH: I'll be keeping watch of father's pulse and respiration during the operation. I am a trained nurse.

XAVIER: A "trained nurse", you say?

RICAHRDSON: Her responsibilities are as great as my own. If Lord Halworth should start to awaken as I operate, Elizabeth will adjust the gas mixture to deepen his slumber. And of course, should his pulse rate and breathing slow down, we lighten the mixture.

XAVIER: Dr. Watson: I presume you are acquainted with the risks. There is yet time to take him to a proper operating room with proper help and proper methods!

RICHARDSON: You may be the Queen's Physician, Xavier, but your ethics are quite doubtful. Lord Halworth is my patient.

XAVIER: Very well. May the consequences be upon your heads!

SOUND EFFECT: HE STALKS AWAY. A DOOR SLAMS

RICHARDSON: I think it would be wise for us to proceed as quickly as possible.

CHARLES: Wait! I want to check all the fittings again! Xavier was handling the valves and the connections. Doctor Richardson, why don't you and Elizabeth go into the study and prepare father while I make sure everything's right.

RICHARDSON: Good idea, Charles. Come along, Elizabeth. Gentlemen . . . you may want to wait in the drawing room until we have Lord Halworth ready for the anaesthesia.

MUSIC: UNDERSCORE

118

WATSON: In the drawing room, Holmes looked out the window at the street below and turned away with a wry smile.

HOLMES: Doctor Xavier is still out there in his carriage.

WATSON: Hoping for failure.

HOLMES: Well, with Halworth's own two children assisting Richardson, I say he couldn't be in better hands.

RICHARDSON: (MOVING ON-MICROPHONE) Everything's ready, John. Lord Halworth's in our impromptu operating room, sedated and drowsy. Charles has checked the equipment, and Elizabeth and I are ready to begin. So, if you'd care to observe . . .

SOUND EFFECT: EXPLOSION

WATSON: Good heavens!

RICHARDSON: The kitchen! Come on!

SOUND EFFECT: TWO MEN RUNNING, THEN THROUGH RUBBLE

WATSON: A ball of flame had curled upward from the operating table and scorched the ceiling. The blast had blown the tanks of gas like bombs! But most terrible of all . . . the blackened body of Lord Halworth was beyond help. And Elizabeth, who had been blown against a counter in the kitchen, was unconscious – severely burned. It was a sight as bad as any casualties I saw in the service. Richardson saw immediately that he could do nothing for Halworth, and we both turned our attention to Elizabeth. Charles dashed in, caught sight of his father and sister, and staggered back, stunned.

MUSIC: BUILDS TO CLIMAX AND CUTS

WATSON: (QUIETLY) After the fire was out, the police took statements. Holmes remained in the ruined kitchen, examining the wreckage. But I took a cab home to Baker Street, where I had two brandies to steady my nerves, and then went to bed.

When I awoke the next morning, Holmes wasn't there, but left a note saying he would meet me at St. John's Hospital. Elizabeth was swathed in bandages and in a private room. Her brother and Dr. Richardson were there with her, and Richardson stepped away and came over to me.

<u>SOUND EFFECT: (BACKGROUND) OLD HOSPITAL EFFECTS</u>

RICHARDSON: She has second-degree burns on her face, neck, and arms, and a broken shoulder and arm. She'll recover, but she'll never look the same again. And I'm responsible!

WATSON: Oh, nonsense. You weren't even in the room. You were with Holmes and me when it happened!

RICHARDSON: Still, it was my experiment. My project. Now it's killed a man and maimed the girl I love! Charles says he'll never forgive me for what I did to his family. I wish I were dead.

HOLMES: (OFF, MOVING ON) (GRIMLY): Oh, there you are. Good morning Watson. Doctor Richardson . . . .

WATSON: Oh, Holmes. Where have you been?

HOLMES: Rather busy, interviewing some of Lord Halworth's staff.

RICHARDSON: Mr. Holmes, I can't tell you how sorry I am –

HOLMES: You needn't be sorry for anything. How is Miss Halworth?

RICHARDSON She has second-degree burns and broken bones. They've given her morphine to help the pain.

HOLMES: Yes, morphine does that quite effectively. Doctor Richardson, There's someone in this hospital who must answer for what happened last night.

RICHARDSON: Someone besides me, you mean?

120

HOLMES: I assure you, Doctor, you bear no blame. The explosion was deliberate.

RICHARDSON: What are you saying?

HOLMES: It was murder.

WATSON: Are you sure?

RICHARDSON: Xavier? Yes! It was Xavier! When he was examining the valve system! I knew he'd try to stop me, but I didn't think he'd go this far!

HOLMES: I see Charles in his sister's room. Since he designed the valve system, perhaps he should know what I found. Can he leave her for a minute?

RICHARDSON: Of course. I'll go fetch him.

SOUND EFFECT: HE HURRIES AWAY

WATSON: (PAUSE) You say you have evidence?

HOLMES: Evidence . . . and a motive. And Charles can cinch this case tightly enough to hand to Scotland Yard on a platter.

WATSON: Charles?

HOLMES: Yes. He built the system. A young man who will take no risks, who will choose the safe way in any enterprise. What did he call himself? Oh yes. *Prudent*. Ah. Here he comes.

CHARLES: (MOVING ON) Oh, Mr. Holmes! Good of you to come! How are you?

HOLMES: My sincere condolences over the death of your father.

CHARLES: Well . . . thank you. It's a terrible shock.

HOLMES: I'm sure it must be. And how is your sister this morning?

121

CHARLES: "Holding her own", the doctors say. Doctor Richardson said you have some kind of evidence . . . ?

HOLMES: Yes I have.

CHARLES: Evidence that proves Doctor Xavier tampered with the equipment?

HOLMES: No, I'm afraid it won't prove that. But it will prove that the explosion was planned and caused . . . by you.

CHARLES: (PAUSE) Is this your idea of humour, Mr. Holmes?

HOLMES: I know what caused the explosion, and I know why it was done. You may remember that right after the blast, I did my own investigation. I was looking for something that shouldn't be there in the kitchen. And . . . I found it.

RICHARDSON: What's that you have?

HOLMES: It's a narrow three-inch strip of abrasive cloth. It was wrapped round the valve on a tank of gas in such a way that when the valve was turned, and the volatile gas leaked out, the grit on the cloth caused a spark that blew it up. It survived the explosion and was still tightly secured around the neck of a valve where I found it.

CHARLES: That's preposterous! There couldn't have been a leak!

RICHARDSON: I never saw it there!

HOLMES: No, because it wasn't there until Charles installed it when he was supposedly checking the fittings, a few minutes before the blast! The same time he put a slit in the rubber gasket.

CHARLES: What absolute rot! My father is dead, my sister is horribly injured, and you say I did it?

RICHARDSON: I think you've made a terrible mistake, Mr. Holmes!

HOLMES: I think not. I've spent the morning speaking with the Halworth legal firm. Lord Halworth was preparing to strip his bank account, against the advice of his bankers and his barristers, to invest his fortune in business with you, Dr. Richardson, and that would have drained away the money Charles had expected to inherit one day.

CHARLES: This is an outrage!

RICHARDSON: Yes! Lord Halworth believed in my process! We named it the Halworth-Richardson System! He literally staked his life on it!

HOLMES: But if he died before he could invest the money, and if Elizabeth were also dead, the Halworth estate would remain intact . . . for Charles to inherit.

RICHARDSON: But the Halworth-Richardson anaesthetic would have made many more millions for Lord Halworth!

HOLMES: If the operation was a success. But that was a chance that Charles Halworth didn't care to take. His butler, the household staff, and even his barrister told me that Charles was frequently at odds with his father . . . and his sister. The invention gave him a perfect way to do away with them both, and profit by it!

CHARLES: The household! They've always been against me! I don't care how famous you may be, you can't prove a thing!

HOLMES: But your sister is still alive, and will be able to testify. I would advise you to keep a close watch over her, Doctor Richardson, until Scotland Yard arrives!

MUSIC: (UNDERCURRENT)

WATSON: And when the case came to the assizes, not only was Charles Halworth indicted, but the Honourable Gordon Xavier, the Royal Physician, was called up to testify as to his interest in keeping the Halworth-Richardson anaesthetic off the market. He wasn't charged with any crime, but his association with the murder of Lord Halworth damaged his career, and soon he was replaced by the Crown.

MUSIC: *DANSE MACABRE* UP AND UNDER

WATSON: This is Doctor John H. Watson. I hope you've enjoyed this story, and I'll have another one for you . . . *when next we meet*!

MUSIC: UP AND OUT

The Adventure of the
Bishop's Ring

CHARACTERS

- SHERLOCK HOLMES
- DR. WATSON
- THE BISHOP
- THE VICAR
- ROBBINS
- MRS. DELAWARE
- LUCY PURSELY

SOUND EFFECT: OPENING SEQUENCE, BIG BEN, STREET SOUNDS

ANNOUNCER: *The Further Adventures of Sherlock Holmes . . . .*

MUSIC: *DANSE MACABRE* (UP AND UNDER)

WATSON: My name is Doctor John H. Watson. For many years I have been privileged to assist my friend Sherlock Holmes as he solved some of England's most baffling crimes. Our clients have ranged from the obscure and humble, to some of the most powerful and wealthy men in the kingdom. But in the case I'm about to tell you tonight, Sherlock Holmes and I found ourselves employed by an official of the Church, in a matter which was never to be publicly acknowledged.

MUSIC: SEGUE TO UNDERCURRENT

WATSON: It was a chill November day in the year 1884. Holmes was feeling downcast. It had been many weeks since he had solved his last case, and he had sunk into a depression which deepened as each day passed without a client. He sat slumped in his chair before the fire, the newspaper carelessly discarded at his side, the lunch things uncollected in a tray on the floor.

MUSIC: FADES OUT

125

HOLMES: (PAUSE) I am a forgotten man, Watson.

WATSON: Nothing interesting in the paper today?

HOLMES: No.

WATSON: Suppose we bundle up and have a brisk walk?

HOLMES: You do as you like. I think I'll stay where I am and conserve my shoe leather. At this rate, I may not be able to buy another pair.

WATSON: Well, exercise stimulates the blood, and blood nourishes the brain.

HOLMES: My brain is of no apparent use to anyone, nourished or not. The devil of it is, Watson, the practice of a skill as exclusive as mine – the world's only consulting detective –

SOUND EFFECT: A KNOCK AT THE DOOR

WATSON: Hmm. Mrs. Hudson must have returned from market. Sit still. I'll get it.

SOUND EFFECT: HE WALKS TO THE DOOR AND OPENS IT

WATSON: Oh! Hello?

BISHOP: Excuse me, are these the lodgings of Mr. Sherlock Holmes?

WATSON: They are.

BISHOP: I beg your pardon for coming unannounced. Your landlady let me in.

HOLMES: (OFF-MICROPHONE) Who is it, Watson?

BISHOP: She had her arms full of groceries and said I might come up by myself. My card.

WATSON: (PAUSE) Oh. My word. Please do come in, sir!

WATSON: You'll forgive the looks of the room. We weren't expecting a guest. Holmes, may I present the Bishop of Downleigh. Reverend, this is Sherlock Holmes, and I am Doctor John H. Watson.

HOLMES: (MOVING ON) Well, well. And is there mischief afoot in the diocese, or have you come to save my soul?

BISHOP: Perhaps I have intruded. If so, I'll withdraw.

HOLMES: No, no, Bishop, that won't be necessary. Pull him up a chair, Watson, and I'll make myself more presentable. (MOVING ABOUT) I have a tendency to scatter things when I am concentrating. Take his coat and hat, that's a good chap.

WATSON: Of course. (EXERTION) Allow me, sir.

BISHOP: Thank you. (EXERTION) You may be wondering why I am not wearing my ecclesiastical clothing.

HOLMES: Obviously, you didn't want to be recognized while calling on me.

BISHOP: That is it exactly.

WATSON: Please, sit down.

HOLMES: Then this is a personal matter.

BISHOP: Correct again.

HOLMES: I am all ears. Please spare no detail.

BISHOP: Well, there has been a theft. The missing object is of great value. I must have it back.

HOLMES: Yes, and the object is – ?

BISHOP: A – ring.

HOLMES: A sacred relic?

BISHOP: No, it belongs to me. It's been handed down through four generations. You see, I am descended from a line of prelates that began with my great-great grandfather. The ring is solid gold. On its face is the form of the cross, and originally it contained one large diamond, where the bars met in the center of the cross. When my great-great grandfather gave it to his son, a second diamond was added. When he passed it on to my grandfather, the Archbishop of York, a third diamond was mounted, and when the ring became my father's, it got its fourth diamond. And now it has five stones.

WATSON: It must be worth a king's ransom!

BISHOP: Its monetary worth is the smallest part of its value to me.

HOLMES: Of course it is. Now, when did you find it missing?

BISHOP: Early this morning.

HOLMES: And the police were called?

BISHOP: No. I don't want any official record of it – don't want a scandal that would embarrass the church. But I felt I needed to take immediate action, so I quarantined the manse and left my vicar in charge while I came to London, praying that you might be able to help.

HOLMES: You quarantined your house?

BISHOP: Well, I'm sorry to say, I have to assume one of the household must have taken the ring as I slept. It was safely in its place just before I retired last night, and then when I arose at six this morning it was gone. And no sign of a break-in. So, as much as I hated to do it, I ordered no one to leave the manse until I return.

128

HOLMES: And who lives there besides yourself?

BISHOP: My vicar, our housekeeper, the cook, and a handyman.

HOLMES: And they all knew about the ring?

BISHOP: I presume they did. But I wear it only rarely, and never during services, of course. One doesn't want to show off.

HOLMES: Where did you keep it?

BISHOP: In a small camphor-wood case on the top of my dresser, which is in a vestibule just off my bedroom.

HOLMES: I must be frank with you, Bishop. In cases like this, it is all too easy to dispose of the stolen property. In fact, the thief may have sold it within an hour of his taking it. We must face the fact that you may never see your ring again.

BISHOP: I know, I know. But still, one must do all one can.

HOLMES: Yes. Now you understand, in order to pursue my investigation, there will be expenses –

BISHOP: Have no concern about that, Mr. Holmes. I am quite prepared to pay whatever you ask. And if you can find the ring for me with diamonds intact, I will gladly reward you with a handsome bonus.

MUSIC: UNDERCURRENT

WATSON: After the Bishop hurried back to catch a train to Downleigh, there was none of the excitement of the chase in Holmes's mood. In fact, until we got on a later train, he scarcely said two words . . . .

SOUND EFFECT: TRAIN (INTERIOR)

WATSON: . . . and then when he did speak, he was grim.

129

HOLMES: It's a fool's errand, Watson. I should resolve never to take a case I have so little hope of winning.

WATSON: But what a credit to you, that you'd try to help him, even if it's hopeless. And you did warn him.

HOLMES: Don't credit me with sympathy or sentiment, Watson. I'm taking this case because I need the money, and what is worse, if I fail, it will do much harm to my reputation. Yes, a fool's errand indeed!

SOUND EFFECT: TRAIN (INTERIOR UP, SEGUE TO)

MUSIC: TRANSITION UNDER:

WATSON: The train arrived at the Downleigh station around four-fifteen, in a pouring rain. Downleigh is a far cry from London and its amenities, and we found no one waiting to meet us, so at last we managed to hire a cab, which plodded its way to an enormous old stone church, next door to which stood a large residence of the same architecture. The door to the manse opened as we approached and a slender stick of a man in a priest's costume rushed out to greet us.

SOUND EFFECT: SEGUE TO RAIN

VICAR: (OFF-MICROPHONE, CALLING) Mister Holmes, is it? And Doctor Watson?

SOUND EFFECT: HOLMES AND WATSON WALKING ON RAINY PAVEMENT

VICAR: (MOVING ON) Do come right in! Filthy weather, isn't it? So sorry we couldn't send for you at the station. The Bishop's trying to keep everyone inside until you've had a chance to interrogate them. My name's Vicar Mason Delaware. I'm the assistant to the Bishop.

SOUND EFFECT: THEY WALK INSIDE, THE DOOR CLOSES (RAIN EFFECT OUT). RAINCOATS BEING REMOVED (UNDER DIALOGUE)

VICAR: How was your journey? It's well past tea-time and we've waited to have ours until you could get here. Oh, here's Robbins to take your things. Yes, Robbins, the umbrellas too. Front hall closet.

SOUND EFFECT: COATS BEING TAKEN OFF (UNDER)

ROBBINS: Yes, sir. (MOVING OFF) I'll just be hanging these things up.

VICAR: Now, gentlemen, if you'll follow me into the front parlor.

BISHOP: (OFF, MOVING ON) Ah, Mr. Holmes and Doctor Watson! Here at last! Would you want a few minutes to freshen yourselves?

HOLMES: No, I prefer to meet the household as soon as possible.

BISHOP: Right you are, right you are. Mason, please bring the others in now. (PAUSE, THEN CLOSE ON) You got here not a moment too soon, gentlemen! I'm afraid there's quite a bad feeling in what was always such a felicitous household!

HOLMES: While the others are assembling, would you show me all of the outside doors?

BISHOP: Outside doors? Why, yes. Robbins can do that. Where's Robbins? Robbins?

ROBBINS: (OFF MOVING ON) Coming, your Reverence. Yes, sir.

BISHOP: Would you be so kind as to show Mr. Holmes the outside doors.

ROBBINS: The outside doors? Why?

BISHOP: He is a detective, Robbins. He's looking for clues!

ROBBINS: Right you are, your Reverence. (MOVING OFF) Well, you seen the front door yourself –

BISHOP: Now why on earth would he want to look at our doors?

131

WATSON: Oh, it's quite simple, actually. He's checking for signs anyone's come in from the rain. You did say you'd ordered everyone to stay inside.

BISHOP: Oh, so I did! And if he saw wet footprints in the house – I say! Extraordinary! Why didn't I think of that? Well, you're an experienced detective right alongside Mr. Holmes, I can see that! Tell me frankly, Doctor: Does Mr. Holmes always get his man?

WATSON: Well, I can say that – in the time we've associated – yes. He's never failed. Of course there's – heh – always the first time.

MUSIC: UNDERCURRENT

WATSON: Presently, the vicar ushered in his wife, Mrs. Delaware – a woman in a severe black dress – and the cook, Lucy, plump, red-faced, all in white, with ringlets of blond curls under her starched white cap. And then the handyman, Robbins, returned with Holmes from the back of the house.

MUSIC: OUT

BISHOP: Ah, very good. We're all here now, I think. Mr. Holmes, Doctor Watson, this is our housekeeper, Mrs. Delaware, our cook, Lucy Pursley, and of course you've met Vicar Delaware, and John Robbins. And did you find any clues, Mr. Holmes?

HOLMES: Only what I expected, Bishop. Now first: Mrs. Delaware.

DELAWARE: Yes sir.

HOLMES: You and the vicar are husband and wife, so I presume you occupy the same rooms?

DELAWARE: Yes, we have an apartment two flights up.

HOLMES: May we see it?

132

VICAR: Of course. Come this way.

MUSIC: BRIDGE

SOUND EFFECT: DOOR CLOSES

VICAR: Look about all you like, Mr. Holmes, Doctor Watson.

DELAWARE: You must forgive the scraps of paper on the table. I'm making Christmas decorations for the childrens' tree at the Orphanage.

WATSON: Oh, I say, that's a charitable thing to do. Good for you!

HOLMES: Mrs. Delaware, at what time did you retire last night?

VICAR: Ah, we retire at ten. We make a practice of going round the house just before bedtime to make sure everything's right.

DELAWARE: And then I lay out the vicar's clothes for the next day.

VICAR: Then we say our prayers and we are in bed promptly at ten o'clock.

DELAWARE: Yes, dear. Mr. Holmes, I know the bishop thinks one of us in the house took his ring, so I invite you to inspect all our belongings. Actually, we haven't much to inspect.

HOLMES: Most obliging. Watson, the pockets and linings of all the clothing hanging in the closet.

WATSON: Righto.

HOLMES: And I will take the drawers of your dresser and night stand.

MUSIC: UNDERCURRENT

WATSON: I must say, I pitied the Delawares. If these were their only possessions, they lived humble lives, indeed. In only a few minutes, Holmes and I had examined every possible hiding

133

place for an object the size and weight of the bishop's ring, and found nothing. We went back down to the parlor, where the Bishop, Robbins, and the cook were waiting.

MUSIC: OUT

HOLMES: Mrs. Pursley, how long have you cooked for this household?

LUCY: (TERRIFIED) It's – it's just going on four years now, sir.

HOLMES: And where did you cook last?

LUCY: Before here? At 'ome for meself and me husbin', rest 'is soul.

HOLMES: And where are your quarters?

LUCY: 'Ere on the ground floor. Me room's next to the butler's pantry.

HOLMES: Hmm. That would be not far from the back door, am I correct?

LUCY: That's right.

HOLMES: In fact, your room is just under the back stairs to the first storey.

LUCY: Yes, sir, it is. Mister 'Olmes, I di'n't steal nuthin', I swear!

HOLMES: Tell us, what did you serve for last night's dinner?

LUCY: Last night's dinner? Uh, roast leg of lamb, gravy, and dumplings.

HOLMES: Excellent. Now let us move on to the handyman. John Robbins, is that your name?

ROBBINS: It is.

HOLMES: What sort of work do you do here, Mr. Robbins?

ROBBINS: Oh, I keeps the grounds, tends the stable, does repairs round the house.

HOLMES: And where do you sleep?

ROBBINS: Above the stable.

HOLMES: And where were you last night?

ROBBINS: I had me dinner here, same as the other folks had, and I might say it was scrumptious good, Lucy! And then I went out to make sure the horse was dry in his stall, and give him fresh hay, then I took meself to bed.

HOLMES: So you were not in the house overnight?

ROBBINS: No, I was up in me own digs. But I will tell ye one thing: About two in the mornin', the horse, he kicks up a rumpus down in his stall.

HOLMES: Oh? Did you go down to see what was wrong?

ROBBINS: Well, no sir, I didn't. I thought it'd be a stray dog or somethin'. But now I'm not so sure I done the right thing.

HOLMES: So when did you enter the house this morning?

ROBBINS: I come down for breakfast like always. Seven o'clock. Lucy has me tea and kippers waitin'.

HOLMES: Now, Bishop. Last night, did you fall asleep promptly?

BISHOP: Yes, I did.

HOLMES: And did you awaken during the night?

BISHOP: Well . . . no.

HOLMES: But you took no sleeping powders?

BISHOP: I don't use them.

135

BISHOP: Very well. Now I think I should like a look at your quarters, Bishop, if you don't mind.

BISHOP: Certainly. My room is one floor above, directly above this room.

HOLMES: Did I see a back stairway, when Robbins showed me the back door?

BISHOP: Yes.

HOLMES: Watson, step into the hall with me. (UP) Excuse me, everyone, for a moment.

SOUND EFFECT: THE TWO OF THEM WALK INTO THE HALL AND STOP

HOLMES: (VERY LOW VOICE) This may not be as difficult as I thought. I will go with the bishop into his room. I want you to stay down here, placing yourself so you can watch the stairway. I'll call the people up, one by one.

WATSON: Yes?

HOLMES: I want you to use your sharpest powers of observation, Watson. As I call each of them, see how they climb the stairs. Watch . . . and listen.

SOUND EFFECT: THEY WALK BACK (UNDER DIALOGUE)

HOLMES: (UP) Now, Bishop, if you will show me your room.

BISHOP: With pleasure. This way.

MUSIC: UNDERSCORE

WATSON: I made myself comfortable on a chair which afforded a view of the stairs, while Holmes and the bishop went to the rear of the house to use the back stairs. As he told me later, he found the bishop's quarters to be a modest bedroom, sparsely

136

furnished. (BEGIN FADE) The walls were lined with books, and a door opened into a small vestibule . . . .

BISHOP: (FADE IN) . . . This is the vestibule I told you about, Mr. Holmes, where I kept the ring.

SOUND EFFECT: DOOR OPENS

BISHOP: . . . and this is the chest of drawers.

SOUND EFFECT: DRAWER PULLED OUT

BISHOP: And the camphor wood box. The ring rested on this silk cushion.

HOLMES: There's no lamp in here.

BISHOP: No. Only the light from that small window, or I bring in a candle. One day we may have gas lighting, but it's far too expensive now.

HOLMES: Tell me, Bishop: Where do the funds come from to operate this home?

BISHOP: Why, the tithes and offerings of the faithful.

HOLMES: And the salaries of your employees?

BISHOP: From the same source. In fact, Mason Delaware is in charge of the offerings. He was a bookkeeper before he took the cloth. Worked under Rector Hastings in Wales for some time. I was lucky to get him. And his wife has been a godsend.

HOLMES: And where did you get the cook and the handyman?

BISHOP: They were faithful members of the diocese who were in need.

HOLMES: Very well, Bishop.

SOUND EFFECT: DOOR OPENS

137

HOLMES: (CALLS, OFF-MICROPHONE) All right, will the Delawares please come up?

BISHOP: You're having them in my room?

HOLMES: Bear with me, bishop. In a minute we'll have the cook and the handyman up here too. But first, I have a short errand.

MUSIC: SHORT BRIDGE

WATSON: I couldn't fathom what Holmes was leading up to, except that I saw on his face the welcome expression that he wears when he knows that he has his man. He came plunging down the stairs and out into the rain. He disappeared round the corner of the house, and was gone a good five minutes.

MUSIC: SHORT BRIDGE

WATSON: Good grief, Holmes, you're drenched!

DELAWARE: May I give him one of your towels, Bishop?

BISHOP: Of course, Mrs. Delaware, you know where we keep them.

HOLMES: Ah, so kind of you.

DELAWARE: (OFF, MOVING ON) Here you are, Mr. Holmes.

HOLMES: Fine. Now here we are, all jammed into the bishop's bed chamber. Mr. Robbins, would you go in the vestibule and open that small window so we can get a breath of fresh air in here?

BISHOP: It won't open, Mr. Holmes. Hinges are rusted or something.

ROBBINS: (OFF-MICROPHONE) Not any more, your worship. It opens fine now. See?

SOUND EFFECT: A SQUEAK AND THE WINDOW OPENS. RAIN EFFECT (UP)

BISHOP: Why, thank you, Robbins. When did you fix that?

138

HOLMES: Yes, that's much better. Now, Watson: I asked you to observe something for me. Would you care to report?

WATSON: Well, uh, here, in front of – everyone?

HOLMES: Oh yes. They'll be fascinated with your powers of observation.

WATSON: Well, you asked me to notice the way everyone climbed up the front stairs.

HOLMES: And?

WATSON: (CLEARS THROAT SLIGHTLY) Well, they all climbed the stairs in a perfectly normal way. But the ninth step creaks.

ROBBINS: He's right. I been meanin' to fix that step!

BISHOP: It does make an irritating noise.

HOLMES: But I'll wager it didn't make any noise at all for one person.

WATSON: Holmes! You knew that all along?

HOLMES: Oh yes. That person couldn't climb to the bishop's bedroom last night using the back stairs because every step squeaks and creaks.

ROBBINS: Aye, I been meanin' to get to that, too.

HOLMES: Oh, but you did a fine job on the vestibule window, Robbins.

ROBBINS: Well, I –

DELAWARE: Robbins – !

HOLMES: You see, it took careful planning and cooperation on the part of all of you. Beginning with . . . Lucy the cook.

139

LUCY: Me?

HOLMES: You cooked a heavy meal last night, with dumplings and gravy. How much sleeping powder did you put in the bishop's portion?

VICAR: Now look here, Holmes!

HOLMES: And you, Robbins, had a story rehearsed. About hearing a noise sometime late last night. To suggest someone tried to break in.

ROBBINS: Wull, it could've been a killer, for all you know!

HOLMES: Ah, but nothing that violent. In fact, the entire plan was so delicate, the slightest hitch could have meant disaster. No, the person who was to climb the stairs and enter the bishop's room had to be very light, to keep the stair from creaking. I don't suppose you weigh more than eight-and-a-half stone, Mrs. Delaware.

VICAR: All right, I've heard about enough of this! I knew what you were up to the minute we came in this room, Sherlock Holmes! Well, this is one case you can't prove! You searched our rooms, you searched our clothes, and you didn't turn up the bishop's ring, did you? No!

HOLMES: I humbly confess, you are correct. You don't have the ring. And neither do you, Mrs. Delaware. Nor do you, Lucy Pursley, and not even you, Mr. Robbins! The ring is not in this house!

VICAR: Your worship, you should order these two back to London with an apology to all of us who serve you so faithfully and ask so little in return!

BISHOP: Oh, shut up, Mason. Let Mr. Holmes finish.

HOLMES: Thank you. No, the ring was not in this house until I went outside just now and retrieved it where it had lain

140

overnight, waiting to be collected and sold no doubt for the gold and diamonds in it. And here it is!

BISHOP: Heavenly saints! Let me see it! Yes! Yes, it's the ring! With all the stones intact! Where on earth did you find it, Mr. Holmes?

HOLMES: In the rain barrel just below the vestibule window. Come.

SOUND EFFECT: TWO MEN WALK BRIEFLY AND STOP

HOLMES: Mrs. Delaware knew where you kept the ring, so she crept into your room as you slept a deep, drugged slumber. She removed the ring and placed it in a tiny paper boat she had made of the heavy paper she is using to make stars for the orphan's Christmas tree. Then she opened your formerly rusted window and sent it sailing down the roof gutter, the ring safely inside. The little vessel hurtled into the gushing downspout and sank into gallons of rain water, where the ring waited for someone to come and get it. Tomorrow. Or the next day.

WATSON: Holmes! How in heaven's name did you figure that out?

HOLMES: Everyone but the bishop himself had a motive to steal the ring. But it would have to be disposed of within hours, even minutes, of the theft.

BISHOP: Just as you told me this morning!

HOLMES: When I looked out the vestibule window and saw the channel of rainwater, it occurred to me that a thing like a ring could survive the journey into the downspout if it were able to float, just long enough to reach the rain barrel. And when I looked a few minutes ago, there was the little paper boat, its voyage finished, floating soggily on the surface of the water. I reached to the bottom and fished out the bishop's ring!

WATSON: We never learned what happened to the household of the Bishop of Downleigh. But the following day a package was delivered to Holmes, and in it, with no note attached, were sufficient pound notes to put a brief wry smile on the face of Sherlock Holmes. And that is the case I call The Adventure of the Bishop's Ring. And I'll tell you another one from my files on the great detective . . . *when next we meet!*

MUSIC: *DANSE MACABRE* AND UNDER

The Adventure of the
Blind Man

CHARACTERS

- SHERLOCK HOLMES
- DR. JOHN H. WATSON
- INSPECTOR LESTRADE
- DR. BAXTER
- WILLIAM WICKERTON
- BLIND MAN
- BARTENDER
- RUSSIAN (IVAN)
- DRIVER
- GREENSMAN

SOUND EFFECT: OPENING SEQUENCE, BIG BEN, STREET
SOUNDS

ANNOUNCER: *The Further Adventures of Sherlock Holmes . . . .*

MUSIC: *DANSE MACABRE* (UP AND UNDER)

WATSON: My name is John H. Watson. Tonight I shall tell you of
one of Sherlock Holmes's most important cases, a matter of
grave national danger, which I have titled, "The Adventure of
The Blind Man".

SOUND EFFECT: CROSSFADE TO QUIET HORSE OR TWO
ON BAKER STREET (UNDER)

WATSON: It began one foggy night on the first of November in the
year 1886. I remember London was in the grip of an icy fog that
night. Holmes and I had eaten a quiet dinner and had drawn our
chairs up to the fire to enjoy our coffee, when a familiar step
was heard on the stair, and an urgent knock on the door told us
we were about to receive a visit from –

HOLMES: Inspector Lestrade!

WATSON: Hmm! Past his working hours, isn't it?

HOLMES: (GETTING UP) Oh, I think he's still working, or he wouldn't come calling at half-past-nine.

SOUND EFFECT: AUTHORITATIVE KNOCK ON THE DOOR (OFF)

HOLMES: (OFF) Coming, Inspector.

SOUND EFFECT: (PAUSE) DOOR OPENED (OFF)

LESTRADE: (OFF) Knew it was me, didn't you? Well, my apologies for the intrusion, Mr. Holmes.

HOLMES: Not at all, Inspector. Come in.

SOUND EFFECT: (OFF) A STEP, THEN DOOR CLOSES

LESTRADE: (MOVING ON) Evening, Doctor.

WATSON: Welcome, Inspector. Here, let me pull another chair 'round by the fire.

HOLMES: And let's rid you of your Mackintosh so you can dry your shirt cuffs.

SOUND EFFECT: TAKING OFF HIS RAINCOAT (UNDER)

LESTRADE: (EXERTION AS HE DOFFS HIS MAC) Ah, you noticed.

HOLMES: Fishing a body out of the Thames, perhaps?

LESTRADE: (PAUSE) How did you know that?

HOLMES: The knees of your trousers are wet, your shirt and jacket cuffs have been soaked, but it hasn't rained in days. Which suggests that you have been kneeling on damp ground and dipping your hands deeply into water, so hurriedly that you paid no attention to the soaking of your clothing. Why would a policeman do that? And why would he come here instead of

144

going home for dry clothes, unless a crime most foul were afoot? Here, let me have your coat.

LESTRADE: All right, all right, have your fun. It was a dead body and it was in the Thames.

HOLMES: (GRAVELY) I never take murder lightly, I assure you. How may I help?

LESTRADE: Because you knew the victim. Jack Campbell.

HOLMES: Jack Campbell? The cut-purse, the armed robber, and burglar. Never turned an honest penny. That Jack Campbell?

LESTRADE: That's him. You were of some help to us in catching him after he robbed –

HOLMES: William Wickerton, the antiquities collector. I remember. How did Jack wind up in the river?

LESTRADE: We know how he got there: His hands and feet were tied and he was dumped. What I want to know is who did it and why.

HOLMES: (MILDLY) And you come to me?

LESTRADE: For just one thing, Holmes. What was he doing with this in his pocket? Your business card!

HOLMES: (BEMUSED) My card? Hmm!

LESTRADE: When did you see him last?

HOLMES: When I turned him over for stealing that box of Roman coins from Wickerton's trophy room. A good five years ago, wasn't it?

LESTRADE: And not since?

HOLMES: Well, he's been in jail all that time, hasn't he? You know, Inspector, in all modesty I must point out that there are people who place some value on celebrity mementoes. No

145

doubt a few of my cards are in circulation. Or perhaps he picked the pocket of a former client of mine, found my card, and kept it to remind him of our last unpleasantry.

WATSON: Or maybe his murderer planted your card on the body, Holmes!

HOLMES: Ah, an interesting convolution. Inspector, where was the body found?

LESTRADE: On the Embankment near the south end of the House of Lords.

HOLMES: And where is the body now?

LESTRADE: At the morgue.

HOLMES: Well, Watson, a distasteful duty awaits us.

MUSIC: BRIDGE

SOUND EFFECT: ECHO

KEEPER: There he is, gents, look all you want. (MOVING OFF) I'll be in the office keepin' warm.

HOLMES: Lestrade, how were his hands and feet bound?

LESTRADE: We've got the rope back at the Yard. Just two lengths of common hemp, ends cut with a sharp knife.

HOLMES: What else was in his clothes besides my card?

LESTRADE: Three-shillings-and-sixpence.

HOLMES: Watson, what about an impromptu examination? How long would you say he's been dead.

WATSON: Well, it's hard to tell with water so cold. I'd say, between twelve and twenty-four hours.

HOLMES: Cause of death?

146

LESTRADE: He was drowned, Holmes. I would've thought you could see that.

WATSON: Oh, not necessarily, Inspector. No wounds on the body as far as I can see, but only an autopsy can say whether he was alive when he went in the water.

HOLMES: When will the autopsy be performed?

LESTRADE: Tomorrow, I suppose.

HOLMES: Tomorrow.

LESTRADE: Well, I can't get one done tonight, can I? It's going on eleven!

HOLMES: Of course. And what's been done with his clothes?

LESTRADE: The morgue keeper can tell you. I don't know where they'd be. What do you want with them, anyway?

SOUND EFFECT: ECHO OUT

MUSIC: UNDERCURRENT

WATSON: Holmes obtained Jack Campbell's clothes and shoes and we took them with us back to Baker Street. Although it was now nearly midnight, Holmes went to work straightaway, drying the poor devil's things in front of the fire. It made a vile smell.

MUSIC: OUT

HOLMES: You see, Watson, what's so intriguing about this is the contradiction. Whoever killed him *wanted* his body to be found.

WATSON: Why do you think that?

HOLMES: There are ever so many ways to hide a body, but a corpse bound hand and foot and floating in the Thames is a better notice than a three-column spread in the papers!

147

WATSON: Notice to whom?

HOLMES: Jack Campbell's friends, perhaps, or potential enemies of the man who killed him. The notice could mean: Warning: you'll get the same as this fellow got!' Or then again, with my card in his pocket, perhaps the warning was meant for me!

MUSIC: UNDERCURRENT

WATSON: Then Holmes became so absorbed in his work that further conversation was impossible, so I toddled off to bed around two. The next morning, I awoke to a smell even worse than the drying of the dead man's clothes the night before!

MUSIC: OUT

HOLMES: (OFF-MICROPHONE) Ah, Watson, you're awake at last! Come see what my chemical analysis has turned up!

WATSON: (A BIT CROSS) Is that what you've been doing all night? Mixing chemicals? It smells like a rotting swamp in here!

HOLMES: (MOVING ON) Our friend the late Jack Campbell was up to no good before his murder. What you're smelling is sulfur, from the flecks of gunpowder I found in abundance in his clothes!

WATSON: From firing a weapon?

HOLMES: No, there was no pattern to it except in the cuffs of his trousers, where it accumulated – as if he had been handling loose gunpowder in some quantity.

WATSON: Well, that's no mystery, Holmes! My army training included cartridge loading. You're bound to spill a few grains when you're loading. This fellow must have been loading cartridges.

HOLMES: A great many of them, if that was the case. Now, let us turn our attention to another ingredient I found traces of.

148

Despite immersion in the Thames, his shirt showed spots where the water had been repelled by some substance which had apparently spattered on it. Here. Let me hold up the shirt.

SOUND EFFECT: SHIRT BEING FLUFFED UP

HOLMES: Tell me what this suggests.

WATSON: Huh! He spilled something all over the front.

HOLMES: Exactly. And when I treated the shirt with a reactive chemical, it turned this pale yellow-green color, which indicates the presence of alcohol, despite being soaked with water. And when I burned a snippet of the cotton in my retort, it produced the flame color of almost pure alcohol. And now, I must ask you to dress quickly and go down to Scotland Yard.

WATSON: Scotland Yard at this hour? Why?

HOLMES: To interview the doctor before he autopsies the body. Encourage him to pay special attention to the stomach and liver. And when you come back, my good friend, you may find me absent. If I am, please wire the results of the autopsy to me in care of the telegraph office in Dawson Street, near Parliament. Now, do hurry, Watson!

MUSIC: FAST BRIDGE

WATSON: I did as Holmes asked, and within the hour I was at the side of a Scotland Yard physician named Baxter, in the dissecting room.

MUSIC: OUT

SOUND EFFECT: (UNDER) OCCASIONAL DELICATE CLINK OF SURGICAL TOOLS

BAXTER: You were quite correct, Doctor. This man didn't drown – there was no water in the lungs. But see what we have here: (CLINK)

WATSON: Ah.

149

BAXTER: He consumed a terrible quantity of alcohol, just before his death. Look at the liver. Engorged. It had no chance to metabolize the alcohol. (CLINK) Toxins spread through the body. The blood vessels opened up. He died of alcohol poisoning. If he wasn't dead when he hit the water with all his pores open, he died of exposure moments after. The Thames runs about fifty-five degrees this time of year. Now, here's another thing: Do you smell alcohol fumes rising from the liver? No. Because what he drank wasn't whisky, wasn't rum, wasn't brandy. Had to be that Russian stuff – vodka! (CLINK) Seen enough?

WATSON: Yes, Doctor Baxter, quite enough. Thank you.

MUSIC: STING TO UNDER

WATSON: I hurried back to Baker Street and found Holmes gone, but a note was fixed to the mantel with Holmes's dagger.

HOLMES: (ON FILTER) *Watson: will be awaiting details of the autopsy. At five o'clock sharp, be in a cab in the alley behind Smith Street near Wharf Row. Be on guard and bring your pistol.*

MUSIC: UNDERCURRENT

WATSON: My pulse quickened as I read the note from Holmes. But no sooner had I folded it into my pocket than Mrs. Hudson appeared at the door to announce a visitor. It was none other than Mr. William Wickerton, the antiques collector who hired Holmes five years earlier to recover the golden serpent of Egypt that had been stolen by Jack Campbell!

MUSIC: OUT

WICKERTON: Holmes not here? Bother! When will he return?

WATSON: I really don't know. But I expect to be in communication with him this afternoon. May I help?

WICKERTON: It's Watson, isn't it?

150

WATSON: That's right.

WICKERTON: Well, they've done it again, Watson! I've been robbed again!

WATSON: You don't say!

WICKERTON: Two bronze Etruscan urns, four-and-one-half-feet tall! 500 B.C.! Utterly priceless!

WATSON: You've alerted the police?

WICKERTON: Immediately. But that was four days ago and they've turned up nothing since. So I thought, well, it was Sherlock Holmes who found the culprit before, why not engage him again? I wonder if it could have been that same thug, Jack Campbell?

WATSON: I just saw him within the hour.

WICKERTON: You did? Where? What was he doing?

WATSON: He was in the London morgue, being dissected. He'd been murdered, and Holmes is on the case.

WICKERTON: On the case of a dead burglar? Come down in the world, hasn't he?

WATSON: (CLEARS THROAT DISAPPROVINGLY) Perhaps if you would give me the particulars – when you notice the theft, how the break-in occurred

WICKERTON: It was four nights ago. Bound and gagged the watchman. The police came, but I've heard nothing from them since. So that's why I came here.

WATSON: Odd I didn't notice anything of it in the papers.

WICKERTON: Oh, the police quashed that up. Didn't want to encourage any more burglars to try their hand.

151

WATSON: The urns: Quite heavy, are they?

WICKERTON: They weigh as much as I do! Took two good men apiece to carry them.

WATSON: What are they worth?

WICKERTON: To a collector or a museum, they're beyond price! But the moment they go on exhibit, of course the game's up! They can't be displayed without bringing down the law! So who the devil would want to steal them?

MUSIC: UNDERCURRENT

WATSON: I took down all the particulars, and hurried out to send a wire to Holmes with the news of the missing Etruscan urns as well as the results of the autopsy. Then I unfolded our large map of London and located Smith Street. It was a short, bending lane half-a-mile or so from the seat of government. It joined Wharf Row, which I was more familiar with – on this thoroughfare were canneries, warehouses, and ship chandleries. I decided to carefully clean my pistol before I loaded it, and waited until just four.

MUSIC: OUT

SOUND EFFECT: HORSE WALKING ON STONE

WATSON: And then I hailed a cab, and some minutes before five, we pulled off Wharf Row into the crumbling alley behind Smith Street. It had grown quite dark, and a cold wet fog was drifting up from the river. I ordered the driver to stop.

SOUND EFFECT: HORSE STOPS

WATSON: At this point, I must rely on what Holmes himself told me had been happening in a pub beyond a dark doorway near where my cab was standing.

SOUND EFFECT: (OFF-MICROPHONE) LOW RUSSIAN VOICES

WATSON: The sign above the door was grimy and almost unreadable. The place was called The Laughing Ram.

<u>SOUND EFFECT: VOICES CLOSER</u>

BLIND MAN: Gent'men, would someone look after gettin' me a pint? Gent'men! Help a poor blind man?

BARTENDER: Get out o'here! We don't take no beggars!

BLIND MAN: I'm not beggin'! You've got eyes, look for yourself! I've got money!

BARTENDER: So you 'ave. I'll take that.

BLIND MAN: Not so fast! Not til I have me drink in me 'and!

BARTENDER: You'll get your drink. First, gimme your coins. (PAUSE) That's right. Now, get out! I'll even point you to the door! Now, out!

BLIND MAN: Hold on! Where's me drink?

BARTENDER: Oh, it's a drink you want? Well, the Thames is just down the street. Keep walkin' and you'll get your drink!

BLIND MAN: Look here! You robbed me! You stole my money!

BARTENDER: What money? Do you see any money? (CRUEL LAUGH)

RUSSIAN: (OFF-MICROPHONE) You! Give him drink!

BARTENDER: Shut up, Ivan!

RUSSIAN: (MOVING ON-MICROPHONE) Give him drink!

BARTENDER: You shut up! This 'ere's my place and I run it like I see fit!

RUSSIAN: (AS HE GRABS BARTENDER BY THROAT) Give – blind man – his – drink!

153

BARTENDER: (STRANGLING) Awright! Awrightl Leave yer ands off me! (MOVING OFF) I'll get him his bloody drink.

BLIND MAN: Thank you, whoever you are! A thousand thanks!

RUSSIAN: I not see you in here before.

BLIND MAN: No, that's right, I don't even know where I am! Just dodgin' the coppers, trustin' society to have mercy on a poor blind beggar.

BARTENDER: (MOVING ON) Awright, yer highness! Here's a pint o' ale!

RUSSIAN: Good. *Karasho*. Drink, old man.

BLIND MAN: (SLURPS HIS ALE) You're a foreigner, ain't ye?

RUSSIAN: Never mind what I am. Drink. Then go.

SOUND EFFECT: VOICES IN BACKGROUND CONTINUE

WATSON: (NARRATING) Holmes told me the old blind man found a bench and sat down, sipping his ale. Customers came in and went out. Many of them were obviously Slavic, and a tough lot. Finally, the beggar stood up and felt his way along the bar.

BARTENDER: And where d'you think you're goin'?

BLIND MAN: Say, have ye' got a loo somewheres?

BARTENDER: Not for the likes o'you. Go out the alley door.

BLIND MAN: Ah. Many thanks.

SOUND EFFECT: MEN IN BACKGROUND LOUDER, CLOSER

BARTENDER: The alley!

BLIND MAN: Aye, the alley.

BARTENDER: (OFF-MICROPHONE, SHOUTS) Someone show the bloke the back door!

BLIND MAN: Ah, never mind. I've found it.

SOUND EFFECT: DOOR TRIED. STUCK, THEN OPENED

BARTENDER: (OFF-MICROPHONE) That's not the alley! Keep that door shut!

SOUND EFFECT: DOOR SLAMS

BLIND MAN: Oh, I'm ever so sorry, gov.

SOUND EFFECT: SHUFFLING STEPS, ANOTHER DOOR OPENS, CLOSES. EXTERIOR AMBIENCE (UNDER). SHUFFLING STEPS ON PAVING STONES

BLIND MAN: (CRYING OUT PITIABLY, SLIGHTLY OFF-MICROPHONE) Blind man! Help a blind man! Blind man! Help a blind man!

WATSON: Good heavens! He's going to walk right into the horse! (CALLS) Watch out, old man!

BLIND MAN: (APPROACHING) Ah, would that be a cab? Would that be a merciful citizen? (LOWER, AND IN HOLMES NATURAL VOICE, PLAYFULLY) Would that be you, Watson?

WATSON: I thought so! What are you doing here, Holmes?

HOLMES: (ALL BUSINESS NOW) Help me in and drive out of here and I'll tell you!

WATSON: (UP) Driver! Take us out of this alley!

SOUND EFFECT: HORSE STARTS PLODDING, THEN A LITTLE FASTER

DRIVER: (OFF-MICROPHONE) Where to now, sir?

HOLMES: To Number 21 Bracken Lane driver!

SOUND EFFECT: HORSE SPEEDS UP

WATSON: Bracken Lane? What's at Bracken Lane?

HOLMES: I haven't told you because there seemed no use in troubling you with it. I keep a room at 21 Bracken Lane.

WATSON: You do?

HOLMES: It's a convenient drop-point for a variety of costume changes. I maintain a decent wardrobe there, so in a few minutes, this raggedy blind man will disappear, and Sherlock Holmes will emerge from a different door.

WATSON: So you go to this place whenever you adopt a disguise? Seems rather unhandy.

HOLMES: It is only one of five safehouses I employ. They are distributed throughout the city.

WATSON: You amaze me!

HOLMES: But to the matter at hand: Watson, your timing and attention to detail was admirable! The telegram you sent has solved the case for me!

WATSON: The murder?

HOLMES: No, I don't know who killed Jack Campbell, but I know why he was killed. Watson, there is a diabolical plot afoot, and you and I must help Scotland Yard to prevent an unthinkable tragedy!

MUSIC: UNDERCURRENT

WATSON: Within the hour, Holmes had changed into his usual tweeds, and once again we employed a hansom to take us across town. Only this time, the pace was slower, as Holmes brought me up to date.

SOUND EFFECT: (BACKGROUND) HORSE AT MODERATE GAIT

HOLMES: First: While you were at Scotland Yard examining the remains of Jack Campbell this morning, I was down at the Embankment where his body was found. The police had trampled any tracks that might have been left, but the location of his body, placed as it was, suggested that he had been killed someplace nearby. And what we observed last night at the morgue and later in my test of his clothes told me he hadn't been in the water for very long, and his death wasn't by drowning, but by the forced ingestion of a lethal charge of a potato-mash liquor. Vodka. The national drink of Russia.

WATSON: Which is what the autopsy doctor said, as well.

HOLMES: And so Campbell's murder may have begun as a drinking bout among people he trusted, probably Russians. But Russian aristocracy would hardly be found drinking with the likes of Jack Campbell.

WATSON: I suppose not.

HOLMES: Well, there is another class of Russian who are emigrating to England: The Nihilists.

WATSON: Who?

HOLMES: The Nihilists. Nihilism is a movement that came from Russia in the eighteen-fifties. They reject all authority, all principle, all beliefs. They've staged acts of terrorism against the Imperial Russian government, and they've been implicated in plots against European governments as well. Some of them are terrorists. And I happen to know that they meet at The Laughing Ram.

WATSON: Then you think Jack Campbell was killed by terrorists?

HOLMES: I think he was used by them, and then killed to maintain secrecy.

WATSON: How would they have used him?

157

HOLMES: As a burglar – to obtain what they needed for their next infernal project. Ah, wait. We're here.

SOUND EFFECT: HORSE SLOWS TO A STOP UNDER ABOVE

MUSIC: STING AND UNDER

WATSON: We had pulled up to the rear gate of the House of Lords, the upper house of Parliament. And standing by the gate was Inspector Lestrade!

SOUND EFFECT: BACKGROUND AMBIENCE

LESTRADE: (UP, OFF-MICROPHONE SLIGHTLY) It's all a false alarm, Mr. Holmes.

HOLMES: How do you mean, Inspector?

LESTRADE: The Crown's own guards have inspected every foot of the passageways under Parliament. All two miles of 'em. No bomb. Nothing out of the way. Me and my men have been all over every foot of all eight acres of the enclosure. Not a mouse could get in without our seeing it.

HOLMES: I see.

LESTRADE: And I've had two men doing nothing but checking the deliveries. Caterer's vans, wagons full of flowers . . . everything's in order for Parliament to sit tomorrow. You got us here for nothing.

HOLMES: (MUSINGLY) Lestrade, did your men inspect the Chamber of the House of Lords as well as Commons?

LESTRADE: Of course.

HOLMES: The assembly room?

LESTRADE: We inspected every square inch of Parliament.

HOLMES: Including that lorry there against the building?

158

LESTRADE: Which? Oh. From the florists. Been bringing in fresh plants and shrubs all day. Yes, we inspected it.

HOLMES: Come along, Watson. You still have your revolver?

WATSON: Well, yes, but –

SOUND EFFECT: STEPS DOWN ONTO PAVEMENT

HOLMES: (EXERTING AS HE GETS DOWN FROM THE CAB) Get your men, Lestrade. Surround that wagon!

LESTRADE: What are you talking about?

WATSON: (ALSO EXERTING) I'm afraid I don't under –

SOUND EFFECT: TWO MEN HURRYING ON PAVEMENT (UNDER)

HOLMES: (SHOUTS AS HE RUNS) You, there! Driver! Hold up!

GREENSMAN: (FAR OFF-MICROPHONE) Who, me?

HOLMES: Stay right there by your wagon!

GREENSMAN: (CLOSER) What are you lot on about?

LESTRADE: Mr. Holmes, I told you! This fellow's already brought in two wagon loads of flowers! He's been thoroughly checked!

SOUND EFFECT: STEPS ALL STOP NOW

HOLMES: Stay there, driver. I'm climbing up on your wagon.

SOUND EFFECT: CLIMBS ONTO WHEEL HUB AND INTO WAGON BOX

GREENSMAN: Who do you think you are?

HOLMES: I'm Sherlock Holmes.

159

GREENSMAN: Right, and I'm the Duke of York.

HOLMES: Come up here, Lestrade.

SOUND EFFECT: SCUFFING ON WOOD

LESTRADE: If you'd be kind enough to let me in on your plan, Mr. Holmes –

HOLMES: Driver: where did you pick up this load of plants?

GREENSMAN: Hey, (SUDDENLY HE DARTS AWAY) You can keep the whole bloody thing! I don't want no problems –

HOLMES: Stop him, Watson!

WATSON: (OFF-MICROPHONE) You there! Stop or I'll shoot!

LESTRADE: Have you finally gone daft, Holmes? What do you think you've captured here? A bunch of shrubbery?

SOUND EFFECT: PAWING THROUGH GREENERY AND BUSHES

HOLMES: The two Etruscan urns stolen from Wickerton Galleries four nights ago. And inside the urns? A couple of small palms have been planted.

WATSON: (MOVING ON-MICROPHONE, SLIGHTLY WINDED) Your men are holding the greens man, Inspector.

LESTRADE: (CALLS OUT) Well, bring him over here!

HOLMES: Yes! We're admiring these trees planted in these old bronze urns! Where did you get them, my man.

GREENSMAN: (OFF) You're all barmy! I didn't do nothin'!

HOLMES: But someone was careless. You see? (EXERTION) You can – lift the tree right out of the urn – like this! The root-ball was resting on –

160

LESTRADE: Hello? What's this rope coming out of the urn?

HOLMES: Rope? Does that look like a rope, Lestrade? Or – a fuse!

LESTRADE: Good Lord!

HOLMES: These urns are packed with black powder. To be rolled under the House of Lords, and touched off by our friend the greens man –

GREENSMAN: No! It wasn't me! All I had to do was bring 'em 'ere! They just paid me to deliver 'em!

LESTRADE: You men! Seal off this area! And not a one of you dare to light up a smoke! Someone come take this fellow away and lock him up until I can interrogate him! (LOWER) And you, Sherlock Holmes . . . .

HOLMES: Yes, Inspector Lestrade?

LESTRADE: How the devil did you know?

HOLMES: When I was impersonating a pitiful old blind man, down at the tavern called The Laughing Ram, half-a-mile from where we're standing, I saw their bomb-making factory. It's in a back room. That's where I think you'll find the murderers of Jack Campbell – and the plotters who wanted to blow up Parliament!

MUSIC: *DANSE MACABRE* UP AND UNDER

WATSON: The following day, Parliament met with its usual pomp and ceremony, with no one the wiser that they all might have been blown to kingdom come, had it not been for my friend, the consulting detective, Sherlock Holmes. And then we went on to another adventure . . . *which I'll tell you the next time we meet*!

MUSIC: UP AND UNDER

The Curse of the Third Sign

CHARACTERS

- SHERLOCK HOLMES
- DR. JOHN H. WATSON
- ROBERT PAIGE – *A young suitor*
- CABBIE – *A typical London cab driver*
- HANLEY – *The butler*
- SIR EDWARD DALRYMPLE
- SOPHIE DALRYMPLE – *Sir Edward's daughter*

SOUND EFFECT: OPENING SEQUENCE, BIG BEN, STREET SOUNDS

ANNOUNCER: *The Further Adventures of Sherlock Holmes . . . .*

MUSIC: *DANSE MACABRE* (UP AND UNDER)

WATSON: (NARRATING) My friend Sherlock Holmes, although an enemy of all wrong-doers, was almost never interested in domestic squabbles which he occasionally was asked to investigate. "People should tend their own gardens," he would say, "and not run for help when weeds begin to grow." It wasn't surprising then, on a cloudless afternoon in July of 1887, that Holmes responded with the single word *"No"* to a telegram that came as he was basking in a wreath of pipe smoke, and appearing, for once, to be in deep contentment.

SOUND EFFECT: BAKER STREET BACKGROUND

WATSON: Just *"No"*? No explanation, Holmes? Seems a little short.

HOLMES: Why waste words on a lover's quarrel?

WATSON: Was that what the telegram was about?

HOLMES: Here, read it for yourself and see what you make of it.

162

WATSON: (READS) *"Urgently request you investigate disappearance of my* fiancée *after misunderstanding. Will pay any fee for her safe return. Will you take my case?"* Signed *Robert D. Paige.*

HOLMES: Yes. Just throw it in the grate, Watson.

WATSON: I don't know . . . Poor young fellow must be desperate to try enlisting Sherlock Holmes at *"any fee"*.

HOLMES: Let him use the police. He's already paying for their services, however incompetent they may be. And I certainly don't want it noised about that now I'm taking on lovers' spats. I won't turn my practice into a clinic for bleeding hearts!

WATSON: Yes, of course. Whatever you wish.

HOLMES: But you disapprove.

WATSON: No, I just happen to feel sympathy for a fellow who's desperate to find a missing loved one. As a matter of fact, I happen to have had some experience along those lines myself in years past.

HOLMES: Well then, there's the answer! Why don't *you* take his case?

MUSIC: UNDERSCORE

WATSON: (NARRATING) And after that, I'm sorry to say that he mooned in our rooms like the sun going behind a cloud. The next half-hour was spent in absolute silence, while Holmes riffled through some books and I read every word in the newspaper I had already perused the night before. Just as the stillness was becoming intolerable, from downstairs came the sound of the bell, Mrs. Hudson's steps to open the door, then a man's heavy tread on the stairs to our rooms.

SOUND EFFECT: KNOCK ON DOOR

HOLMES: He apparently didn't take *"No"* for an answer. (SHOUTS) Sherlock Holmes is not here! Kindly go away!

WATSON: Oh, Really, Holmes!

SOUND EFFECT: WATSON WALKS TO DOOR, OPENS IT

WATSON: Yes? May I help you?

PAIGE: I beg your pardon! The landlady said – that is, I thought –

WATSON: Are you Robert Paige, by any chance?

PAIGE: Yes! Here is my card. Are you Sherlock Holmes?

HOLMES: No, I am Sherlock Holmes. I take it you didn't receive my reply to your telegram?

PAIGE: I did, sir, but –

HOLMES: Was my wording unclear?

PAIGE: Not at all. But forgive me sir, I felt I must explain the circumstances that caused me to seek your help. I truly fear my *fiancée* has experienced some kind of shock that may have changed the direction of her life!

WATSON: Come in, Mr. Paige. I am Doctor John H. Watson, and I'll be glad to hear your story.

SOUND EFFECT: HE WALKS IN

PAIGE: You're very kind, Doctor, but I fear I need a detective.

SOUND EFFECT: DOOR CLOSES

HOLMES: Doctor Watson is far more experienced in matters of the heart than I am.

WATSON: You look a bit unsteady. Would you care for a drink?

PAIGE: Oh, no, thank you. I neither drink . . . nor smoke.

164

HOLMES: But I do, so you may want to conduct your business outside where the air is more to your liking. Regents Park is only a quarter-mile away.

WATSON: *Holmes!*

HOLMES: Merely concerned for the comfort of your guest, Watson.

WATSON: Please have a seat, Mr. Paige. I'll be glad to hear your story.

PAIGE: Very kind of you, Doctor. I take it you know why I wired Mr. Holmes?

WATSON: You had an argument with your *fiancée* and now she's disappeared.

PAIGE: No, no! There was no argument! I'm sure it was just a misunderstanding, and it wasn't with my *fiancée*, but with her father.

WATSON: What happened?

PAIGE: It was this past Tuesday, the morning after I had had dinner with her and her parents. A note was delivered to my office. I brought it with me, if you'd care to read it.

WATSON: By all means.

PAIGE: Here.

WATSON: Hmm! Certainly short enough!

HOLMES: (OFF) Out loud, if you please, Watson.

WATSON: (READING) *"Robert: I am leaving the city. I shall always love you. Pray for me"*. And it's signed with the letter 'S'.

PAIGE: That stands for Sophie. Her name is Sophronia Dalrymple.

HOLMES: Dalrymple? Unusual name. Her father wouldn't be Sir Edward Dalrymple, the architect, by any chance?

PAIGE: Yes! Do you know him?

HOLMES: Only by reputation.

WATSON: What did you do after you received her note?

PAIGE: I went to her house immediately and their butler said the Dalrymples had left, and didn't say when they might be back.

WATSON: Did something happen at the dinner the night before?

PAIGE: I had never met Sophie's parents before, and of course I was nervous, but we had a lovely dinner. Mrs. Dalrymple was charming, and then Sir Edward showed me through their sumptuous home that he designed, and we wound up in his game room. He started reminiscing. He told me how he became an architect, and I told him my father had been a barrister in the firm I work for, and he asked for my card. Then he asked me what my middle initial stands for, and I told him the 'D' stands for *Dunstan*. My full name is Robert Dunstan Paige. When I said that, his whole countenance changed. He looked at me oddly, and then he sank into a chair and his hands began to tremble! Finally, he said he was tired and needed to retire, so I said my goodbyes to Sophie and her mother and went home. And that was the last time I saw Sophie.

WATSON: How did you become acquainted with her?

PAIGE: Well, it happened this way. Nearly two years ago, a friend gave me a ticket to hear the young Polish pianist, Ignace Paderewski, at Covent Gardens, and I was seated next to a lovely young woman who was there with an older lady – her piano teacher as it turned out. As I sat down beside her, for just a moment our eyes met, and I felt an immediate attraction. I couldn't take my eyes off her! All through the first half, I would steal glances at her, and find her glancing at me! At the interval, we stayed in our seats rather than retiring to the lobby, and as we chatted we began to discover how alike we were – the same age, the same interests – it was uncanny! And after the concert

166

resumed, our hands happened to touch, an then they brushed again, and this time I dared to take her hand, and you can imagine my thrill when I felt her delicate fingers entwine with mine! And from that moment on, I couldn't tell you a single note Paderewski played!. When the concert was over, she wrote her address on my program and I gave her my calling-card. We've been seeing each other as often as possible ever since. A year to the day after we met, I proposed and she accepted.

HOLMES: How old are you, Mr. Paige?

PAIGE: Why, I'm twenty-five. I see you're taking notes, Mr. Holmes. Does this mean that you'll help me after all?

HOLMES: We shall see. Are there any obstacles to your marriage?

PAIGE: None that I know of.

HOLMES: Perhaps a past commitment . . . ?

PAIGE: Neither of us have any past commitments.

WATSON: And your parents are agreeable to your plans to marry?

PAIGE: We haven't told them yet. Sophie thought it best to have all her social obligations settled before she leaves home. And I wanted to be sure my mother was in an agreeable state of mind to receive the news. Mother sometimes goes through – difficult moods.

WATSON: And what about your father?

PAIGE: He died seven years ago.

HOLMES: What was his name?

PAIGE: Trevor Paige. He was a barrister at the firm I later came to work for.

HOLMES: We shall do what we can. And we need to study Miss Dalrymple's note, if you'll leave it with us.

PAIGE: Of course, only please don't lose it. And you can't know how relieved I am that you will help me!

HOLMES: You will hear from us shortly.

WATSON: Good day, Mr. Paige.

PAIGE: Good day, gentlemen. And thank you again.

WATSON: Well, Holmes?

HOLMES: The note interests me, and so does the sudden change in Dalrymple's manner. What do you see in it?

WATSON: The two must be connected. Read the note again.

HOLMES: "*Robert: I am leaving the city. I shall always love you. Pray for me.*"

WATSON: By its brevity, she could have been extremely rushed, or possibly she wrote it in secret and didn't want her parents to read it.

HOLMES: Possibly. But what do you make of her salutation? "*Robert*". Not "*Dear Robert*" or any other affectionate term – just "*Robert*". Quite businesslike. Then she wrote, "*I am leaving the city.*" If she knew where she was going, why not say so? Writing to her sweetheart, one would expect her to tell him where she was going, and when she expected to return.

WATSON: If she even knew those things.

HOLMES: Then she wrote "*I shall always love you*". In popular literature, this would be a parting sentiment – something to be said in sadness to someone you don't expect to see again. And her final line: "*Pray for me*" – Was that simply religious litany, or is she facing a serious problem that calls for prayer?

168

WATSON: Holmes! Do you know what it could be? The young lady may be ill, seriously ill! She might have some disease that took a sudden turn for the worse overnight, something that can't be treated in a London hospital! If that's the case, she and her parents might well have taken a boat to France to seek treatment! The French are far advanced in certain medical fields, and the cost of consulting a foreign specialist would be nothing for a wealthy man like Dalrymple.

HOLMES: Hmm. That could certainly explain why she wrote her note. But unfortunately, it still doesn't explain her father's reaction to the name "Dunstan".

WATSON: Then maybe there's no connection after all. Why don't I send a telegram to Robert Paige, asking him if Sophie ever mentioned having a serious medical problem?

MUSIC: UNDERCURRENT

WATSON: (NARRATING) So I sent Paige my question about Sophie's health. But instead of wiring me his reply, within the half-hour he was at our door!

MUSIC: OUT

SOUND EFFECT: DOOR CLOSES SHARPLY (BAKER STREET BACKGROUND)

PAIGE: (BREATHLESS) Forgive my intrusion, Dr. Watson, but your wire alarmed me! I must know what you've found out about Sophie! Is she ill?

WATSON: Calm yourself, Mr. Paige! I didn't mean to imply that she's ill. I only inquired about her health in order to dispose of one possible reason for her sudden departure. It seems reasonable that if she had to leave London so suddenly, there could have been a medical reason, and if that had been the case, it might explain why she wrote *"pray for me"*.

PAIGE: Yes, I see your reasoning. And I have been praying for her almost continuously since her note came, but to my knowledge, she enjoys excellent health.

169

WATSON: I'm delighted to hear it.

PAIGE: Is Mr. Holmes here?

WATSON: He's gone to do some research on your behalf. He said to expect him back around two.

PAIGE: Around two? I would wait for him, but I have to take an important deposition back in the office in half-an-hour. Will you let me know if he makes any progress?

WATSON: Of course.

MUSIC: UNDERCURRENT

WATSON: (NARRATING) After Paige left, there was nothing more for me to do until Holmes returned, so I took the opportunity to lie down on the sofa for a while to consider every possibility that could explain Sophie Dalrymple's mysterious leave-taking and how to find where she had gone. I had been occupied in this pursuit for only a few minutes, with my eyes closed to shut out distractions, when the next thing I knew, Holmes was standing over me.

MUSIC: OUT

HOLMES: Wake up, Watson! It's nearly six. We've missed our lunch and our tea.

WATSON: (WAKING) Umm, there you are, Holmes. Any news?

HOLMES: Bad news for Robert Paige. Sophie Dalrymple will not be marrying him.

MUSIC: VIOLIN STING

WATSON: Say that again, Holmes?

HOLMES: I said Sophie Dalrymple will not become Mrs. Robert Paige.

WATSON: Why? What's happened?

HOLMES: She and her mother are on a ship, bound for America!

WATSON: What? How do you know that?

HOLMES: I have a contact in the Passport Office. It seems Sir Edward exercised his influence and his cheque-book, and was able at the last minute to secure a first-class stateroom on the *Royal Jersey*, which was scheduled to sail from Southampton on Tuesday.

WATSON: They sailed without a word to young Paige at dinner the night before?

HOLMES: She and her mother may not have known they would be leaving the next day. If Paige's account of his conversation with Sir Edward was accurate, the entire complexion of his relationship with the Dalrymples changed when he uttered that name, *Dunstan.*

WATSON: Do you suppose someone named Dunstan was an enemy of the Dalrymples at some time in the past?

HOLMES: That's possible, but remember: All we know about Sophie is what Paige has told us. She may simply have had a sudden change of heart about marrying him and wanted to go as far away as possible, and her mother would naturally accompany her.

WATSON: What a blow to young Paige! I'm not looking forward to telling him.

HOLMES: And he has a thing or two to tell us. But right now, ask Mrs. Hudson to bring us our dinner while I wash London's grime from my face and hands and have a look at *The Evening Standard.*

WATSON: (NARRATING) And Mrs. Hudson, who was accustomed to our irregular hours, laid a table of cold pheasant, Stilton, and a loaf of fragrant bread hot from her oven. Holmes put down the paper and ate hungrily, more to replenish himself than to savor

Mrs. Hudson's cooking. He finished well before I did, glanced at the clock, which was at half-eight, then he rose from the table.

MUSIC: OUT

HOLMES: Well, are you fortified enough to accompany me?

WATSON: Where are you going?

HOLMES: To visit Dalrymple.

WATSON: Tonight? Before dinner, you said he'd be back from Southampton tomorrow!

HOLMES: I said *by* tomorrow. There's a chance he's already returned. * I'll flag a cab while you do something about those flecks of cheese on your moustache.

SOUND EFFECT: * HURRIED STEPS TO DOOR, DOOR OPENS. BACKGROUND FADES OUT (PAUSE) FADE IN: HANSOM CAB UNDERWAY

WATSON: Before we ate, you weren't expecting Dalrymple until tomorrow, and now you think he's already returned? What changed your mind, the pheasant or the Stilton?

HOLMES: (GOOD CHUCKLE) Mark one up for you, Watson! No, as delicious as it was, our repast only satisfied my hunger and not my thinking. You'll recall that before we began dining, I was glancing at *The Evening Standard*? There was a small notice in the shipping news that caught my eye. *Royal Jersey*'s sailing for New York was cancelled due to *"mechanical difficulty"* –

WATSON: What?

HOLMES: – so it is possible the Dalrymples turned round and took a train back to London last night, or stayed the night at a local inn and took an early train back this morning. Bradshaw's shows a northbound leaving Southampton at seven o'clock in the

172

morning, arriving at Paddington at 11:45, and several more trains during the day.

WATSON: But if Dalrymple was trying to hide his daughter, there are many convenient places in this country where she might be hidden in perfect comfort without taking a sea voyage.

HOLMES: But much depends on whose plan it was to hide her from Robert Paige. Was it her father's? Or did she have a sudden change of heart? There's much we don't know.

WATSON: Have you been to Dalrymple's neighborhood before?

HOLMES: Never.

WATSON: Then how did you know where to direct the cabbie?

HOLMES: I make it my business to know every part of London, if not from experience, at least by location. *The Times* published an illustrated story about Dalrymple's town house when it was new, ten or fifteen years ago.

WATSON: Have you ever forgotten anything, Holmes?

HOLMES: Hmm. If I have, I can't remember what it was. Ah, we're there. (UP) This will do, driver.

SOUND EFFECT: HORSE STOPS. THEY EXIT THE CAB. QUIET NATURE SOUNDS

HOLMES: (TO CABBIE) We'll need you to wait, and we'll double your fare.

CABBIE: (OFF) Can't do it, guv'nor. No 'orse-drawn vehicles allowed to stand on this street. Sanitary reasons.

HOLMES: Then if you're told to move on, wait down at the corner in Coldridge Street and we'll find you. Come, Watson.

SOUND EFFECT: MEN WALK ON PAVEMENT (UNDER)

WATSON: These homes are like castles!

HOLMES: And the castle up ahead would be the abode of Sir Edward Dalrymple.

WATSON: You remember it from that old newspaper article? Amazing!

HOLMES: No, from the name carved on this stone gatepost.

WATSON: Oh. Heh-heh. "Dalrymple". Of course. Well, I see he has electricity.

HOLMES: And a telephone, if those wires are any evidence. After you.

SOUND EFFECT: THEY WALK UP SOME BRICK STEPS AND STOP KNOCK ON DOOR WITH A HEAVY KNOCKER

WATSON: What do you suppose it must have cost to build this place?

HOLMES: Estimating real estate values isn't among my talents. Ah, the butler approaches.

WATSON: What? How can you hear that?

HOLMES: I can't hear it, but I can see movement inside through a peephole disguised in this elaborate carving on the door.

WATSON: What? I don't see it.

HOLMES: It's hidden a bit higher than your eye level but visible to a person of my height. If you were to stand on your toes you could see it . . . but now that won't be necessary. Here he is.

SOUND EFFECT: BOLT SLIDES, BIG DOOR OPENS

HANLEY: Yes, gentlemen?

HOLMES: I am Sherlock Holmes and this is Doctor John H Watson. We are here to see Sir Edward Dalrymple. Our cards.

HANLEY: I'm sorry, gentlemen, but Sir Edward has retired for the night.

WATSON: Is he ill? I am a physician . . . .

HANLEY: No, he is not ill. He prefers to retire early.

HOLMES: Be good enough to give him our cards if you please, and tell him we shall call earlier next time.

HANLEY: Very good, gentlemen. Good night.

SOUND EFFECT: DOOR CLOSES

MUSIC: UNDERCURRENT

WATSON: (NARRATING) On our ride back to Baker Street, we had the cabby detour to the home address Robert Paige had written on his business card. There was no answer at his door. It had been a frustrating evening all around. I left Holmes going through some of his files, and I retired, suddenly lonely for my Constance, who was spending the month near Brighton for her health, which had been declining. I was in that twilight between consciousness and sleep, when I thought I heard the door to the stairway open and close, and low voices in the sitting room. I slipped my Eley's No. 2 into the pocket of my robe and stepped down to the sitting room. There, Holmes and Robert Paige were seated, face to face, in front of the fire in earnest conversation.

MUSIC: OUT

SOUND EFFECT: CLOCK

HOLMES: Ah, Watson. Our apologies for waking you.

PAIGE: It's my fault, Doctor. When I saw Mr. Holmes's note on my door, I flew here as fast as my feet would carry me!

HOLMES: When we stopped by on our way from Dalrymple's, Watson, I left a note saying he should come here no matter the hour. Perhaps I didn't mention it.

175

WATSON: You didn't, but now that you're here and I'm awake, what news do you have, Mr. Paige?

HOLMES: We both have news. I told him Sophie's voyage had been cancelled.

PAIGE: And then I told him – I've seen Sophie! She's in her house in Park Terrace!

WATSON: Did you talk with her?

PAIGE: No, no! I couldn't sleep for worrying about her, so – late as it was – I took a cab to Park Terrace and walked up and down, just to be on the street where she lived! She told me once that her bedroom was on the northwest corner of the second story, and to my relief, I saw her lamp was lit and there was someone in her room. There's a large chestnut tree outside her window, and I climbed it in hopes that somehow she hadn't gone after all, and miraculously, there she was!

WATSON: Did you make your presence known?

PAIGE: Oh, no! If I had been caught, I could be prosecuted as a Peeping Tom and my career would be through. I stayed on my perch for an hour, just thrilled to see her, but she was pacing back and forth, back and forth, obviously tormented! What I would have given to have stolen her away and awakened the nearest magistrate so we could be married!

HOLMES: Tell Dr. Watson about the origin of your middle name.

PAIGE: Dunstan is my mother's maiden name. My father chose it, and I was christened Robert Dunstan Paige.

WATSON: Then why did it alarm Dalrymple when he heard it?

PAIGE: I don't know, but I do have a theory. Perhaps some distant person with that same name could have been a threat to Sir Edward at some time. I just want the opportunity to assure him that whatever the name means to him, he has no reason to fear. My mother is a Dunstan from some other branch of the family, or possibly not even from the same family at all!

HOLMES: And you shall have that opportunity tomorrow – correction, *today* – if Dalrymple is willing to see us.

<u>MUSIC: EXCITING, OMINOUS BACKGROUND</u>

WATSON: (NARRATING) The plan was, Holmes and I would return to Dalrymple's home and attempt to see him. If he refused, Holmes would swear out a complaint against him with the Metropolitan Police, charging that an adult woman was being held prisoner in her parents' home, and ask that Inspector Gregson, whom Holmes regarded as the most intelligent of the Scotland Yard detectives, be assigned to the case. But as it turned out, that wasn't necessary.

<u>MUSIC: OUT</u>

<u>SOUND EFFECT: (OFF) DOOR OPENS, MAN WALKS TOWARD MICROPHONE</u>

DALYRMPLE: (SLIGHTLY OFF-MICROPHONE) I am Edward Dalrymple

HOLMES: I am Sherlock Holmes, and this is my associate, Dr. John H. Watson.

DALYRMPLE: And what is your purpose here?

HOLMES: We wish to assure you, first of all, that we come only with the hope of resolving a mystery.

DALYRMPLE: I know of no mystery.

HOLMES: *Dunstan.*

DALYRMPLE: (TIGHTENS) Where did you hear that name?

HOLMES: It is the middle name of our client, Robert D. Paige, as I think you know.

DALYRMPLE: He's your client?

177

HOLMES: A very earnest and honourable young man, if ever I saw one –

DALYRMPLE: I know who he is. So he sent you here?

WATSON: No one sent us here. We are here of our own accord.

DALYRMPLE: (PAUSE) All right, Hanley, we'll be in the drawing room.

HANLEY: Very good, sir.

DALYRMPLE: This way.

SOUND EFFECT: THREE MEN WALK, PAUSE. DOOR OPENS. WALK IN. DOOR CLOSES

WATSON: Let me compliment you on this magnificent home of yours, Sir Edward –

DALYRMPLE: Now what do you know about Dunstan?

HOLMES: We know that Dunstan is Robert Paige's mother's maiden name, and we know that you knew that as well. We know that when you learned that Robert is her son, your entire manner changed. You sent Paige home, and hours later you took your wife and daughter away from London and booked passage for them on a ship sailing to America. But the ship didn't sail.

DALYRMPLE: What are you talking about? The ship sailed. I saw it leave Southampton myself!

HOLMES: You did not, sir. Its sailing was cancelled and your daughter is here!

SOUND EFFECT: (OFF) DOOR OPENS

SOPHIE: (OFF) Father, I heard someone at the door –

DALRYMPLE: Go back to your room, Sophronia!

178

SOPHIE: (MOVING ON) No! I heard Robert's name mentioned! Is he here?

DALRYMPLE: No, and I want you to leave this room right now! We are holding a private conversation! Now leave us!

HOLMES: It's a pleasure to meet you, Sophie. Robert has told us so much about you!

SOPHIE: Robert – ? Told you – ? Who are you?

HOLMES: I am Sherlock Holmes. This is Doctor Watson.

SOPHIE: Sherlock Holmes? Are you really?

DALRYMPLE: All right, I've had enough of your meddling! You two: Get out! Get out of this house before I ring for the police!

SOPHIE: Father, what are you doing?

DALRYMPLE Trying to protect you!

SOPHIE: No! They're not leaving!

DALRYMPLE: Get away from that door!

SOUND EFFECT: DOOR SLAMS SHUT

SOPHIE: No. I have a right to hear what they have to say!

DALRYMPLE: They'll say nothing more or I'll have them thown out!

SOPHIE: Then . . . Mr. Holmes . . . Doctor Watson . . . Robert has hired you?

WATSON: Yes. After he got your note, he rushed here to see *you*, but the butler said you were gone. There was no explanation –

SOPHIE: Yes, I was gone! And I couldn't give him an explanation, because I didn't know why my father put my mother and me on

179

a ship in the middle of the night, saying he wanted to give us a holiday in America! It was a lie, and we knew it!

DALYRMPLE: I did it for your own good, Sophie. You must believe me! For your good! For your mother's good! If you understood what I've been living with – I had to stop you, Sophie! I couldn't let you marry him!

SOPHIE: You can't stop me!

DALYRMPLE: Listen to me! When you told me your plans to marry him, I had no objection. You're twenty-five. You should be married!

SOPHIE: But not to Robert!

DALYRMPLE: No, not to Robert.

SOPHIE: Why? Why? What has he done?

SOUND EFFECT: URGENT KNOCK ON THE DOOR, DOOR OPENS

HANLEY: Forgive me, sir, but Mr. Paige is at the door and he refuses to leave until you speak to him.

SOPHIE: Robert's here? Go let him in, Hanley!

DALYRMPLE: You'll do nothing of the kind, Hanley!

SOPHIE: Then I'll go to him! We'll elope!

DALYRMPLE: You can't! You'll bring disgrace down on our family!

SOPHIE: Go let him in, Hanley!

HANLEY: . . . Sir? What should I do?

DALYRMPLE: (LONG PAUSE) All right, let him in. And may God protect us!

180

HANLEY: Mr. Paige, sir.

DALYRMPLE: All right, Hanley. That will be all. I'll call if I need you.

HANLEY: Yes, sir.

SOUND EFFECT: DOOR CLOSES

DALYRMPLE: I suppose you're proud of yourself, Paige.

PAIGE: Proud of myself? I seem to be carrying some evil around with me that's turned you against me!

SOPHIE: You're carrying no evil, my darling! When we're married, we don't ever have to listen to such foolishness again!

DALYRMPLE: You don't know! Neither of you know what you're doing!

SOPHIE: Then tell us!

(A LONG SILENCE)

HOLMES: Or shall I tell it? (PAUSE) Very well. Robert, your mother, Elsie Dunstan, at one time lived in the Dalrymple's house.

DALYRMPLE: That is a lie! She never lived in this house!

HOLMES: I didn't say she lived in *this* house. She lived in your *previous* house, before this house was built. She was a servant, a girl in her teens.

PAIGE: My mother?

DALYRMPLE: She was one of many servants. I'd forgotten all about her. She wasn't important at all.

HOLMES: But at one time, she was quite important. To you.

181

DALYRMPLE: All right, stop! That's enough!

PAIGE: Oh, no it isn't! I want to hear it all!

SOPHIE: And so do I!

HOLMES: It would be better if *you* told them, wouldn't it, Sir Edward? Why don't you have your butler bring your wife down as well, so the whole family can hear.

DALYRMPLE: My wife knows! (PAUSE) She's always known.

SOPHIE: Known what?

DALYRMPLE: That the young tart fancied me and wouldn't let me out of her clutches! I was just a young man myself . . . I'd had too much to drink one night . . . she threw herself at me . . . .

PAIGE: Just a minute! Who are you talking about?

DALYRMPLE: Elsie. Elsie Dunstan.

PAIGE: My mother?

DALYRMPLE: It was long ago.

HOLMES: Twenty-five years ago?

DALYRMPLE: Yes. . . . .Yes!

SOPHIE: Wait a minute! What are you telling us?

DALYRMPLE: Elsie gave birth –

SOPHIE: Oh, no!

DALRYMPLE: – To twins. She claimed they were . . . mine. But that couldn't be proved! It never could be proved!

HOLMES: But tell us what kind of twins they were.

182

DALRYMPLE: They're called . . . . Fraternal twins.

SOPHIE: Meaning they weren't identical?

DALRYMPLE: That's right. There was a boy . . . and a girl.

PAIGE: Oh my God.

DALRYMPLE: She was a loose woman! They could have been anyone's! I never loved her! I loved my wife! I told her so, over and over! But from that day on . . . . She's never let me forget!

SOPHIE: Then . . . she's not my mother?

DALRYMPLE: Listen to me, Sophie! When I learned Elsie was going to have a child, I paid for everything. I moved her out of our house and found her a decent home. When the babies were born, I had them placed for adoption. A young lawyer adopted the boy, and we adopted you. Your mother and I –

SOPHIE: Only she's not my mother! You're my father but my mother isn't . . . my mother!

DALRYMPLE: Never say that to her! It would break her heart! She's been as good a mother to you as if you were her own flesh and blood! She loves you! I – I love you!

PAIGE: And so where does that leave me?

DALRYMPLE Your father . . . your stepfather . . . adopted you. Gave you his name. But I never knew him. Never knew his name, never knew your name. You see, we adopted Sophie first, and we never visited the orphanage after that.

PAIGE: I see. And did you ever visit my mother after that?

DALYRMPLE: No.

PAIGE: Or me? Weren't you interested in seeing your son?

DALYRMPLE: I made a mistake. I went to church and asked to be forgiven, and I was forgiven, and in time . . . I forgot it and went

183

on with my life. I never dreamed that my daughter and my son would ever meet!

SOPHIE: And fall in love.

PAIGE: Sophie . . . What can we do? (STRICKEN) What can we do?

WATSON: You can love each other as deeply as a brother and sister can love. When you are no longer young, you will still have that love, undimmed by time. What a gift that is! You will always be part of each other.

MUSIC: (UNDERCURRENT)

WATSON: (NARRATING) As Holmes and I rode back to Baker Street, he was silent for a long time. And then . . . .

HOLMES: Where did that come from? That wisdom, that counsel you gave to those poor young lovers?

WATSON: I don't know, Holmes.

HOLMES: Well . . . I think you do.

MUSIC: SEGUE TO *DANSE MACABRE*

WATSON: This is Dr. John H. Watson. I've had many more adventures with Sherlock Holmes, and I'll tell you another one . . . *when next we meet!*

MUSIC: (FADE OUT)

The Sealed Room

CHARACTERS

- SHERLOCK HOLMES – *Thirty-four at this telling*
- DR. JOHN H. WATSON: *Thirty-five at this telling*
- SIR PETER ASHMORE – *Seventy, crusty but enfeebled, highborn wealthy)*
- ELINORE ASHMORE – *Cultured Englishwoman, also speaks French, forty*
- MRS. HUDSON – *A Scot*
- SCRIBNER – *English butler*
- DRIVER – *Cockney cab-driver*
- NAPOLEON BONAPARTE IV – *Eighteen, imperious, deep French accent*

SOUND EFFECT: OPENING SEQUENCE, BIG BEN, STREET SOUNDS

ANNOUNCER: *The Further Adventures of Sherlock Holmes . . . .*

MUSIC: *DANSE MACABRE* (UP AND UNDER)

WATSON: My name is John H. Watson, physician. The events which I am about to relate took place while I was under a burden of grief over the death of my bride of only a year, my beloved Constance. It was just into the year 1888, and that week I had moved my things from Kensington back to the old rooms on Baker Street, which I had long shared with Sherlock Holmes. Holmes was doing his best to console me, though, I must say, it did little good.

MUSIC: OUT

SOUND EFFECT: (OFF) DOOR CLOSES

HOLMES: Ah, Watson. Still sitting by the fire where I left you this morning. Any callers?

WATSON: No.

185

HOLMES: I stopped down in Saville Row. I took your advice and ordered a new hat. You do remember, a year ago, you said I didn't own a decent dress hat?

WATSON: Did I say that? I don't remember.

HOLMES: Well, I've finally done it! Wait 'til you see it! (PAUSE) My dear friend, are you no better today?

WATSON: No, Holmes, I'm afraid not.

HOLMES: (EXASPERATED) This makes me feel quite useless. For seven years we've been close as brothers, and yet I haven't found a way to relieve your melancholy!

WATSON: You can do nothing, Holmes. It will take time.

HOLMES: But seeing patients and treating other people's problems should have been good medicine for you.

WATSON: Physician, heal thyself, eh? Ah, I wish it were that simple. (PAUSE) Do you know what I wish?

HOLMES: Say it.

WATSON: I wish it were the old days. Me, traipsing along on your cases. Possibly adding a tiny bit of assistance here and there, however trivial.

HOLMES: Your assistance was never trivial, Watson, and if you are available once again, I shall be overjoyed to have you at my side. What you need is diversion! Then you'll soon be right again.

SOUND EFFECT: (OFF-MICROPHONE) A TAP ON THE DOOR

HOLMES: Sit still. I'm on my feet.

SOUND EFFECT: HOLMES STRIDES THREE STEPS. OPENS THE DOOR

186

HOLMES: (OFF-MICROPHONE) Yes, Mrs. Hudson?

MRS. HUDSON: (OFF-MICROPHONE) I'm sorry to bother you, Mr. Holmes, but you have two visitors. A gentleman and a young woman. He gave me his card. Here it is.

HOLMES: (PAUSE) Well, well! By all means. Have him up.

MRS. HUDSON: And the young woman?

HOLMES: Of course, the young woman too!

MRS. HUDSON: Right away, sir. And will you be having tea?

HOLMES: No, hold off the tea.

MRS. HUDSON: Very good.

SOUND EFFECT: (OFF-MICROPHONE) DOOR CLOSES. THREE STEPS BACK ON-MICROPHONE

HOLMES: (ON-MICROPHONE) Watson, have a look.

WATSON: Eh?

HOLMES: Our visitor's calling card.

WATSON: Oh. (SHOWS SOME INTEREST) Good heavens.

HOLMES: Yes. Sir Peter Ashmore, head of the Foreign Office! We are about to be honored!

WATSON: I thought you detested politicians.

HOLMES: Politics and politicians are a dragging anchor on the ship of state, but no one this high up would be caught dead consulting a detective unless on a matter of the highest urgency – otherwise he'd have sent a staff member, which suggests that he desires secrecy. Politics or not, this may prove to be irresistible!

MUSIC: (UNDER)

187

WATSON: (NARRATING) In a few moments, Mrs. Hudson ushered in our guests. Ashmore was a thin, pallid-faced man – seventy, I would judge – with a palsy of the hands, which he tried to hide by constantly twisting a large ring round his finger. The woman with him appeared to be in her early forties, with traces of what must have been great beauty when she was a girl. She too was pale, and clung to Ashmore's arm as he spoke.

MUSIC: OUT

ASHMORE: Mr. Holmes, I am Peter Ashmore. This is my daughter, Elinor Ashmore.

HOLMES: Enchanted, Miss Ashmore.

ELINOR: How do you do?

HOLMES: And this is my friend and associate, Doctor John Hamish Watson.

WATSON: Charmed, I'm sure.

ELINOR: Thank you.

ASHMORE: Mr. Holmes, I must speak with you privately.

HOLMES: Certainly. Do sit down – no one will bother us.

ASHMORE: No, no. Privately. With you alone, Mr. Holmes!

HOLMES: Doctor Watson is my trusted associate in all my cases. You may speak before him as you speak before me. Now, what brings you here, Sir Peter?

ASHMORE: This places me in an embarrassing position. Won't you grant me the courtesy of a private audience?

WATSON: (A BIT PUT OFF) Sir, I am a physician and a former officer in the Fusiliers. I assure you I am quite accustomed to keeping confidences –

HOLMES: (TARTLY) – and he is an integral part of my success as a consulting detective. I do not hear cases without him. Now, please do sit down.

ASHMORE: No thank you, I prefer to stand.

ELINOR: No, please sit, father. He's not been well, Doctor Watson. Perhaps you could –

ASHMORE: I don't need a doctor! What I need is a – You should appreciate that I wouldn't be consulting a detective, even one as celebrated as you, if this were not such a delicate – I may say – *critical* matter.

HOLMES: I assure you, this is not the first time a member of Government has been a client. Now, how may I help you?

ASHMORE: Well – (CONFIDENTIAL TONE) I want you to recover something that has been stolen.

HOLMES: And what would that be?

ASHMORE: A vital document.

HOLMES: What sort of document?

ASHMORE: That is a state secret! What's important is, it was taken from a sealed room, and must be found!

HOLMES: A sealed room in the Foreign Office?

ASHMORE: No. In my home.

HOLMES: You keep state secrets in your home?

ASHMORE: Never before, and only this once! I took it with me yesterday afternoon to hand-deliver this morning. I hid it out of sight in an unused room. Then I locked and sealed the only door to the room! I took every precaution!

HOLMES: How did you seal the door?

ASHMORE: With sealing-wax over the keyhole, stamped with my ring. This ring. There is no other like it.

ELINOR: And should anyone try to insert a key, the wax impression of the ring would be spoiled.

HOLMES: And when you went to retrieve the document this morning, you found the wax intact?

ASHMORE: Perfectly intact. But when I went to get the document, it was gone!

HOLMES: I see. Now, it's time you told me what the envelope contained.

ASHMORE: Impossible, Mr. Holmes. I can describe the envelope, but I cannot divulge what was inside it!

HOLMES: Then I regret I will not be able to help you.

ASHMORE: Now look here! There is no need for you to –

HOLMES: Obviously, whoever stole the document knew what he was after and knew how to get it. Unless I know at least as much as the thief knew, I cannot hope to find him.

ASHMORE: You're asking me to compromise a state secret!

HOLMES: It seems to me it was already compromised when you took it to your home.

ASHMORE: Yes, I should have left it in the safe at the Foreign Office, but I can't tell you what was in the envelope.

HOLMES: I see. Then we shall wish you Godspeed in your search.

ASHMORE: No, no! Don't you see – I'm a desperate man, Mr. Holmes. How can I tell the Prime Minister? I shall bear everlasting blame if that letter falls into the wrong hands. It could affect our national destiny!

HOLMES: Then why not go to Scotland Yard?

ASHMORE: Scotland Yard! A platoon of thick-soled constables mucking about? Everyone knowing everything?

HOLMES: And I cannot help you unless I know everything!

ELINOR: Please, Mr. Holmes, my father isn't a well man and this matter is making him sicker by the hour. You surely understand, don't you, Doctor? Mr. Holmes, please do as he asks! Help him find the letter!

HOLMES: I would be more than willing, if I'm given the tools I need to do it.

ASHMORE: (LONG PAUSE, AGONIZED SIGH) Then do I have your word? Both of you? As gentlemen and patriots? That you will hold this matter in strictest confidence?

WATSON: You have our word!

HOLMES: Now I suggest we get on with it.

ASHMORE: Well, as you know, eighteen years ago the last member of the Bonaparte family, the nephew of Napoleon Bonaparte, lost his throne after Von Moltke's Prussians defeated the French at Sedan.

HOLMES: And he died a few years later here in England.

ASHMORE: Yes, in Chiselhurst. His defeat marked the end of French territorial ambitions and the beginning of the German Empire under Bismarck. Louis Napoleon the Third left a heritage of failed ambition and broken promises. But he also may have left something else here in England.

HOLMES: And what might that be?

ASHMORE: A son.

WATSON: I say!

191

ASHMORE: This young man is claiming the right to the French Throne as Napoleon the Fourth, and is secretly planning a coup to overthrow the Third Republic, and establish himself as Emperor of France!

HOLMES: How old is this pretender to the throne?

ASHMORE: Just eighteen.

WATSON: And he wants to be the fourth Napoleon on the throne, eh? Not too ambitious, is he?

ASHMORE: We take him very seriously. He is living right here in London and he has followers. They meet regularly in secret places. He could raise an army of royalists, and the French are ripe for revolt. As you know, when they declared war against Prussia in 1870, they were quickly defeated. They lost Alsace and part of Lorraine, and had to pay a heavy war indemnity to Germany for their trouble. Napoleon the Third was cast out, and three presidents later, Carnot became president. (LOW) But with Carnot as unpopular as he is, if a descendant of Napoleon Bonaparte appeared upon the scene now, with France in upheaval, he could be the rallying-point for a full-scale revolution. And the Foreign Office have reason to believe that, in such a struggle, Bismarck would seize the opportunity to march against France! And on his way, he would swallow up Belgium and Luxembourg! And Britain would be staring across the Channel at a Prussian giant!

WATSON: I see. The stolen letter, then, is a warning to President Carnot, about this new pretender?

ASHMORE: No, we've kept him informed from the first. The letter contains our offer to remove the boy.

HOLMES: Remove him? How?

ASHMORE: We would place him where he would be no threat to Carnot.

WATSON: Banish him to Elba, like his great uncle?

ASHMORE: Hardly. He would be removed from the scene permanently.

HOLMES: (WITH DISTASTE) And in return for this service?

ASHMORE: The French government would share with Britain everything their agents learn about Bismarck's military plans – which would give us priceless advance notice of Prussia's intentions, without risking a single British agent!

HOLMES: What about the mother of this young man?

ASHMORE: We don't know who she was. Just a poor French serving-girl. But Mr. Holmes, such details are quite beyond the scope of your investigation, and so I –

HOLMES: Nothing is beyond the scope of my investigation! I and only I determine what facts I need to know! If you deny me the slightest shred of information, you tie my hands! And so what do you propose to do with this young man? Execute him or lock him up for life?

ASHMORE: One life, in exchange for saving the lives of thousands of men in a preventable war, would seem an acceptable transaction.

HOLMES: Who knows about this offer?

ASHMORE: Only the Prime Minister, and obviously myself. And my daughter. She spends considerable time in Paris, teaching English at *l'Ecole Anglais*, and she brings back invaluable information.

ELINOR: I love both England and France, Mr. Holmes. And I know that any uprising at this time might rupture relations between the two countries, and plunge all Europe into another war!

MUSIC: (UNDERCURRENT)

WATSON: I must say, Elinor Ashmore made a most fetching appeal. She had risen from her chair and stepped closer to

193

Holmes and me, so close that I noticed the scent of her cologne. Most attractive. Then she dropped her eyes and stepped back.

MUSIC: OUT

ASHMORE: I have a four-wheeler waiting in the street. Will you come with us to Belmere before dark?

HOLMES: (PAUSE) Bring our usual kit, Watson!

MUSIC: (UNDERSCORE)

WATSON: The Ashmore mansion, Belmere, loomed above a pond in Kensington. It had three main floors, surmounted by a steep canard roof spiked with turrets and spires. A butler named Scribner greeted us at the door. As we stood in the grand entry hall, I remarked that the house resembled a chateau I had seen in Loire Valley of France before the Afghan war.

MUSIC: OUT

SOUND EFFECT: BIG ROOM REVERBERATION

ELINOR: Yes, in fact it was patterned after Chateau Azay-le-Rideau in the Loire. How clever of you to pick it out, Doctor.

ASHMORE: My daughter is quite expert in all such matters. Now Scribner –

SCRIBNER: Sir?

ASHMORE: The presence of these two gentlemen is not to be discussed in this house or anywhere else. Is that clear?

SCRIBNER: Very good, sir.

ELINOR: Father, I'm going to be late for my class if I don't leave immediately.

ASHMORE: Another night class?

ELINOR: For ambitious office workers hoping for foreign assignment. Will you gentlemen excuse me?

HOLMES: Certainly, Miss Ashmore.

WATSON: Oh, what are you studying?

ELINOR: (NICE LAUGH) I teach French, Doctor Watson.

HOLMES: You teach French to the English and English to the French!

ASHMORE: As I said, she's lived in France on and off for years. Knows the French like a book.

ELINOR: Thank you both for helping my father. And the cause of peace.

WATSON: It was great pleasure to meet you. I hope we shall meek again. *Au revoir.*

ELINOR: *Au revoir*, Doctor Watson.

SOUND EFFECT: HER FOOTSTEPS MOVE OFF

ASHMORE: Comes and goes whenever she pleases! Remarkable girl. Brilliant. Well, come with me. I'll show you the room.

SOUND EFFECT: THREE MEN CLIMBING STAIRS (UNDER)

HOLMES: How large is your household staff?

ASHMORE: Well, there's Scribner. Then there's my housekeeper, the cook, and the groundskeeper.

HOLMES: Have they been with you long?

ASHMORE: All but the housekeeper. I hired her shortly after my wife passed away. Our original housekeeper retired when Evangeline died. Very devoted to her.

195

HOLMES: Why didn't you simply hide the letter in your own bedroom?

ASHMORE: Because I sleep like a dead man. If someone entered my room after I was asleep, I would never know it. Ah. Here we are.

SOUND EFFECT: THEY REACH TOP OF STAIRS. WALK DOWN HALL (UNDER)

ASHMORE: Now, the room is just down this hall.

HOLMES: But I presume you trust your staff implicitly, do you, Sir Peter?

ASHMORE: Yes, of course.

HOLMES: Then, pray tell, why did you think it necessary to seal the room where you hid the letter?

ASHMORE: What?

HOLMES: (IMPATIENTLY) If you had no reason to fear the theft of the letter, why seal the room it was in?

ASHMORE: Good heavens, sir, it's a state secret! One takes every precaution. Here's the room.

SOUND EFFECT: STEPS COME TO A STOP. JANGLE OF KEYS. KEY IN LOCK. DOOR OPENS. THREE MEN STEP IN. DOOR CLOSES (REVERB DOWN)

ASHMORE: (OFF-MICROPHONE) I hid the envelope here, Mr. Holmes, in the bottom drawer of this chest.

SOUND EFFECT: WOODEN DRAWER PULLED OUT

ASHMORE: You see? The drawer has a false bottom. I hid the letter under the false bottom.

HOLMES: I see. You would be surprised at how common false bottoms are.

196

WATSON: Holmes spent little time examining the drawer. Instead, he strode to the fireplace, where he turned up the rugs. His eyes traveled from cornice to cornice, to curtain-rods, to the lounge beneath the window, to the divan and chairs around a low table. Nothing escaped his glance. Then he went to the window again and peered at the sycamore outside, gently tapping a pane here and there.

MUSIC: OUT

ASHMORE: (OFF-MICROPHONE) Nothing's been broken into, as you can see.

HOLMES: So it appears. Watson, will you accompany me outside? And bring the kit.

MUSIC: SHORT BRIDGE

SOUND EFFECT: EXTERIOR

HOLMES: Now, hold my coat.

WATSON: I say, you're not going to climb that tree?

HOLMES: If the thief could do it in the black of night, I should be able to do it in twilight. Hand me my magnifying glass from the kit, Watson.

WATSON: Oh. Yes.

SOUND EFFECT: SATCHEL OPENED

WATSON: Here it is.

HOLMES: (EXERT) And up – I go. (OFF-MICROPHONE) Ah, yes. (MOVING FURTHER OFF) How long has it been since you saw London from a tree, Watson?

WATSON: Be careful up there!

197

HOLMES: Quite delightful up here. (STUDYING SOMETHING) Yes, quite delightful. And very instructive. (MOVING BACK ON-MICROPHONE) I'm coming back down, Watson. Here, take the glass.

WATSON: Yes, I have it.

SOUND EFFECT: BUMP AS HOLMES JUMPS TO THE SOD

HOLMES: (GRUNTS AS HE LANDS)

WATSON: Well?

HOLMES: One of the sixteen small panes of glass in the window was removed, to allow someone to reach in and unlatch it. When the theft was complete, the burglar climbed back through the window and replaced the glass, using glazer's putty to secure it. The putty is still damp.

WATSON: So it was an outside job!

HOLMES: Outside, and inside. Please go down to the road and hail a cab. I'll join you in a minute.

WATSON: Oh? Where are we going?

HOLMES: That is what I am about to find out from Sir Peter!

MUSIC: STING AND OUT

WATSON: Holmes came out of the mansion in five minutes, just as I succeeded in getting a hansom to stop.

SOUND EFFECT: (UNDER) LONDON STREET

DRIVER: (OFF-MICROPHONE) Where to, gov?

HOLMES: (OUT OF BREATH) Lambeth, driver, as fast as you can go!

WATSON: Why are we going to Lambeth?

HOLMES: That's where we shall find the thief who stole the secret paper.

WATSON: How did you find that out?

HOLMES: Ashmore told me.

WATSON: Ashmore! No! Then he knew it all along?

HOLMES: Only he didn't know he knew it.

WATSON: I beg pardon?

HOLMES: He didn't know he knew what he knows.

WATSON: (BEAT) You never change, do you, Holmes? You always do it! Just as you're about to spring the trap and find the guilty party, you become infuriating!

HOLMES: I do?

WATSON: You know you do! You toy with me. When I ask a simple question, you tease me like a cat with a mouse!

HOLMES: Except this cat has a conscience. And in good conscience, I can't tell you my conclusion just yet. But unless this cab goes faster, we may lose this case altogether!

SOUND EFFECT: HE POUNDS ON THE LEATHER CEILING OF THE CAB

HOLMES: (CRIES OUT) Faster, driver! Go like the wind!

MUSIC: FAST MOTIVATION (UNDERCURRENT) FADE TO:

SOUND EFFECT: THE HORSE CHANGES INTO A FASTER GAIT

WATSON: (NARRATING) We flew down Kensington to Knightsbridge, then onto Sloan Street, made a sharp left turn onto Grosvenor Road along the Thames, and here the carriage traffic slowed us down.

SOUND EFFECT: HORSE SLOWS TO A CLIP-CLOP

WATSON: (NARRATING) It had grown dark and the temperature was freezing.

DRIVER: (OFF-MICROPHONE) Lambeth's comin' up, gov. What address?

HOLMES: The Lambeth Academy of Language.

DRIVER: Huh! Never heard of it.

HOLMES: (MUTTERS) I shouldn't wonder. (UP) It would be near Lambeth Road and Millbank, driver. Look sharp for a window sign or doorway!

WATSON: Then we're following Elinor Ashmore!

HOLMES: Or trying to. She had a good head start. From my perch in the tree back at Belmere, I saw her get into a cab.

WATSON: But surely you don't think she stole her father's secret paper?

HOLMES: She arranged it.

WATSON: Then who did it?

HOLMES: Wait a minute! Stop! (SHOUTS) Stop, driver!

SOUND EFFECT: HORSE PLODS TO A STOP. CARRIAGE DOOR OPENS

HOLMES: (EXERTS) We'll walk from here, driver, but don't go away! There'll be extra in it if you follow us!

WATSON: (EXERTING AT THE SAME TIME) Where are we going, Holmes?

HOLMES: (SECRETIVELY:) In the next block, there's a hansom at the curb. A woman just got out and went in one of the doors between shops. And her cab's waiting! I'm sure it's the Ashmore woman!

WATSON: But why are we following her?

HOLMES: Because everything fits.

WATSON: What do you mean by that?

HOLMES: She's practically given us the thief and his motive!

WATSON: Well, she may have given it to you but she didn't give it to me!

HOLMES: Look sharply now! Flat against the wall!

WATSON: Ah! She's coming out of the doorway! With a man!

HOLMES: In a great hurry! (UP) Driver! Let us back in!

HOLMES: (LOUDLY) Head that other cab off if you can! (SOFTER) Watson, there may be danger. I have no doubt he's armed!

WATSON: Is he who I think he is?

HOLMES: We'll know in a moment!

SOUND EFFECT: NOW A SECOND SET OF HOOVES FADES IN, GALLOPING ON PAVEMENT, HORSE NEIGHING (UNDER)

HOLMES: (SHOUTING) Head him off! Force him off the road!

NAPOLEON: (OFF-MICROPHONE, SHOUTS) Get away! Get away! I am desperate! I will kill you!

SOUND EFFECT: (OFF-MICROPHONE) GUN FIRES. HORSE NEIGHS. HORSES PULL TO A STOP

HOLMES: Jump down and seize the woman, Watson! I'll take the man!

SOUND EFFECT: JUMBLED FOOTSTEPS ON PAVING UNDER

WATSON: Madame, are you injured?

ELINOR: No, you fool, I'm not injured, but you will be if you don't let us go!

NAPOLEON: (SLIGHTLY OFF-MICROPHONE) Who are these men?

ELINOR: The ones I told you about!

NAPOLEON: Sherlock Holmes?

HOLMES: (SLIGHTLY OFF-MICROPHONE) At your service!

NAPOLEON: You fool! I will kill you this moment!

SOUND EFFECT: HOLMES'S CANE WHACKS THE GUN OUT OF HIS HAND

NAPOLEON: Ow! My hand!

202

HOLMES: Get his gun, Watson!

SOUND EFFECT: MEANWHILE, UP THE STREET COMES A CARRIAGE (UNDER)

WATSON: (BIG EXERTION) I – I have it!

ELINOR: You don't know what you're doing!

HOLMES: If either of them tries to get away, Watson, shoot them!

WATSON: (BREATHLESS WITH EXCITEMENT) I hope I won't have to do that, but I warn you, *Monsieur et Madame*, I have fought for England before, and I would do it again!

SOUND EFFECT: THE CARRIAGE APPROACHES AND STOPS

ASHMORE: (OFF-MICROPHONE, SHOUTS) Holmes! Watson! Do you have it!

HOLMES: Ah! Sir Peter came, just as I asked him to do.

ELINOR: (AS A MOAN, TO HERSELF) *Mon Dieu*! You've really determined to ruin me, haven't you?

ASHMORE: (MOVING) Do you – have it, Mr. Holmes?

WATSON: Good evening, Sir Peter.

ASHMORE: Who's this – in the cab? Elinor!

ELINOR: Hello, father.

ASHMORE: What are you doing?

ELINOR: You don't know, do you?

ASHMORE: Do you have the letter?

HOLMES: I suspect the letter is moot at this point. Sir Peter, may I present Napoleon Bonaparte the Fourth.

ASHMORE: Is this true?

ELINOR: Yes, father, it's true.

ASHMORE: Well – well, what do you have to do with him?

ELINOR: As Mr. Holmes no doubt deduced: He is my son.

ASHMORE: (PAUSE) I don't believe it. I don't believe it for a moment!

HOLMES: Back at Belmere, Sir Peter, just before we raced after your daughter, I asked you two things: The name of the school where she taught, and you told me it was the Lambeth School of Language. And I also asked you if she had been in France eighteen years ago, and you confirmed that she was. That gave both the opportunity, and the motive, for your daughter to steal your document: To protect her son – Your *grandson*! Napoleon IV!

MUSIC: *DANSE MACABRE* UP AND UNDER

WATSON: The plot to seize Bonaparte the Fourth came to nothing. He returned to France to try to restore the monarchy, but General Georges Boulangel was waging his own revolt against the French government and he, too failed, and fled to Belgium. Madame Ashmore moved out of Belmere to be with her son in the south of France. Holmes bought a new cane to replace the one he broke when he knocked the gun out of young Napoleon's hand. And then we went on to another adventure, which I'll tell you . . . *the next time we meet*!

MUSIC: UP AND OUT

204

The Death of Artemis Ludwig

CHARACTERS

- SHERLOCK HOLMES
- DR. JOHN H. WATSON
- JUDGE
- BAILIFF
- GAVIN
- CAPSTRAW
- HARGRAVE
- ARTEMIS LUDWIG

SOUND EFFECT: SEGUE TO HUSHED COURTROOM

BAILIFF: Do you swear by Almighty God that the evidence you are about to give will be the truth, the whole truth, and nothing but the truth?

HOLMES: I do.

BAILIFF: Please state your name.

HOLMES: Sherlock Holmes.

JUDGE: Mr. Holmes, you are present at these proceedings as an *Amicus Curiae*, a Friend of the Court?

HOLMES: Correct.

JUDGE: Tell us, please, for anyone who doesn't already know, what is your occupation?

HOLMES: I am a consulting detective, your m'Lord.

JUDGE: And you have communicated with the Court to offer information relating to the trial of Emil Capstraw in the death of Artemis Ludwig.

HOLMES: Correct.

JUDGE: And what is this information?

HOLMES: That Emil Capstraw must not be tried for the murder of Artemis Ludwig.

JUDGE: And why not?

HOLMES: Because Artemis Ludwig was not murdered and this trial is a mistake!

SOUND EFFECT: CROWD REACTS. GAVEL POUNDED SEVERAL TIMES

SOUND EFFECT: OPENING SEQUENCE, BIG BEN, STREET SOUNDS

ANNOUNCER: *The Further Adventures of Sherlock Holmes . . . .*

MUSIC: *DANSE MACABRE* (UP AND UNDER)

WATSON: My name is Doctor John H. Watson. I think I may safely say that no man knows Sherlock Holmes better than I do. He sought no public acclaim. In fact, at one time he even turned down a knighthood. But when he read the reports of a murder trial taking place at Old Bailey, he fired off a telegram at once to the judge, was sworn in at the start of the second day of the trial, and immediately turned the courtroom into an uproar!

MUSIC: FADES OUT (UNDER)

SOUND EFFECT: (FADE UP) AUDIENCE TUMULT. JUDGE WHACKS HIS GAVEL AGAIN

JUDGE: Quiet! Or I shall remove the spectators from this room!

SOUND EFFECT: AUDIENCE REACTION DIES

GAVIN: (OFF, MOVING ON) M'Lord!

JUDGE: Mr. Gavin?

GAVIN: May it please the court, as the prosecutor for the Crown, I should like to examine the gentleman myself. In private.

JUDGE: I think not, Mr. Gavin. We shall hear what Mr. Holmes has to say in open court. So proceed with your questions.

GAVIN: Very well. Mr. Holmes. You call yourself a "consulting detective". Will you tell us, please – just what is a "consulting detective"?

HOLMES: I am the last and highest court of appeal in detection.

AUDIENCE: REACTS

GAVIN: Come, come, Mr. Holmes, this is no time for modesty!

AUDIENCE: SCATTERED LAUGHTER

JUDGE: (OFF) Quiet!

SOUND EFFECT: ONE RAP OF A GAVEL

GAVIN: How are you different from a police detective?

HOLMES: Detection ought to be an exact science, and I practice it as such.

GAVIN: And do you say that you are better at detecting than the detectives at Scotland Yard?

HOLMES: Yes.

GAVIN: Oh, I see. And do you say that you have evidence in this matter that Scotland Yard doesn't have?

HOLMES: I simply observe the same evidence with more clarity.

GAVIN: Have you been hired by the defense, Mr. Holmes?

HOLMES: No.

GAVIN: Then what is your interest in this case?

HOLMES: My interest stems from my knowledge of Mr. Capstraw and his peculiar condition.

GAVIN: His condition? Are you a doctor, in addition to your other superior talents?

HOLMES: No, I am an observer of human nature.

GAVIN: And what have you observed in Mr. Capstraw?

HOLMES: That under no circumstances could he have murdered Artemis Ludwig. Not in the conventional sense.

MUSIC: UNDERCURRENT

WATSON: I was sitting in the spectator section as Holmes testified. I had knowledge of Emil Capstraw myself, having been with Holmes on the afternoon when Capstraw first visited us in our rooms in Baker Street many weeks before. He was a distraught young man who stumbled in from the rain and stood before us with his cap in his hand. Holmes was annoyed at being disturbed – he'd been absorbed in research in his clipping files – but his curiosity soon erased his annoyance.

MUSIC: SEGUE TO

SOUND EFFECT: SOFT BAKER STREET (BACKGROUND)

HOLMES: I see you're a teacher, Mr. Capstraw.

CAPSTRAW: Yes, I am! How do you know that?

HOLMES: Oh, the obvious: Chalk dust on the bottom of your jacket cuff where it brushes the slate.

CAPSTRAW: Oh. Of course. And what more do you know about me?

HOLMES: Practically nothing, except that you're left handed, quite near-sighted, and you're in some want. Now how can we help you?

CAPSTRAW: You astonish me, Mr. Holmes! I'd heard you could do that, but . . . is it some kind of trick?

HOLMES: Not at all. The chalk dust is only on your left cuff, your myopia is obvious from your squint, and there's an indentation on the bridge of your nose where you've worn eyeglasses, and your shoes and clothing are badly worn.

CAPSTRAW: Oh. Well, nothing to it then, is there? But you're right on all counts. I've mislaid my eyeglasses, I am as poor as a church-mouse, and I am left-handed. And have you also deduced that I've just lost my situation at Harbison School for Boys?

HOLMES: No, that I didn't know. What classes did you teach?

CAPSTRAW: I taught fifth form. And now that I've lost my job, I'm afraid I won't be able to pay you – that is, if you should agree to help me. And I'm sure that my problem is too trivial to interest you anyway.

HOLMES: We'll discuss that after I hear what you want me to do.

CAPSTRAW: Mr. Holmes, I am being destroyed by a person who was once my greatest helper.

HOLMES: Who is this person? Tell me everything.

CAPSTRAW: His name is Artemis Ludwig. He came to me during the night, a year ago, before I was to hand in a dissertation for my teaching degree. I'd all but given up on it and had fallen asleep at my writing desk, but when I awoke the next morning, there it was – re-written, eloquent, brilliant – far beyond my own abilities.

HOLMES: He came to you during the night? How did he get in?

CAPSTRAW: There's no way to lock the door to my room. I have nothing worth stealing anyway.

HOLMES: You live alone?

209

CAPSTRAW: Yes.

HOLMES: Your address?

CAPSTRAW: Number Nineteen-and-one-half, Orient Street, Lambeth.

HOLMES: How long had you known this fellow Ludwig?

CAPSTRAW: But that's it, sir! I didn't know him! I'd never heard of him! But he must have known of me, because after that first visit, from time to time he would come in during the night and complete my work for me while I was asleep! He'd grade student papers, correct their compositions . . . I didn't even know his name. Then I left a note for him on my desk one night before I went to bed. I just wrote *"Who are you?"* and next morning, he'd written the name, *"Artemis Ludwig"*.

HOLMES: Do you have the note?

CAPSTRAW: Do I have it? No, I threw it away.

HOLMES: Pity. But go on.

CAPSTRAW: Well, I've been writing a textbook on ways to improve education techniques. I was certain that when I had it finished, it would be purchased by the Harbison School and I'd get some money and recognition. But then I began to notice changes were being made in my manuscript. Changes I didn't make! And I knew who was making them. Artemis Ludwig!

WATSON: He did this while you were asleep, you say?

CAPSTRAW: Yes!

HOLMES: Do you sleep in a different room from where you write?

CAPSTRAW: Huh! Hardly. It's a one-room flat half the size of this parlour.

WATSON: Oh, come now, Mr. Capstraw. You never awakened when this chap was working only a few feet away?

CAPSTRAW: I sleep like the dead, Doctor.

HOLMES: Go on with your story, Mr. Capstraw.

CAPSTRAW: Well, yesterday I woke up in the morning as I always do, at six a.m. . . . and my manuscript was gone!

HOLMES: And what did you do then?

CAPSTRAW: I went to school and I went straightaway to Mr. Hargrave, the headmaster, to tell him what had happened, and he as much as called me a liar and a fraud! There on his desk was my manuscript! With Ludwig's name on it!

HOLMES: And?

CAPSTRAW: Well, anyone could see what happened! All the time Artemis Ludwig had been coming into my room and helping me, he'd been stealing from me! Stealing my book! I tell you, I could kill him!

HOLMES: Calm yourself, Mr. Capstraw. Now, tell me the rest of it.

CAPSTRAW: Well, Mr. Hargrave sacked me! Then and there! I was dismissed! And it's all because of Artemis Ludwig! But that's not the worst of it! Mr. Hargrave had already hired someone to take my place! And who do you think it was?

HOLMES: (BORED) Come, come, Mr. Capstraw. The way you tell the story, it was inevitable. Artemis Ludwig has your job. Now what do you want me to do for you?

CAPSTRAW: I want you to force Artemis Ludwig to admit the manuscript is mine, and then I want my situation back.

HOLMES: I am not in that business.

CAPSTRAW: Of course. I knew my troubles wouldn't interest you.

211

HOLMES: Oh, on the contrary, they interest me considerably, but I am neither a policeman nor a labour boss. However, here is what I will do: I will talk to the headmaster and to Mr. Ludwig.

MUSIC: UNDERCURRENT

WATSON: Holmes stood by the window looking down onto the street as our visitor hurried out into the rain, and I thought I heard him murmur "Poor chap". And then he turned away and strode to his closet and put on his long ulster and a close-fitting cloth cap.

HOLMES: Coming, Watson?

WATSON: Where are we going?

HOLMES: To the Harbison School for Boys. Perhaps it's not too late to meet the distinguished Artemis Ludwig in person.

MUSIC: UNDERCURRENT

WATSON: Classes were over at the Harbison School for Boys when our cab let us off in front of an ivy-covered building in Northumberland Street near Charing Cross Station. We walked in and presently we were greeted by a tall, somber-looking gentleman wearing a black frock coat of a style that was in fashion fifty years before.

MUSIC: OUT

HARGRAVE: I am Roderick Hargrave, the headmaster. How may I be of service, gentlemen?

HOLMES: I am Sherlock Holmes, and this is my associate, Doctor John H. Watson.

HARGRAVE: How do you do. Do one of you have a boy in the school?

HOLMES: No, I'd like a word with a new teacher you've hired, a Mr. Artemis Ludwig. Would he be on the premises?

212

HARGRAVE: Excuse me, Mr. Holmes, but I really must ask you to tell me your purpose in this interrogation.

HOLMES: I should like to know the circumstances that caused you to discharge Mr. Capstraw and hire Mr. Ludwig.

HARGRAVE: Mr. Holmes, as headmaster, I have the right to hire and fire as I see fit.

HOLMES: I'm sure you do. But I know only Capstraw's side of his dismissal. I should like to hear Ludwig's . . . and yours.

HARGRAVE: Very well. Capstraw had become quite unsatisfactory. He was often tardy for his classes, he grew slovenly in his appearance, and he was far too lenient in his grades. So when Professor Ludwig became available, I decided that he was much more suitable for this position.

HOLMES: I see. And did Professor Ludwig happen to show you a manuscript of his? A textbook?

HARGRAVE: Yes, he did. I haven't had time to read it yet, but I intend to do so this weekend.

HOLMES: Fine. Now, may we have a word with Artemis Ludwig?

HARGRAVE: (HUFFY) Well, I'll have to go and see if he's still here. Classes ended half-an-hour ago. He may have left. Just wait here, please.

MUSIC: UNDERCURRENT

WATSON: And so we waited. Ten minutes must have passed, and then the Headmaster returned – alone.

MUSIC: OUT

HARGRAVE: (OFF, MOVING ON) It's as I thought – Professor Ludwig has left for the day.

HOLMES: Then perhaps you can give us his home address.

HARGRAVE: That I cannot. He has just come to London from Berlin, and I understand he is staying in a hotel until he can find permanent lodging.

HOLMES: Which hotel?

HARGRAVE: I have no idea. Now, if you'll excuse me . . . (START FADE) I have a great deal of work to do . . . . (PAUSE)

SOUND EFFECT: (FADE UP) HORSE PULLING A CAB

WATSON: Tell me something, Holmes. What is it about this matter that interests you enough to spend your own time and money when there'll be nothing in it for you?

HOLMES: The novelty of it, for one thing. I've never had a case like this. A mysterious scholar who enters a stranger's digs night after night and corrects and then steals a manuscript? And how did Ludwig get to know Capstraw, especially if Ludwig is from Berlin? Why would he help an obscure schoolteacher, a total stranger, then take his job from him? No, there are too many questions to ignore. It's quite irresistable. Besides, I have nothing else to do.

WATSON: Well, if this district is where Capstraw lives, I pity him. So run down . . . Just look at the buildings! Ah, we're turning into Orient Street now.

HOLMES: (UP) Here we are, cabbie! There's Nineteen-and-a-half.

MUSIC: UNDERCURRENT

WATSON: A dark set of stairs led up from the street.

SOUND EFFECT: HOLMES RAPS ON THE DOOR WITH HIS CANE

WATSON: Didn't he say his door had no lock?

HOLMES: He did mention that.

SOUND EFFECT: RICKETY DOOR OPENS WITH A SQUEAK

WATSON: (PAUSE) I say!

HOLMES: (CALLS OUT) Mr. Capstraw! Sherlock Holmes and Doctor Watson!

WATSON: (PAUSE) What a miserable place! Just the one room! A bed, a desk, a table, two chairs, and a gas jet.

HOLMES: There's a sheet of paper on the desk, with an ink bottle on it . . . .

SOUND EFFECT: HOLMES TAKES THREE STEPS

HOLMES: (OFF) It's a note for Ludwig. (READS) *"Artemis Ludwig: Have contacted Sherlock Holmes. He wants to see you. Address is 221b Baker Street in the West End."* And it's signed, *"Emil"*.

MUSIC: UNDERCURRENT

WATSON: Holmes and I hurried back to Baker Street, where he assigned me to await the possible arrival of Artemis Ludwig, and he gave me specific instructions as what to do if Ludwig arrived before he returned. Holmes, meanwhile, said he was off to the telegraph shop and not to expect him for supper. It was past nine o'clock when I heard Holmes's familiar tread on the stairs.

MUSIC: OUT

SOUND EFFECT: DOOR CLOSES

HOLMES: Any visitors?

WATSON: I'm afraid not.

SOUND EFFECT: (UNDER DIALOGUE) HOLMES TAKES OFF HIS ULSTER AND MOVES ABOUT THE FLAT

HOLMES: (IN MOTION) Well actually, I didn't think Ludwig would come, but I needed you to be here in case he did.

215

Meanwhile, I've consulted someone who may be able to add some intelligence to this mystery.

WATSON: Oh? Who is that?

HOLMES: A chap in Vienna. I've been reading some of his work. I wired him the details as we know them and waited for a reply, which came quite promptly and was in English.

WATSON: Really? Who is it?

HOLMES: I doubt his name would mean anything to you, Watson, although he practices on the fringe of your profession. But fortunately my name was known to him. We exchanged two cables apiece.

WATSON: Holmes! In heaven's name, why are you spending all this time and energy –

HOLMES: – Oh, and money! Don't forget the small fortune in telegrams and taxis!

WATSON: Yes! Why are you doing this on a case that isn't really a case at all? No crime has been committed . . . .

HOLMES: Possible plagiarism?

WATSON: Well, but nobody's life is in danger . . . .

HOLMES: Don't be too sure.

WATSON: And your "client" is virtually penniless!

HOLMES: Watson, since all life is an education, I expect to learn a thing or two that may help me earn a handsome fee in some future case. Besides, I'm certain that what we're dealing with here is not exactly what it seems. * Now let us not waste any more –

SOUND EFFECT: * DISCREET KNOCK ON DOOR

HOLMES: I'll get that.

216

HOLMES: (FAR OFF-MICROPHONE) Yes? Oh, a card? A-ha!
Send him up!

SOUND EFFECT: DOOR CLOSES (OFF)

HOLMES: (MOVING ON) The long awaited Artemis Ludwig is
paying us a call!

MUSIC: LOW UNDERCURRENT

WATSON: (NARRATING) And in a moment, a man in his thirties,
dressed in a gentleman's attire, hurried into the room and stood
stiffly before us.

LUDWIG: (OFF) Artemis Ludwig, at your service.

SOUND EFFECT: CLICK OF HEELS

WATSON: (NARRATING) He actually bowed and clicked his
heels!

HOLMES: I am Sherlock Holmes and this is Doctor John H.
Watson. Please have a seat.

WATSON: (NARRATING) Ludwig sat down and removed his gray
kidskin gloves and placed them in his bowler hat, which he held
on his lap.

LUDWIG: My friend Emil Capstraw tells me you wish to see me on
a matter of some importance.

HOLMES: Yes. Thank you for coming.

LUDWIG: My pleasure. Now, what can I do for you, Mr. Holmes?

HOLMES: I have a few questions.

LUDWIG: I shall attempt to answer them.

HOLMES: Mr. Ludwig, there is –

LUDWIG: Ahem. Professor, if you don't mind.

HOLMES: My apologies. Professor Ludwig. There is something that interests me.

LUDWIG: And what is that?

HOLMES: Why did you enter Emil Capstraw's life?

LUDWIG: That is a strange way of putting it.

HOLMES: You stole into his room, improved his literary efforts, and corrected his papers, all in the middle of the night?

LUDWIG: Correct.

HOLMES: And you left after each visit without having awakened him?

LUDWIG: That is also correct.

HOLMES: But then you appropriated his manuscript and claimed it as your own?

LUDWIG: That is *not* correct. The manuscript is mine. Emil constructed a fantasy that he had written it, when in fact, it is my work. One-hundred percent. You see, Emil suffers a mental derangement.

HOLMES: How did you meet him?

LUDWIG: At the Harbison School. After coming here from Berlin where I had been an instructor at a *hochschulen*, I applied for a teaching position at the school but there was nothing open. But that day I visited Emil's classroom and observed him teaching. Quite frankly I was appalled at his unprofessional manner. Knowing that he would never accept my corrections, yet feeling a grave responsibility to the impressionable young men in his class, I took it upon myself to correct his work at night, while

218

he was asleep. He is a deep sleeper and I am by nature a night person, so it was a perfect match

HOLMES: But if I am informed correctly, you left the manuscript in Mr. Capstraw's room.

LUDWIG: As an incentive to Capstraw. And besides, I feared it might be stolen if I kept it at my hotel.

HOLMES: And which hotel is that?

LUDWIG: Well, I've just moved. Now that I am employed at the Harbison School, I can afford better accommodation. Now, if there is nothing else, I must keep an earlier appointment. *Auf Wiedersehen*, gentlemen.

MUSIC: FAST UNDERCURRENT

WATSON: Professor Ludwig left as hastily as he had come, and no sooner had the door closed than Holmes snatched up his own coat and cap!

HOLMES: Watson! Call a cab and meet me in Orient Street! Stay out of sight until you see me arrive! Then do exactly as I say!

MUSIC: UP

WATSON: (NARRATING) I followed Holmes' instructions, and was witness to the climax of the strange case I call "The Death of Artemis Ludwig"!

MUSIC: OUT. (SEGUE TO)

SOUND EFFECT: COURTROOM AMBIENCE. GAVEL RAPPED

JUDGE: Order! Everyone be quiet or I shall clear the court!

SOUND EFFECT: COURTROOM QUIETS DOWN

GAVIN: Mr. Holmes, since you have not been called by counsel for the Crown or for the Defense, you may not be acquainted with the facts in this case, which are these: Artemis Ludwig has

219

disappeared. His clothes, his papers, and his personal effects were found in the ash bin in Emil Capstraw's room. Capstraw tried to cash Professor Ludwig's first pay cheque from Harbison School by forging his endorsement signature. Capstraw had a motive to kill him: Revenge for stealing his manuscript and his job. And lastly, Capstraw himself, when questioned by the police, said he had "done away with Ludwig once and for all". Were you aware of these facts?

HOLMES: Quite aware, Mr. Gavin.

GAVIN: And do you dispute any of them?

HOLMES: Not at all.

GAVIN: Then how can you say that Capstraw "could not have murdered Ludwig", as you claim?

JUDGE: Yes, please tell the court what you mean by that, Mr. Holmes.

HOLMES: Emil Capstraw could not have murdered Artemis Ludwig because Artemis Ludwig never existed!

AUDIENCE: ASTONISHED REACTION

HOLMES: There was no such person as Artemis Ludwig! The man my associate and I met in our rooms, the man hired to teach at Harbison School, the man Dr. Watson and I followed . . . was *Emil Capstraw* in the identity of the fictitious person he fashioned in his mind: *Artemis Ludwig*!

GAVIN: What kind of tommyrot are you saying, Mr. Holmes?

HOLMES: If it please the court, I should like Doctor John H. Watson to be sworn in as a witness.

JUDGE: Oh, go ahead. Every other protocol is out the window! Call him, Bailiff.

BAILIFF: (OFF, SHOUTS) Is Doctor John H. Watson in the court?

220

WATSON: Right here, right here. I'm coming.

AUDIENCE: CONSTANT MURMURNG AS:

<u>SOUND EFFECT: WATSON WALKS TO THE BAR</u>

BAILIFF: Raise your right hand. Do you swear by almighty God that the evidence you are about to give is the truth, the whole truth and nothing but the truth?

WATSON: I do.

GAVIN: State your name.

WATSON: John Hamish Watson.

GAVIN: Occupation?

WATSON: Physician, retired.

GAVIN: Well, what do you have to tell us about the claims made here by Mr. Holmes?

WATSON: Well, after we interviewed the man calling himself Artemis Ludwig, Holmes followed him across town into the room occupied by Emil Capstraw. I was already waiting outside. We followed Ludwig in the door, where he tore off his garments and his blond wig, and became Emil Capstraw again!

GAVIN: Now just a minute! Are you saying Capstraw had been impersonating Ludwig?

WATSON: No. As Holmes pointed out to me, an impersonator pretends to be someone he isn't. Capstraw actually has two distinct identities: That of the humble, impoverished schoolteacher, and that of the arrogant German educator. They both exist within the same body!

<u>MUSIC: OMINOUS (BACKGROUND) IN AND UNDER</u>

WATSON: There followed one of those dramatic moments of which Holmes is so fond. He asked that Capstraw be called to the stand, and in a few moments, Ludwig emerged, and the judge and the banisters fell back in astonishment as the man they thought Capstraw had killed came forth in a torrent of German.

JUDGE: How in blazes did you catch on to this, Mr. Holmes?

HOLMES: It was his shoes and his hands, m'Lord. When Ludwig peeled off his gloves, and as he clicked his heels, my attention was drawn to his hands . . . and his shoes. They were the same, and in the same unkempt condition . . . as were Capstraw's!

MUSIC: SEGUE TO *DANSE MACABRE*

WATSON: (NARRATING) And so the murder charge was dropped and Capstraw – or Ludwig, if you like – was sent to St. Mary's of Bethlehem, the asylum for the insane . . . commonly known by its nickname . . . *Bedlam*.

MUSIC: *DANSE MACABRE* UP

WATSON: This is Doctor John H. Watson. I'll share a further adventure of Sherlock Holmes . . . *when next we meet*!

MUSIC: UP AND OUT

The Mystery of the Patient Fisherman

CHARACTERS

- SHERLOCK HOLMES
- DR. JOHN H. WATSON
- MRS. HUDSON
- HENRY MONCRIEF
- MRS. AMHURST
- HASWELL
- MAN IN THE STREET
- OLD WOMAN IN THE STREET
- THE FISHERMAN

SOUND EFFECT: OPENING SEGMENT, BIG BEN, STREET SOUNDS

ANNOUNCER: *The Further Adventures of Sherlock Holmes . . . .*

MUSIC: *DANSE MACABRE* (UP AND UNDER)

WATSON: My name is Doctor John H. Watson, the associate and close confidante of that most illustrious detective of the nineteenth century, Mr. Sherlock Holmes. You will be aware through my descriptions of his procedures, that Holmes – though he possessed no more than the usual five senses given to us all – had learnt to so attune himself to the use of those senses, that he seemed to possess a sixth sense – which, to the consternation of the regular police, gave him powers of deduction that seemed to border on the supernatural. (Holmes, of course, heatedly denied that.) But sometimes, he knew what was going to happen before it happened . . . .

MUSIC: SEGUE TO HOLMES VIOLIN, SOFTLY IN BACKGROUND

SOUND EFFECT: A LOW FIRE SNAPS OCCASIONALLY. HORSE TRAFFIC ON WET STREET IN BACKGROUND

223

WATSON: I had returned to my old quarters in Baker Street following the death of my dear wife Constance. I'd given up my medical practice, although it would have been beneficial for me, as well as those in need of my services, if I had busied myself treating patients instead of grieving alone. But as it happened, Sherlock Holmes came to my rescue by asking for my assistance in several cases, one of which was the mystery I'm about to relate. Holmes had been playing his Stradivarius by the window as he watched the rain stream down one dark afternoon, when the pensive mood was interrupted by the doorbell . . . .

SOUND EFFECT: DOORBELL RINGS. VIOLIN STOPS

WATSON: Ah, what a pity.

HOLMES: Hmm. Here, take the Strad and the bow, will you Watson, and put them on my bed.

WATSON: Certainly.

SOUND EFFECT: HUSHED STEPS (UNDER)

HOLMES: (OFF) And while you're in there, bring me my waterproof, will you?

WATSON: (UP) Are you going out?

HOLMES: (OFF) Very likely.

WATSON: Hmm. Well then, I'll get mine too.

SOUND EFFECT: WATSON OPENS CLOSET, REMOVES WATERPROOF, CLOSES CLOSET DOOR. HE WALKS BACK INTO SITTING ROOM AND PUTS THE WATERPROOFS DOWN ON A CHAIR

WATSON: (NARRATING DURING ABOVE) I laid the priceless violin on his un-made bed and fetched his rain slicker and my own, while Holmes went round the sitting room turning up the gas lamps.

HOLMES: (OFF, MOVING ON) Now we should be ready to have a good look at our caller, who is obviously here on some urgent mission, by all appearances.

SOUND EFFECT: A MAN'S TAP ON THE DOOR

WATSON: I'll get it.

SOUND EFFECT: DOOR OPENS

WATSON: Yes, Mrs. Hudson?

MRS. HUDSON: A gentleman to see Mr. Holmes. He says his name is Moncrief. He says it's urgent.

HOLMES: (OFF) Show him in, Mrs. Hudson.

MRS. HUDSON: Go right in, sir.

MONCRIEF: (SLIGHTLY OUT OF BREATH) Thank you so much.

SOUND EFFECT: TWO STEPS ON RUG

MRS. HUDSON: Will you be wanting anything, Mr. Holmes? Doctor?

WATSON: No, I think not.

MRS. HUDSON: Very good, gentlemen.

SOUND EFFECT: DOOR CLOSES

MONCRIEF: Then I am addressing Mr. Sherlock Holmes?

HOLMES: At your service. And this is my friend Doctor Watson.

MONCRIEF: How do you do. My name is Henry Moncrief. I apologize if this is an inconvenient time. I'd have waited till morning, but I've decided I can't live another hour without your help!

HOLMES: Which would explain why you had your driver racing up High Street and cutting west to get here.

MONCRIEF: How would you know that?

HOLMES: Oh, by the simplest observation. Your hired coach is a Culligan brougham – the style used only by Marble Arch Livery. You've only just rented it because it isn't yet splashed with much soil from the street. And the fastest route from Marble Arch to our address would of course be by way of the High Street – the only street where a gallop would be possible at this busy hour – thereby saving several minutes by avoiding the Baker Street shopping district. And the poor horse that pulled you here was clearly not accustomed to being driven that hard. But now, why the haste?

MONCRIEF: Mr. Holmes, you take my breath away! You're as clever as they say you are! Let me explain why I sought you out.

HOLMES: Please.

MONCRIEF: But you must promise that you won't dismiss me as a raving lunatic!

HOLMES: I won't dismiss you at all. Please go on.

MONCRIEF: Well I'm being tormented. Followed. Night and day.

HOLMES: Threatened?

MONCRIEF: Not in words, he never speaks. Do you hold with . . . spiritualism?

HOLMES: With spiritualism?

MONCRIEF: Appearances of the dead.

HOLMES: Since none of the dead has ever appeared to me, I've had no experience along those lines.

226

MONCRIEF: Well, neither had I. But in the strictest of confidence, I must tell you . . . Either I am being tricked, or I am being haunted. Now, I am not a type of man given over to his emotions, but in the last month I have come to believe that a man who is dead and buried is pursuing me!

HOLMES: Who would that be?

MONCRIEF: His name is Joseph Amhurst.

HOLMES: Your former business partner?

MONCRIEF: Ah! Then you read the report in the papers at the time?

HOLMES: That's how I recognized your name. He jumped from Waterloo Bridge, I believe, something over a month ago?

MONCRIEF: Yes, the fifth of September. I saw him do it. So I know he's dead. But. . . blast it all! He comes back!

HOLMES: What sort of business are you in?

MONCRIEF: My firm holds various properties to let.

HOLMES: You are a rental agent?

MONCRIEF: That's right. Moncrief and Amhurst.

HOLMES: Were you and Amhurst on good terms at the time of his death?

MONCRIEF: Actually, no. I caught him stealing from me. When I confronted him, he promised he'd pay me back, but we both knew that would be impossible – the amount he'd taken was too great. But he begged me to give him twenty-four hours before turning him in, saying he'd come up with a solution.

HOLMES: So what did you do?

MONCRIEF: I gave him his twenty-four hours. He asked me to meet him on Waterloo Bridge at midnight where he would "make everything right", as he put it.

227

HOLMES: And so . . . ?

MONCRIEF: I met him on the bridge. We spoke for just a minute or so. He begged my forgiveness, and then he suddenly vaulted over the rail.

HOLMES: I see.

WATSON: Uh, May I, Holmes?

HOLMES: Of course.

WATSON: Well, the drop from the bridge to the water wouldn't necessarily be fatal, and last month the Thames wasn't all that cold. We'd had quite a warm spell, if you remember, so a man could survive in the water for some little time. He could have clung to one of the piers that support the bridge, perhaps hailed a passing boat and made it to shore.

MONCRIEF: No, no, no, Doctor. When he jumped he didn't hit the water, he landed on one of those brick piers and dashed his brains out. The water police fished his body out at Blackfriars Bridge and I had the lovely job of identifying it. No, it was him.

HOLMES: And where have you been seeing this, ah . . . ghost?

MONCRIEF: Everywhere! Not an hour ago I saw him on Waterloo Bridge. That's why I finally decided to come to you.

MUSIC: UNDERCURRENT

WATSON: Sherlock Holmes is the least superstitious individual I ever knew. He dismissed the notion that Moncrief was seeing a ghost, and of course I agreed with him. But Moncrief implored us to follow him down to Waterloo Bridge to take a close look at the scene of his partner's death.

MUSIC: OUT

SOUND EFFECT: (FADE IN) CARRIAGE IN MOTION

WATSON: Holmes.

HOLMES: Yes?

WATSON: How did you know we'd have to go out? You asked for your raincoat before we even me Moncrief! Remember?

HOLMES: (WEARILY) Watson, must you make a mystery of everything I do? You'll recall that from our window I saw him dash out of his brougham and run to our door. His horse had been driven at high speed, indicating that whatever he wanted of me, time was of the essence. That being the case, I asked you for my waterproof to save a few moments if I needed to leave at once.

WATSON: (GLUM) Well. Once again you humble me with the speed of your brain.

HOLMES: Not speed alone, Watson. I was thinking ahead. If you were called to see a patient in serious distress, you'd make arrangements in advance for an ambulance to take him to hospital if it were needed, wouldn't you? It's the same thing.

WATSON: (PAUSE) What do you expect to find at Waterloo Bridge?

HOLMES: Nothing.

WATSON: Then, why –

HOLMES: Why go out in this filthy weather? I assure you we are not searching for a ghost. You would do well to bring all your knowledge of the human condition to bear on Mr. Moncrief . . . . (UP) Pull up here, driver, behind that brougham stopping at the end of the bridge, then wait for us here. We won't be long.

MUSIC: SOMBER STING

SOUND EFFECT: HEAVY CARRIAGE TRAFFIC IN THE RAIN

MONCRIEF: Here. It was just here that we had our final interview.

229

HOLMES: Who chose this spot on the bridge?

MONCRIEF: Amhurst. We arrived in separate cabs. As you know, they can't stop on the bridge, so we had them leave us off here and drive on, and we stood here by the rail, talking. And then all of a sudden he sprang up and plunged over the rail.

HOLMES: And how did he jump? Head first? Feet first?

MONCRIEF: I . . . I . . . I really don't remember.

HOLMES: What did you do?

MONCRIEF: I was stunned. I looked over the rail and saw his body strike the pier and bounce off into the river.

HOLMES: How could you have seen that, at midnight?

MONCRIEF: Well, we were right under this double street lamp, and there were lights along Victoria Embankment and in Somerset House there on the shore.

HOLMES: Did anyone else see it happen?

MONCRIEF: Well, I did see a fisherman down on the Embankment. He was the only other living soul who could have seen it. Then a hansom came by a minute later and I flagged it down and told the driver to find a policeman, and he must have done, because one showed up shortly afterwards.

WATSON: And this is where you think you saw Amhurst's ghost today?

MONCRIEF: Yes! He was perched on the rail, right here where we're standing, hanging onto this double lamppost . . . waiting for me to come by!

HOLMES: Were you alone?

MONCRIEF: No, I was riding in a cab with a business acquaintance.

HOLMES: And did he see the ghost as well?

230

MONCRIEF: I suppose not.

HOLMES: The other times. Tell me about them.

MONCRIEF: He shows up anywhere . . . everywhere. Just a glimpse of him. Haymarket. Foley Street Mews. . . just anywhere. I catch sight of him and then he's gone.

HOLMES: Have you attempted to speak to him?

MONCRIEF: (PAUSE) No. (PAUSE) You think it's all in my mind, don't you?

HOLMES: I have made no conclusion. There is much more to learn, but I prefer to learn it somewhere other than in the middle of a bridge in a driving rain. Suppose we retire to your offices.

SOUND EFFECT: RAIN SEGUE TO

MUSIC: UNDERCURRENT

WATSON: Moncrief and Amhurst did business out of a modest three-room suite on Sabine Road in Lavender Hill.

MUSIC: FADE OUT

MONCRIEF: Can I offer you some tea? Or something stronger? I'm going to have a drink.

HOLMES: Nothing for me.

WATSON: I'm a bit chilled. Perhaps a spot of tea?

MONCRIEF: I'll put the pot on. Miss Railton usually takes care of the tea but she leaves at five. I'll only be a second.

SOUND EFFECT: (BACKGROUND) POURING WATER INTO TEAKETTLE. PUT KETTLE ON A HARD SURFACE

HOLMES: (OVER SOUND EFFECT) This photograph on the wall. Two men shaking hands in front of this building. I take it the other fellow is Amhurst?

MONCRIEF: (OFF) Oh that, yes. We had that made when we went into business together.

HOLMES: He looks a bit older than you.

MONCRIEF: He was.

HOLMES: Just how did you find out that Amhurst was stealing from the company?

MONCRIEF: (OFF) Well, every night I tally the receipts against the cash on hand. Some of our tenants began to fall behind in their rents, or so Amhurst said. He told me not to worry, that he'd take stern measures to get what was owed to us. But the shortages continued for weeks and months and got worse! Finally, I went to some of our delinquent tenants myself, and that's when I found that they'd been paying Amhurst but Amhurst had been pocketing the money. (MOVING ON) Well, at first Amhurst denied it, but I persisted and finally he broke down and admitted he'd stolen the money. Over a thousand pounds in all. Said he'd had debts he had to pay. Begged me not to turn him in. But I told him we were quits. Bloody awful scene. He did have a wife to support. I suppose I could have given him another chance, but who wants to be in partnership with a crook? Anyway, that's when he asked me to give him twenty-four hours. I thought perhaps he'd return some of what he'd taken from the business. . . . Excuse me, you sure you wouldn't like a drink, gentlemen?

MUSIC: UNDERCURRENT

WATSON: It was all too clear that Henry Moncrief felt responsible for Ainhurst's suicide. That would account for his seeing what he took to be the ghost. After we left Lavender Hill, Holmes and I had supper at the Holborn Restaurant, and he outlined a simple plan.

MUSIC: SEGUE TO

HOLMES: What Moncrief wants is for me to rid him of his guilt over his partner's demise, but no one can do that for him.

WATSON: I quite agree.

HOLMES: So I'd like you to be at his side wherever he goes tomorrow, and if Moncrief sees someone he thinks is his dead partner, you'll follow him and learn his true identity. Then, when Moncrief finally admits that his mind has been playing tricks on him, it would seem to me that our job is done. What do you think?

WATSON: It seems that would be all we can do.

HOLMES: And see if you can locate Amhurst's widow, and get what you can from her. In the meantime, will make a few inquiries of my own, and then tomorrow night we'll compare notes.

MUSIC: UNDERCURRENT

WATSON: So before Moncrief opened his office the next day, I called on Mrs. Joseph Amhurst. She lived in a comfortable house in Upper Norwood.

MUSIC: OUT

MRS. AMHURST: You work with Sherlock Holmes? Is he looking into the death of my husband?

WATSON: It's not that, exactly.

MRS. AMHURST: Then what is it?

WATSON: I wonder if I might ask you to tell me everything your husband told you about the last few days of his work with Mr. Moncrief?

MRS. AMHURST: That's what the police asked. I can only tell you what I told them. He was upset about something, he wouldn't say what. I gathered it had to do with something personal between the two of them.

WATSON: But he never said what that was.

MRS. AMHURST: Joseph always protected me from his business worries. That's the kind of husband he was to me.

WATSON: Very considerate. What was his age at the time of his . . .
.

MRS. AMHURST: Fifty.

WATSON: Now, forgive me, this is a very delicate thing to ask you and I hope it won't seem rude of me, but I should like to know if you and Mr. Amhurst were happy in your marriage.

MRS. AMHURST: Very happy.

WATSON: And he wasn't in any kind of financial difficulty that you know of?

MRS. AMHURST: No, Doctor Watson, he left me quite well off. Perhaps you should talk to our solicitor, Mr. Haswell in Regent Street, if you have any more questions.

SOUND EFFECT: STORMY CITY PERSPECTIVE THROUGH WINDOW

HASWELL: And the purpose of your inquiry is?

WATSON: Sherlock Holmes is looking into the Amhurst matter, Mr. Haswell.

HASWELL: Good! Maybe we'll get to the bottom of it then!

WATSON: Sir?

HASWELL: I happen to know that Scotland Yard hasn't closed the book on Joseph Amhurst's death. How did Holmes get into it?

234

WATSON: Well, he's . . . acting for a client. That's really all I can say.

HASWELL: Mrs. Amhurst?

WATSON: I, uh, really can't say. Mr. Holmes has established a rule that he never discloses the name of his clients.

HASWELL: Who does he think he is, a solicitor? Well, never mind. I'll tell you this much, Doctor Watson. The facts don't fit. Amhurst wasn't the suicidal type. And he certainly wasn't a thief.

WATSON: But the police haven't made any charges.

HASWELL: No. They need evidence. Let us hope your Mr. Holmes sheds some new light on this tragedy.

SOUND EFFECT: CARRIAGE IN STREET, (INTERIOR)

MONCRIEF: Keep a sharp lookout, Doctor. He could be on the sidewalk, or crossing the street . . . He could be anywhere!

WATSON: You seem to be most afraid of seeing the ghost on Waterloo Bridge, Mr. Moncrief.

MONCRIEF I suppose that's because that's the last place I saw him alive.

WATSON: Well, we're only two blocks from the bridge.

MONCRIEF: I know.

WATSON: What sort of clothes would this ghost be wearing?

MONCRIEF: Oh, he wore what any gentleman wears in business. Black coat and trousers. A black hat . . . something like this one I'm wearing.

WATSON: Amhurst seemed a bit taller than you, in that photograph.

235

MONCRIEF: He was. And he wore a beard and moustache. Look, you watch the street and I'll watch the sidewalk on the left.

WATSON: Right. And if either one of us spots someone you think looks like Amhurst, I'll take out after him. Although I'm not as fast as I once was. When I was in the army, I –

MONCRIEF: Look! There! I think that's him! The tall man! Standing in the crowd!

WATSON: I see him! Driver, stop the cab!

SOUND EFFECT: HORSES HOOVES STOP. WATSON GETTING OUT OF CAB, ONTO STREET. LONDON STREET IN BACKGROUND

WATSON: Stay there!

SOUND EFFECT: WATSON TROTS ON STREET

WATSON: (OUT OF BREATH, TO HIMSELF) Wait! Where is he? Where'd he go?

SOUND EFFECT: STEPS STOP

WATSON: I don't see him! (UP) Excuse me . . . did you see a tall man in black? He was just here on the curb . . . .

MAN: I didn't see no one.

WATSON: Madam! Pardon me! Did you see where that tall man went? He was standing right here

OLD WOMAN: What are you talking about? I didn't see anyone.

WATSON: I see. Thank you. Sorry.

SOUND EFFECT: WATSON WALKS BACK TO THE CAB, GETS IN

WATSON: (EXERTION AS HE GETS IN AND SITS DOWN) I'm sorry. I lost him.

236

MONCRIEF: He disappeared, didn't he? Just like he always does! But now at least you've seen him! You know he's real! (UP) All right, driver.

SOUND EFFECT: CAB STARTS UP AGAIN

WATSON: He could have gone into one of those doors.

MONCRIEF: How does he know where I'll be? That's what I want to know! If it's a living person, how does he know how to find me? But if it's a ghost. . . I'll never be rid of him!

WATSON: Mr. Moncrief, I will stake my career in medicine and my years investigating crime on one thing: There is no such thing as a ghost! Your mind is playing tricks on you.

MONCRIEF: You think I'm crazy, don't you? . . . Well, maybe I am. He's driven me to it! I don't know how much longer I can go on.

WATSON: Are you married, Mr. Moncrief?

MONCRIEF: No! I was. She left me. It's been years. No woman will have me! It's all right. I'm happier by myself.

WATSON: Whom do you talk to? Whom have you told about seeing your ghost?

MONCRIEF: No one! Not one living soul! Not one – living – soul.

WATSON: We're onto Waterloo Bridge now.

MONCRIEF: I'm not going to look! I'm going to shut my eyes!

WATSON: Please, Mr. Moncrief –

MONCRIEF: Yes! I should have done this before! I won't open my eyes until we're off the bridge! Tell me when we're off the bridge, Doctor Watson!

WATSON: Really. Now, I'm going to write a prescription for some medicine I want you to take that will ease your anxiety. When we're through collecting rents today, I want you to stop by a chemist's and have him –

MONCRIEF: (PAUSE) Yes? What? What is it? Did you see something?

WATSON: (SHAKEN) Uh, it's nothing. Just, uh . . . keep your eyes closed, Mr. Moncrief. We'll be off the bridge in a minute.

MUSIC: UNDERTONE

WATSON: I didn't tell Moncrief, but just as we were passing the center of Waterloo Bridge, I saw a figure dressed in black, squatting on the rail, hanging onto the double lamp post . . . in the same spot where Amhurst had jumped to his death! I rode with him to three addresses where he picked up his rent money, and then he dropped me off at 221b Baker Street. To my surprise, although it wasn't yet four o'clock, Holmes was there.

MUSIC: OUT

HOLMES: Ah, Watson. Did you meet the widow Amhurst?

WATSON: Yes, I did.

HOLMES: And did you chaperone Henry Moncrief on his rounds?

WATSON: Yes, I've just come back.

HOLMES: Well . . . ?

WATSON: Mrs. Amhurst says her marriage was a happy one, and her husband left her well off. She did say he seemed to have had something on his mind prior to the night of his death but he wouldn't say what it was. She referred me to her solicitor, a Mr. Haswell.

HOLMES: And did you see him?

WATSON: Yes. He doubts that Amhurst committed suicide, and he said Scotland Yard is still investigating, which I didn't know.

HOLMES: Interesting. And what else? You're saving the best for last, aren't you?

WATSON: What do you mean?

HOLMES: You have more to tell. Oh, come, Watson. I can read you like a book.

WATSON: Well, I may have seen him myself.

HOLMES: Who?

WATSON: I saw someone who vaguely fit Amhurst's description and I gave chase, but he vanished. And then, as we crossed Waterloo Bridge, I saw – well, I saw someone again who fit the description. Perched on the bridge rail, right where Amhurst jumped.

HOLMES: And how did Moncrief react to that?

WATSON: He didn't see him. He had his eyes shut.

HOLMES: Too bad. Well, are you now converted to a belief in ghosts? Shall we book a seance or two?

WATSON: Don't make light of it, Holmes. I don't know what I saw, but I did see someone . . . and I know that Moncrief isn't having delusions!

HOLMES: And I agree.

WATSON: You do?

HOLMES: I've spent an informative day myself. The result of which I expect will bring this case to a conclusion tonight . . . with your help.

MUSIC: UNDERCURRENT

239

WATSON: Holmes then busied himself with writing materials and a concoction of foul-smelling chemicals for the next hour. Then he made up a small parcel and gave it to a delivery boy he often hired, along with a generous tip.

HOLMES: And now, what say we see if Mrs. Hudson has any of that mutton left over. I'm ravenous, and we have work to do at midnight!

WATSON: By ten o'clock we had finished our supper, chatting about inconsequential things. Finally he suggested I get into my warmest clothes and some wading boots . . . and bring my gun.

MUSIC: OUT

HOLMES: By no later than eleven, Watson, you are to take up a position just east of the north end of Waterloo Bridge, down on the Victoria Embankment in front of Somerset House. Conceal yourself and keep watch.

WATSON: Keep watch? For what?

HOLMES: A solitary fisherman.

WATSON: At that hour?

HOLMES: You don't know what he's fishing for.

MUSIC: MYSTERIOUS UNDERCURRENT

WATSON: And so, at twenty-minutes-to-eleven, I left Holmes and took a cab down through Bloomsbury to Waterloo Bridge. Fog was rolling down the Thames, forming haloes of light round the streetlamps. I found a nesting place beneath the stonework at the end of the bridge, and settled in to wait for – I didn't know what. Fifteen minutes later, a fisherman lumbered down to the Embankment. He carried a wicker creel and a jointed fishing pole, which he patiently assembled. Then he dropped his line in the water and sat on the edge of the seawall. He was an older man, wearing a hood over his head. In a few minutes, another man walked down from the road toward the fisherman, approaching from the back. I crept out of my hiding place and

240

followed him. The fog was wafting up from the river. Then, the newcomer spoke.

SOUND EFFECT: RIVERBANK SOUNDS

MONCRIEF: Well, a boy delivered your putrid note and I'm here.

FISHERMAN: I see you are, Henry. My apologies for the smell. Everything I touch smells that way . . . now.

MONCRIEF: I've hired Sherlock Holmes. If you're real, he'll get you.

FISHERMAN: Even Sherlock Holmes can't help you now.

MONCRIEF: You . . . your voice doesn't sound the same.

FISHERMAN: Being dead changes one, Henry. You'll find that out.

MONCRIEF: I don't believe you! Let me see your face!

FISHERMAN: You don't want to see my face, Henry. There's not much left of it after what you did.

MONCRIEF: You left me no choice! You were going to report me!

FISHERMAN: So you went from thievery . . . to murder.

MONCRIEF: What do you want?

FISHERMAN: I want to hear your confession. It may help save your soul – if you have one.

MONCRIEF: And then you'll let me alone? Say you'll let me alone!

FISHERMAN: You won't ever see me again.

MONCRIEF: All right! I stole from the company! I stole your half of the earnings! And then . . . when you found me out . . . .

FISHERMAN: Yes?

241

MONCRIEF: . . . I lured you out here to the bridge and . . . and I smashed your head with a hammer and pushed you into the river! There! I've confessed! Now let me go!

HOLMES: (NATURAL VOICE) I think not. (CALLING OUT) Watson! Train your gun on him!

MONCRIEF: Sherlock Holmes! You! You tricked me!

HOLMES: Along with six Scotland Yard policemen made up to look like your victim. Ah. And here they come now.

SOUND EFFECT: POLICEMENT APPROACHING.

HOLMES: You see, Watson, I learned that Scotland Yard had been laying their own trap for Moncrief, stationing men along his usual routes through London, dressed as Amhurst had dressed.

WATSON: And your plan to force Moncrief to admit his guilt was the final touch.

HOLMES: Yes, but you and I will no doubt be called as witnesses for the Crown, and Moncrief s defense will surely be the insanity plea.

WATSON: But if he *was* insane, it was his own crime that had driven him mad.

HOLMES: Yes, Watson. But either way, a grim lesson to those who would commit murder: The evil that men do lives on – after the deed.

MUSIC: *DANSE MACABRE* UP AND UNDER

WATSON: And this is Doctor John H. Watson. I'll have another Sherlock Holmes adventure to tell you . . . *when next we meet*!

MUSIC: UP AND OUT

The Woman from Virginia

CHARACTERS

- SHERLOCK HOLMES
- DR. JOHN H. WATSON
- MRS. HUDSON
- LOWELL WALDRON – *A wealthy upper-class Englishman, age about 60. Robust nature*
- EVAN WALDRON – *His son, twenty-seven, demanding and spoiled, a wastrel and whiner*
- ALICE ROYCE / LUCY BLAKE – *A cockney actress (Lucy) who portrays an American girl (Alice)*

SOUND EFFECT: OPENING SEQUENCE, BIG BEN, STREET SOUNDS

ANNOUNCER: *The Further Adventures of Sherlock Holmes . . . .*

MUSIC: *DANSE MACABRE* (UP AND UNDER)

WATSON: My name is John H. Watson, and I have the honour of being the chronicler of the famous consulting detective, Mr. Sherlock Holmes, with whom I shared lodgings at 221b Baker Street, London. The story I shall tell you now, I have titled, "The Woman From Virginia", and it began one pleasant April afternoon in the year 1889.

SOUND EFFECT: UNDER: BAKER STREET SOUNDS

WATSON: It was one of those unexpectedly balmy spring days, just before tea, when the yellow tile of the building across the street reflected the sun so brightly that it illuminated our sitting room as if a powerful electric lamp were focused on us.

SOUND EFFECT: HOLMES PLAYING CONEMPLATIVELY IN BACKGROUND

WATSON: Holmes and I hadn't spoken for some minutes, both being lost in a contemplative mood. Personally, I enjoyed those rare moments when no business pressed upon me. Holmes, on the

243

other hand, had restlessly tried the papers, then a book, and finally picked up his Stradivarius and stood at the mantel, improvising a tune, to drain away some dills unspent nervous tension.

SOUND EFFECT: VIOLIN STOPS

HOLMES: (SLIGHTLY OFF-MICROPHONE) Another hour gone. At times like these, how I envy the cobbler, or the green-grocer!

WATSON: Whatever for?

HOLMES: Because the cobbler always has another pair of boots to work on, and the green-grocer can snip radish tops or sprinkle his spinach. They don't have to wait for events.

WATSON: (CHUCKLING) They do if no one wants his boots repaired or needs vegetables.

HOLMES: My meaning, Watson, is that they can prepare their shops for the next day's business, which surely will come as long as people walk and eat! But in my specialty, being the world's only consulting detective, I must wait for events to happen! And it drives me to distraction, this idleness!

WATSON: Not much different from the life of a private physician, seems to me. Have to wait 'til someone gets sick or breaks his leg.

HOLMES: But the doctor is merely a mechanic who fixes things the way he's been trained. I, on the other hand, must attack each case with a fresh analysis of the facts, taking innumerable factors into consideration, human nature being infinitely variable. A doctor can spend his idle hours reading medical books, while I can do nothing until a fresh case presents itself

WATSON: Poor Holmes! But given the state of human nature, I would expect you won't be long without a commission.

SOUND EFFECT: DISCREET KNOCK ON DOOR

WATSON: There, you see, Holmes! What did I tell you?

244

HOLMES: It's probably just Mrs. Hudson with our tea.

SOUND EFFECT: DOOR OPENS

HOLMES: (DISAPPOINTED) Ah, Mrs. Hudson. Right on time.

SOUND EFFECT: (UNDER) TEA TRAY JIGGLES SLIGHTLY

MRS. HUDSON: Good afternoon, Mr. Holmes. Doctor Watson. Your tea.

HOLMES: Yes, bring it in.

MRS. HUDSON: And a telegram. I'll just put the tea things down here.

SOUND EFFECT: TEA TRAY SET DOWN

HOLMES: The telegram! Let's have it!

MRS. HUDSON: Here you are, sir. The boy just brought it.

SOUND EFFECT: LIGHT ENVELOPE TORN OPEN, LETTER UNFOLDED

MRS. HUDSON: Will there be anything else, gentlemen?

HOLMES: Yes! Just wait a moment while I read this. Ah!

WATSON: Something interesting?

HOLMES: Here. Read it out loud while I write a reply. Sit down, Mrs. Hudson. Have some tea.

MRS. HUDSON: Oh, no thank you, sir. I only brought the two cups.

HOLMES: Read it, Watson!

WATSON: *"Mr. Sherlock Holmes, London: Desperate emergency at Tunbridge Wells. Life at stake. Dare not involve police. Come at*

245

once and name your price. Cable acceptance by return wire. Lowell Waldron, Amblehurst." Who is Lowell Waldron?

HOLMES: I don't know. But we're certainly not going to travel all the way down to Kent without more information. Let me just fmish my scribble, here . . . . Ah. How does this sound: "*Kindly furnish references, particulars. Will await reply, Sherlock Holmes.*"

WATSON: That should do it.

HOLMES: Please have this sent as soon as possible, Mrs. Hudson. Is the boy still waiting?

MRS. HUDSON: He's downstairs.

HOLMES: Then give him this and let him keep the change. And tell him to wait for the reply and hurry back here when it comes.

SOUND EFFECT: COINS

MRS. HUDSON: Very good, sir. (MOVE SLIGHTLY OFF) Will you be eating supper here tonight?

HOLMES: That depends on Mr. Lowell Waldron, the telegraph, and the British Railway.

MRS. HUDSON: Yes, sir. I'll send the boy off at once.

HOLMES: Please do.

SOUND EFFECT: DOOR CLOSES

HOLMES: "Name your price", eh? I like the sound of that.

MUSIC: UNDERCURRENT

WATSON: Within the next hour, Lowell Waldron replied that a young American woman who had been visiting Amblehurst had been kidnapped, and a ransom note had arrived. The note warned that to notify the police would assure that the woman would be killed! And as for his personal references, Waldron said he was

246

one of the underwriters for Lloyd's, and a trustee of the Bank of England! Which was good enough for Holmes.

SOUND EFFECT: ENGLISH TRAIN ARRIVING

WATSON: We took a seven o'clock train from Waterloo station, and pulled into Tunbridge Wells just after nine. A sturdy gentleman with a bristling white moustache and tweed cap, coat, and britches made his way toward us as we stepped down from our car.

LOWELL: (SECRETIVELY LOW) Holmes?

HOLMES: Indeed. And you're Mr. Lowell Waldron?

LOWELL: Yes. Thank you for coming. Not a moment to lose.

HOLMES: My associate, Doctor John Watson.

LOWELL: Most honored, I'm sure. Please come this way.

MUSIC: MOTION BRIDGE (UNDER)

WATSON: We rode in a splendid carriage through the mild country night, while Waldron recounted what had happened at Amblehurst.

MUSIC: OUT

SOUND EFFECT: HORSE AT A FAST TROT

LOWELL: The young lady's name is Alice Royce. Family owns half the tobacco grown in Virginia. My son met her when he was on holiday in the States last year. Been writing to her ever since. Then she turned up in London last fortnight, and Evan invited her down. Quite a fetching girl, actually. Evan's quite gone on her.

HOLMES: I see. Now, about the kidnaping?

247

LOWELL: It happened yesterday. She'd been out riding with Evan. On the estate. We have two-hundred-and-eighty acres. Evan was showing her around. Well, he'll tell you the rest.

HOLMES: Is Evan your only child?

LOWELL: No. My older son Charles lives in London with his wife. I'm teaching him the banking business. Ah, we're almost there.

MUSIC: SWEEPS UP AND UNDER – A SCENIC MOTIF

WATSON: And in a minute, Amblehurst came into view. By then it had grown quite dark, but we could see a huge dark block of a place, sitting on a rise of ground bordered by a stand of white birches along the roadside. We turned in at the gate and drove another two-hundred yards to the grand entrance, and as we pulled up, a young man in his twenties rushed out to meet us with a lantern.

MUSIC: OUT

EVAN: Father! Were you followed?

LOWELL: I don't think so.

HOLMES: You may rest your mind. We were not followed.

LOWELL: My son, Evan.

EVAN: Hullo.

LOWELL: These gentlemen are Mr. Sherlock Holmes and Doctor John Watson. Help us down, Evan.

SOUND EFFECT: THE THREE MEN GET DOWN FROM THE CARRIAGE

HOLMES: Thank you.

EVAN: I may as well tell you right off. It was a mistake for father to hire you, Mr. Holmes. The fiends who kidnaped Alice said they'll kill her if we tell the police! And you're such a famous detective, if they find out you're here, all is lost, don't you see?

HOLMES: We've taken great pains to avoid attracting any attention.

LOWELL: Excuse my boy, Mr. Holmes. He's not usually so rude!

SOUND EFFECT: FOUR MEN WALKING ON STONE, THEN INSIDE. LARGE DOOR CLOSES

LOWELL: I'll have your things taken up to your rooms. And you'll be wanting your dinner.

HOLMES: At the moment, no. First, it is paramount that we learn exactly what happened last night.

LOWELL: Of course. We'll talk in my study. Right this way.

SOUND EFFECT: FOUR MEN WALKING ON HARD SURFACE; STOP. DOOR OPENS. STEPS IN, DOOR CLOSES

HOLMES: Now, then. Evan –

EVAN: Yes, Mr. Holmes?

HOLMES: Tell us precisely what happened last night.

EVAN: Well, after we'd had dinner, I wanted to show Alice 'round the estate while it was still light.

HOLMES: What time would this have been?

EVAN: We left the house at eight.

HOLMES: You were riding?

EVAN: Yes. I gave her a gentle little Arabian mare, and I was on Racer, my thoroughbred. Well, we'd gotten down near a stand of trees at the southeast corner of the property, about half-a-mile from the house, when all of a sudden, these two men rode out of the trees and dashed right up to us! One of them made right for me, and the other one rode up beside Alice. She was a few

249

lengths behind me at that moment. One man grabbed my reins and shoved a gun in my face! I heard Alice scream, and the next moment this other ruffian had galloped off with Alice on his horse. She was struggling and fighting him all the way as they disappeared into the wood.

HOLMES: And the man with the gun?

EVAN: He kept it aimed right at my face, and then he made me get down. I had no choice. It was that or be shot! He slapped Racer on the flanks and made him run away. Then he threw me the note, and said if I ever wanted to see the girl again, to follow the instructions to the letter! And then he spurred his horse and dashed into the wood after the other man.

HOLMES: I see. And the note?

EVAN: Yes. Here it is.

HOLMES: Thank you. (READING) *"To get her back, put two-hundred used fifty-pound notes in a bag. Saturday at 10 P.M. Place bag at north gate pillar. If I am followed, girl will die."* I'll need to study this.

EVAN: I don't know what you have to study it for. It's plain enough!

HOLMES: Tell me now, Evan: Did you recognize either of these men?

EVAN: No, but we've had poachers on the land, and last month father warned them off with a few shots to scare them away. My guess is, that's who they were – poachers, back for revenge.

LOWELL: No, no. Poachers steal to eat. They're not the class of crook to kidnap someone. Wouldn't you agree, Mr. Holmes?

HOLMES: I've had very little experience with poachers, Mr. Waldron. At the moment, I'm more interested in a description of the men.

EVAN: The one who attacked me had a black moustache, heavy black brows. Wore a hat like a chimney sweep wears – you

250

know, a battered opera hat, it looked like. His coat was long and black. And he spoke like a Cockney. I couldn't get a good look at the other one.

HOLMES: Did you try to pursue them?

EVAN: It was useless. By the time I got Racer to come back, they'd gone. I wouldn't have known where to look. Besides, I wasn't armed. Mr. Holmes: Alice is the dearest thing in life to me. Do you think you can get her back?

HOLMES: One way or another, the lady will be returned. Now tomorrow morning, I'll need you to show me where the abduction took place. And meantime, see that no one tramples the area. And Mr. Waldron –

LOWELL: Yes?

HOLMES: In the event that we fail to find Alice Royce before the deadline, will you have the required ransom available?

LOWELL: I don't keep that much money on hand. I'd have to go to London.

HOLMES: Then I think it would be prudent to do so tomorrow.

MUSIC: SHORT STING, SEGUE TO

SOUND EFFECT: OCCASIONAL TABLE SOUNDS (UNDER)

WATSON: (EATING) This is excellent beef, Mr. Waldron.

LOWELL: Glad you enjoy it. Hope you'll excuse Evan, gentlemen. Hasn't had much of an appetite since the kidnaping.

WATSON: Well, who could blame him? Poor fellow, his fiancée snatched right out of his very arms – er, so to speak.

HOLMES: Mr. Waldron, tell me what you can about Miss Royce.

LOWELL: Well, she's a lovely girl. My late wife would have adored her. Daughter of a prominent Virginia tobacco family, and fairly

251

well-educated by American standards, I should say. Very well-to-do.

HOLMES: Have you communicated with her family?

LOWELL: Never have, no, but Evan stayed with them in Virginia when he was on holidays last year. Told me all about them.

HOLMES: And I take it you approve of her as a potential daughter-in-law?

LOWELL: Her family controls a good share of the Virginia tobacco crop. If our two families were connected – well, it could be mutually advantageous. The Bank is always on the lookout for interesting investment opportunities, and Alice tells us the Royces are planning to expand their holdings. I think the Bank would like to provide the financing. Yes, a good match all round, it seems to me. If we can just get her back!

MUSIC: UNDERCURRENT

WATSON: At around eleven, Holmes and I retired to our rooms, which adjoined with a connecting door between them. I'd gotten into my night clothes when Holmes tapped on the door and came in, wearing his mouse-colored dressing gown, and he flopped down carelessly in a chair by a window. He had the ransom note in his hand.

MUSIC: OUT

WATSON: What do you make of it, Holmes?

HOLMES: Have a look at the note. Tell me what *you* think.

WATSON: Hmm. Well, the words are printed in pencil. And the bottoms of all the letters are level, as if a straightedge had been used. To disguise his hand, you think?

HOLMES: Yes, go on.

WATSON: Well, the note's very terse. *"To get her back, put two-hundred used fifty-pound notes in a bag."*

252

HOLMES: Yes. Why does he specify that the fifty-pound notes be used, not new?

WATSON: Because the serial numbers on two-hundred used bills wouldn't be consecutive, as on new ones. Makes tracing them impossible.

HOLMES: Good man, Watson! Now, a common thug or an inexperienced one might not have thought of that, but our man did. Go on.

WATSON: Well, the rest of it reads: *"Saturday at 10 P.M. Place bag at north gate pillar. If I am followed, girl will die."*

HOLMES: A clever choice, ten o'clock on a Saturday night. This is church-going country, and there should be no traffic on the roads and lanes that late on Saturday night. And the stone gate pillar on the north side of the driveway is the better one because it's well shaded by the birches and covered with climbing ivy, making a safer spot for concealing the money-bag than the south gatepost, which is bare stone. Whoever devised this plot is acquainted with the neighborhood.

WATSON: But it shouldn't be hard to collar the fellow who picks up the money. How's this: We have two men on fast horses hidden by the road. When the guilty party rides up and snatches the money-bag, we snatch him!

HOLMES: Well and good, but if the kidnapers are serious, there will be a second conspirator waiting somewhere for his partner to bring the money, and if he doesn't, I would fear for the lady's life.

MUSIC: MOURNFUL MOTIF (UNDER)

WATSON: Well, Holmes went back to his room and I went to bed and fell asleep, wondering: Was I going to see Sherlock Holmes defeated at last?

MUSIC: OUT

253

WATSON: After an almost sleepless night, I awoke when I heard the household stirring below, and I got up and rapped on Sherlock Holmes's door. It was seven-thirty, much earlier than he likes to rise at home. Finally he replied through the door, saying he would meet me downstairs, which he did some fifteen minutes later. He looked tired and haggard, and he hadn't shaved.

HOLMES: Good morning, Evan. Where is our host this morning?

EVAN: My father is taking an early train to London, to go to the bank for the ransom money, thank God. Mr. Holmes . . . .

HOLMES: Yes, Evan?

EVAN: Let me appeal to you: Leave now, and let my father pay the ransom! Otherwise, you know what they may do to Alice! I beg of you!

HOLMES: I understand your feelings. But give me another hour to see the place where she was abducted. If there are no clues there, Watson and I will do as you ask.

EVAN: Well, then let's go. It's about half-a-mile, just over the ridge by a grove of oak trees.

MUSIC: OMINOUS MOTION (UNDER)

WATSON: We tramped across the meadow, Holmes in the lead, his head down, watching for any telltale sign. He walked slowly with his hands behind him, while Evan and I were a few feet back.

MUSIC: OUT

SOUND EFFECT: MEN WALKING THROUGH STRAW AND WEEDS

EVAN: (UP) What worries me is, they could be in the trees this very minute, watching!

WATSON: I'm sure Holmes has weighed the possibilities.

EVAN: If it's your reputation you're worried about, Mr. Holmes, you can be assured my father and I won't broadcast your failure. Or is it your fee that you're afraid to lose?

WATSON: I say! There's no cause for rudeness, my good man!

EVAN: (CHOKING BACK A SOB) Oh . . . I'm sorry! Forgive me! It's just that I'm so terrified that –

HOLMES: (OFF-MICROPHONE) Hold up.

SOUND EFFECT: STEPS STOP

HOLMES: (SLIGHTLY OFF-MICROPHONE) This, I take it, is where you and Miss Royce were stopped by the two horsemen.

EVAN: That's right!

HOLMES: Yes. The hoofprints match your description of the scene. And here are the tracks of two horses heading into the oak grove.

EVAN: Yes, that's right. Does this help in some way, Mr. Holmes?

HOLMES: (GLOOMILY) No. No, it only confirms what you described.

EVAN: Then please go back to London! I'll fix it up with my father. I'm sure he'll pay whatever you ask.

HOLMES: There will be no fee. Come along, Watson. I've done all I can do here.

MUSIC: STING TO BRIDGE AND UNDER

WATSON: To say I was stunned would be putting it mildly. In all the years I've worked alongside Sherlock Holmes, this was the first time he has ever admitted defeat. I couldn't think of anything to say that would comfort him. We walked back to the mansion in silence. Evan seemed geatly relieved, and was almost cheerful.

MUSIC: SEGUE TO

255

WATSON: We were driven to the railway station at Tunbridge Wells by the Waldron's stable man. Holmes was absolutely silent. And then, after we got off at the station . . . .

HOLMES: (CHEERFUL) It's a lovely morning, Watson, and that walk in the field has given me a lion's appetite! Let's find ourselves some bangers and eggs and good strong coffee, what say?

SOUND EFFECT: THEY WALK ON PAVEMENT (UNDER)

WATSON: But we'll miss our train!

HOLMES: There will be another one. But breakfast first. Let's try that inn across the way. You'll notice they have a telegraph station. I'm expecting a wire.

WATSON: Here? Why would you be getting a telegram here?

HOLMES: Because I sent one from here last night.

WATSON: You did? You came into town? When?

HOLMES: At midnight.

SOUND EFFECT: STEPS STOP, DOOR OPENS, WALK IN, CLOSE DOOR. LIGHT CONVERSATION IN BACKGROUND

WATSON: (HUSHED TONE) At midnight? I thought you were in bed and asleep at midnight!

HOLMES: I haven't slept since we left London. (UP) Ah, my good man. Is there a telegram for Holmes?

MAN: Yes sir, it just came in. Here you are.

HOLMES: Thank you.

SOUND EFFECT: RIPPING OPEN FLIMSY ENVELOPE

256

HOLMES: (PAUSE) A-ha! (CHUCKLE) Well, Watson. Now for some breakfast.

SOUND EFFECT: (UNDER) THEY WALK TO A TABLE AND SIT

WATSON: Why did you come here at midnight, and without telling me? I'd have been glad to come with you.

HOLMES: There was no need to rob your sleep. And I did have company.

WATSON: Who drove you?

HOLMES: Mr. Lowell Waldron himself. Fine chap. We had a very instructive conversation.

WAITRESS: Hello, sirs. What'll it be?

HOLMES: Three large breakfasts, please. And a pot of coffee. A third party will be joining us shortly.

WAITRESS: Very good.

WATSON: A third party?

HOLMES: Yes. One of the players in the case.

WATSON: I thought you're abandoning the case?

HOLMES: No, Watson. I've solved the case.

WATSON: You've solved it? After all that despair back at Amblehurst?

HOLMES: Quite necessary. Here. Perhaps this telegram will explain.

SOUND EFFECT: FLIMSY PAPER UNFOLDED

WATSON: Good heavens, it's a transatlantic cable! From Richmond, Virginia! (READING) *"To Sherlock Holmes, Tunbridge Wells,*

257

England. Party in question unknown here, regards, Clarence Martin, Manager, Royce Tobacco Growers."

HOLMES: Yes. There is no Alice Royce.

WATSON: Then who is she?

HOLMES: Shall we find out?

WATSON: What do you mean?

HOLMES: She's taken lodging right here in the inn. Under an assumed name, of course.

WATSON: How do you know that?

HOLMES: Only one unattached female registered here Wednesday night. And this is the only inn. Ah, here comes our friend.

WATSON: Good grief! Waldron! I thought he'd gone to London.

LOVELL: (MOVING ON) Here I am, Mr. Holmes. Good morning, Doctor.

HOLMES: Here is the reply to my wire. Read it for yourself

LOWELL: (PAUSE) I see. How did you know she was an imposter?

HOLMES: I suspected her at first, because well-bred young women seldom travel overseas alone – even Americans.

LOVELL: She was after her fortune, wasn't she? Thought she'd marry into money, so she passed herself off as an heiress and romanced my poor naive son! Well, I'd have found out soon enough!

HOLMES: Possibly when it was too late. Now, if you're ready, Mr. Waldron, she's upstairs in Room One, registered as Lucy Blake.

MUSIC: STING

SOUND EFFECT: KNOCK ON DOOR. DOOR OPENS

ALICE: (GASPS) – You?

LOVELL: Hello, "Alice".

ALICE: You've – You've come to rescue me! Oh, thank goodness!

SOUND EFFECT: STEPS IN, DOOR CLOSES

HOLMES: Your performance is over, Miss Blake.

ALICE: Who are these men?

LOVELL: Sherlock Holmes, England's finest detective, and his friend Doctor Watson.

ALICE: Then we must hurry away before those terrible kidnapers come back!

HOLMES: I think we'll stay here a while.

ALICE: No, you can't! They'll kill you! They'll kill us all! Let me go! Put me on a train to London! I'll be safe there!

WATSON: I hear someone's coming up the stairs, Holmes!

ALICE: It's him!

HOLMES: Quiet, all of you! Watson, Waldron, into the vestibule! Miss Blake, there is no possible escape for you unless you cooperate fully. If you do, we may let you go. Now – Receive your visitor as if we weren't here!

SOUND EFFECT: TAP ON DOOR

HOLMES: (WHISPERS) Open it!

SOUND EFFECT: DOOR OPENS

EVAN: (BREATHLESSLY) Lucy! I've got great news! The old man's gone to London for the money! We'll be out of it and away by ten tomorrow night!

259

LUCY: (NOW IN COCKNEY DIALECT) I – I don't think so, Evan.

EVAN: Why? The plan worked perfectly! Sherlock Holmes gave up! The old man's getting us ten-thousand pounds!

LOVELL: The "Old Man" is right here. And all you'll be getting is the back of my hand! You're a poor excuse for a son. Or a man!

EVAN: Oh, yes, that's right! You never cared about me! It was Charles! Charles gets everything, I get nothing! Well, I met Lucy in a London music hall and I coached her to play Alice.

LUCY: Yeah, and I done all right! I think the old man even fancied me!

LOVELL: You little guttersnipe! Get me out of here, Mr. Holmes.

SOUND EFFECT: DOOR SLAMS. THREE MEN WALKING DOWNSTAIRS

WATSON: Holmes, tell me! When did you suspect Evan was in on this?

HOLMES: From the beginning, Watson. But this morning when we saw the hoofprints he said were from the kidnapers' horses. We had a heavy dew last night. Those hoofprints were made after the dew fell. And all by one horse. I'm truly sorry, Mr. Waldron.

MUSIC: *DANSE MACABRE* UP AND UNDER

WATSON: Now you can see that my title for this adventure, "The Woman From Virginia", was a bit of irony on my part. But Holmes marked this case a success, and Mr. Waldron rewarded him quite handsomely. As for Evan? At last report he was seen hanging around the stage door at a certain music hall in London. I hope you've enjoyed this story, and I'll tell you another case of Sherlock Holmes . . . *when next we meet*!

MUSIC: UP AND OUT

The Adventure of the Samovar

CHARACTERS

- SHERLOCK HOLMES
- DR. JOHN H. WATSON
- MARY MORSTAN WATSON
- CHRISTINE – *Mary's school chum. They have similar backgrounds*
- MR. HARRIER – *Scholarly, frail, mid-sixties, upper-class British*
- ANTON BOROCHEV – *Gruff-sounding Russian*

SOUND EFFECT: OPENING SEQUENCE, BIG BEN, STREET SOUNDS

ANNOUNCER: *The Further Adventures of Sherlock Holmes . . . .*

MUSIC: *DANSE MACABRE* (UP AND UNDER)

WATSON: My name is Doctor John H. Watson. For many years I was a close companion of Sherlock Holmes. However, in the spring of the year 1889, Miss Mary Morstan agreed to be my wife, and I moved out of the lodgings I had shared with Holmes on Baker Street to a flat above the practice I'd purchased in Paddington. It was while Mary and I were living there that the occurrence I am about to relate brought me back into close contact with the great detective, and the dangerous circumstances which arose from what seemed a commonplace crime.

SOUND EFFECT: CITY PARK, 19th CENTURY

WATSON: It was a fine evening, just twilight on July the 2nd. After my office hours, Mary and I often liked to stroll through Paddington Park. On this particular occasion we had just decided to buy our supper from a street vendor, but as we approached his cart, Mary suddenly seized my hand.

MARY: John! You see that woman in black who just passed by? I know her!

WATSON: Which woman?

MARY: The one pushing a perambulator. It's Christine Tedding, I know it is! Good gracious! It's been ten years! Come, let's stop her!

SOUND EFFECT: STEPS HURRY ON PAVING

MARY: (UP) Excuse me! Excuse me, madam!

SOUND EFFECT: STEPS COME TO A STOP

MARY: Pardon me, but aren't you Christine Tedding?

CHRISTINE: I – I beg your pardon?

MARY: Christine? It *is* you! I'm Mary Morstan! From the boarding school in Edinburgh! Don't you remember?

CHRISTINE: Oh! Oh, yes, of course! Mary Morstan! I didn't know you at first!

MARY: How lovely to see you! Oh, this is my husband, John Watson. John, Christine was one of my best friends through my teen years.

WATSON: Pleasure, I'm sure.

MARY: Well, and I see you've started a family! Is it a boy or a girl?

CHRISTINE: A boy.

MARY: Oh, let me see him!

CHRISTINE: Well, actually, I keep this dark netting over the carriage because the baby's eyes are sensitive to light. The doctor was quite firm about it

WATSON: Yes, I'm quite familiar with that condition. Photophobia, it's called. Rather rare in infants but not uncommon.

MARY: John's a doctor.

CHRISTINE: Oh. Well, I'd love to talk with you, but I really must be getting back. Oh, I think he's awake. Hello, darling. Are you hungry? (SHE TURNS AWAY AND MAKES A BABY'S CRYING NOISE) Yes, mama will take you home and feed you.

MARY: Of course, we mustn't delay you. But Christine, do call on us sometime soon. John, give her your card.

WATSON: Oh. Yes. Of course. Here you are.

MARY: We live in Norfolk Square. And you must live nearby yourself.

CHRISTINE: Oh! "Doctor John H. Watson". Well, I, uh – I really must be getting back. (FADING) Pleasure to have seen you. I do hope we run into each other again, sometime.

SOUND EFFECT: HER FOOTSTEPS FADE AWAY

MARY: (PAUSE) How curious.

WATSON: Eh?

MARY: When we were girls, she was fun-loving and amusing and a constant chatterbox. Now, she seems – a bit distant.

WATSON: It's not unusual for a mother to be protective, especially if her infant has some abnormality.

MARY: Oh, poor Christine. Do you suppose he's deformed?

WATSON: She probably doesn't want our sympathy.

MARY: I know, but – when we were girls, she was always putting on plays, taking different characters – now it's almost as if she didn't want to talk to me!

WATSON: (CHUCKLING) Come on, Mary. I'm the one who writes about Sherlock Holmes, remember?

MUSIC: UNDERCURRENT

WATSON: My modest medical practice occupied me for most of the next day, but the fate that governs our lives must have been alerted by my mention of Sherlock Holmes, for Holmes was soon to reappear at our doorstep, and any concern about Mary's old school friend was forgotten. Mary was determined to make a mystery out of our brief meeting with the former Christine Tedding, and the next afternoon while I was seeing a patient, she walked by herself to Paddington Park hoping to see her again. When she returned after dark, I admonished her about being out alone.

MUSIC: OUT

MARY: Oh, John, don't scold me, you really mustn't worry. Perfectly respectable women travel all over London by themselves these days.

WATSON: Yes, and so does Jack the Ripper.

MARY: Oh, that was last year! Besides, Paddington Park isn't exactly Soho, is it? And it's full of people day and night. Anyway, Christine didn't show up. Here, I bought you the paper to read while I see about supper.

WATSON: Thank you. I was going to go out for one.

SOUND EFFECT: HE UNFOLDS A NEWSPAPER

MARY: (MOVING OFF) Perhaps you never had an old chum you cared about and lost track of, and then have him turn up in some kind of distress, * and not be able to be of any assistance.

SOUND EFFECT: * (OFF) A KNOCK ON THE DOOR

WATSON? Now who can that be?

MARY: Jack The Ripper no doubt, saying he's sorry he missed me!

264

SOUND EFFECT: SHE WALKS OFF, OPENS THE DOOR OFF

MARY: (FAR OFF-MICROPHONE) Why, Mr. Holmes!

HOLMES: (FAR OFF-MICROPHONE) Good evening, Mrs. Watson. Ah, just back from Paddington Park, I see. Is your good husband at home?

MARY: Why, yes. Won't you come in.

SOUND EFFECT: HE STEPS IN, DOOR CLOSES (OFF). STEPS ON-MICROPHONE (UNDER)

MARY: (MOVING ON-MICROPHONE) But how on earth did you know I was at the park, Mr. Holmes? Did you see me there?

HOLMES: (MOVING ON-MICROPHONE) No, I was nowhere near it. (ON-MICROPHONE) Ah there, Watson!

WATSON: Holmes! I haven't seen you since Boscombe Valley! What a surprise! Welcome old chap!

MARY: May I bring you some tea, Mr. Holmes? Of course it's supper time now. Perhaps you'll join us.

HOLMES: So it is. Yes. I'd be glad to join you. One has to eat somewhere.

MARY: (FADING) I'll just go and see what I can offer you, if you'll excuse me.

HOLMES: (CALLING) Oh, and it was the petals, Mrs. Watson!

MARY: (OFF-MICROPHONE) What?

HOLMES: There were cherry blossom petals on the collar of your coat and hat, which you hadn't had time to take off or you'd have noticed them. Flowering cherries are found nowhere else in this area but in Paddington Park, and just now they're losing their blossoms. That's how I knew where you'd been just before I called. Elementary, really.

265

MARY: (OFF-MICROPHONE) Of course. I should have known.

<u>SOUND EFFECT: (OFF) KITCHEN DOOR CLOSES</u>

WATSON: (CHUCKLING) Still up to your old tricks, I see, Holmes.

HOLMES: Keen observation is not a trick, but a necessity of my profession, as it is in yours. Now, Watson, to the problem at hand. A burglary took place in this neighbourhood yesterday afternoon.

WATSON: Yesterday? Really! I haven't had a chance to look at tonight's paper.

HOLMES: You won't find notice of it in the paper because the victim didn't report it to the police. He reported it only to me.

WATSON: Oh?

HOLMES: We've exchanged telegrams twice today. In his second wire, he explained it might have international repercussions if the theft became public knowledge. Well, generally as you know, burglary and other low-class crimes bore me because they seldom test my skills, but in this instance, I was intrigued, because the burglar acted in broad daylight and carried off only one thing: A samovar.

WATSON: A samovar? One of those Russian tea-kettles?

HOLMES: Well, a samovar is a bit more elaborate than a tea-kettle, Watson. Quite a noble piece of workmanship.

WATSON: Yes, but why steal a samovar and nothing else?

HOLMES: Indeed. And when we learn that, we'll find the thief.

WATSON: That is intriguing!

HOLMES: Then you'll join me in my little inquiry?

266

WATSON: Holmes! You know nothing would please me more!

HOLMES: Excellent. The burglary was committed at the home of a language professor at Dean's College, Mr. Thomas Harrier. He lives at 29 Charter Oak Lane. That's only a few blocks from here. I told him I'd visit him this evening.

MUSIC: STING TO UNDERCURRENT

WATSON: After supper under threatening skies, Holmes and I took umbrellas and walked over to Charter Oak Lane. Number 29 was a tall, narrow edifice with four wooden columns intended to suggest Grecian architecture. Double front doors stood atop a rise of six steps, and behind this facade lurked a succession of small dark rooms. Mr. Harrier guided us through them until we reached his office. There, he stood behind a desk piled high with books and papers, and drew his shawl around his narrow shoulders as if to begin a lecture.

MUSIC: OUT

HARRIER: Until 1840, you see, this was a private library. Then a sanitarium, and at last, a small school of some kind. When the landlord put it on the market five years ago, I bought it for a song and moved in with all my books.

HOLMES: Yes. Now Mr. Harrier, tell us please about the missing samovar.

HARRIER: It was made of brass, it stood around twenty-five inches, and was quite heavy. I kept it here in this cabinet, along with the silver service you see here.

WATSON: Sterling silver? Very handsome.

HARRIER: Worth much more than the samovar. So why didn't the blackguard take my silver as well as the samovar?

HOLMES: How did you acquire the samovar?

HARRIER: Well, it didn't belong to me, you see. I was keeping it for a Russian chap called Valery Tamarov. He said he'd come

267

to London to escape the agents of the Czar. But he was penniless, so I hired him for next to nothing to help me translate some rare books dating back to the beginning of the Romanov Dynasty.

HOLMES: Why did Tamarov want you to keep the samovar?

HARMER: Well, he had no permanent address, you see. I don't know where he stayed one night to the next, poor devil. He'd been here scarcely a week and then on Friday he didn't turn up, and now his only valuable posession is stolen! I fear for his life.

WATSON: What is so valuable about this particular samovar?

HARRIER: All Tamarov would say was that it was meant to be a gift to Czar Alexander the Third, and that if it was known to be on British soil it could provoke grave consequences between Russia and England, and that if he was found with it, he'd be killed!

HOLMES: And you said in your wire that the theft occurred sometime yesterday afternoon.

HARKER: Yes. I was out of the house between two-thirty and eight. I teach a late class at the college on Tuesday and Thursdays, you see – seldom get back before eight because I like to stop off for supper at Falstaff's on East High Street before coming home, and then I generally work here in my study until I nod off. So the thief had more than five hours, you see.

MUSIC: UNDERCURRENT

WATSON: Holmes and I inspected the doors and windows, then we made a room-to-room survey led by Mr. Harrier with a lamp. At last we came to an unused back room.

MUSIC: OUT

SOUND EFFECT: DOOR OPENS

WATSON: Hmm. What's that I smell in here? Mold, isn't it?

HARRIER: Yes, it's always damp in here. I've never found a use for this room, so I never have a fire in here.

<u>SOUND EFFECT: HOLMES WALKS AROUND THE ROOM</u>

HOLMES: (OFF-MICROPHONE) And this door in the corner?

HARRIER: Oh, that's just a closet. Never use it.

<u>SOUND EFFECT: (OFF) HOLMES OPENS THE CLOSET DOOR</u>

HOLMES: (OFF) (PAUSE) Well, here's where your moldy smell comes from. A-ha! Come have a look in here!

<u>SOUND EFFECT: THE TWO MEN WALK TO THE CLOSET</u>

HOLMES: Were you not aware that there is a loose panel in the back wall of the closet?

HARRIER: A loose panel? By Jove! Well, that's where the damp's been coming from!

HOLMES: And something more than the damp has come in, I daresay. May I have that lamp?

HARRIER: Here you are.

HOLMES: (MOVING ABOUT) Yes. A two-foot wide section of the wall swings up. It's hung on two leather hinges. And from this closet it's only a step to the ground and the pathway in back. Ah, and there's a bit of earth no doubt tracked in by the burglar. Yes, still moist.

HARRIER: So that's how he got in!

HOLMES: And got out with the samovar.

HARMER: But – good heavens! I didn't know about this hole in my wall! I wonder how long it's been here?

269

HOLMES: For some years, from the look of it. By its narrow size, I would suppose this little escape was used by students when this house was a school. The wonder is that you haven't had more unwelcome visitors.

HARRIER: By heaven! I'll have a carpenter seal that up first thing in the morning!

MUSIC: UNDERCURRENT

WATSON: Holmes took the lamp and some newspapers round to the narrow path which ran behind the house. A fine mist was falling. The secret door was almost invisible unless one knew where to look. He placed the lamp on the ground, spread out the newspapers, and got down on his hands and knees to inspect the space just below the door.

MUSIC: OUT

SOUND EFFECT: FAINT LONDON BACKGROUND

HOLMES: A-ha. Yes!

WATSON: You found footprints?

SOUND EFFECT: HE STANDS UP, BRUSHING OFF HIS HANDS AND TROUSERS

HOLMES: Footprints, yes, and something better. Mr. Harrier, are there children living in this neighbourhood?

HARRIER I never hear any. Why? You surely don't think a child did it?

HOLMES: I never dismiss any possibility until it becomes an impossibility.

WATSON: This Russian fellow who's missing: Do you think he might have come back and taken it?

HARRIER: Tamarov? Why would he sneak in and steal it when all he had to do was ask for it and I'd have given it back to him?

270

HOLMES: What size of fellow was he?

HARRIER: Oh, normal size – shaped something like Doctor Watson here. Perhaps just a bit thinner.

MUSIC: UNDERCURRENT

WATSON: I returned home and told Mary all that had gone on, and around ten o'clock we retired for the night. But the next morning, I had barely dressed when Holmes was at the door!

MUSIC: OUT

SOUND EFFECT: DOOR OPENS

HOLMES: Watson! Our simple case of burglary has turned deadly!

WATSON: What do you mean?

HOLMES: A man's corpse was dumped in front of my door in Baker Street last night. He'd been fiendishly tortured. Even though the clothes were blood-soaked, there was no mistaking that they were foreign. I notified the police immediately and then took a cab to Harrier's place and brought him to the morgue, and he instantly identified the body. As I suspected, it was the Russian, Tamarov!

WATSON: Good Lord!

HOLMES: Watson, this was meant as a warning. We're dealing with an adversary who will stop at nothing. He knows we're on his trail, and I have no doubt he would kill to keep us from learning more!

MUSIC: UNDERCURRENT

WATSON: Who was this desperate killer? We were soon to learn the answer. But before that, Holmes and I made a discovery about our client, Professor Harrier, which changed the complexion of the whole case. Holmes had been holding a cab while we talked, and he urged me to come with him back to Mr.

271

Harrier's residence, where he feared Harrier was ill from the shock of having to identify Tamarov's battered corpse. And when we saw him, he certainly was agitated.

MUSIC: OUT

HARRIER: I swear to you, I had no idea I was helping seal the poor fellow's doom when I agreed to decode the samovar!

HOLMES: Decode the samovar? You told us you were translating rare books.

HARRIER: I lied. The samovar held the names of several men, encrypted in a very novel kind of code.

HOLMES: And you were able to decode them?

HARRIER: I pray you will keep this in confidence: In addition to my work at the college, I sometimes work for the War Office as a code analyst.

HOLMES: Then decoding the samovar was an official assignment?

HARRIER: Yes. That's why I couldn't have the police in, you see. This was all *sub rosa*. Otherwise there could be an international incident!

WATSON: Mr. Harrier, I'm going to give you some powders to help you relax.

HOLMES: Mr. Harrier – those names on the samovar – ?

HARRIER: The leaders of a secret Russian revolutionary society. The men who were responsible for the murder of Czar Alexander II in St Petersburg eight years ago! They were inscribed on the samovar in the most devilish code I've ever seen. The samovar was a sort of icon, you see, a sacred thing to the insurrection. Tamarov stole it away from them on orders of the Czar, and the Czar didn't know who could decode it, so he appealed to our government for help, and the War Office called me to try. In secret, of course.

272

WATSON: Do you have any water handy?

HARRIER: What? Oh, here, in this decanter.

WATSON: Very good. I'll prepare the powders for you to drink.

<u>SOUND EFFECT: GLASS DECANTER UNSTOPPED. POUR INTO GLASS. THEN STIRRED, ALL UNDER DIALOGUE</u>

HOLMES: (OVER SOUND EFFECT) So Tamarov stole the samovar from the revolutionists, and now the revolutionists have stolen it back.

HARRIER: And these men will stop at nothing, Mr. Holmes! On either side, these Russians will stop at nothing!

<u>MUSIC: UNDERCURRENT</u>

WATSON: Meanwhile, the sky grew dark over London and a heavy rain began to fall. I returned home and closed up my practice for the day, having seen not a single patient, and sat with Mary in our front room. And then a cab pulled up in front of the house. I ordered Mary to hide in the back bedroom, and I stepped to the mantelpiece and pulled my Adams six-shot revolver from its case, and stood back from the window. A black-cloaked woman emerged from the cab and hurried up to our door!

<u>MUSIC: OUT</u>

<u>SOUND EFFECT: TAPPING ON THE DOOR</u>

WATSON: Female or not, I greeted the visitor with a gun in my hand!

<u>SOUND EFFECT: DOOR OPENS</u>

CHRISTINE: Doctor Watson? Doctor, it's Christine, Mary's friend. We met in the park the other day, remember? You gave me your business card. Why do you point that gun at me?

WATSTON: Oh! Oh yes, of course! I didn't recognize you. Please, come in!

SOUND EFFECT: SHE STEPS IN. THE DOOR IS CLOSED

WATSON: Uh, please excuse me, I ah, thought you might be someone else. It's all right. Now, what can I do for you? Is your baby ill?

CHRISTINE: Yes, dreadfully ill! He's burning up with fever, and his breath is raspy. And he's coughing and won't stop crying!

WATSON: Do you have no regular physician?

CHRISTINE: Well – we're new to the district.

WATSON: Ah.

CHRISTINE: But I thought, with you being Mary's husband and a doctor and all –

WATSON: Of course. Where is the child now?

CHRISTINE: We have rooms in Brixton Road.

MARY: (OFF, CALLING) John? Is that Christine I hear?

WATSON: (CALLS BACK) Yes, she says her baby is sick.

MARY: (MOVING ON) Oh, Christine! I'm so sorry!

CHRISTINE: Hello, Mary. Have I come at a bad time?

MARY: No, no, of course not.

CHRISTINE: But the gun – ?

MARY: Don't worry about it. John has been helping Sherlock Holmes investigate a crime! .

CHRISTINE: Really! Sherlock Holmes! I've heard of him! How exciting that must be!

274

MARY: Christine, you're drenched! Did you walk?

CHRISTINE: No, no, I hired a cab.

WATSON: Mary, I'm going to go see her baby. Here, take the gun, and don't let anyone in until I get back.

MARY: No, I want to come with you, John. I'll feel safer beside you. And Christine may need me.

CHRISTINE: No, really, Mary! You mustn't trouble yourself.

MARY: I've helped John before. Please, John?

WATSON: Well – then fetch my bag for me, Mary. It's in the bedroom.

MARY: (MOVING OFF) I'll be right back.

MUSIC: UNDERCURRENT

WATSON: And in a few moments we had locked the house and hurried out to a waiting cab. The three of us crowded in, and Christine gave the driver her address.

HOLMES AS DRIVER, OFF-MICROPHONE: 137 Brixton Road, right you are.

SOUND EFFECT: CAB INTERIOR, HORSE TROTTING

MARY: (PAUSE) Well, we have so much to tell each other, haven't we, Christine? Where did you go after we graduated?

CHRISTINE: I've been many places since then.

MARY: And your theatrics – did you keep them up? You were so funny!

CHRISTINE: No, I've found other things to do.

MARY: And you've married! I'm sure John and I will be thrilled to meet your husband.

CHRISTINE: And I'm sure he'll be thrilled to meet you both.

MUSIC: (SEGUE TO UNDERCURRENT)

WATSON: In a few minutes the cab drew up before a dilapidated three-storey building. Christine led us into the ground floor hallway and to a door at the back, which admitted us to a barren room. A perambulator stood against the far wall. And beside it stood a man in his shirt-sleeves.

MUSIC: OUT

SOUND EFFECT: DOOR CLOSES

ANTON: (OFF) Who is this woman?

CHRISTINE: His wife. She insisted on coming. But it may be better this way.

ANTON: You fool woman! Can't you follow orders?

SOUND EFFECT: HE WALKS OVER AND SLAPS HER

CHRISTINE: (SCREAMS IN PAIN)

ANTON: Now we have two to get rid of!

WATSON: I say. how dare you strike that woman!

ANTON: Shut up! You saw what I did to that traitor Tamarov!

MARY: John, open your medical bag. She may be hurt!

MARY: But – where's the baby?

CHRISTINE: Oh, Mary, you stupid cow! There is no baby! There never was! How else was I to get the samovar from Harrier's house to ours?

276

MARY: But you had a baby in the pram yesterday! I heard him!

CHRISTINE: You heard me! You forget, I could make all kinds of voices when we were doing our plays in school! I could fool anyone!

SOUND EFFECT: POLICE WHISTLE. POLICEMAN POUNDS ON DOOR

HOLMES: Come in, Officer! Everything's under control!

MUSIC: *DANSE MACABRE* UP AND UNDER

WATSON: – as indeed it was. As Holmes explained later, when the cab brought Christine Tedding to our door, Holmes changed places with the driver and had the driver notify the police, who followed Christine's cab. Christine and Borochev were charged with burglary and murder. Christine is now in the Tower of London, and Borochev was deported to Russia, where the Czar no doubt took great pleasure in his execution. I hope you've enjoyed this story, and I'll tell you another case of Sherlock Holmes . . . *when next we meet*!

MUSIC: UP AND OUT

The Adventure of the Seven Shares

CHARACTERS

- SHERLOCK HOLMES
- DR. JOHN H. WATSON
- MARY WATSON
- TRUAX – *Solicitor*
- BARMAID
- GROOM
- CABMAN
- CONSTABLE

SOUND EFFECT: OPENING SEQUENCE, BIG BEN, STREET SOUNDS

ANNOUNCER: *The Further Adventures of Sherlock Holmes . . . .*

MUSIC: *DANSE MACABRE* (UP AND UNDER)

WATSON: I wonder how many friendships between bachelors have been mortally wounded when one of the men marries? My name is Doctor John H. Watson. My friend Sherlock Holmes was perhaps the most celebrated bachelor of his time, and he was vigorously opposed to marriage, and to women, for that matter, owing, I suspect, to a dreadful childhood. But I, on the other hand, have always enjoyed the company of the fairer sex, and none more ardently than Mary Morstan, whom I married in 1889. After that, I saw much less of Holmes. Mary and I had set up housekeeping in Paddington, where I re-opened my medical practice and often spent cozy evenings by the fire, editing my notes on some of Holmes's more interesting cases, with Mary's considerable help. One such evening, she brought up a ticklish point.

MUSIC: (FADE)

MARY: What do you think Mr. Holmes would say if he knew you were letting me read what you've written about him before it goes to your publisher?

WATSON: Well, Holmes has always been ambivalent about my writing.

MARY: Mr. Holmes would be angry if he knew I had anything to do with your stories, wouldn't he?

WATSON: I don't think he'd like it if you were to suggest that I alter the facts in his cases.

MARY: Have I ever done that?

WATSON: No, of course not.

MARY: I think he resents me.

WATSON: Nonsense.

MARY: Well, what else am I to think? He's never once come calling since you moved out of Baker Street.

WATSON: Holmes isn't the type to come calling. As long as I've known him, he never paid a social visit to anyone, without a scientific motive behind it. I think he's quite oblivious to common social practices.

MARY: All the same, I'm sure he thinks it was disloyal of you to marry. Do you miss him?

WATSON: Do I miss him? How can I answer that? I admired his skills, he was the most fascinating . . . the most aggravating . . . the, uh —

MARY: There! You see? You do miss him terribly, don't you? And I've come between you.

WATSON: My dear, life is a series of phases. As a bachelor, I shared part of my life with Sherlock Holmes, but that phase is over, apparently. And now I've entered this wonderful new phase, with you.

MARY: Oh, John! Were you not ready for marriage again? Should we have waited? With your first wife so recently gone –

WATSON: Really, Mary, what good can come of all this?

SOUND EFFECT: AN IMPERIOUS RAP ON THE DOOR WITH A CANE

MARY: Good heavens, who can that be, at this hour?

WATSON: A patient, no doubt. Sit still, I'll see who it is.

SOUND EFFECT: HE WALKS TO THE DOOR AND OPENS IT

WATSON: Holmes!

HOLMES: Are you busy, Watson?

WATSON: Why, no. Come in. Come right in! * You'll never believe it, but we were just talking about you!

SOUND EFFECT: * UNDER AT "YOU'LL". HE WALKS IN, DOOR CLOSES

WATSON: We were just saying, we haven't seen you for a long time –

HOLMES: Are you up to a night of following a fellow who may be involved in murder? I need someone of average stature and common appearance, someone it would be hard to describe later, and naturally I thought of you. You do have some dark clothing, I imagine –

MARY: (INTERRUPTING) Good evening, Mr. Holmes.

HOLMES: Good evening, Mrs. Watson. Now, Waston, while you're on the tail of this chap, I'll be –

MARY: (INTERRUPTING) Would you care for a cup of tea?

280

HOLMES: Any other time, Mrs. Watson, but I'm afraid we haven't time for tea. Anything dark will do, Watson. Do you still have that black coat with the missing button on the left cuff?

WATSON: Yes, wear it all the time. Where would we be going?

HOLMES: I will spend the night in Camberwell. You will follow our man from Paddington Station and observe all that happens.

WATSON: Camberwell? Where you solved that poisoning last year?

HOLMES: Yes, but there is no connection. Now, I must urge you to hurry. I have a cab waiting to take us round to the station.

MARY: Just a minute, Mr. Holmes! Does John not have a choice in this matter? I didn't hear him agree to this midnight foray.

WATSON: It's all right, Mary. (MOVES OFF) I'll only be a minute, Holmes.

SOUND EFFECT: DOOR CLOSES

MARY: So you're sending my husband after a murderer.

HOLMES: You heard me incorrectly, Mrs. Watson. I said the quarry may be involved in murder. It's my job to prevent murder. It may have escaped your notice as you've read Watson's chronicles of my efforts, but a fair share of the cases I have solved have resulted in lives saved.

MARY: I am suitably chastened, Mr. Holmes.

HOLMES: And which of my cases do you have there on your lap?

MARY: Oh. It's the one John calls "The Reigate Squire".

HOLMES: Ah. And are you correcting errors in the manuscript?

MARY: Why, no. The writing is entirely John's, Mr. Holmes. He enjoys sharing it with me, that's all.

281

WATSON: (OFF, MOVING ON) Will this do, Holmes?

HOLMES: Admirably, Watson. Add a black bowler and you're ready.

WATSON: My bowler. Yes, my black bowler. Where did I put it?

MARY: I'll fetch it for you, dear.

SOUND EFFECT: SHE WALKS OFF. DOOR OPENS (OFF)

WATSON: (SECRETIVELY) I'm taking this along too, just in case. I thought a good little pistol would be a comfort in my pocket.

HOLMES: Let us hope you won't need it. But since we're dealing with the greatest of motives for murder, who can say?

WATSON: Is our man a killer?

HOLMES: He may be. Or he may be a victim. Or both.

SOUND EFFECT: MARY WALKS BACK ON (UNDER)

MARY: (MOVING ON) Here you are, dear. I must say, you'll look quite smart as you follow your quarry.

WATSON: Yes, thank you so much, Mary. Well, Holmes?

HOLMES: Then we'll be off.

MUSIC: UNDERCURRENT

WATSON: (NARRATING) And with that, Sherlock Holmes led me into his investigation of one of the most cold-blooded of crimes.

MUSIC: UP AND OUT

WATSON: To my surprise, when Holmes and I hurried out to the cab at my gate, there was a man waiting for us inside.

HOLMES: Get in, Watson, and let me introduce you to Mr. Jacob Truax, the solicitor for the Luscombe brothers of Camberwell. Mr. Truax, my friend, Doctor John H. Watson.

TRUAX: So kind of you.

WATSON: My pleasure.

HOLMES: (UP) To Paddington Station, driver!

SOUND EFFECT: HORSE STARTS TO PULL CAB

HOLMES: Mr. Truax engaged my services a few years ago on behalf of another client of his. You were living away from Baker Street at the time, Watson, with your first wife, I believe.

WATSON: Ah. Well, I'm delighted if I can be of service.

TRUAX: I'm afraid I've cooked up a most volatile recipe for conflict.

HOLMES: We haven't much time, so I suggest you explain the situation to Watson as quickly as possible.

TRUAX: Yes. Well, the Luscombe family own large cattle holdings in South Africa, in the Transvaal. These holdings are a closely-held trust in which the seven living members of the family own all the shares. But the business has lost money for the past two years. The drought, you know. But now, they've received an offer to purchase their holdings. I'm sorry to say, the Luscombes seldom agree with each other on anything, but the offer to take the business off their hands at a fair price met with almost unanimous approval. The one exception was Clive Beckwith, their cousin. He lives in the Transvaal and runs the cattle holdings, and he refuses to sell his shares.

HOLMES: And unless he sells, there can be no purchase.

TRUAX: Exactly.

WATSON: But why wouldn't he want to sell a losing business?

283

TRUAX: Well, it would put him out of a job, for one thing. But more than that, some years ago there was a bitter falling-out between Beckwith and the Luscombe brothers. It grew worse after their father, Angus Luscombe, passed on, and not long afterward, the Luscombes tried to buy Beckwith out, but he wouldn't sell. Said they were trying to cheat him. There was an exchange of angry letters between John, the eldest of the brothers, and Beckwith. It concluded with Beckwith inviting John Luscombe to South Africa, where Beckwith said he would shoot him dead on sight!

WATSON: Oh, I say! Do you think he meant it?

TRUAX: Having met the man, I wouldn't put it past him.

HOLMES: And now, Beckwith is back in England and coming here.

TRUAX: Yes. The by-laws require him to attend a meeting with the other shareholders so that a vote can be taken. Any shareholder not present for this meeting – unless physically unable to attend – must automatically forfeit his shares in the company. Beckwith sailed on the third, and his ship arrived at Liverpool yesterday. I met him at the dock. I must say, he is a fearsome person. I offered him assistance, but he shoved me aside and said that he was well able to "do what must be done" himself.

HOLMES: Which you dutifully reported to the Luscombe family.

TRUAX: Yes, and now their tempers are at hair-trigger! I truly believe John Luscombe may well try to kill Beckwith before he kills one of them! And nothing would please them more than to have one fewer partner with which to share the proceeds of the sale! That's why I called you, Mr. Holmes.

HOLMES: So here is my plan. Mr. Truax has determined that Beckwith is on the train from Liverpool that will stop at Paddington Station in . . . what's the time now? In fourteen minutes. You, Watson, will board that train and ride it the five miles to Kennington Park station – the station nearest to Camberwell. Beckwith will get off. You will shadow his every step. He may engage a room for the night at the Lambeth Inn near the station. Its rates would suit a man of mean circumstances. But unless he sleeps until morning, I must know everything he does for the nine hours before he is to arrive at Camberwell tomorrow.

WATSON: Wherever he goes, I'll be behind him. You may rely on it. How will I know him?

TRUAX: Your man is about forty, tall and wiry, of a nervous and erratic disposition. His left leg is shorter than the right, so he limps. He is dark-haired, well-tanned, with a full beard.

HOLMES: But Watson, he is almost certain to be armed, and he has a vile temper, so do nothing that will put yourself in danger.

WATSON: Don't be concerned, Holmes. I can take care of myself.

HOLMES: Very well . . . .

SOUND EFFECT: HE RAPS ON THE LEATHER CEILING WITH HIS CANE

HOLMES: (UP) Pull up here, driver!

SOUND EFFECT: CARRIAGE PULLS TO A STOP

WATSON: And where will you be?

HOLMES: I will be making the coach house my base of operations. It's all arranged with the Luscombes' groom, a man named Maples. Now, on your way, Watson!

MUSIC: BRIDGE. SEGUE TO

SOUND EFFECT: OLD ENGLISH TRAIN ARRIVES

WATSON: Just a few minutes after Holmes and Truax drove away, the Liverpool train pulled in and I got aboard in a compartment near the head of the train. Ten minutes later, we pulled in to the Kennington Park station and I was among the first to step onto the platform. There were only a few travelers, it being the middle of the night, but I soon spotted Clive Beckwith. He was just as Truax had described him: A tall bearded man with a pronounced limp, and a determined look on his face. He carried a Gladstone as an overnight bag. I let him pass, then as he rounded the corner to the street, I began to follow.

SOUND EFFECT: QUIET STREET SOUNDS BLEND WITH

MUSIC: SOFT UNDERCURRENT

WATSON: There was only one cab at the stand, and Beckwith took it. What was I to do now? At midnight in this end of town there wasn't another cab in sight . . .

SOUND EFFECT: WATSON TROTTNG ON PAVEMENT (UNDER)

WATSON: . . . so I trotted after it, hoping he wouldn't look back and see me. But in another block, the cab stopped in front of the Lambeth Inn, just as Holmes had surmised.

SOUND EFFECT: HIS STEPS DROP TO A WALK, PER DIALOGUE:

WATSON: Beckwith stepped down from the cab, took his bag, paid the driver, and limped in the door, never turning to look my way. I paused for a minute, then walked up to the inn and looked through the glass in the front door. Beckwith had just turned away from the front desk and was climbing the stairs. I was relieved that he had taken a room for the night, but to assure that he had no other plans, I waited across the street for a light to go on in the upstairs window, which it soon did. Then I caught a glimpse of Beckwith pulling off his coat. There was no doubt he was retiring. In another three minutes, he turned down the light.

SOUND EFFECT: STEPS TO A DOOR, DOOR OPENS UNDER DIALOGUE

WATSON: And then I hurried across the street and entered the inn. A barmaid, no doubt the innkeeper's wife, was just about to lock the door for the night.

BARMAID: Sorry, it's past closin' time, and if you're looking for a room, I just rented me last one not five minutes ago.

WATSON: That's all right. Tell me – are these the only stairs to the upstairs floor?

BARMAID: These stairs 'ere? Why'd you want to know that? You a 'tec?

WATSON: No. As a matter of fact, I'm a doctor.

BARMAID: So what's it to you about the stairs?

WATSON: To, uh – to make sure there is an escape route if there should be a fire. I have an elderly friend – one of my patients – who may want a room here. I'm only concerned with his safety.

BARMAID: Well, we aven't had no complaints that I know of. Now, like I say, I'm lockin' up, so you'll 'aye to be on yer way.

MUSIC: UNDERCURRENT

WATSON: I was rather pleased with myself for improvising a plausible reason for asking about the stairs. I left the inn and took up a position across the street again. Fog was beginning to drift in. I thought of my cozy hearth, and Mary, and how I would have much preferred to be snug under a coverlet in my own little cottage, instead of standing in a cold dark street with the damp seeping into my bones, keeping watch on a man who was probably that minute drifting comfortably off to sleep in his room across the street.

SOUND EFFECT: FAINTLY IN BACKGROUND: A CHURCH CLOCK TOLLS ONE

WATSON: It had just gone one o'clock when I decided there was no need to keep watch over a slumbering man, so I started off through the silent streets to find Holmes. Moonlight bathed the wisps of fog in eerie luminescence. After walking about a mile, I came to a walled mansion. Iron gates were hanging agape off rusted hinges. I walked into a courtyard strewn with branches

287

and leaves. There was a dim light in the coach house, which stood to the side of the main building. Behind the coach house was a stable, as is customary in this type of urban estate. I rapped on the coach house door, and Holmes opened it on the instant.

SOUND EFFECT: QUIET (EXTERIOR BACKGROUND)

HOLMES: Watson! What are you doing here? Come in and shut the door!

SOUND EFFECT: HE STEPS IN. DOOR CLOSES

HOLMES: This is Maples, the keeper of the Luscombe's livery and my gracious host for the night. Maples, meet my friend Doctor Watson.

MAPLES: Evenin'.

WATSON: How do you do?

HOLMES: We will both be wanting some good strong hot coffee.

MAPLES: Aye. (FADING) I'll put the pot on.

HOLMES: Now, by your presence, Watson, I presume you have much to report, or you wouldn't have left your surveillance.

WATSON: (A BIT TAKEN ABACK AT HIS MANNER) Well, I followed Beckwith to the Lambeth Inn. He went to bed. There seemed nothing for me to do –

HOLMES: And how do you know he went to bed?

WATSON: Well – I saw him. I saw him go up the stairs, light a lamp in his room, take off his coat, and –

HOLMES: And undress and get into bed?

WATSON: Well, no, I couldn't see that much. But he put out the lamp and I watched his room for the better part of an hour and nothing more happened. And he couldn't have left the room because there's only the one staircase –

HOLMES: And you don't think he knew you were watching him?

WATSON: I'm sure he didn't.

HOLMES: I see. Now tell me, Watson, everything you observed about him from the first moment he stepped off the train.

WATSON: Well, he was dressed in a wrinkled black frock coat and pants that were a bit too short. His boots were scuffed. He bore an intense expression on his face.

HOLMES: And he carried with him – ?

WATSON: What?

HOLMES: Surely he had luggage.

WATSON: Oh! Nearly forgot! Yes, he carried a Gladstone.

HOLMES: Light or heavy?

WATSON: Light, I'd say.

HOLMES: Hmm. Go on.

WATSON: He took a cab and rode to the Lambeth Inn, just as you suspected. Then I –

HOLMES: He took a cab. Where was the cab?

WATSON: It was in the street outside the station.

HOLMES: Only one cab was waiting?

WATSON: Yes, only the one.

HOLMES: I see. He took the cab. And then what?

289

WATSON: I ran after the cab, but it only had a short way to go to the inn. Beckwith got out and went into the inn, rented a room, and went up the stairs. I waited outside for three minutes, then I went in and spoke to the innkeeper's wife. She said she had just rented her last room and was closing for the night. I asked her if there were any back stairs to the upper story rooms, and she said there were not. She asked if I were a detective, and I said no, I'm a doctor, and I was trying to determine if her rooms were safe in event of a fire. (Rather clever, I thought.) And then I went outside and took up a position across the street from the inn. And you know the rest.

HOLMES: And you saw nothing unusual in any of your observations?

WATSON: Unusual? In what way, Holmes?

HOLMES: Did you not think it was curious that a cab might be meeting a midnight train at a residential station? Or that Mr. Beckwith would spend the money to hire that cab to take him barely a mile to a cheap inn?

WATSON: Well, I suppose it's quite painful for the man to walk any great distance, with one leg shorter than the other.

HOLMES: Yes, of course that could be it. No reason for you to suspect otherwise.

WATSON: Holmes, if I've missed something –

HOLMES: You've done your work well, Watson. In fact, you have provided me with some important keys.

WATSON: I have?

SOUND EFFECT: DOOR UNLATCHED

JOHN: (OFF-MICROPHONE) Hello? Everything right in here?

HOLMES: Ah. Come in, Mr. Luscombe. And you may put away that gun.

JOHN: (MOVING ON) I saw someone come onto the property.

HOLMES: It was my partner, Doctor John Watson. Watson, this is John Luscombe, most senior of the Luscombe brothers. I tells me your cousin has taken a room at the Lambeth Inn.

SOUND EFFECT: DOOR CLOSES

JOHN: Is that so? You're sure?

WATSON: Quite sure. I saw him go up and get ready for bed.

JOHN: Well, then I guess there'll be no fireworks tonight. You can't trust a man who threatens to kill you, Mr. Watson. And all we want is to pay him a fair price for his shares. He's a queer duck, Beckwith. Never knew anyone like him.

HOLMES: I suggest you retire and get your sleep. Watson and I will be your watchdogs until the meeting is over tomorrow.

MUSIC: UNDERCURRENT

WATSON: John Luscombe bid us goodnight and went back into the house. Maples brought steaming cups of coffee which warmed me nicely. When I finished mine, Holmes stood up.

MUSIC: OUT

HOLMES: And now, I regret to do it, but I must send you back out into the foggy night, Watson.

WATSON: Eh? Where do you want me to go this time?

HOLMES: Back to the inn. Walk carefully. You may encounter Beckwith coming this way, and you don't want to be seen. Commence to follow him as you did before. Be on your guard every moment.

MUSIC: URGENT UNDERCURRENT

WATSON: I did as Holmes asked. The fog was lying heavily on the road, but not as much as a rabbit stirred as I walked back to the inn. I took up my post again across the street. Time and again I felt myself nodding off, but I was able to remain alert. Beckwith's window remained dark. But in an hour or so, I began to notice a faint glow, like a sunrise, except this was to the south. The fog seemed to be turning orange! I looked in the direction from which I'd come, and the orange light grew brighter and flickered! Something was on fire! I stood in the street, feeling helpless, when suddenly I heard a horse galloping out of the fog! It was pulling a four-wheel carriage, and it drew up in front of the inn! The driver sprang down and rushed up to me!

MAPLES: Mister Watson! It's me, Maples, from the Luscombe estate! Your friend Mister Holmes told me I'm to get the constable and you and him's to come to Camberwell on the double! Somethin' terrible's happened!

MUSIC: STING, SEGUE TO

SOUND EFFECT: A HORSE GALLOPING OFF WITH A WAGON

WATSON: While Maples went for the constable, I hammered on the door to the inn.

SOUND EFFECT: (ALL UNDER) HE POUNDS ON THE DOOR TO THE INN. PAUSE, THE DOOR OPENS

BARMAID: (OFF-MICROPHONE) What's all the racket?

SOUND EFFECT: HE STOMPS UP THE STAIRS QUICKLY

WATSON: I pushed past the startled woman and bounded up the stairs. Beckwith's room was the first to the left at the landing. I tried the knob and it was unlocked! And just sitting up in the bed was a young man I'd never seen before!

MICK: (DAZED) Here, what do you want?

WATSON: Who are you? Where's Beckwith?

MICK: What d'you mean, breakin' into a man's bedroom like this?

292

WATSON: Beckwith! What have you done with him?

MICK: Listen here, you've got the wrong room! Now get out before I call the constable!

BARMAID: (OFF, MOVING ON) I'm sorry, guy, I couldn't stop 'im! Just what do you think you're doin', anyway? Wakin' up the whole bleedin' household!

WATSON: (OUT OF BREATH, DESPERATE) Just tell me: The man who took your last room tonight – where is he?

BARMAID: You're lookin' at 'im. It was 'im!

WATSON: No! This man isn't Beckwith!

BARMAID: I don't know any Beckwith. This is Mick Thomas, the cabbie!

MUSIC: STING TO UNDERCURRENT

WATSON: I'd been fooled! By some magic, Beckwith had escaped! Maples was waiting in the street with the constable. He went upstairs and brought Thomas down, and we raced back toward the blaze of Camberwell! The four-story building was all but consumed when we turned in the drive.

SOUND EFFECT: IN BACKGROUND – ROARING FIRE

WATSON: Silhouetted against the flames was a man standing by the coach house. A second man sat on the ground with his head in his hands. A third man lay on the ground. As we drove up, Sherlock Holmes turned to look at me, a stricken expression on his face. Beside him sat John Luscombe.

MUSIC: OUT

SOUND EFFECT: FIRE UP

CONSTABLE: All right, what's happened here?

HOLMES: A tragedy. A fatal tragedy.

WATSON: Who is this man on the ground? Beckwith?

HOLMES: Yes. That's Beckwith.

JOHN: (SLIGHTLY OFF-MICROPHONE) I shot him. I saw him in the drawing room, with his coal oil. He'd drenched everything and just as I fired, he tossed a match. The room was a sheet of flames. It took Mr. Holmes and me to drag his body out before the whole house went up!

WATSON: Good heavens! What about your brothers?

JOHN: Mister Holmes and I tried to wake them before the fire got to the second story. But I'm sorry to say . . . we failed.

HOLMES: All of the men perished.

JOHN: We may not have got along, but we loved each other!

WATSON: Holmes, I – I must take much of the blame for this tragedy!

HOLMES: Why, Watson?

WATSON: After I left my observation of Beckwith's room, he must have slipped away. Then the innkeeper rented that room to Thomas, the cab driver here, and Beckwith was free to do his fiendish work.

HOLMES: But that's not quite what happened, Watson. Tell us, Mr. Thomas, why you happened to be sleeping in the inn tonight.

MICK: All right. He's dead so it don't matter any more. I was told to be at the station by midnight, to pick up a man with a limp. When he gets in the cab, he gives me a false beard to wear, then we trade coats, and when we get to the inn, it's me that gets out and books a room, and it's him who drives off in my cab. He give me twenty quid and promises the rig will be back by sunrise.

CONSTABLE: Why would this Mr. Beckwith burn down the house?

JOHN: He wanted all the money from the sale of our property in South Africa. I'm afraid it's that simple. Our solicitor can tell you: Beckwith threatened to kill me.

CONSTABLE: Mick, you didn't know what Beckwith had in mind?

MICK: I swear! I didn't know a thing!

CONSTABLE: Well, looks as if there's nobody to arrest, then.

HOLMES: Perhaps, Constable, you might want to question John Luscombe.

JOHN: What are you saying?

HOLMES: Where did the coal oil come from?

JOHN: Beckwith obviously brought it in the cab he drove out here!

HOLMES: Did you have coal oil in your hansom, Mr. Thomas?

MICK: Me? No!

HOLMES: No. I inspected the cab which was left in the trees west of the house. There was no smell of coal oil in the cab, but I noticed a faint trace of it on your dressing gown, Mr. Luscombe, when you came to the coach house tonight. You were wearing it when you brought the coal oil from wherever you'd hidden it, into the room where you and Beckwith had conspired to set the house ablaze!

JOHN: Conspired? Why would I conspire with Beckwith?

HOLMES: Didn't you and Beckwith plan all along to get rid of those bothersome brothers of yours, so you two could split the proceeds of the sale? And after Beckwith played his role just as the two of you planned it, didn't you shoot him – presumably to stop him from burning your house down – so he would never confess your conspiracy?

CONSTABLE: (PAUSE) Mr. Luscombe, I think you'd better come with me to headquarters. I'm sure the inspector will have some questions to ask you.

MUSIC: *DANSE MACABRE* UP AND UNDER

WATSON: John Luscombe was brought to trial, and with the testimony of Sherlock Holmes and myself, was found guilty on seven counts of murder, and was hanged. And so ends "The Adventure of The Seven Shares". But I'll tell you another story from the life of Sherlock Holmes . . . *when next we meet*!

MUSIC: UP AND OUT

The Head of Jean Malreaux

CHARACTERS

- SHERLOCK HOLMES
- DR. JOHN H. WATSON
- EDMUND STANSFIELD – *Wealthy impresario, fifty-to-sixty, highborn English*
- CHARLOTTE STANSFIELD – *His nineteen-year old daughter, willful and spoiled*
- MRS. DOLAN – *Old woman from Ireland, blunt spoken*

SOUND EFFECT: OPENING SEQUENCE, BIG BEN, STREET SOUNDS

ANNOUNCER: *The Further Adventures of Sherlock Holmes . . . .*

MUSIC: *DANSE MACABRE* (UP AND UNDER)

ANNOUNCER: *The Further Adventures of Sherlock Holmes*

WATSON: My name is Doctor John H. Watson. The story I'm about to tell you tonight might not have happened if Sherlock Holmes hadn't been bored. His *ennui* had set in after he solved the case I called "The Man With the Twisted Lip". Scotland Yard had requested his help on a missing persons case but Holmes declined. Two or three other commissions came, but he said he wasn't interested. So you can imagine my surprise when, early in September in the year, after receiving a telegram, Holmes brightened up.

MUSIC: OUT

SOUND EFFECT: BAKER STREET BACKGROUND (CLOCK, TRAFFIC)

HOLMES: How would you like a change of scene, Watson?

WATSON: What change of scene is that?

HOLMES: Oh, getting out of town, eating some good country cooking, with sparkling company, and a mystery to solve.

WATSON: Elaborate.

HOLMES: The place I have in mind is the coast of Sussex. The sparkling company will be provided by one Edmund Stansfield, the noted impresario – and since he is notably rich and fat, he must set an exceptional table.

WATSON: What about the mystery?

HOLMES: Here, read his telegram.

SOUND EFFECT: TELEGRAM HANDLED

WATSON: (READS) *"Mr. Sherlock Holmes,"* et cetera et cetera . . . *"Outrageous occurances at my estate. Decapitated head victimizing my daughter"* . . . Good heavens! . . . *"Local police no use. I am prepared to pay whatever you ask. Edmund Stansfield, Seacliff Manor, Worthing, Sussex"*. Why, this sounds like a Halloween prank! Are you sure this is worthy of you?

HOLMES: Why not? How many times will I have the opportunity of facing down the supernatural? At the very least, our coffers will be enriched by a wealthy client.

WATSON: Oh, I'll tag along if you're serious about this, but –

HOLMES: Excellent! According to Bradshaw's, we want to take the one o'clock train from Marylebone to reach Worthing in the daylight. I'll wire Mr. Stansfield to expect us.

SOUND EFFECT: BACKGROUND FADES OUT. INTERIOR, TRAIN RUNNING

WATSON: You are unpredictable, Holmes. Recently you've turned down murders and missing person cases, but now you hire on to chase a ghost! Why?

HOLMES: I can give you three reasons. One, I expect to charge a handsome fee commensurate with the degree of my annoyance,

298

which is high. Two, the victim of the prankster is a young woman, and surely you of all people should want to help the fairer sex. And three, in his reply to my wire, Stansfield claimed that the head his daughter saw at her window was that of none other than the famous French maestro and composer, Jean Malreaux, who, you'll remember, was separated from his head by the French government several months ago.

WATSON: I read about that! He shot two men, didn't he?

HOLMES: An oboe player in London and a French guard in Paris. The French weren't so concerned over one English oboeist more or less, but they took umbrage over the killing of one of their gendarmes. And so Monsieur Malreaux's career ended under the guillotine. He became more famous in death than he ever was in life.

WATSON: Then what's his head doing in Worthing?

SOUND EFFECT: TRAIN WHISTLE. ALL BACKGROUND FADES OUT. FADE IN COUNTRY SOUNDS. HORSEDRAWN SHAY HAULS TO A STOP. MEN STEP DOWN OUT OF THE RIG

WATSON: (EXTERIOR) Hmm. Seacliffe Manor is big enough, isn't it?

HOLMES: And quite overgrown. Strange. One would hardly imagine that a wealthy master would tolerate an unkempt estate.

SOUND EFFECT: THE SHAY STARTS UP AND FADES AWAY. MEN WALKING ON GRAVEL

WATSON: (NARRATING) As we approached the front door, it opened, and instead of a butler, an old woman dressed in black, even to her gloves, stepped out to meet us.

HOLMES: (EXTERIOR) (UP) Good afternoon! Is this the Stansfield residence?

MRS. DOLAN (EXTERIOR) (OFF) It is. And you've come down from London?

299

HOLMES: Correct. I believe Mr. Stansfield is expecting us.

MRS. DOLAN: (CLOSER) That he is. And so is his daughter. Just you wait till she tells you her story! Oh. I'm Mrs. Dolan, the housekeeper. I've read about you two in the papers. It's Mr. Holmes and Mr. Watson?

WATSON: Er . . . Doctor Watson.

MRS. DOLAN: They say you've caught a lot of men, but have you ever caught a *dead one*?

HOLMES: No, this will be my first.

MRS. DOLAN: *If* you catch him! (SECRETIVELY) Back in County Cork, I've seen me share of things like this, y'know!

STANSFIELD: (OFF TO ON) Gentlemen! I see you've met Mrs. Dolan. I am Edmund Stansfield. Thank you for coming. Which of you is Sherlock Holmes?

HOLMES: I am Sherlock Holmes. This is my associate, Doctor John H. Watson.

STANSFIELD: It's a privilege to meet you both. I appreciate men of your standing agreeing to help in this bizarre situation.

HOLMES: We have agreed to help only because of your standing.

MRS. DOLAN: I'll be taking your bags up to your rooms.

WATSON: Er . . . Mrs. Dolan, shouldn't a butler be carrying those?

MRS. DOLAN: We've got no butler.

WATSON: No butler?

STANSFIELD: He left us. I expect to hire another one any day now. Well, shall we go in and talk about why you're here?

MUSIC: STING

STANSFIELD My daughter will be here presently. She's the one who's been seeing the, uh, head.

HOLMES: You haven't seen it?

STANSFIELD No, I have not, and I doubt that I shall. But others in the household believe in it. I've lost Stinson, a butler I've had for going on ten years. Both maids and our groundskeeper quit. I had to double my cook's wages or she'd have quit too. They're locals, and they tend to be superstitious. All I have left are Mrs. Dolan and the cook, and they're both well along in years.

WATSON: And Mrs. Stansfield . . . ?

STANSFIELD My wife died four years ago.

WATSON: Oh, I'm sorry to hear that. My condolences.

HOLMES: Mr. Stansfield, how long has the apparition been seen?

STANSFIELD For about the last fortnight.

HOLMES: Now, please tell me everything you can about the late Monsieur Malreaux.

STANSFIELD: Well, as you may know, Jean Malreaux was a noted composer and conductor from France, who concertized all over Europe. I brought him over here to appear in England and Wales conducting the Royal Philharmonic. Every single one of his performances were sellouts! His likeness was displayed in Madame Tussaud's museum!

HOLMES: Yes, so I've read.

STANSFIELD: But . . . as I soon learned, Jean Malreaux was an outrageous womanizer. He was in his mid-forties, very handsome and elegant, and he had his pick of unattached females everywhere we went. London was our last stop on the

301

tour and I held a press reception for him at the Langham, and took my daughter along. That was a fatal mistake!

HOLMES: In what way?

STANSFIELD: As you will see, Charlotte is a beautiful girl, and the moment I introduced her to Malreaux, he began to shower her with attention, to the exclusion of everyone else in the ballroom! Charlotte had never experienced such flattery before, although she was always popular in school. Well, by the time the evening was over, she was thoroughly smitten with him! I forbade her to see him again, but it did no good. Charlotte was visiting him in his rooms at the Langham the afternoon he shot Fletcher Abbott. The concert tour was cancelled. The papers had a field day. Even the Tussaud Gallery removed him!

HOLMES: And what about Fletcher Abbott? The papers all printed different stories.

STANSFIELD: Fletcher was in love with Charlotte and she returned his feelings. He learned where she was and went to the hotel to confront Malreaux in a jealous rage. Abbott was a good oboe player but an even better pugilist, and he knocked Malreaux down, whereupon Malreaux took a pistol and fired it at him, killing him instantly.

WATSON: And your daughter witnessed all this?

STANSFIELD: Yes. Malreaux fled the hotel, leaving Charlotte with the body of her former sweetheart and begging her to lie to the police about what she had witnessed. But to her credit, she told them the truth. She wasn't held.

HOLMES: And Malreaux managed to flee back to France?

STANSFIELD: Fled back to France, but was seized the next day by the Parisian police, who put him in a room for questioning by two men who'd come over from Scotland Yard. Then suddenly he broke away, dashed into the street, hoping to escape. A French policeman tried to stop him, and Malreaux shot him dead! And so he was tried and found guilty of murder, which in France means death by the guillotine.

WATSON: And how did your daughter react to all this?

STANSFIELD: As you can imagine, she was devastated. Her new love kills her old love, then kills again and is beheaded! The papers ate it up! Tussaud's wanted to put Malreaux and Abbott in a special exhibit, which I was able to discourage.

HOLMES: But what about the others in your house who've left your employ. Did any of them see the head?

STANSFIELD: No, but they were afraid of seeing it. As I say, they tend to be superstitious in this neighbourhood.

SOUND EFFECT: (OFF) QUICK RAP ON DOOR, DOOR OPENS

CHARLOTTE: (OFF-MICROPHONE) Father? You wanted to see me?

SOUND EFFECT: BOTH MEN GET OUT OF THEIR CHAIRS

STANSFIELD: Yes, Charlotte. We're going to end this siege and restore some sanity to the place. This is Mr. Sherlock Holmes and Doctor John Watson. Gentlemen, my daughter.

WATSON: A pleasure.

HOLMES: Miss Stansfield.

CHARLOTTE: (VERY SUBDUED) How do you do?

STANSFIELD: I've sent for Mr. Holmes because he is the best detective in all of England, and if anyone can get to the bottom of this mystery, he can!

CHARLOTTE: There is no mystery. I betrayed a man who loved me, and he has returned from Hell to haunt me. If it hadn't been for father bringing him here to England, and for me to capture Jean's heart, he would be alive today.

HOLMES: Miss Stansfield, please describe exactly what you've seen at your window. Leave out no detail, however small.

303

CHARLOTTE: To what end, Mr. Holmes? A tormented spirit can't be driven away by mortal man. Mortal law no longer applies to Jean Malreaux.

STANSFIELD: Now look here, Charlotte – I've persuaded these two gentlemen to come down here and help you! You must cooperate!

CHARLOTTE: No one can help me. And I desire no help. I only wish that Fletcher could also come back! They are the only two men I have ever loved, or ever shall love!

HOLMES: Miss Stansfield! If I could prove to you that the image you have been seeing is not supernatural, wouldn't you be relieved?

CHARLOTTE: Relieved? Of what, Mr. Holmes?

HOLMES: Of your fears. Your feelings of guilt. Your melancholy!

CHARLOTTE: No! If this is to be my lot in life, it is no worse than I deserve, so I'll pay the price.

STANSFIELD: You see, gentlemen, what I'm up against? I can't make her understand that she's not to feel guilty for anything!

WATSON: In my practice, I've seen those who find pleasure in guilt.

CHARLOTTE: I'm not here to get pleasure, doctor.

HOLMES: Will you at least answer a few questions about this spectre that you've seen?

CHARLOTTE: Yes, I suppose so.

HOLMES: Good. Describe the head in detail

CHARLOTTE: It is the head of Jean Malreaux. What more can I say?

HOLMES: Where does it appear?

CHARLOTTE: At my bedroom window. Every night at nine.

HOLMES: *Every* night, with no exception?

CHARLOTTE: Every night.

HOLMES: And always exactly at nine o'clock.

CHARLOTTE: Yes.

HOLMES: And so you go to your bedroom each evening, and wait for the head to appear?

CHARLOTTE: Yes.

HOLMES: Are you always alone in your room at those times?

CHARLOTTE: Yes, after the third appearance when the help quit.

HOLMES: When the head makes its appearance outside your window, does it move?

CHARLOTTE: It . . . seems to float in the air. It twists and turns, and then when it's level with my window, it moves close to the glass and looks at me! The first and second nights it appeared, I fainted . . . dead away! And then ever since, I wait for it to come to me. Some nights he seems to smile at me, but other nights he won't even look at me.

HOLMES: How long does it remain?

CHARLOTTE: I'm not conscious of the time – perhaps two or three minutes.

HOLMES: And when it goes away, how does it move?

CHARLOTTE: The same way as when it came. It just vanishes.

HOLMES: May I see your window?

CHARLOTTE: (PAUSE) I suppose you may. I'll show you the way.

MUSIC: UNDERCURRENT

WATSON: (HUSHED) There was no doubt the young woman was under an emotional strain. As she led us through the house and up the vast stairway, she told us how she had described the appearance to the two maids and the butler, and they stood at her bedroom door on the third night and saw the appearance themselves, after which they turned in their notices.

MUSIC: OUT

SOUND EFFECT: ECHOING FOOTSTEPS CLIMBING STAIRS

HOLMES: I take it, then, that Mrs. Dolan hasn't seen the floating head?

CHARLOTTE: No. But she believes in it. She says visits by restless spirits are quite common in Ireland. My bedroom is just down this hall, gentlemen.

SOUND EFFECT: STEPS IN HALL, COME TO A STOP

CHARLOTTE: Here we are.

SOUND EFFECT: DOOR OPENS

CHARLOTTE: And there's the window.

SOUND EFFECT: HOLMES: WALKS SHORT DISTANCE. STOPS

HOLMES: (OFF-MICROPHONE) Do you ever open the window?

CHARLOTTE: No, I leave it closed. I am subject to colds.

SOUND EFFECT: HOLMES WALKS SLOWLY BACK ON-MICROPHONE

HOLMES: Thank you, Miss Stansfield. I think I've seen everything I need to see. Now I should like to visit the ground outside your window.

CHARLOTTE: You will understand if I don't accompany you?

HOLMES: By all means, you should conserve your energy for the next appearance of Monsieur Malreaux's head.

MUSIC: STING

WATSON: Holmes, Mr. Stansfield, and I went outside to examine the ground just below Charlotte's second story window . . . .

SOUND EFFECT: RURAL BACKGROUND, STEPS ON GROUND (UNDER)

WATSON: The house was built of smooth river rock, and over the years, deposits of moss had turned the rock green and slippery. Holmes didn't hesitate. He pulled off his shoes, undid his garters, and removed his stockings. Then, barefoot, he proceeded to scale the rock wall, clinging with his toes and his fingers, until he was just under Charlotte Stansfield's window.

STANSFIELD: I never saw anything like it! He climbed that wall like a cat!

WATSON: More like a monkey, actually. Leather shoe soles can't find purchase on anything slick like that rock, so he . . . apes the apes, as he says . . . Heh heh . . . (UP) Find anything, Holmes?

HOLMES: (OFF-MICROPHONE) Yes! Coming down!

SOUND EFFECT: THUMP AS HE HITS SOFT GROUND & LEAVES AND WALKS ON-MICROPHONE

HOLMES: (ON-MICROPHONE) Very interesting.

STANSFIELD: What did you find on the wall?

HOLMES: Nothing but moss.

307

STANSFIELD: No clues, then?

HOLMES: On the contrary, the absence of clues can be a clue in itself. Now we know that, however the prankster did it, he didn't do it from below. The moss has never been touched. So let us retire to the roof.

MUSIC: UNDERCURRENT

SOUND EFFECT: MAN CLIMBS LADDER UNDER AT *

WATSON: We entered the enormous attic from stairs at the end of the upper hallway. The attic was stuffed with old furniture and box after box of stored goods. There was an aisle through the jumble that ended at a ladder. * Stansfield climbed it, produced a key, and unlocked a padlock, which freed a trap door to open onto the roof. Then he stood aside. Holmes stopped and knelt down over a piece of the slate roofing and brushed something into his hand and put it in his pocket. Then he walked to the western edge of the roof. He stood there for close to a full minute. Then he got down on his hands and knees and bent forward until his head and shoulders were extended beyond the wall.

STANSFIELD: (EXTERIOR) (SHOUTS) Be careful not to fall, Mr. Holmes! I don't want another death on my hands!

WATSON: Oh, he's remarkably sure-footed. Holmes has the most precise control of his muscles and nerves of any man I've ever known.

STANSFIELD: He must have! Climbing walls, hanging in space! Well, he's apparently seen all he wanted. Here he comes back already.

SOUND EFFECT: (FADING BACK ON) STEPS ON SLATE

HOLMES: (FADING ON) On the parapet there's a small quantity of recently dried blood.

STANSFIELD: Blood? Are you sure? How recent?

HOLMES: Recent enough to suggest it could belong to the trickster. Who else comes up here?

STANSFIELD: No one. There is no way onto the roof other than the route we've just taken, and as you noticed, climbing into the attic raises quite a clatter.

WATSON: And then there's the climbing back down again.

HOLMES: I'm sorry to dispute you, but there is another way to get onto this roof if you're agile enough. You have a handsome row of poplar trees by the east side of the house, and as you can see, several of their branches extend over the roof.

STANSFIELD: So you mean to say that someone could climb a tree, drop onto the roof, do his trick, and go back the same way he came?

HOLMES: The trees are thick with leaves at this time of the year, so they offer good concealment to anyone climbing in them.

WATSON: But hold on, Holmes – How could someone climb a tree carrying a burden the size of a human head, even if it's a fake?

HOLMES: Suppose he wasn't carrying it?

WATSON: What do you mean?

HOLMES: I hope to make that clear later tonight. Why don't you and Mr. Stansfield go back down. I'd like to spend another few minutes up here looking about.

STANSFIELD: Look as long as you like, Mr. Holmes. Just make sure you don't fall off the roof!

MUSIC: UNDERCURRENT

WATSON: Dinner that night was as informal as an indoor picnic. The cook brought in the courses herself, and Mrs. Dolan went round the table, ladling a hearty stew of lamb, pork, and vegetables onto our plates. Then to my surprise, she seated herself at the table, like a member of the family rather than part of the household staff. She had changed to a dark blue costume, with matching gloves. Conversation was sparse. There seemed to be an air of expectation, punctuated by the chiming of a clock every quarter-hour. When it rang, Stansfield said . . . .

SOUND EFFECT: (UNDER) SOUNDS OF EATING STEW

STANSFIELD: Well, your spectre will start his performance in fifteen minutes, Charlotte, if he's on time tonight.

CHARLOTTE: Father! Could you for once not ridicule? Mr. Holmes, I want you and Doctor Watson to be in my room so you can see him for yourself. Then you'll know I'm not making this up.

HOLMES: Thank you, Miss Stansfield. I was about to ask your permission to do just that. Will you be joining us, Mr. Stansfield?

STANSFIELD: No! I won't give whoever's doing it the satisfaction!

CHARLOTTE: You just don't want to admit that it's real!

STANSFIELD: Ghosts are not real, Charlotte!

MRS. DOLAN: Now hush you, girl. If your pa is afraid of ghosty things, it's not his fault! He wasn't brought up a believer!

STANSFIELD: I think that will be all for tonight, Mrs. Dolan. Thank you for serving us, and goodnight. Sleep well.

MRS. DOLAN: (PAUSE) Yes . . . good night to you all.

SOUND EFFECT: CHAIR MOVED. SHE WALKS SLOWLY OFF-MICROPHONE

WATSON: (PAUSES) Mrs. Dolan seems quite far along in years to be doing such housework. Is she in good health?

STANSFIELD: Strong as a mule and just as stubborn! I think she was actually glad when Stinson quit me and she took on some of his duties.

WATSON: Your former butler?

STANSFIELD: That's right.

CHARLOTTE: If you'll excuse me, I think it's time I went up to my room now.

STANSFIELD: Oh yes, my dear. We mustn't make you late for your *rendezvous*!

CHARLOTTE: Are you gentlemen coming?

HOLMES: Yes, we'll be right along

SOUND EFFECT: CHAIR MOVED BACK

CHARLOTTE: Father, are you sure you won't come this time?

STANSFIELD: Quite sure, thank you.

CHARLOTTE: (SIGH) All right

SOUND EFFECT: SHE WALKS AWAY

HOLMES: (AFTER A PAUSE) Why *won't* you join her, Mr. Stansfield?

STANSFIELD: Why? Because I think the girl is part of the scheme!

HOLMES: What scheme?

STANSFIELD: A scheme of revenge, that's what scheme! I introduced her to Malreaux and she fell in love with him. She's got it in her head that was my fault! Malreaux killed her other suitor, Fletcher Abbott – that was my fault. And when Malreaux was executed for killing a French policeman, why of course, somehow that was my fault too!

WATSON: So you think she is behind all these appearances?

STANSFIELD: Yes, Doctor, I'm afraid I do.

311

HOLMES: Have you told her your suspicions?

STANSFIELD: Oh yes. Of course she denied it, but by then she'd gotten the help so rattled, they quit – superstitious lot! That was her work entirely! I'm sorry to say, Charlotte is headstrong and willful, with a disobedient streak. Of course, with no mother around to raise her properly, and with me away so much of the time, it may be that in some ways I am guilty.

HOLMES: Then who did raise her?

STANSFIELD: Mrs. Dolan. That's why she eats at our table. She's like one of the family.

HOLMES: Mr. Stansfield, if you're convinced that your daughter is responsible for these appearances, do you still want me to expose the sham, even if it implicates your daughter?

STANSFIELD: Yes! That's why I wanted you here!

HOLMES: Then I misunderstood your request for my assistance. What I thought was a need to put a stop to a nuisance, is in reality just a family dispute!

STANSFIELD: No, no! I must have an end to the mystery!

HOLMES: You shall have an end to it tonight. I shall be very much surprised if the floating head appears again after tonight!

MUSIC: OMINOUS UNDERSCORE

WATSON: Holmes and I made our way upstairs. Just as we reached the upper hallway, Holmes looked at his watch.

MUSIC: OUT

HOLMES: I have three minutes before nine. There's something I've got to see. You go ahead to Miss Stansfield's room, Watson, and I'll join you shortly.

WATSON: Well, all right. I do hope you'll be back in time!

HOLMES: Oh, don't worry, I shan't miss it.

WATSON: (NARRATING) I knocked on Miss Stanbury's door and she promptly opened it. There was only one small lamp burning on a night table, illuminating a bedside clock. Aside from that, the room was in darkness. The window, which faced west, showed only the last lingering traces of twilight.

CHARLOTTE: He'll be here in two minutes by my clock.

WATSON: I certainly hope Holmes gets here before then.

CHARLOTTE: Well, at least you'll see what I've been seeing.

WATSON: (PAUSE) Have there been any other supernatural occurrences during these last few weeks?

CHARLOTTE: I don't know, doctor. If there have been, nobody would believe them. Mortals cannot begin to imagine what spirits do . . . or can do. There's no use trying.

WATSON: (NARRATING) I could see that Charlotte Stansfield was becoming increasingly nervous. Unless she was a remarkable actress, I was convinced that she wasn't part of any kind of trick, as her father thought. She now stood as rigid as a sentry, gripping the brass bedstead.

CHARLOTTE: One minute!

WATSON: For a woman who had fainted twice upon seeing the head of her lover at her window, she now trembled with sheer anticipation of seeing it again. Her breath came more and more rapidly. The seconds ticked by. I heard a slight noise in the hallway, and then . . . .

SOUND EFFECT: A DISTANT CLOCK STARTS CHIMING. A RAP ON THE DOOR

CHARLOTTE: (GASPS) Oh, no! Who can that be? Don't answer it!

SOUND EFFECT: HARDER RAP ON THE DOOR

313

CHARLOTTE: Go away!

SOUND EFFECT: THE DOOR OPENS

HOLMES: I take it the moment has arrived to witness the return of Jean Malreaux's head?

CHARLOTTE: Be still! Please! Close the door and be perfectly still!

HOLMES: Just as you wish.

SOUND EFFECT: THE DOOR CLOSES

WATSON: (NARRATING) She never took her eyes from the window. Holmes stood beside me in the darkness with his hands behind his back.

SOUND EFFECT: CLOCK FINISHES STRIKING

WATSON: No sign of the head?

CHARLOTTE: Be still!

WATSON: (WHISPERING) Is he usually right on time?

CHARLOTTE: Yes! Nine o'clock every night! (PAUSE) Well, apparently he's not coming. And you probably are thinking the whole thing is a humbug!

HOLMES: Oh, don't give up so quickly, Miss Stansfield. Turn up the lamp, will you, Watson? The missing head . . . is missing no more. I brought it with me.

CHARLOTTE: (SHRIEKS, AND SHRIEKS AGAIN)

WATSON: From behind his back, Holmes produced an alarmingly realistic head, complete with hair and glistening eyes!

CHARLOTTE: What . . . what are you doing with that?

314

HOLMES: Is this what you've been seeing? Don't turn away, look at it closely. Is this what you thought was Jean Malreaux's head?

CHARLOTTE: It *is* Jean Malreaux's head! Where did you get it? How did you get it?

HOLMES: From a box in the attic, where it was stored between its nightly appearances.

CHARLOTTE: No!

HOLMES: The complexion is beginning to disintegrate slightly. You see, it's made of wax.

WATSON: Like a figure in Madame Tussaud's gallery!

CHARLOTTE: Wax?

HOLMES: And neatly done, too, except for the wear and tear.

SOUND EFFECT: DOOR OPENS

MRS. DOLAN: What's happened? Did the head appear?

HOLMES: Oh yes. The head appeared.

MRS. DOLAN: Did it now? And are you gentlemen satisfied?

HOLMES: Perfectly, Mrs. Dolan. I've been admiring the workmanship. Observe the detailed eyebrows and lashes.

MRS. DOLAN: (PAUSE) Where did you get that?

HOLMES: Right where you've been keeping it, in the attic.

MRS. DOLAN: Me? You're daft! I don't know anything about it!

HOLMES: Please don't bother to deny it. On the roof I found bits of flesh-colored wax. So I stayed behind this afternoon while Watson and Mr. Stansfield returned to the downstairs. I followed a tiny trail of wax droppings to a box amid a pile of others in the attic, and there I found the wax head and the sharp

315

piano wire hooked to it, with a bit of blood on it from the cut on your hand which you concealed with your gloves. You might let Dr. Watson have a look at it. Then I urge you to come downstairs with us and explain to Mr. Stansfield why you undertook such an ambitious project.

SOUND EFFECT: (FADE IN UNDER) TRAIN INTERIOR

WATSON: What did Mrs. Dolan hope to get out of such an elaborate hoax?

HOLMES: She did it solely to frighten Charlotte.

WATSON: Why?

HOLMES: Mrs. Dolan strongly disapproved of Charlotte for her romance with two men at the same time. And when she read that Malreaux's likeness had been banished from the museum and would be destroyed, she saw a chance to attack Charlotte's conscience by playing on her superstition and guilt. Somehow, she obtained the wax head.

WATSON: So Mrs. Dolan didn't actually commit any crime!

HOLMES: None.

WATSON: But it won't be easy for her to find another situation.

HOLMES: Oh, she won't need to! I think Mr. Stansfield will keep her on. She taught his daughter a valuable lesson. Now, I'm going to sleep the rest of the way home.

WATSON: Oh, one final thing, Holmes. You haven't mentioned – did Stansfield pay you as handsomely as you expected?

HOLMES: In terms of the seriousness of the case, I would say he overpaid me. In fact, my only disappointment was the dinner, but we'll make up for that with a bucket of oysters, a brace of grouse, and a bottle of a nice white wine!

MUSIC: *DANSE MACABRE* UP AND UNDER

WATSON: This is Doctor John H Watson. I have many more stories of Sherlock Holmes, and I'll tell you another one . . . *when next we meet*!

MUSIC: UP AND FADE

The Tuttman Gallery

<u>CHARACTERS</u>

- SHERLOCK HOLMES
- DR. JOHN H. WATSON
- MARY WATSON
- INSPECTOR GREGSON
- VOLAND – *Neutral middle-class Brit, sixty*
- QUAYLE – *Fusty sixty-year-old*
- PYNE – *Grouchy, low-class, fifties*
- MRS. VOLAND – *Grieving middle-class widow, sixties*
- KEEPER – *Middle-class, friendly, late middle age*
- MAN
- WOMAN

<u>SOUND EFFECT: OPENING SEQUENCE, BIG BEN, STREET SOUNDS</u>

ANNOUNCER: *The Further Adventures of Sherlock Holmes . . . .*

<u>MUSIC: *DANSE MACABRE* (UP AND UNDER). FADE TO</u>

<u>SOUND EFFECT: HUSHED CROWD IN MUSEUM (ON FIRST ECHO)</u>

VOLAND: . . . . and we find ourselves once more at the entrance. This will conclude our museum tour for this evening, ladies and gentlemen. We thank you for your patronage and we do hope you'll visit The Tuttman Gallery again. Are there any final questions?

MAN: (OFF) Well, who's to say all these fantastic creatures ever really lived? I mean, they could just be dummies made up by a taxidermist, couldn't they?

VOLAND: Sir, each and every one of the specimens you have seen was alive when captured by Mr. Tuttman.

WOMAN: But you said there aren't any more like them anywhere in the world, so how are we to know?

VOLAND: Madame, this is not the P. T. Barnum circus. It is the private collection of Mr. Cyril Tuttman, who devoted his life and his fortune to the discovery of the rarest animal life on the planet! You may have every confidence that the animals on display here are genuine in every respect. Now . . .

SOUND EFFECT: BIG OUTER DOOR OPENED

VOLAND: . . . I bid you all a pleasant evening, and a good night.

SOUND EFFECT: CROWD MURMURS ON ITS WAY OUT

VOLAND: Come again! Be sure to tell your friends. Good night.

SOUND EFFECT: THE DOOR CLOSES AND IS BOLTED. VOLAND WALKING ON MARBLE FLOOR (UNDER) HE SNAPS OPEN HIS POCKET WATCH

VOLAND: Nine-twenty!

SOUND EFFECT: POCKET WATCH SNAPPED CLOSED

VOLAND: I never do get them out of here on time. Well, Bob's late again, so I'll have to turn down the lamps myself.

SOUND EFFECT: STEPS PAUSE

VOLAND: (PENSIVE SIGH) One down, thirteen to go.

SOUND EFFECT: HE STARTS WALKING AGAIN, PAUSES

VOLAND: Two . . . three . . . four . . . there, the lobby's dark.

SOUND EFFECT: HE STARTS WALKING AGAIN, PAUSES

VOLAND: It would be nice if they'd put in electric lights. Just turn a switch and you'd be done.

VOLAND: Ah. There's the smell again. Odd no one mentions it.

SOUND EFFECT: HE WALKS (UNDER)

VOLAND: I suppose some of these beasts want a good cleaning. If they weren't dead, they'd do it for themselves like my cat, I suppose.

SOUND EFFECT: STEPS STOP. (OFF) A SOUND LIKE A BUMP ON WOOD

VOLAND: Hello, what's that? (PAUSE) (UP) That you, Bob? (LOUDER) Bob? (PAUSE) Hmm!

SOUND EFFECT: HE STARTS WALKING AGAIN

VOLAND: Maybe it wasn't a door. Maybe it . . . .

SOUND EFFECT: STEPS STOP

VOLAND: I don't think I'll turn down any more lights.

SOUND EFFECT: THE SOUND AGAIN

VOLAND: Bob? Is that you?

SOUND EFFECT: ANIMAL RUNNING TOWARD HIM WITH RUMBLING GROWL

VOLAND: Oh my God! Oh my God! (SCREAMS HORRIBLY)

WATSON: My name is Doctor John H. Watson, and the Sherlock Holmes adventure I have for you tonight took place in the autumn of the year 1889. I no longer lived in our old digs in Baker Street, having married and started up my medical practice again in Paddington. But Holmes and I remained the closest of friends, and I joined him in many an investigation, with the approval of my wife, Mary. On the particular night when this case began, we had just retired at ten, when, at ten-fifteen, a cab

320

clattered to a stop outside, and a cane rapped * smartly on our door.

SOUND EFFECT: *PER DIALOGUE ABOVE – CANE RAP ON DOOR

MARY: Who can that be at this hour?

WATSON: Who is it usually?

SOUND EFFECT: SHEETS TURNED BACK

MARY: Sherlock Holmes?

WATSON: In this neighborhood, at this time, with a stick instead of knuckles? It's Holmes or the police.

SOUND EFFECT: CANE RAPS AGAIN

WATSON: (UP) I'm coming, I'm coming! Just putting on my dressing gown!

SOUND EFFECT: SLIPPERED FEET HURRY, STOP. DOOR OPENS

WATSON: Holmes?

HOLMES: A thousand apologies, Watson.

WATSON: Come in, come in.

HOLMES: How quickly can you be dressed?

WATSON: Why . . . three or four minutes. What's the matter?

HOLMES: Murder most foul, Watson. Scotland Yard is panting to tramp all over the scene but, to his credit, Tobias Gregson has roped it off until I join him with you and your medical bag. Go on, get dressed and I'll wait in the front room. (OFF-MICROPHONE SHOUTS) Wait for us, Cabbie! We won't be a minute.

HOLMES: Now, while you dress, I'll tell you what I know: The killing took place shortly past nine tonight at Tuttman's Gallery, a museum in Threadneedle Street. The body – that of a guide at the museum – was found by the night watchman who sounded the alarm. I wouldn't have known a thing about it but for the fact that I was riding home from a lecture at Lloyds when a Black Maria passed me on Leadenhall Street, turned the corner and pulled up in front of the museum. I saw it was Gregson and he invited me in. Are you hearing me?

WATSON: (FAR OFF-MICROPHONE) Yes, perfectly. Go on.

HOLMES: The room where the slaughter occurred is a large gallery with stuffed animals placed around a pool.

WATSON: Did you say slaughter?

HOLMES: You'll see what I mean. Are you almost ready?

WATSON: Just pulling on my boots.

HOLMES: We must hurry, Watson. Whoever or whatever killed the guide is still at large!

MUSIC STING: SCENE BEGINS ON FIRST ECHO

SOUND EFFECT: (BACKGROUND) SEVERAL POLICEMEN IN DISTANT INTERIOR

GREGSON: Good evening, Doctor Watson.

WATSON: Good evening, Inspector Gregson.

GREGSON: I suppose Mr. Holmes has prepared you.

WATSON: Prepared me? Well, he –

GREGSON: It's not a pretty sight.

HOLMES: Murder never is. The first thing, Watson, is to ascertain how the victim was killed.

GREGSON: Come on into the main exhibit room. Ever been here before?

WATSON: Not I.

GREGSON: Well, the gallery looks like a jungle clearing, dirt path and all. Watch where you step.

SOUND EFFECT: THREE MEN WALKING ON FLOOR, THEN ONTO DIRT

HOLMES: Who found the body?

GREGSON: The night watchman. The victim's name is William Voland. He was found in this room we're going into. Step carefully now. (CALLS OUT) Can you turn the gas up as high as it goes, Mr. Quayle?

QUAYLE: (FAR OFF) Of course.

SOUND EFFECT: STEPS STOP

WATSON: My word! It's like a jungle clearing in here, even to the humid air! And look at all the animals around a pond . . . even a mannequin of a native with his spear . . . Wh . . . What's all this? Good heavens!

GREGSON: Now, Doctor, I need you to tell me: Are these all parts of one man, or more than one? And are any parts missing?

WATSON: (CLOSE, INTIMATE NARRATION) Never, not even in the Battle of Maiwand, had I seen such carnage! I shan't attempt a detailed description of the scene that met my eyes, but the room was like a slaughterhouse. While I tried to mentally reconstruct the remains into some semblance of their natural condition, Holmes made a thorough inspection, at one point lowering himself to stretch upon the earthen trail under the trees beside the pond. Then he got up and followed the trail to the back of the room and left it through a door. When I had

323

accumulated as much information as possible from the remains, I joined Holmes and Gregson in an office off the lobby. The man who had turned up the gas jets was there, steadying himself beside a desk, looking quite ill.

GREGSON: This is Mr. Quayle, the manager of the museum.

HOLMES: And I am Sherlock Holmes, and this is Doctor John H. Watson.

QUALYE: So good of you to come, gentlemen.

GREGSON: Any conclusions, Mr. Holmes?

HOLMES: The absence of a second set of footprints is interesting.

GREGSON: And Doctor? What are your conclusions?

WATSON: The remains are that of one man, but some organs are missing.

QUALYE: Oh my word! Poor Voland!

HOLMES: It appears he was attacked near the edge of the pool, but crawled round, trying to get away, and then he fell and could rise no more. A quantity of bloody water has washed away any tracks.

QUAYLE: Oh, Lord have mercy!

HOLMES: And Watson, you no doubt observed there is no evidence that Mr. Voland's struggle for his life took him near either entrance?

GREGSON: Well then, how did the killer get out? He'd have had blood on his shoes.

HOLMES: We will know that when morning comes and the gallery will be brighter. Also, I noticed someone's been through the victim's clothes.

GREGSON: That was me. Voland had a purse with six pounds, half-a-crown, and two shillings in it, a key to the museum and a house key, and a small list of items he apparently intended to buy at an apothecary's shop. The motive wasn't robbery.

HOLMES: But he had no watch?

GREGSON: No, there was no watch.

HOLMES: Curious. What's the name of the man who found him?

QUAYLE: His name is Bob Pyne. He's the night watchman. He rushed over to my house. I live just next door, you see.

HOLMES: And it was you who called the police?

QUAYLE: Yes. I called the police straightaway and came right over.

HOLMES: Kindly tell me about this museum, Mr. Quayle, if you feel able.

QUAYLE: Well . . . the Tuttman Gallery is maintained by a trust from the estate of Cyril Tuttman, a world explorer who was born in a house that stood right here where the Museum now stands. Near the end of his life, he established the museum to house the rare specimens he'd encountered during his several expeditions.

HOLMES: Those on display in the gallery?

QUAYLE: Those and more that are in storage. Species of exotic animal life: Birds, reptiles, mammals of the most bizarre kinds . . . many that were thought to be extinct, or which have since become extinct. He had them stuffed and mounted in realistic poses, and placed in settings faithful to their natural habitats. It's quite instructional.

HOLMES: Many of the specimens are completely unfamiliar to me.

QUAYLE: Many of them are mutations of rare species, and some of them in fact were thought to have died out millennia ago. The

325

sabre-tooth tiger, a unique species of ape, the forty-foot python
–

LESTRADE: Strange it's not on the tourist circuit, like Madame Tussaud's.

QUAYLE: Call it a private hobby, if you will, that outgrew Tuttman Hall, which was his private residence . . . and so Mr. Tuttman purchased his old birthplace – renovated it from basement to attic, and turned it into a kind of preserve, being careful not to change its outward appearance, so that on its facade it still appears like a large private home. And he considered his patrons as guests more than customers. It was his idea that we keep a guest register, and have every visitor sign it.

GREGSON: Yes, I've checked it. Twenty-four people came through on this date. It shows their names and addresses and the time they took the tour. My men will be interviewing the night patrons first thing in the morning.

HOLMES: May I see that?

QUAYLE: Of course. Take it.

SOUND EFFECT: HEAVY SCRAPBOOK PLACED ON DESK. ITS THICK PAGES TURNED

QUAYLE: You see, here they are. The time the tour began, the time it ended, the time he locked up. Mr. Voland was very careful about his record keeping.

HOLMES: And since I see that your lobby has no clock, Mr. Voland obviously carried a watch, which is now missing.

GREGSON: You're right. So the killer took it.

HOLMES: But left the money? Interesting. So according to the register, the last tour of the evening concluded at 9:20. And then Mr. Voland was through for the night?

GREGSON: I've already been over all that with Mr. Quayle. Voland locked up, went through the museum turning off the gaslights, and was on his way through the gallery to exit the building through the back door when he was attacked.

HOLMES: And how long would it take him to lock up and turn off the lights?

QUAYLE: Not more than five minutes, I should say.

HOLMES: So at around 9:25, that would place him in the gallery.

QUAYLE: Uh . . . I suppose so.

HOLMES: And where is the night watchman now?

GREGSON: Pyne? He was in such a state of hysteria, it was no good asking him any questions, so I let him go home.

HOLMES: Very sympathetic of you, Inspector, but I think I'd like to have a word with him before he drinks himself to sleep.

GREGSON: What do you mean by that?

HOLMES: Perhaps you noticed his locker in the back room, the one marked with his name on it?

GREGSON: I haven't been there yet.

HOLMES: It would appear Mr. Pyne passes the lonely hours by reading naughty magazines while drinking cheap whisky.

QUAYLE: Is that so! Well! I shall look into that!

HOLMES: Don't be too harsh on him, Mr. Quayle. Spending the night in a place like this would drive anyone to drink.

MUSIC: OMINOUS UNDERSCORE

WATSON: Holmes obtained Robert Pyne's address, and we took a cab into Lambeth, found the narrow old alehouse over which the night watchman had his rooms, mounted the creaking stairs, and knocked on his door. The door opened only a crack, through which an alarmed and bloodshot eye appeared.

327

PYNE: What do you want?

HOLMES: Just a moment of your time, Mr. Pyne. My name is Sherlock Holmes and this is Doctor John Watson. We've just come from the museum and I need to talk with you.

PYNE: No! I don't want to talk about it!

HOLMES: I know you've had a terrible shock tonight, but we must ask you a few questions. May we come in?

WATSON: (NARRATING) He opened the door and we entered his sorry quarters. Mr. Pyne was in his nightshirt. The room was dominated by an unmade bed, sheets and blankets tumbled together. On a stand beside the bed was an oil lamp, which offered the only illumination, and beside the lamp was a bottle of whisky, more than half gone.

SOUND EFFECT: DOOR CLOSES

WATSON: (NARRATING) He took up the lamp, holding it in his shaking hand, and faced us so that his back was to the bed-stand, a maneuver I assumed was designed to hide the whisky bottle from our view.

HOLMES: I'll be quite brief, Mr. Pyne. When did you arrive at the museum tonight?

PYNE: When? Urhh . . . nine o'clock.

HOLMES: Nine o'clock. You're sure about that?

PYNE: That's when I start me work.

HOLMES: Mr. Pyne. If you arrived at the museum at nine o'clock, then you were there when William Voland was killed, weren't you? In fact, you must have heard what happened. Perhaps you even saw what happened!

PYNE: I did not! 'E was already dead when I come in the gallery.

HOLMES: No, that won't do, Mr. Pyne. We know he was alive at 9:20. Between 9:20 and 9:25 p.m., he was attacked and mutilated! So if you were in the museum at nine o'clock, you knew what was happening! Or . . . perhaps . . . you're the killer!

PYNE: Are you crazy? It wasn't me! I wasn't there!

HOLMES: You just *said* you were there at nine.

PYNE: All right! So I was a few minutes' late!

HOLMES: How late?

PYNE: Nine-twenty-five. I got there at nine-twenty-five. That's the truth, so help me!

HOLMES: How did you know what time it was when you got there?

PYNE: Well . . . by me watch.

HOLMES: May I see your watch?

PYNE: Urhh . . . .

HOLMES: Is there something wrong? Where do you keep your watch, Mr. Pyne? (PAUSE)

SOUND EFFECT: THREE STRIDES

HOLMES: (OFF) I wager you would keep something as valuable as a watch here, in your night-stand!

SOUND EFFECT: HE YANKS A WOODEN DRAWER OPEN

PYNE: You got no right to do that!

HOLMES: Ah. A watch in a gold case. And inside . . . .

SOUND EFFECT: HOLMES WALKS BACK ON MICROPHONE

329

HOLMES: . . . Yes, inside are the owner's initials. But they're not your initials, are they, Mr. Pyne? The initials are *W.V.*

PYNE: I bought it at a pawn shop!

HOLMES: *W. V.*! The initials of William Voland! You stole this watch from the body of your co-worker, William Voland, didn't you?

PYNE: I didn't go near 'im! . . . What was left of him!

HOLMES: Then where did you find this watch? (PAUSE) It will do you no good to lie, because your lies will only build your gallows, Mr. Pyne!

PYNE: It's God's truth, so help me! The watch was in the gallery, right by the door when I went in.

HOLMES: And so you pinched it.

PYNE: I was goin' to turn it in! But the next second, I saw what else was there.

HOLMES: Interesting. The watch stopped at 9:25!

PYNE: Huh! It must be broke.

HOLMES: Well, at least, Watson, this more or less verifies the time of the murder. Now, tell us, Mr. Pyne, when you came to work, how did you get into the museum?

PYNE: The same way I always do. Through the alley door.

HOLMES: Was the alley door open or closed when you came in?

PYNE: Closed.

HOLMES: And was it locked?

PYNE: Yes, same as always. So I took me key and unlocked it, just like I always do.

HOLMES: And when you got inside, you closed the door?

PYNE: And locked it again.

HOLMES: And then what did you do?

PYNE: Went to me locker and hung up me coat. Then I went into the gallery and . . . I swear, I knew somethin' was wrong the second I opened the door!

HOLMES: Mr. Pyne, tell me everything you can recall, no matter how trifling!

PYNE: Well, it was the smell.

HOLMES: What smell?

PYNE: Ever been to the zoo? It was like that. The gallery don't ever smell like that, just the stale water smell.

HOLMES: And so, you went into the gallery.

PYNE: And I wish I hadn't. 'Scuse me, gent'men . . . I need a bit o' this!

SOUND EFFECT: HE PULLS THE CORK FROM A BOTTLE AND GLUGS DOWN A GOOD SLUG, NOISILY

HOLMES: Now, Mr. Pyne, you saw no one in the gallery?

PYNE: Nobody alive.

HOLMES: And then what did you do?

PYNE: I ran next door to tell Mr. Quayle.

HOLMES: And did you close and lock the alley door as you left?

PYNE: I . . . I don't remember. Maybe I didn't. But by then it was too late anyway, wasn't it?

MUSIC: UNDERCURRENT

331

WATSON: The sky was just getting light as we left the watchman, shivering in his nightshirt and finding solace in his bottle. We circled round to Scotland Yard and found Inspector Gregson in his office, his tie loosened and his face deeply lined with fatigue.

MUSIC: OUT

GREGSON: The worst part of my job is telling someone their loved one is dead.

HOLMES: You've been to see Voland's family.

GREGSON: His widow. She wanted me to take her to see him. I had to tell her I couldn't, but I didn't tell her why.

HOLMES: Did you inquire as to whether Mr. Voland had any enemies?

GREGSON: Come on, Mr. Holmes. An enemy who'd kill him and tear him apart? The Volands lived a quiet life in a modest middle-class neighborhood, on a pension from a steamship company. He worked at the Tuttman Museum as an unpaid lecturer.

HOLMES: I should like to pay Mrs. Voland a visit at some point.

GREGSON: I'll write down her address.

HOLMES: Thank you.

GREGSON: So you've been to the watchman's place, have you?

HOLMES: Yes. He seemed to be recovering.

WATSON: With a little help from the bottle.

GREGSON: Then he wasn't much good to you.

HOLMES: On the contrary, Inspector. He said the gallery smelled like a zoo last night when he walked in and saw the scene.

GREGSON: Huh. The only animals in that place haven't been alive for a long time.

HOLMES: The smell was present at the time of Voland's death, but it had disappeared by the time we got there.

GREGSON: Well, I didn't notice it. And if there was something there, how'd it get in? And how'd it get out?

SOUND EFFECT: FADE IN – TROTTING HORSE PULLING CAB UNDER

WATSON: (PAUSE) I don't know about you, Holmes, but I'm left with a very uneasy feeling. What motive would justify tearing a man limb from limb?

HOLMES: What if there was no motive?

WATSON: There had to be a motive. Even the insane find motives to justify their irrational acts.

HOLMES: Very well, let us examine possible motives for what was done to Mr. Voland. Anger?

WATSON: I suppose, in an extreme case. But the killer would have to have been violently insane to have done what he did.

HOLMES: I fear you've come close to the truth, Watson. There is little doubt that we are not searching for any ordinary kind of killer!

MUSIC: UNDERCURRENT

WATSON: (NARRATING) As dawn broke over London, the coroner finished his grim work in the museum and two men from the morgue carted away the mortal remains of William Voland. Holmes retired to Baker Street, and I found a cab to take me back to Paddington, where I let myself in as quietly as possible, but found Mary wide awake.

MUSIC: OUT

MARY: Did you have an exciting time of it, John?

WATSON: Exciting? It was the most brutal murder I've ever seen.

MARY: Can you tell me about it?

WATSON: No, I don't want you to know about it. Besides, look at the time.

MARY: It's all right. I've been dozing off-and-on since you left. Shall I make some coffee?

WATSON: No. All I want is to sleep and forget what I've seen.

MUSIC: LOW UNDERCURRENT

WATSON: (NARRATING) I'm not usually given to dreaming, but when I finally dropped off, I experienced the horror of what I had seen in the Tuttman Gallery over and over again. I felt as if I was trapped in that abattoir, and no matter which way I turned, some unknown slayer kept pursuing me! And then he shook me and shook me . . . and suddenly I was awake and Mary was crouched over me on my bed!

MUSIC: OUT

MARY: John! Wake up!

WATSON: What?

MARY: You were thrashing about and groaning!

WATSON: I was?

MARY: You were having a nightmare!

WATSON: I'm sorry, my dear . . . .

MARY: I've never seen you like this before!

WATSON: I've never seen what I saw before! Not even in war!

MARY: Then you mustn't go back. You mustn't go back with Sherlock Holmes. At least not on this case.

WATSON: Oh, but I must.

MARY: Why? Out of loyalty? If anyone owes loyalty, it's *he* who owes it to *you*! You've made his name a household word, and I have no doubt it's brought him a fortune! You're such a gentle, sweet man, John, and this work is for men with coarser sensibilities. Why torture yourself?

WATSON: Mary, I've been with Holmes against desperate men and mad men and every type of predator, and I like to think I may have added at least a small bit of help in bringing them to justice. (BRIGHTER) And besides, who was it wthat encouraged me to keep working with him?

MARY: But not if it does this to you!

WATSON: I'm sorry, Mary. As much as the case revolts me, it also fascinates me. And now, the real work begins. We'll be interviewing the widow today, and inspecting the scene of the crime in the most minute detail, and I believe I am of some assistance in these things. So . . . . now I'd appreciate a cup of coffee. And your trusting patience.

MUSIC: UNDERCURRENT

WATSON: (NARRATING) I left Mary pouting. Oh, I knew she was concerned for me, but I had to see this thing through. And so I took a cab to Baker Street, and found Holmes gone. But a note was tacked to his door, which read, *"Watson: Meet me at the Gallery"*, which I did. Shafts of pale morning light streamed into the room through many skylights in the roof, flooding through the dust in the air and illuminating what looked like a tropical jungle. Then in the shadows there was a sudden movement! I admit I felt a pang of terror, thinking it was the mannequin come to life! But then I recognized the figure of Sherlock Holmes in his overcoat and cap, on his hands and knees under a massive palm tree, his magnifying glass in hand.

335

MUSIC: OUT

ECHO THROUGHOUT SCENE

WATSON: I came as soon as I saw your note.

HOLMES: (ALMOST WHISPERING) I'm onto something, Watson. You see all these trees and plants? They are artificial, of course, but look at the earth around them.

WATSON: What about it?

HOLMES: Footprints – made by a large, bare foot.

WATSON: I can't make them out.

HOLMES: This display was installed several years ago, and has been collecting dust ever since. In time, dust covers everything, whereas in nature, rain and wind disperse the dust that falls. But these footprints have pressed the dust into the earth and the moisture from the artificial pond has helped keep their form. But here's something else. There are other sets of prints, deeper than the footprints, which appear to be those of some different kind of animal. In fact, I wouldn't call them footprints at all. See? A pair of them here . . . and here . . . and over here . . . .

WATSON: But were these prints made recently, then?

HOLMES: Very recently. And many of them contain traces of *blood*!

WATSON: So there were two different creatures in here!

HOLMES: Possibly. Now: Observation number two. Look at the bark of these trees.

WATSON: Hmm. Artificial. And they need a good dusting too.

HOLMES: Yes, but feel their texture.

WATSON: Hmm. It's rather rough. Like the real thing, I suppose.

336

HOLMES: The trees are spaced closely. Whoever left these footprints undoubtedly brushed against the trunks. I've been inspecting them for bits of cloth.

WATSON: Did you find some?

HOLMES: Not a piece of fuzz or fabric or lint. But what I did find was this . . . which I have put in this envelope.

SOUND EFFECT: OPENS THE FLAP OF SMALL ENVELOPE

WATSON: What's in here? Looks like a long hair. That's all you found?

HOLMES: I can hardly wait to put it under my microscope!

QUAYLE: (OFF) I say! Who's there?

WATSON: Doctor John H. Watson.

QUAYLE: (OFF) Oh. Watson . . . Watson . . . You were with Sherlock Holmes last night.

WATSON: That's correct. Holmes is right here . . . in the jungle.

HOLMES: (LOUDLY) It's quite all right, Mr. Quayle. Inspector Gregson arranged for us to inspect the scene of the crime.

QUAYLE: (MOVING ON) Oh, yes, now I remember! Of course, I knew you were coming. Thousand pardons. So much has happened . . . how are you, Doctor? Mr. Holmes. Are you finding anything?

HOLMES: Very little, so far.

QUAYLE: Did you see the morning papers? There must be fifty people outside at this very moment, clamoring to get in and see where it happened! They have no interest in science, only in sensation!

337

HOLMES: (MOVING ON) I believe you mentioned that you live next door, Mr. Quayle. Would it be convenient for us to go there for a brief chat?

QUAYLE: Why . . . I suppose so. Museum's closed all day anyway. Yes. We'll go to my place.

ECHO DIES TO ZERO

SOUND EFFECT: TEA SOUNDS

HOLMES: Now, last night you told us that Mr. Tuttman bought the house next door to this one and turned it into a museum.

QUAYLE: That's right.

HOLMES: Were you living in this house at the time?

QUAYLE: No. You see, Cyril Tuttman and I were friends from school, close friends. When he built the museum, he asked me to run it for him, and he bought this house next door for me to live in.

HOLMES: Mr. Tuttman must have been quite wealthy.

QUAYLE: Oh yes, he was. Shipping. Owned several vessels.

WATSON: I must say, those animals you have in the gallery are very real looking, but they're not like any I've ever seen.

QUAYLE: Nor ever will see again. I may have mentioned last night that Cyril Tuttman was a great naturalist. Went places that aren't on any map. Lived with aborigines, learned their lingo, and collected animals no scientist even knew existed. Exotic species of every kind.

WATSON: Well, why didn't he place these in the British Museum? After all, that's the greatest museum in the world.

QUAYLE: They wouldn't have him.

WATSON: Why not?

QUAYLE: They said he couldn't prove where he'd been, or that the specimens were authentic, just because he went by himself and paid for his expeditions with his own money! Wasn't sponsored by any prestigious society or famous organization.

HOLMES: Mr. Tuttman is dead now, I take it?

QUAYLE: Died in '85. His estate provided a trust to run the museum and pay the expenses. I'll stay on as long as I'm able. But after that . . . . well, it'll all be gone. Tuttman was no fool. He knew some sharp businessman would turn this into a sideshow. He often said, "I don't want this to become a Tussaud's with animals instead of celebrities".

HOLMES: And you draw a salary from the trust, I presume?

QUAYLE: Yes, a modest salary.

HOLMES: You've been very kind, Mr. Quayle, to give us your time. Incidentally, whom do you think killed Mr. Voland?

QUAYLE: I have no idea. I don't know how he got in the place or got out again. Or why he'd do such a thing. Bill Voland didn't have an enemy in the world.

MUSIC: FAST, SHORT BRIDGE

MRS. VOLAND: My husband didn't have an enemy in the world. I can assure you of that, Mr. Holmes. We were married more than forty years . . . (BREAKS DOWN) . . . and he made friends wherever we went. He loved people and people loved him. That's why he took the position as a docent in the museum. Not for the money. We had enough to live decently . . . (BREAKS DOWN)

HOLMES: (SYMPATHETIC) And had Mr. Voland been acquainted at all with Cyril Tuttman?

MRS. VOLAND: Acquainted? He worked for him for years in the shipping business. Why, William wouldn't have put in the time

339

and effort that he did if it weren't for his respect for Cyril Tuttman.

HOLMES: What sort of work did he do for Mr. Tuttman?

MRS. VOLAND: He was his head accountant.

HOLMES: Then was it Mr. Tuttman himself who hired your husband as a guide?

MRS. VOLAND: He wasn't a guide, Mr. Holmes, he was a docent! He never took a penny for all the lectures he gave, every day. He knew more about the specimens in the collection than anyone except Cyril Tuttman himself!

HOLMES: How did he get on with Mr. Quayle?

MRS. VOLAND: William never spoke much about him. Mr. Quayle was in his office during the day, and William came in near the end of the afternoon to conduct his tours. And once a month he did the books.

MUSIC: UNDERCURRENT

WATSON: (NARRATING) Holmes and I left the Voland home and stood somberly at the curb, waiting for a hansom. Holmes had that absorbed, distant expression on his face that meant his mind was churning over the intelligence we now had accumulated. I waited patiently beside him. And then finally, as an empty cab approached, he said – without turning toward me –

HOLMES: This thing is more devilish than I thought. We have work to do tonight, Watson.

MUSIC: STING AND UNDER

WATSON: He was silent as we rode to Baker Street. I made no attempt at conversation, for I could see that he was organizing our next moves. There was now an urgency in Holmes. Through the earlier parts of his investigation of the slaying at the Tuttman Gallery, he had been concerned mainly with examining small details. But now he had formed them all together in his mind and was ready to bring his investigation to a close. When we arrived at Baker Street, Holmes immediately took his microscope from its case and set it up on the dining table. He removed the hair he'd taken from the gallery, pulled a hair from his own head, and placed them side by side between two glass slides, which he then clamped on the stage beneath the microscope's lens. He twisted the focusing knob, and then held it still.

MUSIC: OUT

HOLMES: (PAUSE) Ah. Just as I thought. Come have a look, Watson.

SOUND EFFECT: WATSON MOVES TO THE TABLE

HOLMES: We must face it: William Voland was not murdered!

WATSON: *What?*

HOLMES: No. Murder is defined as one human being killing another. Mr. Voland was not killed by a human being.

WATSON: I thought that was what you were coming to. The animal footprints and all . . . .

HOLMES: You can see the difference in the hairs. The one from Tuttman's jungle exhibit is almost twice as thick as mine. It's an animal hair, and there were many more of them.

WATSON: What kind of an animal?

HOLMES: The animal that brushed against the man-made trees and left his prints in the dirt doubtless is the animal that killed Mr. Voland.

WATSON: How can you be sure?

HOLMES: Remember that I could find no fuzz, no lint, no thread of material stuck to the trees? And yet the footprints indicated that someone – or some *thing* – had moved through the stand of trees and would have certainly brushed against the tree trunks?

WATSON: Yes?

HOLMES: There was no residue of cloth because the individual in the artificial forest wore no clothing. It was an animal, a large animal, large enough to have left its hair on the tree five-and-one-half feet off the ground. And it was strong enough to kill and rend a human body limb-from-limb in five minutes or less!

WATSON: But Holmes, I inspected the remains, as you know, and I found definite signs that something with a blade on it inflicted the fatal blow!

HOLMES: There is an order of ape, first discovered in Africa around forty years ago, that is quite large. Males can weigh over four-hundred pounds.

WATSON: The gorilla!

HOLMES: Precisely.

WATSON: But how would a gorilla get into a museum?

HOLMES: Only with human help. And that, we must discover . . . tonight.

MUSIC: STING

SOUND EFFECT: SCOTLAND YARD OFFICE NOISES (BACKGROUND)

GREGSON: A gorilla?

HOLMES: Yes, Inspector. The footprints, the hairs on the tree bark, possibly the smell Bob Pyne mentioned, the brute force in the attack on Voland . . . they all point to a massive animal, an animal with opposable thumbs.

GREGSON: Opposable thumbs?

HOLMES: Even as you and I have. Makes it possible to grasp a weapon. All apes have them.

GREGSON: Well, it'll be easy enough to find out if there's a gorilla on the loose, which I doubt. But I'll send a man to the London Zoo and see if they're missing one.

HOLMES: I think I'd rather have Watson do that, while I'm occupied elsewhere for a while. Do you mind taking a trip to the zoo, Watson? You'll know all the right questions to ask. When you're done with that, meet me at Baker Street at six.

SOUND EFFECT: BACKGROUND FADES. FADE IN – ZOO BACKGROUND, GORILLA CAGE

KEEPER: Yes, sir, these are African gorillas. Their home is the rain forest of central Africa.

WATSON: What hideous monsters!

KEEPER: Well, it's all in one's point of view, I suppose. I always tell people, to a gorilla, a man looks frightening.

WATSON: You, eh . . . wouldn't be missing one, would you?

KEEPER: Missing one? What do you mean?

WATSON: Did any of them ever get away?

KEEPER: (CHUCKLE) Oh, I see. No, they're actually quite content here.

WATSON: These are the only ones you've had?

KEEPER: No, we've sold pairs of them to zoos in Berlin and Amsterdam.

WATSON: Pairs of them?

KEEPER: Gorillas are like you and me. They can get lonely. In their native habitat they live in groups. There's always a leader, who

343

makes all decisions for the tribe . . . sees they're safe from danger.

WATSON: What possible danger could a gorilla fear?

KEEPER: Well, some African tribes hunt them for food. The gorilla's greatest enemy is man.

WATSON: I should think it would be the other way round.

KEEPER: No, no. These big fellows may look fierce, and they use their frightening appearance to scare off attackers, but in fact, they're really quite gentle.

WATSON: They have hands – something like a human's – so could a gorilla use a weapon?

KEEPER: We don't really know. I suppose it's possible.

WATSON: What do they eat?

KEEPER: In the wild, they're herbivorous. They'll eat fruit, leaves, and bark.

SOUND EFFECT: BACKGROUND FADES TO ZERO

(PAUSE)

SOUND EFFECT: MANTEL CLOCK STRIKES SIX . KNOCK ON THE DOOR. STEPS. DOOR OPENS

HOLMES: Ah, Watson. Prompt as always.

SOUND EFFECT: HE WALKS IN. DOOR CLOSES

WATSON: Yes. Well, no gorilla is missing from the zoo, and they aren't fierce unless attacked. And they don't eat meat.

HOLMES: Quite right. My mistake. I sent you on a fool's errand.

WATSON: Then it wasn't a gorilla that left that hair?

344

HOLMES: Oh yes, it was gorilla hair. But while you were at the zoo, I found out that the reconstruction at Cyril Tuttman's place on Threadneedle Street was a bit more elaborate than merely turning a house into a museum. The place next door, where Mr. Quayle lives, was remodeled at the same tune. Quite a project, according to his neighbors. And so we are going back for another visit tonight . . . after the museum is closed. We will both take torches this time . . . and pistols.

MUSIC: STING

SOUND EFFECT: LONDON CITY BACKGROUND

HOLMES: Here we are. The alley door.

SOUND EFFECT: CANE RAPPING ON HEAVY DOOR

HOLMES: (LOW, EXTERIOR) Are you prepared, Watson?

WATSON: (LOW, EXTRERIOR) Prepared for what? You haven't said a word to me since we started here!

SOUND EFFECT: DOOR UNLOCKED AND OPENED

PYNE: Eh? Who's there?

HOLMES: Sherlock Holmes and Doctor Watson, Mr. Pyne.

PYNE: Oh, it's you two. We're closed for the night.

HOLMES: Yes, we know. Let us in, please.

PYNE: I can't. It's against the rules.

HOLMES: Ah, against the rules? Like stealing a dead man's watch?

PYNE: (PAUSE) Come on in.

SOUND EFFECT: THEY DO COME INSIDE. DOOR CLOSES. CITY BACKGROUND OUT

PYNE: What do you want?

HOLMES: We want to go into the gallery again.

PYNE: All right, this way.

<u>SOUND EFFECT: THREE MEN WALKING. STOP. ECHO THROUGHOUT SCENE. THREE MEN WALK IN, DOOR CLOSES</u>

HOLMES: Now: Mr. Pyne. Besides this back door, and the door to the lobby, is there any other door to the gallery?

PYNE: No sir.

HOLMES: But of course there must be.

<u>SOUND EFFECT: MOVING THROUGH THE JUNGLE</u>

WATSON: Holmes! Look! Look at the statue of the spear-carrier! (EFFORT) The spear comes loose!

HOLMES: Yes. First thing I checked. Clean as a whistle. No sign of blood on it.

WATSON: Oh. Then exactly what are we looking for in this jungle?

HOLMES: A trap door in this artificial ground. A camouflaged exit.

WATSON: Are you sure we should be tramping around in here? Won't we be destroying more footprints?

HOLMES: That doesn't matter anymore. What does matter is finding a passageway out of this gallery. Ah!

<u>SOUND EFFECT: STEPS STOP</u>

HOLMES: Look!

WATSON: It's a door in the wall!

HOLMES: Of course! I'd been looking in the wrong place!

346

WATSON: A stairway!

HOLMES: (CALLS) Mr. Pyne!

WATSON: Huh! Where did he get to? He was with us a minute ago.

HOLMES: I suspect he's gone next door to report our presence to
   Mr. Quayle. Unless I am very much mistaken, this stairway
   goes to an underground passage between the museum and
   Quayle's house. While I follow it, I want you to go back out of
   this jungle and wait for whatever I may scare into that passage!
   I don't know how long I'll be gone, but be ready to escape into
   the locker room and bolt the door. And Watson . . . have your
   gun in hand and be prepared for anything!

WATSON: (Narrating) With that warning, Holmes disappeared
   through the side door and into the blackness beyond, while I
   backtracked through the man-made jungle. I skirted the small
   pond and planted myself some ten yards from the door in the
   back of the gallery. The only light was the dim blue of the night
   sky that came through the skylights. It grew still in the vast
   room. And then I decided it would be wise to make sure that the
   back door was unlocked, so I walked the thirty feet or so . . .

SOUND EFFECT: HE JIGGLES THE DOOR HANDLE

WATSON: (FLAT) . . . but it was locked from the other side!

SOUND EFFECT: HE TROTS ON DIRT (UNDER)

WATSON: (FLAT) My heart lurched. That door was supposed to be
   my escape route! I set out along the trail that wound through the
   trees and the strange animals posed among them, in mounting
   fear that I might have no way to get out if I had to! Why had the
   night watchman locked me in? Perhaps the front entrance was
   unlocked . . . yes, that had to be it. But when I got to the
   massive double doors that opened into the lobby . . . .

WATSON: (FLAT) It was locked! I was locked in!

SOUND EFFECT: HE HAMMERS ON THE DOORS

WATSON: (ECHO) Mr. Pyne! Unlock these doors!

WATSON: (FLAT) Then I listened in silence to hear any sign that the watchman had heard me, but there was nothing.

SOUND EFFECT: HE WALKS ON THE DIRT TRAIL (UNDER)

WATSON: (FLAT) All I could do was to follow Holmes's orders and resume my post. It dawned on me that, whatever was to follow, Bob Pyne knew full well that he had me trapped in here.

SOUND EFFECT: STEPS STOP

WATSON: (FLAT) And then, I noticed a faint movement somewhere out of the corner of my eye. I stopped and scanned the jungle forest. Nothing moved. All was still. And then! There it was again! What caught my eye was a twinkle of stars reflected through the skylights into the water of the pond. There was a disturbance somewhere beneath the surface! The pond had been as flat as a mirror a minute before, but now there were ripples running across the surface! Were there fish in the pond? A bit of life in this gallery of the dead?

SOUND EFFECT: A SPLASH OF WATER IN THE POND

WATSON: (FLAT) Somewhere in the darkness beneath the trees, the sound of a body moved in the water! Now the ripples were ten inch waves travelling out of the blackness and lapping against the side of the pond, at my feet! Now the pond seemed to be rising! Something was plowing toward me through the water! I stepped back from the edge of the pond, the gun in my hand.

SOUND EFFECT: CROCODILE EMERGES, HISSING

348

WATSON: (FLAT) And then I saw it! The knobbed, leathery hide of the largest crocodile anyone had ever seen! It slithered up the side of the pond, its jaws spread three feet apart, its short legs driving its thrashing body directly for me! Aiming my gun with both hands, I fired into the monster's gaping maw!

SOUND EFFECT: SEVERAL PISTOL SHOTS

WATSON: (FLAT) But the shots had no effect! It kept coming! I had only one chance of escape, and that was to run into the jungle forest and find the hidden door!

SOUND EFFECT: WATSON PLOWS THROUGH THE BRUSH (UNDER)

WATSON: (FLAT) The huge beast was crashing through the trees behind me! I considered climbing one of them, but then remembered they were only stage scenery, too flimsy to support my weight! My torchlight played through the trees and threw shadows on the black wall. And then, with the fetid breath of the crocodile near enough to feel, part of the wall opened only ten feet ahead of me!

HOLMES: (OFF-MICROPHONE) Watson! Here I am! Hurry!

SOUND EFFECT: WATSON CRASHES ONTO SOLID FOOTING AND THE DOOR CLOSES

WATSON: (GASPING WITH RELIEF) Holmes! It was a crocodile! The biggest one in the world!

HOLMES: Yes, I saw it go into the water in the cellar beneath Quayle's house! He breeds them there, and he sent the brute through an underground canal into the gallery in search of fresh meat!

WATSON: I shot it five or six times and it still kept coming!

HOLMES: Well, if you didn't finish it off, Inspector Gregson has armed men in Quayle's house and they'll attend to it. Now, if you're up to it, let's take this underground passage next door and join them.

GREGSON: I'm surprised at you, Mr. Holmes . . . using your old friend as crocodile bait!

HOLMES: Nothing of the kind, Inspector. When I discovered the secret passageway from the gallery into Quayle's house, I expected to confront Mr. Quayle with my evidence and discover the beast he'd sent through the tunnel to kill Mr. Voland. I hadn't counted on another tunnel . . . an underground canal!

WATSON: Yes! I thought you were preparing me to meet a gorilla!

HOLMES: And well you might have. That was what poor Voland saw, last night, as he was preparing to lock up.

WATSON: A gorilla?

HOLMES: Quayle, wearing a gorilla skin, complete with the feet!

WATSON: No!

GREGSON: Oh, yes. Hoped he'd frighten Voland to death. Didn't work. Tried to strangle him. Didn't work. Finally grabbed the spear and stabbed him instead.

WATSON: You'll have to explain, I'm afraid. It's not clear to me at all!

GREGSON: Mr. Holmes? You did most of the research,

HOLMES: As you know, Mr. Voland kept the books for the museum. He began finding substantial sums of money unaccounted for, which he traced to Quayle. Quayle feared arrest and disgrace, so he devised a plan to kill Voland.

GREGSON: He came through the passageway into the gallery last night in the gorilla costume, and waited for Voland to close the place up. He counted on the night watchman to be late as usual, so hee knew he'd have enough time to kill Voland.

HOLMES: He stabbed him with the spear the mannequin carried, no doubt washed the blood off it in the pond, and put it back in the hand of the statue.

GREGSON: Then he drags the bleeding body over by the pond, the crocodile smells the blood, and comes up into the pond and . . . does what crocodiles do.

HOLMES: Which he claims wasn't part of his plan.

WATSON: But what about the locked doors to the gallery?

HOLMES: Once we were inside, Pyne locked us in, not knowing about the secret side door. Then he went round to tell Quayle we were trapped.

GREGSON: And that gave Quayle a chance to turn loose his crocodile. But testimony from the two of you will help us put Mr. Quayle away for a long, long time.

HOLMES: One would hope. Well, Watson, I've imperiled your home life long enough. It's back to Paddington for you, and your serene domesticity.

MUSIC: *DANSE MACABRE* UP AND UNDER

WATSON: I hope you've enjoyed this story, and I'll tell you another case of Sherlock Holmes . . . *when next we meet*!

MUSIC: UP AND OUT

The Adventure of the Lonely Harvester

CHARACTERS

- SHERLOCK HOLMES
- DR. JOHN H. WATSON
- INSPECTOR GREGSON
- CHRISTINE RYAN: *From the Midlands*
- MRS. RYAN: *From the Midlands*
- EVANGALINE: *From a working-class family*
- TRIXIE: *From a working-class family*
- OFFICER: *A sturdy London bobby*
- TOM: *Midlands accent*

SOUND EFFECT: OPENING SEQUENCE, BIG BEN, STREET SOUNDS

ANNOUNCER: *The Further Adventures of Sherlock Holmes . . . .*

MUSIC: *DANSE MACABRE* (UP AND UNDER)

WATSON: My name is Doctor John H. Watson, and it has been my privilege to document the achievements of the original consulting detective, Mr. Sherlock Holmes. Many of the cases in which I collaborated with Holmes put my medical experience to use, and none more so than a curious series of crimes that took place in London during the fall of 1889. Although by then I had married and moved out of the flat I had shared with Holmes on Baker Street, we still worked together as occasion demanded. And such was the case I have titled "The Adventure of the Lonely Harvester".

MUSIC: FADES OUT

WATSON: It had been a fine day in mid-October. I'd shut up my surgery rather early for want of patients, and my wife Mary and I were enjoying the twilight in our parlour in Paddington –

SOUND EFFECT: (OFF) FRANTIC KNOCKING BY A WOMAN

WATSON: – when someone knocked on our street door, the kind of frantic knock which usually means an emergency.

MARY: (OFF) My goodness!

WATSON: Yes?

MRS. RYAN: Please, sir, are you the doctor?

WATSON: Yes, I'm Doctor Watson.

MRS. RYAN: We tried your downstairs door but no one answered.

WATSON: The surgery is closed, but how can I help you?

MRS. RYAN: This is my daughter. A man tried to chloroform her! She's still quite weak!

WATSON: Chloroform? Yes, yes, bring her right in!

WATSON: Let's have a look at you. What's your name, my dear?

CHRISTINE: Christine.

WATSON: Well, Christine, let's go down to my surgery so I can have a good look at you.

MARY: I'll go down and light the gas.

WATSON: Thank you, Mary. Come along, Christine. And Mrs. . . . ?

MRS. RYAN: Oh, I'm Mrs. Ryan.

353

WATSON: How did this happen?

MRS. RYAN: We were over in the park. Christine was riding the carousel, and I was sitting on a bench reading, when I looked up and saw her fall to the ground, and a man was hurrying away!

SOUND EFFECT: THEY WALK, THEN DOWN THE STAIRS

MARY: (CALLS, OFF) Mind the stairs! They're quite steep.

WATSON: And was she unconscious?

CHRISTINE: It was like I went to sleep for a minute. Will I die?

WATSON: No, my dear, you're getting better right now. Have you called the police, Mrs. Ryan?

MRS. RYAN: No! All I could think was to get her to a doctor. Our regular doctor is in Wellington Street, but I remembered I'd seen your sign the other day and you were closer . . . .

WATSON: Well, I'm glad to be of help, but with children being abducted right and left all over town, I think you should speak with a policeman as soon as possible.

MRS. RYAN: Yes, I'm sure. We live just the other side of the park.

SOUND EFFECT: STEPS STOP

WATSON: Well, here we are. Now I want you to sit up on the examining table, Christine.

CHRISTINE: All right.

WATSON: That's the girl. Now, tip your head so you're looking at that lamp. That's right. (LONG PAUSE) Well, the eyes are tracking normally. Is your vision normal, Christine? Can you see all right?

354

CHRISTINE: I think so.

WATSON: Well, no permanent damage was done.

MRS. RYAN: Oh, thank God.

WATSON: Well, my girl, you seem healthy enough otherwise. Not dizzy or anything?

CHRISTINE: I was, but I'm not any more.

WATSON: Good. And just how old are you?

MRS. RYAN: She's nearly nine.

CHRISTINE: I can still go to the Halloween party, can't I?

MRS. RYAN: She's invited to a party tomorrow and all her friends will be there.

WATSON: Oh, you'll go to your party and have a splendid time.

MRS. RYAN: I don't know . . . I don't feel I should be letting her out of my sight, after this.

CHRISTINE: Oh, mama!

WATSON: Now, Christine, tell me everything you can about the man who did this. What did he look like? Was he tall or short?

CHRISTINE: He was kind of tall.

WATSON: As tall as I am?

CHRISTINE: Yes, I think so.

WATSON: Did he seem as old as I am?

CHRISTINE: I don't know.

WATSON: Well, did he look as old as your daddy?

CHRISTINE: I don't know. I haven't seen my daddy.

MRS. RYAN: Her father has been away a long time on business.

WATSON: Oh, I see. Well, was there anything you especially remember about this man?

CHRISTINE: Well . . . he had very blue eyes.

WATSON: And what did he say to you?

CHRISTINE: I don't remember. He just held out a bag of candy, like he wanted me to go with him, but I wouldn't, and then he grabbed me and put a cloth right over my face and I couldn't breathe. I fell down and mama came, and the man ran away.

WATSON: Mrs. Ryan, you'll want to get this information to the police as soon as possible.

MRS. RYAN: Of course. So she's all right, then?

WATSON: I think so. If she didn't lose consciousness, there's no reason for concern.

MRS. RYAN: Oh, I'm so relieved. Thank you, Doctor. Now if you'll give me your bill, I'll send you a cheque.

WATSON: Oh, there'll be no charge.

MRS. RYAN: But I'll be glad to pay you. My husband sends money to his bank all the time.

WATSON: No, no. Just, uh . . . give this girl a good meal.

MRS. RYAN: Yes, of course. We're just on our way home. Now thank the doctor, Christine.

CHRISTINE: Thank you.

WATSON: And Mrs. Ryan, you should report this to the nearest policeman right away. What with so many little girls being taken . . . well . . . .

356

MRS. RYAN: Yes, I will, and I'm ever so grateful. Now we must be going. We've already interrupted your evening.

WATSON: It was no trouble at all. Only too glad to help. Here, this way out . . . .

SOUND EFFECT: WALK A FEW STEPS, DOOR UNBOLTED, OPEN DOOR. LONDON STREET (BACKGROUND)

MRS. RYAN: Good evening, Doctor.

WATSON: Let me stop a cab for you.

MRS. RYAN: Oh, no, we'll just walk home.

CHRISTINE: Can't we take a cab, mama? Just this once?

MRS. RYAN: No, we'll walk. (MOVING OFF) Come along, Christine. (OFF) Good night, Doctor, and thank you again.

WATSON: (UP) You're sure you don't want a cab?

MRS. RYAN: (OFF) No, thank you. We'll be fine.

SOUND EFFECT: (PAUSE) HE STEPS BACK INTO DOORWAY, DOOR CLOSES. STREET BACKGROUND DROPS

MARY: Well, that was interesting.

WATSON: Wasn't it! She may have seen this man who's been taking all those children!

MARY: No, I mean, Mrs. Ryan not hiring a cab, and her daughter acting as if she'd never ridden in one!

WATSON: Yes, I did notice that.

MARY: And her mother made a point of saying they live "on the other side of the park", and her husband "sends money to his bank". People of real means don't need to impress anyone. And

357

that dress the girl was wearing had been mended several times. John, they're poor and she's trying not to show it!

WATSON: Mary, you're as observant as Sherlock Holmes! Hmm. I suppose I should stop round to Baker Street in the morning and tell him about this.

MARY: Why not go tonight? And I'll go with you!

MUSIC: UNDERCURRENT

WATSON: And so we locked the house and went to Baker Street immediately.

MUSIC: SHORT VIOLIN BRIDGE

SOUND EFFECT: DOOR OPENS

HOLMES: Ah, it's you, Watson. And Mrs. Watson! Come in! You know Inspector Gregson, of course.

SOUND EFFECT: (UNDER DIALOGUE) HE WALKS IN, DOOR SHUTS

WATSON: Of course. Good evening, Inspector. This is my wife, Mary.

GREGSON: A pleasure, Mrs. Watson.

HOLMES: What brings you two out on a chilly evening?

MARY: I'm afraid I urged John to come right over after what happened.

HOLMES: And what was that?

WATSON: A few minutes ago, I treated a little girl in my surgery who had been approached by a man who then tried to chloroform her!

MARY: And since there've been these abductions, we thought you'd want to know.

358

GREGSON: I should say we do! That's why I came round to see Mr. Holmes tonight. He's working with us on this case.

HOLMES: Yes, I took an interest in it after reading the accounts in the papers. Where did this happen, Watson?

WATSON: Paddington Park, near the carousel.

GREGSON: Did she describe the fellow?

WATSON: She said he was about my height and had vividly blue eyes. He approached her with a bag of candy, and when she wouldn't go with him, he took hold of her and put a chloroformed cloth over her face. She fell to the ground unconscious, the attacker fled, and her mother revived her.

HOLMES: Candy? She was sure it was candy?

WATSON: Well, that's what she said.

HOLMES: Interesting!

GREGSON: Yes. Do you have the name of the victim?

WATSON: Christine Ryan.

GREGSON: (TAKING IT DOWN) Christine Ryan. Age and description?

WATSON: She's almost nine. Height perhaps four-and-a-half feet, light brown hair . . . .

MARY: More blond than brown, actually. And she's rather small for her age.

HOLMES: And a bit thin, would you say?

MARY: Why, yes! How did you guess?

HOLMES: Did she have brown eyes?

MARY: Yes! How amazing!

WATSON: Holmes, how do you know all this?

HOLMES: The kidnapper seems to prefer thin, blond-haired girls with brown eyes.

GREGSON: And you took down the Ryan girl's address, of course?

WATSON: Her mother just said they live on the other side of Paddington Park from my place. Since there was no need for me to call on her, I didn't ask for her address.

GREGSON: I'm sure the men on that beat will know the family.

MARY: Only they may not really live In Paddington at all.

HOLMES: Oh? Why is that?

WATSON: Well you see, Mrs. Ryan mentioned that her husband has been away for a long time on business, and sends money home regularly, as if to imply they were people of some means –

MARY: But they're not. Her clothes were mended and a bit shabby. And when John suggested they take a cab home, Mrs. Ryan said no, they'd walk.

WATSON: And the girl spoke as if a cab ride would have been a rare treat.

HOLMES: Did the mother pay you for the visit?

WATSON: No, I wouldn't charge for that.

MARY: But she said she'd gladly send you a cheque. That's when she said her husband sends her money to the bank.

HOLMES: Hmm. Now Inspector, since Watson and his wife have brought us this information, and since I intend to press him into service on this case, it would be useful for him to know all that the Yard knows about it.

GREGSON: Well, we haven't a lot to go on. Over the past two weeks there've been five girls taken and returned, apparently unharmed, about an hour later.

MARY: Unharmed? Are you sure?

GREGSON: Yes. They all were taken as they were walking in the street or playing. The girls all seem to fit the description you've given of the Ryan girl. And all of the girls went willingly with the man. I suspect they were all too hungry to be suspicious. And they were all given tarts to eat.

WATSON: But now the rascal must be desperate if he's using chloroform!

GREGSON: The man who chloroformed the Ryan girl may not be our man. There's a certain class of deranged criminal who is stimulated to copy sensational crimes they read about in the paper. We told the reporters the man gave candy to the girls, when in fact it had been tarts. I think the Ryan girl might have been in grave danger if something hadn't scared this fellow off. I believe he was not the same man who snatched the other girls. He might well not have returned her!

WATSON: Yes, I see –

HOLMES: In addition to which, the carousel is nowhere near a road where a carriage could be waiting. At any rate, Watson, I need your help this very night, and with your wife's agreement, perhaps you could take her home and return as quickly as possible.

WATSON: Would you mind, Mary?

MARY: Oh no, I quite understand. Take me right home, John.

MUSIC: UNDERCURRENT

WATSON: Half-an-hour later I was back in Baker Street, learning the rest of what was known about the bizarre kidnappings.

MUSIC: OUT

361

HOLMES: Now, Inspector Gregson, tell Watson what you told me.

GREGSON: Well, I've interviewed the five girls who were abducted, and their stories are all identical. The man offers them a tart and promises them another if they take a ride with him. He uses a closed carriage – some sort of coach. He drives it himself. What we didn't tell the papers is that, once the girl is inside, he lowers the side curtains, and while the horse pulls the carriage through the streets, he has the girl remove her shoes and stockings.

WATSON: Oh, heavens. One of those!

HOLMES: Wait, Watson. Now tell what the fellow does then, Inspector.

GREGSON: Well, he looks at their feet. He just looks at their feet. And then he has them put their stockings and shoes back on, and drives them back to where he picked them up.

WATSON: And he doesn't . . . harm them in any way?

GREGSON: Apparently not. Some of the girls thought it was an adventure. Some say they quite liked the man – thought he was funny.

WATSON: Well, he should be in Bedlam. It may be only a matter of time before this creature does some real harm.

HOLMES: He may have a mental fixation compelling him, but he may have a good reason for doing what he does.

WATSON: A good reason? What could be a good reason for such behaviour? In my medical experience, anything of this sort would call for immediate hospitalization in the criminal ward!

HOLMES: I have a theory in mind, but I must talk with as many of the girls as possible. Can you supply me with their addresses, inspector?

GREGSON: Well, you're welcome to my notes on my interrogation .
   . . .

HOLMES: And I'm sure they're quite complete. I'd just like to see these girls for myself.

GREGSON: Then I'll be round first thing in the morning, Mr. Holmes, and we'll see them together.

MUSIC: UNDERCURRENT

WATSON: Early the next morning, I returned to Baker Street to find Holmes dressed and impatient to interview the five girls. We had coffee, and then Inspector Gregson arrived in a four-seat coach with the Scotland Yard emblem on the door. Our first stop was at a squalid house in Camden Town and a girl named Alice, who described her captor as a dust-man. Then to Hackney, where a delightful urchin called Gwen said the man looked as poor as her own father. By nine, we were in a working-class neighborhood of Bethnal Green to meet Barbara, and then, on to Waltham Stowe and a girl called Evangeline.

MUSIC: SEGUE TO

SOUND EFFECT: WORKING-CLASS NEIGHBORHOOD

EVANGELINE: He said he had more tarts in his carriage if I'd take a ride with him, so I said, "Why not?"

HOLMES: What did his carriage look like?

EVANGELINE: Black. And sort of . . . tatty.

HOLMES: Tatty?

EVANGLINE: Like it needed fixing. Everything was loose. The roof flapped.

HOLMES: I see. Now Evangeline, how would you describe the man's voice?

363

EVANGELINE: Oh, he's not from around here. He talked funny, like.

HOLMES: He made you laugh?

EVANGELINE: Naow! He talked different, like he was from another part of the country!

SOUND EFFECT: BACKGROUND FADE

WATSON: And thence to the Docklands, to interview a girl called Trixie.

SOUND EFFECT: (FADE UP) HARBOUR SOUNDS

TRIXIE: . . . And then after he's had a look at me feet, he thanks me and says to put me shoes back on.

WATSON: And that's all he did, Trixie?

TRIXIE: God's my witness. I thought 'e must be a doctor or som'fin'. Only his shoes wasn't good enough for a doctor.

WATSON: (AMUSED) No, Trixie, I doubt he was a doctor.

GREGSON: Thank you, young lady, that will be all. Now, mind you don't take food or rides from strangers!

HOLMES: Oh, one other thing. Did you notice a smell about him?

TRIXIE: A smell?

HOLMES: Cologne? Tobacco? Anything like that?

TRIXIE: He smelled like – like hay. You know – like out in the country.

SOUND EFFECT: BACKGROUND UP AND FADE OUT. HORSE PULLING CARRIAGE IN CITY STREET

HOLMES: A most productive morning, Inspector.

GREGSON: Was it? Frankly, I don't see what you've uncovered that isn't right here in my notes.

HOLMES: Your notes are perfectly adequate, as far as they go.

GREGSON: Well? What did you learn from all this?

HOLMES: Watson?

WATSON: What?

HOLMES: Your professional observations on these five children?

WATSON: Well, they were all sallow-complexioned. Too much breathing-in the fumes of the city.

HOLMES: And?

WATSON: And they all showed signs of improper nutrition. Bowed legs, mis-shapen arms, poor teeth . . . .

HOLMES: And . . . ?

WATSON: Well, they obviously bore a superficial likeness to one another - their age and size, their hair color . . .

HOLMES: And so why would our mystery man hunt out only these slightly deformed youngsters who all look a bit alike, eh? And why his interest in their feet?

WATSON: I think you're barking up the wrong tree, Holmes. You're looking for a sensible answer when it's clear to me that we're dealing with mental depravity here! His fascination with their feet should tell you: This man is insane!

HOLMES: Then why didn't he examine the feet of children from middle-class homes? Why has he preyed only on the poor?

WATSON: Because they were the most vulnerable! Surely that should be obvious to you! Rich children can play in supervised yards, behind fences. The poor must play in the street! These hungry little waifs are the only children this monster could hope to capture!

HOLMES: Watson, I salute you. Your scope of the facts is most commendable, but your conclusions are wrong.

WATSON: Wrong? How are they wrong?

HOLMES: You shall see for yourself in the hours just ahead. Inspector?

GREGSON: Yes?

HOLMES: We must find Mrs. Ryan. And we must locate the bank near Paddington where she may have an account. Have your men do that. I shall wait by my telephone for your call. But in the meantime, I will be totally immersed in the daily newspapers.

MUSIC: UNDERCURRENT

WATSON: And we rode back to Baker Street with Holmes absorbed in thought, with an eager smile playing about his lips. We spent the rest of that afternoon in Holmes's rooms in Baker Street, which were now covered in a white blanket of newsprint. On the way home, he had stopped at a newsvendor's and purchased back-copies of every London paper. Now, he sat cross-legged in a chair, ripping apart one edition after another.

SOUND EFFECT: (IN BACKGROUND) GREAT FLURRY OF NEWSPAPERS

WATSON: Holmes? . . . Holmes? . . . Holmes!

HOLMES: Unless you have something of immeasurable importance to say just now, pray don't say it.

WATSON: I was merely going to offer to help you look for whatever it is you're looking for.

HOLMES: It would take me longer to explain what I'm looking for, than the time it would save if you were looking for it too.

HOLMES: I'll get it, Watson, I'll get it!

SOUND EFFECT: PAPERS RUMPLE AS HE GETS TO HIS FEET. RING ENDS AS HE PICKS UP THE PHONE

HOLMES: Holmes here . . . Excellent! And what about the bank? . . . I see. Where are they coming from? . . . Scotland. Bring Mrs. Ryan and daughter here to Baker Street tonight! . . . No, six o'clock is too early. Can you make it eight? . . . Good, then eight it is. Any luck finding the coachman? . . . Keep trying. He'll be somewhere in the east end. And when your men find him, bring him straight here!

SOUND EFFECT: TELEPHONE HUNG UP

HOLMES: Gregson has located Mrs. Ryan and her daughter.

WATSON: So I gather. Are they coming here?

HOLMES: At eight. I need more time to read the agony columns.

MUSIC: UNDERCURRENT

WATSON: The hours dragged by. I felt completely useless. As much as I wanted to help Holmes in his search, he wouldn't tell me what he was looking for. And then, as I was standing at the window, watching twilight fade into darkness and the lamps go on in the street . . . .

MUSIC: OUT

SOUND EFFECT: HORSES IN STREET, SOFTLY

HOLMES: (OFF-MICROPHONE) Yes! At last! Here he is!

WATSON: What is it?

HOLMES: *"Joan, searching for 'C'. Able to help. Want to come home. Send address box 395!"* Signed, *"Thomas"*.

WATSON: There must be a hundred advertisements like that in the papers.

HOLMES: Not like this one. Help me clean up this mess, Watson! They'll be here in an hour!

MUSIC: STING

SOUND EFFECT: KNOCK ON DOOR

HOLMES: Ah!

SOUND EFFECT: HE STRIDES TO DOOR, OPENS IT

GREGSON: Mr. Holmes . . . .

HOLMES: Yes, yes, Inspector, come right in. And come in, Mrs. Ryan and Christine.

SOUND EFFECT: THREE PEOPLE WALK IN AND CLOSE DOOR (UNDER)

HOLMES: I believe you already know Doctor Watson.

MRS. RYAN: Doctor! What are you doing here?

WATSON: I'm a close associate of Sherlock Holmes, Mrs. Ryan. I told him about Christine's experience.

HOLMES: Yes, and with your information, I believe tonight we may solve these matters. Now, Watson, let's find chairs for our guests.

SOUND EFFECT: ASSORTED STEPS, FURNITURE MOVES (UNDER)

MRS. RYAN: But the inspector didn't tell us why you wanted us here.

GREGSON: Mr. Holmes assists the Yard from time to time.

368

HOLMES: Yes, and I have something I want you to do for me, Christine. Will you kindly remove your shoes and stockings?

MRS. RYAN: What? Whatever for?

HOLMES: If it would make you feel more comfortable, I'll have Mrs. Hudson come in.

CHRISTINE: I don't mind. I'll take them off.

GREGSON: Is this absolutely necessary, Mr. Holmes?

HOLMES: If you want to solve this case, it is.

CHRISTINE: Take my stockings, mama.

MRS. RYAN: Christine! What are you doing wearing those old stockings!

CHRISTINE: There!

HOLMES: Now, may I look at your feet?

CHRISTINE: All right.

HOLMES: Thank you. How did you lose the last two toes on your right foot?

MRS. RYAN: She was only a baby . . . there was an accident.

SOUND EFFECT: KNOCK ON DOOR

HOLMES: Inspector, will you get that? It may be one of your men.

SOUND EFFECT: HE WALKS TO THE DOOR AND OPENS IT

OFFICER: Is Mr. Sherlock Holmes here?

GREGSON: I'm Chief Inspector Gregson.

OFFICER: Oh. Yes sir. I'm PC Newbold, Metropolitan Police, sir. I was told to bring this man up here if we found him.

HOLMES: Yes, bring him in, Constable. I'm Sherlock Holmes.

SOUND EFFECT: TWO MEN WALK IN AND DOOR CLOSES

HOLMES: Do you know this man, Mrs. Ryan?

MRS. RYAN: What are you doing here? Why are you in London?

CHRISTINE: Who is it, Mama?

TOM: Is it you, Christine? Is it really you?

CHRISTINE: Who is this man?

TOM: I'm your dad, Christine. I've been looking for you and your mum for so many years . . . .

GREGSON: According to the Imperial Bank, for the past seven years, a Thomas Ryan has been sending a small amount of money every month to the account of Joan Ryan, from somewhere in Scotland. We just learned that today.

TOM: I've done fairly well with the farm, Joan. Sending a few pounds was all I could do after you left me. Not that I blame you for leaving, after the accident and all . . . .

HOLMES: And was that the accident that injured Christine's foot?

MRS. RYAN: You were drunk, Torn, and you had a knife and one night you threatened me with it while I was changing the baby. You were aiming for me, but you missed me and struck her! That was the "accident". I packed up and left that very night.

TOM: And I haven't touched a drop since that night, so help me!

HOLMES: And you ran an advertisement but got no response.

TOM: I had to find my wife and my baby! I didn't have their address, or any idea what Christine would look like now, seven years later, but . . . I thought of a way to find her: Find a little girl with that terrible injury!

370

GREGSON: It's my duty to inform you at this point, Mr. Ryan, that anything you say may be taken down and used against you in a court of law. You're guilty of at least five counts of molestation and kidnapping.

TOM: I didn't harm any of the girls, Christine. I was just looking for you.

MUSIC: UP AND UNDER

WATSON: And later, after Gregson took the Ryan family away, I asked Holmes to tell me how he knew who was abducting the girls, and why.

HOLMES: I knew the abductor was looking for a mark of some kind on the feet of a certain physical type of girl who lived in poor circumstances. He was seeking a child of poverty. Why? No poverty-stricken parent could pay a ransom. It had to be a quest by a family member. An estranged father, for example. And then the advertisement in the agony column: "*Searching for 'C'*" – Christine begins with a *C*. And "*want to come home*". A wayward son? A derelict husband?

WATSON: Then he wasn't the man who tried to chloroform Christine.

HOLMES: Most assuredly not. That had to be someone who read the newspaper accounts and tried to re-enact the crime that made headlines. A sick mind, and a dangerous one.

WATSON: But if he hadn't made his attempt, and if Mrs. Ryan hadn't come to me, Christine wouldn't have found her father. You know, Holmes, maybe everything always works for the best.

HOLMES: I wouldn't rob you of your idealism for the world, Watson. Now let's have dinner.

MUSIC: *DANSE MACABRE* UP AND UNDER

WATSON: This is Doctor John H. Watson. Be sure to join me for another Sherlock Holmes adventure . . . *when next we meet*!

MUSIC: UP AND FADE

The Man Who
Believed in Nothing

CHARACTERS

- SHERLOCK HOLMES
- DR. JOHN H. WATSON
- MRS. HUDSON
- REVEREND KENNETH PAIGE – *Distinguished Vicar of a small old Anglican church in the town of Harrow. Well-educated, British, Age sixty*
- ALICE VAN METER – *Choir director and organist for the church. Age thirty-seven, single*
- REVEREND HARRY LANTRY – *Assistant Pastor. Mild-mannered, frail, Age thirty-five*
- MATRON – *Head nurse of a British Mental Hospital. Age sixties*

SOUND EFFECT: OPENING SEQUENCE, BIG BEN, STREET SOUNDS

ANNOUNCER: *The Further Adventures of Sherlock Holmes . . . .*

MUSIC: *DANSE MACABRE* (UP AND UNDER)

WATSON: My name is Doctor John H. Watson. To some of you who have followed my stories about Sherlock Holmes, it may seem that his services were always in constant demand. However, in the fall of 1889, despite having solved the hideous killing in the Tuttman Gallery several weeks earlier, Holmes experienced a period of inactivity. In the first week of December, I had just attended a patient whose condition had worsened, and now required immediate admittance to a sanitarium. Being only half-a-mile or so from Baker Street – and needing a change of mood – I decided to stop around at 221b for a visit with Holmes.

MUSIC: OUT

MRS. HUDSON: Oh, it's Doctor Watson! Come in, Doctor! How nice to see you!

WATSON: It's good to see you, Mrs. Hudson. How have you been?

SOUND EFFECT: DOOR CLOSES. STREET SOUNDS DOWN

MRS. HUDSON: Oh, still hale and hearty, thanks be. And yourself? You're looking fine!

WATSON: I've been quite busy lately. Is Holmes in?

MRS. HUDSON: Yes, he's in. I was just going up to collect his breakfast dishes. (LOW) You know, Doctor, for the past fortnight, he's been in one of his gloomy spells. But then a letter came this morning, and I think he's back to his old self.

WATSON: A letter, eh?

MRS. HUDSON: By special messenger, at six a.m.! It must have been good news, because he began to bustle about, and I even heard him whistling. He never whistles.

WATSON: Well, we know he has his moods, but give him a juicy case, and he's right as rain.

SOUND EFFECT: TWO PEOPLE CLIMBING STAIRS

MRS. HUDSON: And how is your wife these days?

WATSON: Mary? She's in excellent spirits, I'm glad to say. Today she's poring over a cook book, planning what to serve for Christmas.

MRS. HUDSON: Ah, then she likes to cook, does she?

WATSON: (CHUCKLES) Can't you tell? I've had to buy new suits!

SOUND EFFECT: STEPS STOP. MRS. HUDSON TAPS ON DOOR. PAUSE, THEN DOOR OPENS

HOLMES: Watson! Come in. I was just thinking about you.

WATSON: Hello, Holmes. I was just in the neighbourhood –

HOLMES: – visiting a highly contagious patient.

WATSON: Now how on earth can you tell?

HOLMES: (CHUCKLES) The marks from the sanitary mask are still impressed on your face.

WATSON: Eh? They are? I must have tied it too tightly.

HOLMES: And by the evidence of your new clothes, your practice must be flourishing. Feel free to take the breakfast tray, Mrs. Hudson

MRS. HUDSON: (MOVING OFF) Yes, I'll only be a moment.

WATSON: And how is it with you, Holmes?

HOLMES: My life has become a study in boredom. Scarcely a whisper of interest from anyone since that museum horror. But then this morning, a glimmer. A letter came from out of town, making me think of you and your predilection for idylls in the country.

MRS. HUDSON: (FAR OFF) Well! I see for once you ate every scrap!

SOUND EFFECT: (FAR OFF) DISHES STACKED

HOLMES: And Mrs. Hudson, I shan't be dining here for the rest of the day, so you are now free to go and buy out the stores.

MRS. HUDSON: Buy out the stores, indeed!

SOUND EFFECT: (UNDER ABOVE) MRS. HUDSON WALKS OFF, PLATES JIGGLING. DOOR OPENS. SHE GOES OUT. DOOR CLOSES.

WATSON: You *are* in a chipper mood. Is it the letter?

HOLMES: Like to hear it?

WATSON: Certainly.

SOUND EFFECT: NOTE HANDLED

HOLMES: (READING) *"Dear Mr. Holmes: Knowing of your most excellent reputation in solving all manner of difficulties, may I trouble you to consider helping us locate one of our clergy who is missing? He is quite disturbed, and I fear he may try to harm himself. It is urgent that he be found before a tragedy takes place, and it is equally urgent that this matter remain confidential, for reasons which I will explain in detail if you will grant us the goodness of your help. I prayerfully await your earliest reply, for time is of the essence, and a life may hang in the balance. May God bless you. Most sincerely, The Reverend Kenneth Paige, Vicar of the Anglican Church of Harrow."*

WATSON: Well. What do you think?

HOLMES: I sent a telegram this morning, telling him I would be there this afternoon. You wouldn't like to come with me, would you? I may need your medical knowledge, and I am almost certain that you won't be chased by a crocodile this time. Of course, with a busy practice like yours . . . .

WATSON: Nonsense. Old Jackson would be glad to take my patients for a day or so, and Mary is so busy with her shopping, I doubt she'd even notice I'm gone. Of course I'll come with you, Holmes! With pleasure!

MUSIC: UNDERCURRENT

WATSON: It was late afternoon when Holmes and I arrived in the Middlesex town of Harrow. The church stood on a road of gabled houses. On one side was a small cemetery, and on the other was a large two-story house. It was here that the Reverend Paige had arranged to meet us. He welcomed us into a darkly-panelled study, warmed by a wood fire.

376

MUSIC: OUT

PAIGE: So terribly good of you to come so promptly. May I offer you tea or coffee? Or we do have some hot mulled wine.

WATSON: Well! After a chilly trip, that would make me most wel–

HOLMES: Perhaps later, thank you. Now, about the missing man. How long has he been gone?

PAIGE: Since last night.

HOLMES: You've called the police?

PAIGE: No, as I mentioned in my letter, this is a . . . delicate matter.

HOLMES: Delicate in what way?

PAIGE: Well, Father Lantry certainly wasn't in his senses when he left.

HOLMES: Oh?

PAIGE: Miss Van Meter tells me she found him in a despairing mood last evening, before our service. They spoke for a few minutes, then went their separate ways. Then, at just before seven, when I entered the sanctuary to prepare for Vespers, I discovered the gold altar cross and a pair of silver candlesticks were missing. Well, of course the first thing that entered my mind was that we'd been robbed!

HOLMES: The church isn't kept locked when it's not in use?

PAIGE: No. Parishioners may need to come into the sanctuary at any time for prayer or meditation. But, thinking we'd had a burglar, I immediately went to the sacristy to see if anything there was missing, and a silver communion chalice was gone, along with the morning's collections!

WATSON: Oh, I say. What a shame.

HOLMES: And what about the missing man?

377

PAIGE: Father Lantry didn't turn up for Vespers, so I conducted the service by myself. But immediately after the benediction, I hurried up to his room to see if he was ill. And there . . . I found the missing items. Now you see why I must shield Father Lantry form any public shame.

HOLMES: Tell me all you can about him.

PAIGE: Well, he grew up in this parish, and came out of the seminary and served as a deacon. Then he accepted a call to replace the chaplain at Blackwall Prison, but that turned out to be too much for him.

HOLMES: In what way?

PAIGE: Associating with that low class of men every day caused him to doubt his faith, and that brought on a nervous collapse. He resigned his post as chaplain, and the Diocese decided it would be best if he were put under treatment at a mental hospital. Parkhurst Hospital, in the West End.

HOLMES: Be more specific about what brought on his condition and what it did to him.

PAIGE: Well, many of the prisoners he ministered to – or tried to minister to – had committed unspeakable crimes. They were such brutal men that, no matter what Henry did, it seemed to do no good. The anger and the violence he encountered eventually broke his spirit. But in hospital, he seemed to have convalesced well, so we welcomed him back to the parish, and found quarters for him right here in the vicarage.

HOLMES: I take it he's unmarried?

PAIGE: Oh, yes.

ALICE: (OFF) Father Paige?

PAIGE: Oh, yes, Alice, come right in. Gentlemen, our choir director and organist, Miss Alice Van Meter. Alice, these are the gentlemen who so graciously came up from London to help us. May I present Mr. Sherlock Holmes and Doctor –

ALICE: Doctor Watson? It's Doctor Watson, of course! (MOVING ON) Excuse me, I can't believe I'm actually in the same room with Sherlock Holmes and Doctor Watson! I've read everything about you, Mr. Holmes!

HOLMES: Most kind of you.

WATSON: I'm glad you enjoy the stories.

PAIGE: Now, Alice, I've been telling the gentlemen about what happened last night, and I thought they might have some questions for you.

ALICE: I'll tell you all I can, gentlemen.

HOLMES: The Vicar was saying Mr. Lantry spent some time in mental hospital.

ALICE: Ten months and a week, to be exact.

PAIGE: But he gradually improved, and seemed to be anxious to resume his duties in the Parish. We thought he was getting along rather well.

HOLMES: The Vicar tells me you spoke with Mr. Lantry last night, shortly before he turned up missing.

ALICE: Yes.

HOLMES: Did you have any concerns about him at that time?

ALICE: Yes, I did. But . . . well, he spoke to me in confidence.

PAIGE: If you can throw any light on our search for him, my child, you ought to realize that his safety is of paramount importance. Please tell us what he said.

ALICE: Well, as you know, he'd been struggling with his faith, and . . . and he'd had another of his blank spells. He's been having them right along, but he didn't want you to know.

HOLMES: Describe these spells.

ALICE: He forgets whole hours of time. He . . . he won't remember doing this or that . . . . It's as if his mind went to sleep for a short time, and then woke up again.

HOLMES: Watson? Have you ever heard of this?

WATSON: Well, it's rare, but not unheard-of. The literarure mentions it from time to time, but I haven't seen it personally. It may be what they call a "fugue" state.

PAIGE: Is it considered a form of insanity?

WATSON: Well, you know there's no reliable measure for insanity. There's a broad line between normal and abnormal behaviour.

HOLMES: What brings on these "fugues"?

WATSON: Sometimes it's a shock of some sort. And typically he won't remember the cause when he comes out of it.

HOLMES: And so Mr. Lantry confided in you that he was having these mental lapses. What else?

ALICE: He . . . he was terribly disillusioned by his work with the prisoners. I think he questioned why God would permit Man to do such horrible acts.

HOLMES: Are you saying he lost his faith?

ALICE: I . . . Yes. I supposed that's what it comes down to.

HOLMES: May we see his room?

PAIGE: Certainly. Just follow me.

ALICE: May I come too?

PAIGE: Of course.

SOUND EFFECT: (UNDER) GROUP ASCENDING STAIRS

WATSON: The priest's room was upstairs in the back. It had a thin rug on the floor, curtains at the window, a narrow cot, a chair, and a writing desk, with a painting of *"The Last Supper"* hanging on the wall. The room was dominated by a heavy mahogany armoire.

SOUND EFFECT: STEPS STOP

HOLMES: Where did you find the missing goods?

PAIGE: There, in the armoire. Go on, open the wardrobe doors. You see, all his clerical garb is hanging there. Two complete sets – that's all he had. So he left here wearing layman's clothing.

MUSIC: UNDERCURRENT UP AND UNDER

WATSON: Holmes pulled open the drawers beneath the wardrobe. They were empty. He stood quietly in the middle of the room for several seconds. Then, he walked to the cot and carefully lifted the blanket, then the pillow, and then the thin mattress, and there – under the mattress – lay a single sheet of paper. He picked it up.

MUSIC: OUT

SOUND EFFECT: SINGLE PAPER FLEX

HOLMES: Half-a-sheet of cheap writing paper, torn in half down the middle. Would you recognize Mr. Lantry's handwriting?

PAIGE: I think so.

ALICE: *I* would.

HOLMES: Is this his writing?

SOUND EFFECT: PAPER FLEX

381

ALICE: Yes, it's his. But what's this he's written?

HOLMES: It appears to be a list.

PAIGE: What does it say? "*God, self, humanity, country, royalty . . .*"

ALICE: ". . . *Government, education, money, science, intelligence,* (PAUSE) . . . *love* . . . ."

PAIGE: "*Law, loyalty, honesty, sympathy, and service to others.*" What is this?

HOLMES: Things people believe in, it would seem.

PAIGE: Why would he have written this?

HOLMES: I'm more interested in what he wrote on the half that was torn away.

WATSON: How do you know he wrote anything on the other half of the paper?

HOLMES: Because, Watson, here . . . on the very edge where he tore it, is the start of another line of writing. You see it?

WATSON: Oh! I'd missed that.

PAIGE: He may have thought better of what he wrote and thrown the other half away.

ALICE: Mr. Holmes, how in the world did you know to look under his mattress?

HOLMES: I thought he might have left a note before he left, and the only place to hide one in this room – if not in the armoire – was in or under the bed. Now: Would you, by any chance, remember what Mr. Lantry was wearing when you saw him last night, Miss Van Meter?

ALICE: Why, he was still in his vestments.

382

HOLMES: Does he own a coat?

ALICE: Yes.

HOLMES: And a hat?

ALICE: Yes.

HOLMES: Then where are they?

ALICE: Why, I don't know.

HOLMES: Well, I think, for the moment at least, we may discard any fear that he's taken his life. He would hardly go to the trouble to dress against the weather if he went outdoors only to commit suicide.

MUSIC: UNDERCURRENT

WATSON: But the question remained, where *had* the Reverend Lantry gone – and why? Holmes requested a private interview with Alice Van Meter, and the two of them went down to the sitting room by themselves for a few minutes while I had coffee with the Vicar. Afterward, Holmes joined me in the study. The Vicar excused himself to attend to some parish business. Holmes paced around the study in an impatient mood, puffing on his pipe. And then suddenly, he whirled and smote his forehead.

MUSIC: OUT

HOLMES: Of course! I think I know where he is!

WATSON: Where?

HOLMES: Watson, make our goodbyes to the Vicar, while I see about hiring a carriage to take us to the train station.

SOUND EFFECT: FADE UP – TRAIN IN MOTION

WATSON: We were able to catch a southbound train at 5:05 p.m., which made many stops on its way to London. During the trip, Holmes appeared to have fallen asleep. But then he said, without opening his eyes –

HOLMES: Go on, Watson. I'm not asleep, and you're about to burst like a tea kettle. I can feel the pressure from here, so ask away.

WATSON: Well! To begin with, where are we going?

HOLMES: To Notting Hill. To the Parkhurst Hospital. That's where I believe we shall find Reverend Lantry.

WATSON: What makes you think that?

HOLMES: The hospital was his first place of refuge after quitting his job as a prison chaplain. But when he left there, he may have still felt he'd lost his faith. No doubt he feels a great confusion and guilt. Where else to go but back to Parkhurst? But Watson, if I'm right and we find him, I have reason to believe we can help him!

MUSIC: UNDERCURRENT

WATSON: We got off the train at Notting Hill Station and took a hansom to Ladbroke Road, where there stood a manor house with a sign saying "*Parkhurst Hospital*". We approached the matron on duty at the front desk.

MUSIC: OUT

MATRON: May I help you?

HOLMES: We are here to visit a patient. Henry Lantry.

MATRON: Your names?

HOLMES: Sherlock Holmes.

WATSON: Doctor John H. Watson.

MATRON: Oh. Has Reverend Lantry been your patient, Doctor?

WATSON: Uh, why, uh . . . .

HOLMES: Doctor Watson is here in a consulting capacity. He is a specialist, as am I.

MATRON: I see. Well, if you'll excuse me for a moment, gentleman –

SOUND EFFECT: SHE GETS UP AND WALKS OFF. DOOR OPENS AND CLOSES

WATSON: (LOUD WHISPER) Consulting capacity?

HOLMES: Perfectly truthful. We *are* consulted by clients all the time, aren't we?

WATSON: Well, yes, I suppose that's right. But what if they don't let us see him? He may be too ill . . . or he may not want to see anyone.

HOLMES: Our mission was to find him, and apparently we've done that. But there is more to learn about this, which will be of some use to the Vicar . . . .

SOUND EFFECT: (OFF) DOOR OPENS AND CLOSES. WOMAN WALKS ON

MATRON: This way please.

MUSIC: UNDERCURRENT

WATSON: She led us into a comfortably appointed office, where we waited a moment or two, and then she returned, with a pale, thin, haunted-looking man. He barely spoke as we were introduced. The matron remained in the room.

MUSIC: OUT

LANTRY: What do you want with me?

HOLMES: We want to help you.

385

LANTRY: They all want to help me, but there is no help, not for me. How did you know where to find me?

HOLMES: A fortunate assumption. Reverend Lantry, I think I –

LANTRY: Don't call me that! Don't call me Reverend, not any more.

HOLMES: Very well, Mr. Lantry. I think I know why you left the parish so suddenly. You believed you had stolen money and valuables from the church while you were not aware of what you were doing. And when you came to your senses and found these things in your room, you decided to leave and come back here before you did something else, perhaps something worse.

LANTRY: I don't know how you would know that.

HOLMES: We found the note you left.

LANTRY: The note?

HOLMES: This.

SOUND EFFECT: PAPER CRINKLES

HOLMES: You did leave this under your mattress?

LANTRY: I . . . forgot I left it there.

HOLMES: What did you do with the other half of the page?

LANTRY: How did you know there was another half? I was going to burn it. Destroy it! But I kept it. I don't know why. The madness, perhaps.

HOLMES: Do you still have it?

MATRON: It's with his things. Do you want me to get it, Henry?

LANTRY: Yes, you might as well.

MATRON: I'll be right back.

SOUND EFFECT: A STEP. DOOR OPENS. STEP OUT. DOOR CLOSES.

HOLMES: Are you treated well here?

LANTRY: As well as I deserve.

WATSON: Look here, Mr. Lantry . . . Holmes has information that will relieve your mind.

LANTRY: Nothing will relieve my mind! I've been cursed by Blackwall Prison! I went there to bring God to the inmates, but the inmates took God away from me!

HOLMES: But they couldn't do that, could they? Didn't Saint Matthew quote God as saying, *"I am with you always"*?

LANTRY: Matthew 28, Verse 20. *"I am with you always."*

HOLMES: *"Even unto the end of the world."*

SOUND EFFECT: DOOR OPENS. STEP IN. DOOR CLOSES

MATRON: Is this what you want?

SOUND EFFECT: PAPER UNFOLDED

LANTRY: Yes.

HOLMES: May I see it?

LANTRY: Here.

HOLMES: Hmm. Now it makes sense. The list I found on the left hand side of the paper has a list of things to believe in.

LANTRY: Things I *ought* to believe in . . . things I *used* to believe in! Mr. Holmes, I left the chaplaincy in Blackwall with no belief left in me! It was burned out of me! I struggled day after day, but I felt like an empty shell! So one night, I wrote down the things I ought to believe in, starting with God, so I could think and pray about them. Then, on Sunday evening, after talking with Alice . . . Did you meet Alice . . . ?

HOLMES: Yes, we met her.

LANTRY: Well, I went up to my room and took out the list . . . and I saw that I had written something opposite each of the objects of belief! While I was out of my senses! It was so horrible, I tore it away!

HOLMES: But look, Mr. Lantry. Look at these two lists. The right column isn't your handwriting.

LANTRY: Oh, I'm afraid that it was my hand, guided by the Devil! Look what I wrote! Opposite *"Service to Others"*, I wrote *"Waste of Time"!* "Opposite *"Law"*: *"A contrivance of the ruling class"*! Opposite *"Love"*: *"Animal Emotion"*, and worst of all, opposite *"God"*: *"Superstition"*! I came back to my room and found what I'd done – stolen the cross and the rest – and knew I had to leave right then!

MUSIC: UNDERCURRENT

WATSON: We were allowed to spend the night talking with Lantry. It wasn't until eight o'clock the next morning that the doctor in charge permitted us to take Henry Lantry back to Harrow with us. And it was noon when we got back to the church, and Holmes asked the Vicar to meet with Lantry and me in the study, and for Alice Van Meter to join us and bring her notes for the upcoming Christmas program.

MUSIC: OUT

PAIGE: I'm overjoyed to have you back with us, Henry, and we shall do everything possible to make things just as they were before.

HOLMES: Or possibly not.

PAIGE: What do you mean? Father Lantry seems to be quite himself again!

388

LANTRY: I may still have occasions when I go blank, but my doctor tells me these will gradually go away. But during the past few hours, Mr. Holmes made several things clear to me, and now I must make *everything* clear. Alice?

ALICE: Yes, Henry?

LANTRY: I told Mr. Holmes about our conversation on Sunday.

ALICE: You did what?

HOLMES: He told me how you had thrown yourself at him, Miss Van Meter.

ALICE: Why, you surely don't believe that!

HOLMES: Didn't you tell him that you could bring him health and happiness if you would marry?

ALICE: We discussed our understanding, yes, but –

LANTRY: We had no understanding, Alice, but you were so determined that we should be married –

ALICE: Don't think I haven't had a lot of chances! Every bachelor in this parish wants to marry me! But I saved myself for you, Henry!

HOLMES: And how did this conversation end, Mr. Lantry?

ALICE: You won't tell him that, Henry! You mustn't!

LANTRY: She kissed me. I didn't expect it, but . . . she kissed me!

HOLMES: And then what happened?

LANTRY: I was so dazed, I didn't remember anything until I found myself back in my room. And I opened my armoire and I saw the cross and the chalice and the candlestick! Of course, I thought I'd taken them from the sanctuary myself, without

389

realizing it. So I knew I should leave and go back where I couldn't do any more harm. I went back to Parkhurst.

HOLMES: How did those items get from the church and into Mr. Lantry's room, Alice?

ALICE: He took them! He'd been in the prison too long, you see, and it turned him into a criminal! I tried to protect you, Henry!

HOLMES: May we see your notes for the Christmas service?

ALICE: What?

HOLMES: The notes you shared with me during our talk a few minutes ago.

SOUND EFFECT – RUSTLE OF PAPERS

ALICE: Here.

HOLMES: Now, Mr. Lantry, the half-page you tore away because you thought you had written it?

LANTRY: Yes, here it is.

SOUND EFFECT – SINGLE RUSTLE OF PAPER

HOLMES: Compare the handwriting, Reverend Paige.

PAIGE: (PAUSE) The writing on the right half is different.

HOLMES: Now, compare it to Alice's writing.

PAIGE: This *is* Alice's writing!

HOLMES: Mr. Lantry listed the things he believed in. He'd shown you his list. He told you where he kept it. You took the opportunity to add to it, at the time you hid the objects from the church in his armoire, hoping Mr. Lantry would think he had written it, just as you hoped he'd think he'd stolen the goods! It was all part of your plan of revenge because Mr. Lantry refused to marry you. Isn't that right?

390

ALICE: (PAUSE) I forgive you, Henry. You're not in your right mind. After we're married, I'll take care of you.

PAIGE: Alice . . . my child . . . you'd better come with me now.

ALICE: (FADING OFF) You don't need to be afraid anymore, my darling. I'll protect you. I love you! I've always loved you . . . .

PAIGE: (OFF) Come along, Alice

ALICE: (OFF) They're evil men, Henry! Like the men in the prison —

SOUND EFFECT – DOOR CLOSES

MUSIC: UNDERCURENT

WATSON: The Vicar had a long talk with Alice Van Meter. More than that we weren't told. But it was enough to satisfy Holmes, and we returned to London on the next train. A few days later, we received an invitation to come back to Harrow for the Christmas Service at the church. To my surprise, Holmes said that he'd be there . . . if my wife and I would come with him. Which, I'm happy to say, we did.

MUSIC: *DANSE MACABRE* UP AND UNDER

WATSON: This is Doctor John H. Watson. I had many more adventures during our long friendship, and I'll tell you another one – *when next we meet*!

MUSIC: UP AND FADE

The Estonian Countess

CHARACTERS

- DR. JOHN H. WATSON
- MRS. HUDSON
- MYCROFT HOLMES
- TEMPLETON – *Diogenes Club Servant*
- COUNTESS MARIE VALMIERA OF ESTONIA – *A noblewoman from Northern Europe*
- BLAKE – *Pinkerton Agent*

SOUND EFFECT: OPENING SEQUENCE, BIG BEN, STREET SOUNDS

ANNOUNCER: *The Further Adventures of Sherlock Holmes . . . .*

MUSIC: *DANSE MACABRE* (UP AND UNDER

WATSON: My name is Doctor John H. Watson. As those who have followed my writings know, the date of May the fourth, 1891 was one of the darkest days of my life. It was on that day, on a cliff overlooking Reichenbach Falls in Switzerland, that my dear friend Sherlock Holmes had a final confrontation with the evil Professor Moriarty. The two men were locked in a mortal struggle on a ledge high above the falls, when they tumbled into the abyss and disappeared. No bodies were ever recovered. There followed, for me, the most dismal period of depression. Though I am a surgeon and familiar with human loss, for a time I simply ceased all normal function. I retired from my medical practice, returned to Kensington, and saw virtually no one for months. Mary, my wife, had gone to the country to visit old friends and I felt quite alone. And then one afternoon, a most surprising and welcome visitor called at my door.

MUSIC: OUT

SOUND EFFECT: DOOR OPENS. STREET (BACKGROUND IN)

MRS. HUDSON: Doctor Watson?

WATSON: Mrs. Hudson! Upon my soul! Come in! Come right in!

SOUND EFFECT: SHE WALKS IN, DOOR CLOSES (STREET OUT)

WATSON: How are you? Let me take your coat.

MRS. HUDSON: And how have you been keeping, doctor?

WATSON: Ah . . . well, missing the old days, Mrs. Hudson.

MRS. HUDSON: Indeed, and so am I.

WATSON: Oh, please! Where are my manners! Do sit down. Can I bring you some tea?

MRS. HUDSON: I won't have the time, I'm afraid. There's a cab waiting. I've come at the request of Mr. Holmes.

WATSON: Mr. Holmes? Good heavens! – You don't mean –

MRS. HUDSON: Mr. Mycroft Holmes, I mean.

WATSON: Oh, yes, of course. His brother.

MRS. HUDSON: Well, you know about the fire in Baker Street.

WATSON: Yes, Moriarty did it the night before Holmes and I left for Europe on our last trip together.

MRS. HUDSON: Well, did you know that Mr. Mycroft Holmes has had the damage repaired? Paid for it himself and had everything put to rights, so it looks just the way it did when you and Mr. Holmes were living there!

WATSON: No!

MRS. HUDSON: Well, he did. Of course, I never saw the man, but he sent 'round decorators, paperhangers, carpenters, glazers – you never saw such a great mob of workers! And in a week it was just like before, and not a farthing's cost to me!

WATSON: How amazing!

MRS. HUDSON: And he sends me a cheque every month for the rent!

WATSON: He does?

MRS. HUDSON: Oh, yes. I'm not to let the rooms out to anyone!

WATSON: What a touching thing to do! Trying to keep the memory of his brother alive.

MRS. HUDSON: Well, now here's why I've come to see you, Doctor Watson: This morning I heard from Mr. Mycroft. It seems that he wants you to move back into 221b.

WATSON: Move back in?

MRS. HUDSON: And he told me to ask you to go and see him today!

MUSIC: UNDERCURRENT

WATSON: And so began the strangest adventure I had ever lived since first meeting Sherlock Holmes. For what Holmes's older brother asked me to do was outrageous! I made my way from Kensington to Whitehall at twilight, arriving just as the street lamps were being lit. Lamps glowed in the upper windows of Mycroft Holmes's office, and a butler showed me into the rooms without a word. It was the first time I'd been there since Reichenbach Falls.

MUSIC: OUT

MYCROFT: (OFF) Come right in, Doctor. That will be all, Templeton.

TEMPLETON: (OFF) Very good, sir.

SOUND EFFECT: (OFF) DOOR CLOSES QUIETLY

MYCROFT: Have you had your tea?

WATSON: Well, no.

MYCROFT: Templeton has laid out a rather elaborate one. Sit down and share it with me.

WATSON: Thank you.

<u>SOUND EFFECT: WATSON SITS, TEA SERVICE (UNDER)</u>

MYCROFT: You're not taking care of yourself, Doctor. You've lost weight and you're paler than normal. You should either learn to cook or hire someone to fix your meals while your wife's away.

WATSON: How could you know she's away?

MYCROFT: You didn't shave this morning, your collar's rumpled, your tie's not straight, and your shoes aren't polished. Mrs. Watson wouldn't have let you out of the house looking that way. How is she, by the way?

WATSON: She's had some heart palpitations, but she refuses to concern herself about it. She's gone to visit friends for a few days.

MYCROFT: Well, her absence comes at a convenient time, actually. I need you to do something for me.

WATSON: I will be glad to have something to do. What is it?

MYCROFT: Impersonate Sherlock.

WATSON: (LONG PAUSE) I beg your pardon?

MYCROFT: As Mrs. Hudson no doubt told you, I've had your old rooms in Baker street restored to their original condition. I would like you to take up residence there, temporarily, and be prepared to receive a very important visitor, who will think that you are my brother.

WATSON: But –

MYCROFT: I'll tell you what she'll say to you, and what you will say to her. The entire encounter should take half-an-hour of your time.

WATSON: You – you can't be serious!

MYCROFT: I am always serious.

WATSON: But who is this person?

MYCROFT: She is a noblewoman from Northern Europe. You will refer to her as "Countess".

WATSON: Excuse me, sir, but this strikes me as a . . . a . . . well, to pretend to be Sherlock Holmes would be –

MYCROFT: An absolute necessity.

WATSON: I – I'm sorry, but I don't feel I could do such a thing.

MYCROFT: Sherlock would want you to do it.

WATSON: I can't believe that!

MYCROFT: Depend on it.

WATSON: But I don't look anything like he looked. I'm older . . . .

MYCROFT: The Countess never saw him. She comes from a country where Sherlock was unknown and the news of his death was never published. She knows of him only from your magazine stories, but on that basis she absolutely insists on dealing through him. Her mission to London is of critical importance to three nations including England, and if she can't deal personally with Sherlock Holmes, I fear the course of history may be drastically altered.

WATSON: Have you spoken with her?

MYCROFT: No. She's been in America. She sent a letter to Sherlock, which was forwarded to me. I receive all of Sherlock's mail now, of course. I cabled her a reply on the tenth and she sailed from New York the next day, so she's due to dock at Liverpool tomorrow. She'll be here the next morning and I'll take her to Baker Street after lunch. Oh, and of course I'll give you a copy of her letter.

WATSON: Good heavens, this is all happening too fast! I'm not up to this! Look here, you're his brother! Why don't you impersonate him yourself?

MYCROFT: Because I'm greeting her at the dock and she will know I'm Sherlock's brother.

WATSON: But what if she sees through my impersonation?

MYCROFT: Remember, all she knows about Sherlock Holmes is what you've written. Just follow your own words and it will come off splendidly!

MUSIC: STING, TO UNDERCURRENT

WATSON: It seemed I had no choice, so I agreed to attempt the deception. As twilight darkened into evening, Mycroft Holmes unfolded all the bizarre circumstances . . . .

MUSIC: FADE OUT (UNDER)

MYCROFT: The Countess is descended from generations of Estonian rulers.

WATSON: Oh, she's Estonian?

MYCROFT: Yes. But Estonia has been overrun by neighboring states for centuries. First the Danes, then the Germans, then Poland, then Sweden, and Sweden gave Estonia to Russia at the end of the Great Northern War. And then Peter the Great, the Czar of Russia, married an Estonian girl, and she was the grandmother of the Countess you are going to meet day after tomorrow.

WATSON: Does this Countess have any ruling authority?

MYCROFT: In Russia, no, but she is the hereditary leader of the Estonian loyalists because she is a descendant of the Czarina.

WATSON: Oh. I see.

MYCROFT: Now: here's the problem: The Countess is convinced that a revolution is coming in Russia, and with it, a chance for freedom for Estonia. But if it is to be successful, an army must be trained and weapons must be purchased and smuggled into Estonia, and the Countess is coming here to try to arrange this. But it would have to be done in secret, so as not to incite an incident between Russia and England.

WATSON: But would Victoria ever agree to such a thing? Would Parliament?

MYCROFT: Well, if I trotted the proposition through the palace, then it wouldn't be a secret any more, would it? No, the Countess insists she will deal only in secret, and only with – as she put it – "the brilliant and incorruptable . . . Sherlock Holmes!"

WATSON: Well, what do you think he would have done?

MYCROFT: He would consider her proposal, and then agree to contact some influential men in the War Office, who may provide a cadre of officers in mufti to do some training in Estonia, but not with British arms, so as not to upset France. Men can deny what they are – guns cannot. That's what Sherlock will offer her.

WATSON: But he never had the authority to speak for England!

MYCROFT: No, he didn't. . . . But I have.

MUSIC: SNEAK IN UNDERCURRENT

MYCROFT: Now, here is what I want you to do. First, move your things into Baker Street and become familiar with the rooms again.

WATSON: But why don't you just bring her here to Whitehall?

398

MYCROFT: Oh, I shall. But then we'll adjourn to Baker Street to discuss her proposal with "Sherlock".

WATSON: Is that her idea?

MYCROFT: Of course. Remember, we're dealing with a woman as well as a Countess, a woman who has fallen in love with the mystique of Sherlock Holmes and everything about him! And you've made Baker Street as real to her as he is!

MUSIC: UP AND UNDER

WATSON: At this point, Mycroft Holmes gave me the Countess's letter to study. After I made several notes, we spent the rest of the evening rehearsing my part in this subterfuge. The next morning, I visited 221b Baker Street myself, for the first time since Reichenbach Falls.

MUSIC: OUT

MRS. HUDSON: It's just like it was when you and Mr. Holmes lived here, Doctor.

WATSON: Yes. Well, almost. It was always a bit untidy.

MRS. HUDSON: Oh, my yes. He wouldn't let me touch a thing of his. So I have straightened things up a bit.

WATSON: He kept his pipe tobacco in an old slipper. Do you know what became of it?

MRS. HUDSON: That filthy old slipper? I put it away in the drawer right there.

WATSON: Would you get it out? And he kept his correspondence fastened to the mantelpiece with a dagger, if you remember.

MRS. HUDSON: Yes, I polished the dagger and put it away – it was terribly tarnished.

WATSON: Let's have it up on the mantelpiece, too.

399

MRS. HUDSON: Very good . . . .

MRS. HUDSON: There. The slipper . . . And the dagger.

WATSON: Right. I think he kept them – just there. Yes. I must say, it's as if Holmes might walk in the door at any moment . . . . (SIGH) How I wish he would.

WATSON: Mrs. Hudson turned away then, and left me alone in the room. The new paint had obliterated the smoky aroma that had clung to everything when Holmes lived here, so I smoked pipefuls of tobacco as I investigated the closets, and found not only a collection of Holmes's clothes and shoes, but garters, shirt studs, and collars in the drawers of a chiffonier in his bedroom. My melancholy returned.

WATSON: Another day of coaching from Mycroft Holmes, and then, Thursday dawned, after a night of little sleep. I paced 'round the parlor, smoking, watching the traffic in the street, and then, at just past three in the afternoon, a carriage drew up below. The sturdy figure of Mycroft Holmes alighted, then another man wearing a derby helped a woman out of the carriage, a slender woman dressed in a fashionable costume of deep purple, fully veiled. While the man looked up and down the street, she paused and looked up directly at my window, and brushed back the veil as if to get a better view. She saw me and our eyes met. A trace of a smile lit her face.

WATSON: Mrs. Hudson let the visitors in and ushered them up to our door. First to enter was the hawk-faced man wearing a derby. He nodded to me, said nothing, but walked round the room, peered into the bedrooms, and inspected the closets while

400

the Countess and Mycroft Holmes waited in the doorway. Then he walked past me and handed me a calling-card.

BLAKE: Good afternoon, Mr. Holmes. My name's Blake, from the Pinkerton agency in New York. All right, Countess, come on in.

<u>SOUND EFFECT: THREE PEOPLE WALK IN AND CLOSE DOOR (UNDER)</u>

WATSON: (NARRATING) I caught Mycroft's eye. His expression told me he hadn't expected the bodyguard.

COUNTESS: Are you Sherlock Holmes?

WATSON: (CLEARS HIS THROAT) At your service, madam.

MYCROFT: Sherlock, I have the honor to present Countess Marie Valmiera of Estonia.

WATSON: A distinct honor, Countess. Won't you sit down?

COUNTESS: Thank you.

<u>SOUND EFFECT: GENERAL BODY MOVEMENTS</u>

COUNTESS: Now, please explain. What is this deception?

WATSON: I – I beg your pardon?

COUNTESS: In New York and aboard the ship, there is talk everywhere that Sherlock Holmes is dead!

MYCROFT: (PAUSE) I . . . must confess, the deception was my doing.

COUNTESS: And why did you do this?

MYCROFT: To protect you, Countess, to assure the utmost secrecy. If it were thought that my brother is dead, obviously you couldn't be consulting him.

COUNTESS: But then at some point, you will come back to life, no?

401

WATSON: What? Oh, yes! Yes, of course!

MYCROFT: After an appropriate interval.

COUNTESS: I see. Very clever. Well, while you are "dead", Mr. Sherlock Holmes, I would like to make use of your influence, as I mentioned in my letter.

WATSON: I understand that you expect a revolution in Russia?

COUNTESS: Yes. It isn't only the people of Estonia and Latvia who are languishing under the Czars. Throughout Russia, the intellectuals, as well as the peasants and factory workers, are ready for an uprising. When that happens, that will be the moment for Estonia to awaken and join them! We have thousands of able-bodied men who love Estonia and long to be free, but they must be trained and they must have modern weapons, which only England can supply!

WATSON: Madame Countess, if it were possible to arrange assistance for your people, what benefits would there be to England?

COUNTESS: Benefits? You talk of benefits? You are the strongest nation on the face of the earth! England has an obligation to help civilized, downtrodden peoples achieve freedom!

MYCROFT: I'm sure that Sherlock agrees, but as a representative of Her Majesty's government, I must remind you of the delicate relations between London and Moscow . . . .

COUNTESS: Delicate relations? In 1855, you defeated Russia in the Crimean War and made them give up Bessarabia! And when Alexander the Second went to war to get it back, British and Austrian troops stopped him from entering Constantinople! It seems to me that England has nothing to fear for supporting a revolution!

MYCROFT: Supporting reforms is one thing, but a revolution is something else. In the ten years since Alexander the Second was assassinated, any number of revolutionary societies have been formed in Russia. England cannot be allied with any of them.

COUNTESS: Sherlock Holmes: does your brother speak for you as well as for England?

WATSON: Yes, he does.

COUNTESS: Well! I came here hoping you would consider the needs of my people and apply your great skills to help us . . . but now it seems it is your brother I should have been talking to all along! By the way – your friend, Doctor Watson. Where is he?

WATSON: Watson is minding his medical practice in Kensington.

COUNTESS: He doesn't share your rooms, then?

WATSON: Uh, not since his marriage.

COUNTESS: I should like to speak with him. Can you arrange that?

WATSON: Speak with Watson?

COUNTESS: Yes. It is only through his stories in *The Strand* magazine that I became acquainted with you and your work as a consulting detective.

WATSON: Well, I'm sure Watson would be most flattered to know –

COUNTESS: But now I find that his description of you was inaccurate.

WATSON: You do?

COUNTESS: You don't look the way he described you. And you don't seem the commanding and incisive figure – do I use the right word? – that one would be led to expect of Sherlock Holmes.

WATSON: I'm sorry to have disappointed you, Countess.

403

COUNTESS: It is of no matter. I will deal with whomsoever has the will to help my people. That is why I was in America, and that is why I will travel the world until I can find the resources we need! I am ready to leave, Mr. Blake, if you will help me up.

BLAKE: Yes, ma'am.

WATSON: Uh . . . Countess . . . .

COUNTESS: Yes?

WATSON: I see you have difficulty standing. And I also perceive that you are in severe pain from an inflammation of your joints, particularly those of your hands.

COUNTESS: What do you know about my hands? I'm wearing gloves.

WATSON: Your constant rubbing of your knuckles, an unconscious act you performed throughout our interview, is a sign even a layman could recognize. But what concerns me now is your use of a very dangerous drug.

COUNTESS: I use no drug!

WATSON: You use laudanum, and you mix it with alcohol. And you use too much of it.

COUNTESS: My physician prepares it for me! How do you know all this?

WATSON: If you've read what Doctor Watson has written about me, you should know that where others may see, I perceive.

COUNTESS: Mr. Blake, I am finished here. Take me down to my carriage!

MUSIC: UNDERCURRENT

WATSON: She walked out of the room on the arm of the Pinkerton man, with Mycroft Holmes following, and I assumed my part in

404

his charade was over. As the door closed, I sank into Holmes's chair by the hearth, feeling quite let down and wanting a glass of something myself. But two minutes later, there was a knock at the door . . .

SOUND EFFECT: RAPID KNOCK, DOOR OPENS

WATSON: . . . and Mycroft stode into the room, flushed and intense.

SOUND EFFECT: STEPS IN, THE DOOR CLOSES

MYCROFT: Bully! Absolutely bully! You pulled it off better than I dreamed!

WATSON: I did?

MYCROFT: Your last-minute diagnosis was brilliant! As she got into the carriage she said she knew Sherlock Holmes is a man to reckon with! How did you know she was taking laudanum?

WATSON: You could smell it. Laudanum is a tincture of opium.

MYCROFT: Well, how did you know she uses alcohol?

WATSON: Laudanum is made of powdered opium softened with water and then mixed with alcohol. It's very dangerous. We seldom use it any more.

SOUND EFFECT: KNOCK ON THE DOOR

WATSON: My word, who's that?

MYCROFT: I don't know. I'll get it.

SOUND EFFECT: A STEP TO THE DOOR, DOOR OPENS

MYCROFT: Mr. Blake!

BLAKE: May I have a word with you gentlemen?

MYCROFT: I thought you were taking the Countess to her hotel.

BLAKE: I will be, but I told her I'd left my hat here.

WATSON: Oh? Oh! So you did. Here . . . here you are.

BLAKE: I left it on purpose. I wanted to talk to you in private for a moment.

SOUND EFFECT: DOOR CLOSES

BLAKE: She's not working for Estonia, she's working for an outfit called the Second International.

MYCROFT: The Second International?

WATSON: What's that?

MYCROFT: Karl Marx founded the First International. It was a revolutionary movement that united many European socialist groups.

BLAKE: Right, but it collapsed, and two years ago, a lot of these same socialists founded the Second International, and she joined them to use her reputation in Estonia to round up the guns for a revolution against Imperial Russia. She wanted American help and we turned her down. Now she wants English help – through the back door, as it were – and that's why she thought she could work something out with you two. But I guess you saw through that. You didn't give her what she wanted. I expect Washington will be glad of that . . . if they ever find out.

MYCROFT: You're no Pinkerton man, are you, Mr. Blake?

BLAKE: Sure I am.

MYCROFT: Not working for the American government?

BLAKE: Well, not officially. But Pinkertons have their own intelligence department when we work overseas.

MYCROFT: I thought as much.

BLAKE: Well, anyway, I thought you gentlemen ought to know . . . if you didn't already. And by the way, Sherlock, you had her dead to rights on that stuff she takes. The laudanum. I didn't know what it was, but she takes it all the time.

WATSON: Well, whatever she may be, she's putting her life in danger by using it.

BLAKE: Maybe I can get her to stop. . . . Well, I'd better get back to the Countess. Nice to meet you both.

SOUND EFFECT: DOOR OPENS

BLAKE: I guess what that Watson fellow says about you is pretty much right on the barrelhead, Sherlock. Oh. And if you gentlemen ever come to Washington, look me up.

SOUND EFFECT: A STEP, DOOR CLOSES

WATSON: (PAUSE) Interesting chap.

MYCROFT: Americans. So direct. Plain and straightforward.

WATSON: Mr. Holmes? Did you know the Countess was counterfeit?

MYCROFT: Oh, she's not counterfeit. She's who she said she is.

WATSON: But did you know she was part of this – this –

MYCROFT: Second International? No. But it all comes to the same thing, doesn't it? England doesn't support revolutions. Good heavens . . . Look what happened in the American colonies!

MUSIC: *DANSE MACABRE* UP AND UNDER

WATSON: It was the first and last time that I would be asked to impersonate Sherlock Holmes, and I was most uneasy throughout the experience, for it seemed almost indecent to his memory, and to my regard for him. Of course, at that time, in 1891, I had no way of knowing that Sherlock Holmes would return after a three-year hiatus, and that his brother was the only other person on earth besides Sherlock Holmes himself to know that he had survived Reichenbach Falls. But that's a story I've already written. There are many more, and I hope you'll be with me again when I tell you another one.

MUSIC: UP AND FADE

Appendix

The Further Adventures of
Sherlock Holmes:
Radio Logs

The Further Adventures of Sherlock Holmes ran on *Imagination Theatre* as part of its rotating line-up of shows from March 3rd, 1998 to August 6th, 2017. Initially, all of the episodes were written by founder Jim French. However, beginning with episode 037, "The Strange Case of Lord Halworth's Kitchen", Mr. French welcomed other authors into the stable by co-writing a script with Gareth Tilley. Episode 041, "The Amateur Mendicant Society", featured the first non-French solo script by Matthew J. Elliott, who would go on to become the primary script writer for the show.

Additionally, from November 20th, 2005 to January 24th, 2016, Matthew would write the scripts for *Imagination Theatre*'s presentation of the entire Sherlock Holmes Canon, *The Classic Adventures of Sherlock Holmes*. This accomplished several firsts, including being the first time that these adaptations had all been done by the same writer, the first time that they had been performed by the same two American actors, John Patrick Lowrie and Lawrence Albert as Holmes and Watson, respectively, and the first time that the entire Canon had been performed in this way in its entirety on American Radio.

Additionally, these episodes, when combined with those making up the entire run of *The Further Adventures of Sherlock Holmes*, have made John and Larry the longest running Holmes and Watson in American Radio, and have given Larry the distinct honor of portraying Dr. Watson the longest in any format.

For such a large body of work, the number of writers involved was actually quite small:

- Jim French
- Matthew J. Elliott
- Larry Albert
- John Patrick Lowrie
- Gareth Tilley
- Matthew Booth
- J.R. Campbell

413

- Jeremy B. Holstein
- Roger Silverwood
- Teresa Collard
- John Hall
- Steven Phillip Jones
- Daniel McGachey
- Iain McLaughlin and Claire Bartlett
- David Marcum

After *Imagination Theatre* closed its doors in early 2017, fans were bereft. But then, without warning, a "lost" broadcast, No. 129, "The Strange Case", appeared. It was written by Iain McLaughlin, and considered too good to waste. It was recorded in mid-2017, and broadcast on *Imagination Theatre*'s *YouTube* website in August.

And even that isn't the end. In September 2017, the cast reassembled to record a new Holmes adventure, one of several that are planned during 2017 and 2018.

The Further Adventures of Sherlock Holmes

No.   Episode Title – Date (Month/Day/Year) – Author(s)

001   The Poet of Death – 03/08/1998 – Jim French
002   The Sealed Room – 06/21/1998 – Jim French
003   The Adventure of the Blind Man – 07/12/1998 – Jim French
004   The Woman from Virginia – 08/02/1998 – Jim French
005   The Adventure of the Seven Shares – 09/20/1998 – Jim French
006   The Adventure of the Painted Leaf – 10/25/1998 – Jim French
007   The Secret of the Fives – 11/29/1998 – Jim French
008   The Quartermaine Curse – 02/14/1999 – Jim French
009   The Adventure of the Bishop's Ring – 04/18/1999 – Jim French
010   The Adventure of the Samovar – 08/08/1999 – Jim French
011   The Adventure of the Red Death – 09/26/1999 – Jim French
012   The Adventure of the Silver Siphon – 10/31/1999 – Jim French
013   The Dark Chamber – 02/27/2000 – Jim French
014   The Ragwort Puzzle – 03/26/2000 – Jim French
015   The Adventure of the Mind Reader – 04/23/2000 – Jim French
016   The Gambrinus Cure – 07/02/2000 – Jim French
017   The Billingsgate Horror – 10/29/2000 – Jim French
018   The Adventure of the Missing Link – 11/26/2000 – Jim French
019   The Adventure of the Edison Sender – 03/25/2001 – Jim French
020   The Estonian Countess – 05/27/2001 – Jim French
021   School for Scoundrels – 07/15/2001 – Jim French
022   The Adventure of the Dover Maiden – 08/19/200 – Jim French

023   The Adventure of the Wycliffe Codicil – 09/23/2001 – Jim French

024   The Tuttman Gallery – 10/28/2001 – Jim French

025   The Bee and the Spider – 11/18/2001 – Jim French

026   The Man Who Believed In Nothing – 12/23/2001 – Jim French

027   The Death of Artemus Ludwig – 01/13/2002 – Jim French

028   36 Thayer Street – 02/17/2002 – Jim French

029   The Adventure of the Farnham Grange – 03/17/2002 – Jim French

031   The Adventure of the Lonely Harvester – 07/28/2002 – Jim French

030   The Strange Death of Lady Sylvia Eichorn – 08/25/2002 – Jim French

032   The Mystery of the Patient Fisherman – 10/27/2002 – Jim French

033   The Wizard of Baker Street – 12/15/2002 – Jim French

034   The Diary of Anthony Moltaire – 01/19/2003 – Jim French

035   The Singular Affair of Madame Planchette – 02/16/2003 – Jim French

036   The Bardsley Triangle – 04/13/2003 – Jim French

037   The Strange Case of Lord Halworth's Kitchen – 05/18/2003 Jim French and Gareth Tilley

038   The Adventure of the Voodoo Curse – 06/22/2003 – Gareth Tilley

039   The Mystery of the Ten Pound Notes – 07/27/2003 – Jim French (from a story by Gareth Tilley)

040   The Adventure of the Great American – 08/24/2003 – Jim French

041   The Amateur Mendicant Society – 09/28/2003 – M. J. Elliott

042   The Adventure of the Tontine – 10/26/2003 – Jim French

043   The Goldolphin Arabian – 11/23/2003 – Jim French

044   The Living Weapon – 12/28/2003 – M. J. Elliott

045   The Blackmailer of Lancaster Gate – 01/25/2004 – M. J. Elliott

046   The Problem of Pennington Flash – 02/22/2004 – M. J. Elliott

047   The Adventure of the Forgotten Throne – 03/28/2004 – Lawrence Albert and Gareth Tilley

048   The Speaking Machine – 04/25/2004 – Jim French

049   The Adventure of the Serpent's Tooth – 05/16/2004 – M. J. Elliott

050   The Dreadnaught Papers – 06/27/2004 – Jim French

051   The Covetous Huntsman – 07/25/2004 – M. J. Elliott

052   The Master Craftsman – 08/22/2004 – Jim French

053   The Margate Deception – 09/26/2004 – M. J. Elliott

054   The Head of Jean Malreaux – 10/17/2004 – Jim French

055   The Ripper Inheritance – 11/28/2004 – M. J. Elliott

056   The Bonesteel Covenant – 12/26/2004 – Jim French

057   The Great Ansceni – 01/16/2005 – Lawrence Albert and Gareth Tilley

058   The Adventure of the Vampire's Kiss – 02/13/2005 – Matthew Booth

059   The Tragedy of Saxon's Gate – 03/27/2005 – Matthew Booth

060   The Winterbourne Phantom – 04/24/2005 – M. J. Elliott

127   The Adventure of the Bitterest Season – 12/25/2016
128   The Moriarty Conclusion – 02/19/2017 – M. J. Elliott

Imagination Theatre "closed" in early 2017. However, later that year, it returned with the following Holmes adventures, with more promised in the future . . . .

129   The Strange Case – 08/06/2017 – Iain McLaughlin
130   The Adventure of the Cruel Miracle – 10/28/2017 – M. J. Elliott
131   The Autumn of Terror (Part I) – 01/12/2019 – M. J. Elliott
132   The Autumn of Terror (Part II) – 01/19/2019 – M. J. Elliott
133   The Autumn of Terror (Part III) – 01/26/2019 – M. J. Elliott
134   The Autumn of Terror (Part IV) – 02/02/2019 – M. J. Elliott
135   The Autumn of Terror (Part V) – 02/09/2019 – M. J. Elliott

The Further Adventures of Sherlock Holmes
will continue . . . .

The MX Book of New Sherlock Holmes Stories
Edited by David Marcum
(MX Publishing, 2015-   )

"This is the finest volume of Sherlockian fiction I have ever read, and I have read, literally, thousands." – Philip K. Jones

"Beyond Impressive . . . This is a splendid venture for a great cause! – Roger Johnson, Editor, *The Sherlock Holmes Journal,* The Sherlock Holmes Society of London

Part I: 1881-1889
Part II: 1890-1895
Part III: 1896-1929
Part IV: 2016 Annual
Part V: Christmas Adventures
Part VI: 2017 Annual
Part VII: Eliminate the Impossible (1880-1891)
Part VIII – Eliminate the Impossible (1892-1905)
Part IX – 2018 Annual (1879-1895)
Part X – 2018 Annual (1896-1916)
Part XI – Some Untold Cases (1880-1891)
Part XII – Some Untold Cases (1894-1902)
Part XIII – 2019 Annual (1881-1890)
Part XIV – 2019 Annual (1891-1897)
Part XV – 2019 Annual (1898-1917)
Part XVI – Whatever Remains . . . Must be the Truth (1881-1890)
Part XVII – Whatever Remains . . . Must be the Truth (1891-1898)
Part XVIII – Whatever Remains . . . Must be the Truth (1898-1925)

In Preparation
Part XIX – 2020 Annual

. . . and more to come!

The MX Book of New Sherlock Holmes Stories
Edited by David Marcum
(MX Publishing, 2015-   )

Publishers Weekly says:

Part VI: *The traditional pastiche is alive and well . . . .*

Part VII: *Sherlockians eager for faithful-to-the-canon plots and characters will be delighted.*

Part VIII: *The imagination of the contributors in coming up with variations on the volume's theme is matched by their ingenious resolutions.*

Part IX: *The 18 stories . . . will satisfy fans of Conan Doyle's originals. Sherlockians will rejoice that more volumes are on the way.*

Part X: *. . . new Sherlock Holmes adventures of consistently high quality.*

Part XI: *. . . an essential volume for Sherlock Holmes fans.*

Part XII: *. . . continues to amaze with the number of high-quality pastiches . . .*

Part XIII: *. . . Amazingly, Marcum has found 22 superb pastiches . . . This is more catnip for fans of stories faithful to Conan Doyle's original*

Part XIV: *. . . this standout anthology of 21 short stories written in the spirit of Conan Doyle's originals.*

Part XV: *Stories pitting Sherlock Holmes against seemingly supernatural phenomena highlight Marcum's 15th anthology of superior short pastiches.*

The MX Book of New Sherlock Holmes Stories
Edited by David Marcum
(MX Publishing, 2015-   )

MX Publishing

MX Publishing is the world's largest specialist Sherlock Holmes publisher, with several hundred titles and over a hundred authors creating the latest in Sherlock Holmes fiction and non-fiction.

From traditional short stories and novels to travel guides and quiz books, MX Publishing caters to all Holmes fans.

The collection includes leading titles such as *Benedict Cumberbatch In Transition* and *The Norwood Author*, which won the 2011 *Tony Howlett Award* (Sherlock Holmes Book of the Year).

MX Publishing also has one of the largest communities of Holmes fans on *Facebook*, with regular contributions from dozens of authors.

www.mxpublishing.co.uk (UK) and *www.mxpublishing.com* (USA)

CPSIA information can be obtained
at www.ICGtesting.com
Printed in the USA
LVHW111511301019
635835LV00002B/50/P

9 781787 054912